PAC NOR
WOLVES

05

THE STRYKER

BOYS OF
RICHLAND
x x x

*Gabriel
Herrera*

A NOTE FROM THE AUTHOR

This story is so incredibly special to me. What Gabriel and Cecilia go through... it's a lot.

If you're new to my Boys of Richland series, while not required, I recommend you start with The Savage so you can see what it all begins. If you've read it already, welcome back.

I hope you enjoy this next chapter in Gabriel and Cecilia's story.

xx Daniela

TRIGGER WARNING

The Striker is recommended for mature readers 17+
If you don't have any triggers, turn the page and enjoy.
If you do, check out the list below and make sure this book is
a good fit for you!

The Striker deals with sensitive subject matter including but
not limited to, suicide, suicidal thoughts, grief, bullying, and
sexual assault.

Please read responsibly. If it gets to be too much, you can put
the book down, take a break, or walk away.

The Striker much like other books of mine deals with social
issues and real-world problems. Some of your views may
differ from those of my characters and that is entirely okay.
But please don't message me to tell me "I'm wrong" about a
particular social issue. I'm not here to convince you one way
or the other. Your opinions are your own.

The Striker is not a standalone novel.
Gabriel and Cecilia's story begins with
The Savage and continues here in The Striker.
It will conclude in The Replay.

1
GABRIEL

"Gabe, man. You gotta talk about this," Felix says, concern creasing his forehead as he lingers in my doorway.

"I'm fine," I grunt, shoulders hunched without looking up. No way in hell am I about to rehash how Cecilia ripped my heart out and stomped on the pieces.

Sharing my fucking feelings isn't going to make what I'm dealing with any better. In fact, I'm ninety-nine-point-nine-percent positive it will only make things worse.

Felix steps further into my room, persistent bastard that he is. "You've been a ghost for weeks. I know something happened with you and Cecilia, but when any of us so much as says her name, you either bite our heads off or you shut down. What gives?"

I rake both hands through my hair, emotions churning violently in my gut. *That's because she ended things.* What a fucking joke. I don't even know why I'm so torn up about this.

About her. It doesn't make any sense. But nothing about my feelings for Cecilia made sense. They didn't need to.

She was just ... fuck. I don't even know. She was her, and I was me, and together, we fit. We just fucking fit.

I told her I loved her. Me. I said those three fucking words. Words I've never said to any other girl before. I handed her my still-beating heart and let her carve it up as she saw fit, trusting that she felt the same way I did.

Idiot.

I don't know what I was thinking. I trusted the girl who snuck beneath my armor when no one else could. And when I laid myself bare at her feet, she told me to walk away. Like severing this connection between us is so damn easy.

Maybe for her, it is. But it's not like that for me.

I can't stop caring about her with the flip of a switch. If it was that easy, I wouldn't feel like this. Like my fucking soul is cannibalizing itself, leaving behind a gaping wound in my chest.

I fucking hate it.

I rub at the ache beneath my ribs, desperate to ease some of the pain.

We weren't dating. She wasn't my girlfriend. We were just ... *fuck.*

Even now, I don't know how to describe what we were.

And a part of me thinks I never needed to.

I didn't need a label to know it was special. That what was going on between us was different. More than anything I'd ever had before with another woman. But for some irrational reason, it sort of pisses me off that I can't even call her my ex. As far as anyone else can tell, we were never anything.

"Just leave it alone," I snap, hands clenching at my sides to hide their faint tremor. I can't keep reliving the worst day of my goddamn life. Not if I want to keep what's left of my sanity.

Heavy footfalls sound down the hall before Julio—another of my roommates—fills the doorway just behind Felix, brow furrowed. The combined weight of their stares makes my skin prickle uncomfortably.

Christ. They're turning into mother fucking hens.

"For fuck's sake," I mutter under my breath, shoulders tensing. There goes any chance at privacy. I'm trying to sort through the tangled mess in my head, and I don't need a goddamn audience for it.

The weekends are the only reprieve I get from seeing her, and this weekend came and went too goddamn fast.

I'm trying to amp myself up for today—Monday—and these assholes won't leave me the hell alone.

"You've been moping around for weeks," Julio says bluntly, always one to cut right to the chase. The guy doesn't even start off with a good morning. "You're not the only one who lives here, cabrón." —fucker— "So, spill. Why have you been an absolute dick, lately?"

I flip my best friends off, jaw tight. I don't care if I'm being a moody bastard right now. I think I've earned the right to work through this on my own terms, without either of them scrutinizing my every move.

Julio's dark eyes flash with frustration, clearly not on the same page. "Can you at least pretend to be a functioning human long enough to welcome Deacon? The guy *you* invited to move into nuestra casita." *—our home—* "He's going to be here any minute and you need to get whatever stick you have up your ass, out."

Shit.

I forgot he was moving in today. I scrub my hand over my face and try like hell to shove my feelings back into their box.

Deacon's a freshman transfer from Suncrest U. We met when he helped friends of ours fork our soccer field.

A prank in retaliation for one of Julio's fuck ups. I silently eye the fucker. Maybe I should remind him of how not so long ago he was dealing with a mess of his own, too. And what did he do when Felix and I suggested we hash it out?

He told us to back the fuck off.

And we did.

I'd love to give the asshole a reminder, but knowing Julio the way that I do, it would just make him dig deeper. He's a stubborn bastard like that. Always wanting to peel back everyone's fucking trauma, except for his own.

I sigh. The Deacon thing can't be avoided. I made a bet with the guy after he helped Allie, Bibiana, and Kasey fork our field. If he scored a goal against me, we'd clean up their mess. If he missed, they were cleaning up after themselves.

Long story short, he scored. Talk about a blow to my fucking ego. But after seeing the guy's kick, we recruited him onto our team. Who knew the cocky footballer would be a legit *fútboler.*

Convincing him to change sports and switch schools seemed like a good idea at the time. Now I'm not so sure. The timing is absolute shit if you ask me.

The idea of slapping on a polite smile as I make stilted small talk makes my insides twist up even more. I can't handle this shit. Not today. Not when I have to see her in less than an hour.

Low voices drift down the hall as the front door opens. It's Atticus—roommate number three—giving Deacon the grand tour. I should make an effort to welcome the guy. I know that. But the mere idea of exchanging pleasantries and pretending I'm not imploding on the inside feels fucking impossible right now.

Fuck. When did I become such a little bitch?

I've been through tough shit before. Carlos's suicide. My parents divorce. Real shit.

So why the hell is it so goddamn hard to function now?

I stare out my bedroom window. The sun is shining. The autumn leaves have turned from green to a multitude of yellows, reds, and oranges.

By all accounts it's a beautiful day.

And it's a lie.

How can I act like everything's fine when it fucking isn't? When every word out of Cecilia's mouth echoes endlessly inside of my head?

"And this is Gabe's room," Atticus tells him once they reach my door. "Hey, man," Atticus greets me, hand raised in the air.

Breathe, I tell myself. Say hello. It's not that hard. Only ... it is.

My molars grind together, jaw locked tight.

Felix jumps to the rescue, playing the gracious host while I avoid eye contact and remain stubbornly silent. *Fuck this shit.*

"Hey! Atticus giving you the grand tour?" Felix asks. "Has he shown you the garage? No?"

Deacon responds, but I can't make out his words over the ringing in my ears. I don't want to do this. I'm not ready to see her again. I need more time.

"Bro, it's perfection. We always kick it in there. Come on, I'll —" Their voices fade as Felix steers Deacon and Atticus down the hallway and toward the back door, granting me a temporary reprieve.

A second later, the door clicks shut, leaving me alone with Julio's scrutinizing stare once more. He stays propped just inside my doorway, the wooden door closed at his back and his tattooed arms crossed over his chest.

The weight of his gaze bores into me as the silence stretches tight.

I grit my teeth, resentment simmering beneath my skin. It's not that much to ask to be left alone.

"Get your shit together, man," Julio says, tone harsh with judgment.

I bristle, hands clenched into fists at my sides. "You don't know what I'm dealing with, J," I fire back.

Julio has no goddamn idea what it's like to put yourself out there. To lay your feelings bare, only to have them stomped on and dismissed without a second thought. How could he? The guy hasn't been in a serious relationship in ... well, ever. And whatever spark he did have with a certain someone—she who will not be named—he snuffed out.

It was his call. His choice.

I wasn't afforded that luxury.

Julio steps further into the room, eyes searching mine for answers I don't have. "Then talk to me. I've always had your back, but I can't do anything if you shut me and everyone else out."

I scrub both hands roughly down my face, throat tightening around all the things I want to say, but can't seem to voice.

He's not wrong. I've been pushing him and the others away when I know all they want is to help me. Problem is, I don't want their help. I don't want to deal with any of this.

"I don't even know how to process this myself right now," I force out hoarsely, unable to meet his gaze. "Let alone talk through it. What Cecilia said ..." I trail off, shaking my head as the echo of her words threatens to drag me back down into the abyss.

Fuck.

What is wrong with me? I don't get like this. Not over a girl. I'm not this guy. Never have been. So why the fuck is this shit hitting me so goddamn hard?

Julio grips my shoulder, his palm rough and warm. Grounding. "Tell me what happened, man. Start there."

Sucking in a sharp breath, I shake my head.

"Come on, man. Try." Knowing Julio, he's going to keep poking until I cave. May as well get it over with now and just tear off the damn band-aid.

"She ended things. Said she didn't want this. Didn't want me." I repeat Cecilia's speech aloud for the first time, and with each word I say, I watch as Julio's expression sinks more and more into one of pity.

I don't want his pity. Though it's obvious I have it.

I force out the last of my words, making sure to get it all out. If pushed again, I won't be able to rehash this shit a second time. Just voicing her rejection aloud leaves me raw. Wounded.

But there it is. All of it. I don't leave a single detail out.

My pathetic confession hangs heavy between us. Admitting it out loud doesn't grant the respite I think either of us hoped for. It only intensifies the crushing weight on my chest. Why do people think talking about this kind of shit will make them feel better? It doesn't.

Fuck.

I rub a hand over my chest.

It hurts. This feeling. It fucking hurts, and I need to figure out some way to make it go away.

Julio squeezes my shoulder, tone softening. "Damn. I'm sorry, man. I know how much she meant to you."

Does he, though? My throat tightens around the bitter lump expanding inside my throat. Cecilia isn't some casual fling I can move on from overnight. She's so much more than that. She's ... everything.

"I thought we had something real. Something that could go the distance." My voice cracks on the admission. But I saw a future with this girl. "I know she has shit to deal with. Of course, I know that. But ..." I hang my head. "It felt real. It felt like more than just ... I don't know." I rub the back of my neck. "Guess it was all one-sided. Whatever it was. She made it crystal clear where she stands."

Julio nods, eyes shining with sympathy. "I know it's hard to hear, but maybe this is a good thing. I hate to see you hurting like this. We all do. But you said it yourself, she's got her own shit to work through. Letting her go sounds like the right call."

I jerk sharply out of his grasp. "Letting her go?" I repeat incredulously. As if my feelings for Cecilia can be boxed up and set aside like this week's trash. "Are you fucking with me right now?"

His dark brows draw together.

I'm not letting her go. Julio's one of my best friends. He's not supposed to tell me to move on. He's supposed to, I don't know, give me advice or some shit on how to get her back.

"You're an asshole," I tell him.

Resentment simmers in my veins. I know why Cecilia is pushing me away. She's scared of needing someone. Scared of relying on me too much to keep her demons at bay.

But she shouldn't be. And yeah, she ended shit, but I'm not giving up on us that easily. Right?

Right.

The more and more I think about it, the more determination settles in my bones. I'm not going to just lie down and let her push me out of her life. Not when she's shut out everyone else around her.

She doesn't get to dictate my feelings.

This is bullshit.

I refuse to be just another person who's abandoned her when things get too hard. I'm not about to be added to the growing list of people she can't depend on or open up to. Nah. Not happening.

Cecilia's let me in before.

An idea forms in my mind.

She'll let me in again. This is only a setback. Cecilia needs to know I won't bail. That I'll put in the work. That I'll be there when she needs me, no matter what.

"You don't get it." If anyone could understand, I thought it'd be Julio. "She needs me right now, even if she won't admit it. I can break through her walls again if I try hard enough. I can fix this. Fix ... us."

My voice trails off as I realize how weak and desperate I sound.

I don't care.

Cecilia is worth fighting for. What we have, it's worth going all in on. I have to believe that. Because, fuck, I don't know how I'm supposed to go on myself if I don't.

Julio's shoulders slump in defeat, and he walks back to the door with a heavy sigh. "I know you love her," he tells me.

If he knew what I felt for her, he wouldn't tell me to let her go.

"But don't let this destroy you, too. Not after how much *you've* been through. How far *you've* come."

My jaw flexes.

He hesitates by the door, turning back to face me. Doubt shadows his dark brown eyes and I can see how much he's weighing his words. "I know it doesn't feel like it right now, but moving on is for the best. I truly believe that. You've already been through hell yourself. With your brother. And then all the bullshit with your parents. Taking on Cecilia's trauma too—" He shakes his head. "That's a lot for anyone to handle. Even you. You're not invincible, Gabriel. You bleed red just like the rest of us."

My jaw clenches, teeth grinding together hard enough that pain shoots up behind my eyes. But I remain silent. I let him speak his mind, as misguided as he is. Julio needs to get it out of his system.

He runs a hand through his short-cropped hair. "I'm just saying, sometimes love means knowing when to walk away. Cecilia has a mountain of issues to work out alone before she can handle being in a relationship again. Sometimes it's just ..." He hesitates. "The right girl and the wrong time." I get the feeling we're not only talking about my relationship now.

"She doesn't have to go through it alone. Not when she has me."

He nods his head and gives me a sympathetic look. "You're my best friend. My brother. I don't want to see you wrecked when you win her back, only for her to break it off again later on down the road. It'll hurt that much more. We both know that girl isn't ready for anything serious right now."

I stare back at him, anger simmering beneath my skin even as I fight to keep my expression carefully blank. I don't want him to know how much this hurts—his lack of support. How it fucking guts me. Because yeah, he is my best friend. My brother. We're ride or die. *Familia* to the bitter end. Which is what makes all of this that much worse.

After a painfully long moment, Julio turns back to the door with a disappointed shake of his head. "Just think it over," he says quietly. "Sometimes it's better to make a clean break now than to drag it out. It'll save both of you a lot of pain in the end."

2
CECILIA

"**Y**ou can do this," I remind myself, clutching my books tighter to my chest. The bell is going to ring any minute, which means if I don't walk inside right now, I'm going to be late.

I can do this. Deep breaths. Things are going to get better.

I know they will.

Right? I mean. They have to. Gabriel can't hate me forever, right?

God, I hope not.

Sucking in a lungful of air, I walk toward my first class, eyes glued to my feet.

I bump into a hard body, and my heartbeat stutters. An involuntary reaction.

A knot forms in the pit of my stomach.

Before I can react, large hands grip my upper arms to steady me. Revulsion spirals through me at the unwanted touch, and I wrench myself away, skin crawling.

Breathe. I remind myself. You're at school. It's fine. Just breathe.

"Sorry. Excuse me," I choke out, trying not to let this frazzle me, but when I look up to see who I ran into, I recoil.

Austin Holt leers down at me, blocking my path. I jump, barely stifling a shriek as he looms over me, his hulking frame casting me in shadow. I can't breathe with the heavy weight of his stare dragging over me.

No.

What does he want from me now?

I cross my arms, hugging myself tight as I retreat further into the corner in a vain attempt to make myself smaller.

Invisible.

Anything to avoid notice.

But I'm never that lucky.

Nausea and panic rise like twin tides set to drown me. I squeeze my eyes shut, fighting to stay afloat amidst the waves. His cologne assails my senses. It's thick and cloying. Like an Axe body spray commercial gone wrong.

Memories flicker across my closed eyelids.

Hands pulling at my clothes. A heavy weight pinning me down to the bed.

No. No. No.

Do not go there. You're not there. You're here. At school. You're safe. Austin can't hurt you here.

Except, he already has.

Just a few weeks ago, Austin slammed my head into the wall outside the campus pool. Both in retaliation and warning.

He doesn't care where he is when he hurts me or who might see it. An audience doesn't stop Austin. It never has. In fact, I'm almost certain he craves the attention. The impunity.

I can't breathe. I can't—

"Cece," he drops his voice low in an almost seductive drawl. "Fancy seeing you here." An arrogant smirk twists his mouth, and I tighten my arms around myself, fighting off a shiver.

He reaches a hand toward me, and I take an involuntary step back, sinking into the nearby wall. My heart pounds in my chest. Why won't he just leave me alone? I can't— I shake my head. I just can't. Not today. Not ever.

Fuck.

I avoid his probing gaze.

Austin scrutinizes me like I'm a butterfly pinned to the wall.

Maybe if I refuse to engage, he'll get bored and move on. That's it. I just have to keep it together long enough for him to get bored. Austin wants a reaction out of me.

I won't give him one.

"Aw, don't be like that," he croons, planting one muscular arm on the wall beside my head. He leans in close enough for me to get another whiff of his cologne. To see the blond stubble lining his jaw.

I clench my teeth to keep them from chattering and stare at the stupid puka shell necklace around his neck.

Austin presses into me until my back is flush with the wall, caging me in place as students rush by, oblivious. Their voices fade into the background noise beneath the roaring of blood in my ears.

They see us. Of course they do. But with the way we're positioned, Austin and I look like secret lovers. They don't see him as the monster and me, his unwilling victim. But that's exactly what we are. Austin Holt will never be anything but the monster in my nightmares, and I hate him for it. I hate him for breaking me. For stealing bits and pieces of who I am. For turning me into this ... this shell of a person. He ruined everything.

I swallow down my scream.

He ruined me.

The urge to cry for help overwhelms me, but fear locks up my throat, leaving me mute and trembling.

Austin's smile twists cruelly as he places a fingertip beneath my chin and forces my eyes up to meet the arctic chill of his pale blue gaze.

"Wha... wha... what do you want?" I stumble over the words.

Dammit. I'm stronger than this.

Don't show him your fear. Don't give him what he wants.

Austin's fingers shift until he's cupping my jaw, but the hold isn't gentle. It's possessive. Controlling. Bile rises in my throat.

"I've been thinking about you," he says. "Have you been thinking about me, too? About our night together?"

Tears well in my eyes.

"I've been thinking about that night a lot lately. Especially since you've needed near constant reminders about our little ..." he pauses until my eyes flicker to his, fingers digging painfully into my skin, "arrangement."

His breath ghosts over my cheek as he leans in to whisper near my ear, "I'd hate to resort to more extreme measures to keep this pretty little mouth shut, Cece. So tell me, are you behaving yourself? Or should we revisit our night together? You know, for old times' sake."

Tears blur my vision, but I blink them back, refusing to show any more weakness in front of this monster than I already have.

His finger trails from my chin down my throat in a perverse caress.

Revulsion and nausea roil inside me.

"I'm doing what you asked," I choke out in a ragged whisper. "I've kept my mouth shut. I haven't said a word since ..." I trail off, unable to get the words out, but he knows what I mean. He knows I haven't said a word about the assault since the morning after it happened. Not since I realized no one was going to believe me. Not the school. Not my friends.

And if they don't believe me, why bother going to the police?

Austin knew before he ever laid a hand on me that he'd get away with it. But it took me losing everything to come to that same realization.

Statistics for rape victims are deplorable in the United States. Richland is no exception.

One in every six women in the U.S. has been a victim of sexual assault. I'm not special here. Just a member of a club I wish I'd never been a part of.

Suncrest U did a study a while back that found less than six percent of reported rapes in the United States lead to an arrest. Less than one percent lead to a conviction. And only half a percent of those convictions result in jail time.

And that's not even including the over sixty percent of rapes that aren't even reported. Ones like mine.

It shouldn't surprise me that Austin and his friends got away with what they did to me. I'm just another statistic. A silent, forgotten number that society couldn't care less about.

Austin clicks his tongue, straightening as his smile sharpens with cruelty. "Keep it that way. Your boy is sniffing around my business. Get him to stop or—" He lets the threat hang in the air between us.

"I broke things off," I tell him, hating the way that admission tastes on my tongue. My heart squeezes. Just thinking about Gabriel, about the look on his face when he told me he loved me, it twists something inside of me.

I look down at my chest, searching for the blood I know should be pouring out of my heart. It feels like someone's stabbed a blade deep in my chest. There's nothing there. But the pain is real. This ache. Austin found a way to take yet another thing from me.

He tilts his head, a curious glimmer in his eyes. "Trouble in paradise? Lover boy unable to—" He makes a crude motion with his hips, grinding into me. "—satisfy you?"

"Get off of me," I shriek. Bracing both hands against Austin's chest, I push with all my might.

He doesn't even sway.

My breath seizes in my lungs. He's too close. He's going to ... no. He can't. He—Urgh!

A mocking chuckle pours out of him.

Fear skitters down my spine. I need to get out of here. But I can't move. I can't breathe. And I'm trapped between the wall and Austin's body. My breathing grows labored, the sound loud in the near-empty hallways.

Where did everyone go? There were more people before. Did the bell ring and I somehow missed it?

"Is that what happened, Cece? Did you realize you need a real man to—"

"Get the fuck away from her," an all too familiar voice bites out. The next thing I know, Austin is thrown back away from me and slammed into the wall across from me. His body bounces off the wall, a small grunt hissing past his lips.

My eyes jerk to familiar pools of amber right before Gabriel tears his furious gaze away from mine, only to shove his face into Austin's. "I told you to stay the fuck away from her," Gabriel snarls, fists twisting into the collar of Austin's polo shirt.

Gabriel looks two seconds away from punching Austin in the face, but he can't.

Not here.

There's too much at stake for him.

"Gabe—" I start.

"Or what?" Austin bites back. "Last I heard, she dumped your ass. So, why don't you mind your own business?"

Gabriel's nostrils flare and he draws his fist back, but before he can swing, I lunge for it. Wrapping my hands around his wrist, I pull down on his arm, praying he won't shrug me off.

"He isn't worth it," I tell him, my voice pleading.

Austin's grin widens. "You sure about that?" His eyes rake me up and down with clear interest as bile scorches the back of my throat.

The first bell rings, a shrill alarm reminding me to get to class. Only I can't just walk away from this. Not knowing that as soon as I turn my back, Gabriel will punch Austin in the face. He'd happily be the one to deliver the first blow.

It's what Austin wants. I can see it in his eyes. He wants Gabriel to punch him, which means he already knows the repercussions Gabriel will face.

I can't let Gabriel throw his future down the drain. Austin's parents are lawyers. They'll go straight to the Dean's office—guns blazing—and have Gabriel expelled.

Screw him.

Austin doesn't deserve that satisfaction. He's ruined enough lives as it is. I won't let him destroy Gabriel's.

"What's it gonna be, Hererra?" Austin taunts. "You gonna defend your girl, or are you gonna walk away like a scared little bitch?"

Gabe bares his teeth but eases back, his entire body vibrating with barely tempered restraint.

Austin's hands raise in mock surrender even as his smile remains cold and satisfied. He tips an imaginary hat my way. "The bitch route it is. Good thing you cut this one loose." He chuckles. "See you around, Cece. Enjoy class." He turns to saunter down the now empty hall and disappears around the corner just as the late bell rings, his jaunty whistle echoing back to Gabriel and me where we stand.

I slump against the wall, shaking and fighting back irrational tears. I'm going to be sick. Or pass out. Or both. Now that the adrenaline is leaving my system, I'm falling apart fast.

Fuck.

Why won't Austin just leave me alone? What is it going to take? I've done everything he's asked. There's nothing left for me to give. No further concession I can make.

Pulling in one gasping breath after another, I close my eyes, counting down from one hundred to quell the rising panic threatening to choke me. If Gabriel hadn't been here ... No. I can't think about that right now.

I'm fine. Austin is gone. I'm going to be fine.

Deep breath in. *Exhale.* Deep breath out.

My hands tremble as I smooth back my long brown hair, my fingers unsteady.

I avoid Gabriel's searching gaze, instead staring down at the Volcom graphic on my oversized T-shirt. It hangs off one shoulder, exposing more bare skin than I'd like. Should have stuck with a sweater.

I cross my arms over my chest and try to stop shaking.

Gentle fingers under my chin tilt my head up. I nearly flinch away but remind myself this isn't Austin. It's Gabe. And Gabriel is safe. He won't hurt me. Even though when we last spoke, I was the one to hurt him.

His honey-gold eyes bore into mine, his jaw clenched. "Are you okay?"

I open my mouth but can't find any words. I manage a slight nod. A lie. But denying that I'm all right won't help either of us right now.

Gabriel's nostrils flare, a muscle in his cheek feathering. I can see the effort it takes to rein in his anger. He doesn't like my response. He doesn't believe me.

His thumb brushes my cheek. A barely there caress before dropping away. My heart plummets, and already I mourn the loss of his touch.

"Come on," he says roughly. "Let's get you to class."

He turns on his heel, shoulders rigid, but keeps his steps short. A way to ensure I'm able to keep up with his longer stride.

I trail after him. My legs are unsteady, and my gut churns with all the words left unsaid between us. Gabriel isn't supposed to save me. I'm not his responsibility. Not anymore.

I just wish I was strong enough to save myself.

3
CECILIA

The day drags on at a snail's pace. Sitting through my first class of the week with Gabriel is uncomfortable, to say the least. There's this heavy tension hanging between us, and despite the weeks that have passed, it never seems to abate.

He still sits beside me, just like before—when he bothers to show up to class at least. And I know the classes he's missed lately are because of me. But even when he's here, he doesn't look at me. Doesn't flash me that crooked smile of his. He doesn't try to pull me into conversation.

I used to hate that. Hated that he wanted to be friends. That he tried to pull me out of my shell. But this ... this is so much worse.

It's a painful, suffocating silence.

The weight of unspoken words fill the space where casual banter used to flow, and by the time the bell rings signaling the end of class, I'm desperate for a reprieve from it.

Only there isn't one. Gabriel and I have two classes together today, and I get the feeling that the next one will be even worse. I don't know how to fix this. And if I'm honest, I'm not entirely sure I want to.

He isn't supposed to be my friend. He isn't supposed to be my anything.

Mom used to say, *time heals all wounds*.

Time hasn't helped me recover from what Austin did to me, but maybe with enough time, I can heal from this. From losing Gabriel.

The semester will end soon enough and with us no longer seeing each other, there's no reason for him to be in any more of my classes. He won't need to insert himself into my life. He won't drag me to his practices or drop in at my parents' house unannounced.

We won't cross paths every day. There's a good chance we can go an entire semester without even seeing one another.

Maybe then it will hurt less. That's all I can hope for these days.

After I gather my things, Gabriel walks beside me in silence, keeping pace with my shorter steps. I don't know why. He isn't talking to me, so why walk with me to class when he can easily outpace me?

But this has become a routine of sorts.

He shadows me but doesn't talk to me. He sits by me but never looks at me.

It's infuriating. Meanwhile, I can't help but steal glances at the hard line of his jaw, the furrow between his dark brows.

What is he thinking?

Is he angry? He looks it. But whether his anger is directed at me or someone else, I don't know. He might still be pissed about Austin. Though that was an hour ago. Maybe someone or something else is on his mind right now?

We've drifted apart in such a short span of time that I don't know how to read him anymore.

But I miss him. And I hate that I miss him because I have no right to. Not when I'm the one who pushed him away.

Part of me wishes I could slip my hand into his like I used to, and have things go back to the way they were before I opened my mouth and ruined everything.

But I can't. Life doesn't work that way. And it wouldn't be fair to him.

I told myself I wouldn't be selfish. Not when it comes to him.

We walk into our next class, and just like before, Gabriel claims the seat beside me. Our second class goes by much like the first, our professor droning on about this week's lecture. I'm barely paying attention, too caught up in watching Gabriel from the corner of my eye.

He looks as miserable as I feel. Is he sleeping okay? Are those dark circles or just shadows under his eyes?

Is this what it'll be like from now on? Gabriel spoke to me earlier in the hall when he defended me against Austin. A part of me thought it would continue. That this strange silent treatment thing going on between us would finally come to an end.

At least, I hoped it would.

Gabriel takes methodical notes beside me, his attention locked on the front of the room.

It's like I don't even exist.

Of my three classes, two of them are with him, and while I can't stand this weird limbo we're stuck in, I still dread when class comes to an end. Gabriel will go off to soccer practice, and I'll drag myself back home, where I know I'll overthink and second-guess my decision to break things off between us for the hundredth time.

I need a distraction. Some way to quiet my racing thoughts before I completely lose it. A swim, or maybe a run? It's days like this when I'm reminded of the fact I no longer have friends.

Joelle and Kim dropped me as soon as Austin drew battle lines in the sand. They were shitty friends. But they were the only ones I had and an irrational part of me misses them. Misses having someone to call and confide in.

The bell rings, jolting me from my thoughts. Our professor announces what chapters we'll need to have read by tomorrow, and everyone begins shuffling their things into their backpacks, eager for freedom.

I shove my own books haphazardly into my bag, refusing to let my eyes drift back to Gabriel. I can't stomach seeing that closed-off look of his aimed my way. Maybe I should make an appointment with my counselor. See if I can make some changes to my schedule before the semester ends.

I might have to take a zero since the withdrawal date has already passed, but it might be worth it. It's not like I'm in a rush to graduate or anything.

My phone chimes, and I look down at the screen, seeing the email alert from another of my professors.

Dear Students,

Class is canceled today and tomorrow due to an unforeseen personal matter. Please read up on last week's assignments. We will have a quiz on Wednesday on the materials we've been covering. It is weighted at 15% of your final grade. I encourage you to study in an effort to be prepared.

Regards, Professor Bowman.

My shoulders slump. *Great.*

Gabriel hovers beside me, his movements slow as though he's waiting for me. I try not to read into it. He's always walked me to my last class of the day when he's here, regardless of how tense things are between us, but it's canceled today.

Do I tell him?

No.

It's presumptuous to assume he'll want to walk me to class today, isn't it?

It is.

I'll just head to my Jeep and see what he does. Maybe he'll go the opposite direction as soon as we exit the classroom.

I don't know. And I hate not knowing.

We exit the building side by side, silence stretching between us. He's still following me, but we're not going in the direction of my class, and he hasn't asked me why. He also hasn't moved to head for the locker rooms, which are on the opposite end of our campus.

He just wordlessly walks beside me.

I want to bridge this gaping chasm between us, but I don't know how.

Or if he even wants me to try.

Lost in my thoughts, I don't see Felix bounding up to us, or the guy trailing close behind him. But I do notice when Gabriel stiffens beside me, coming to a stop. My footsteps falter beside him.

"Cecilia!" Felix greets me with a grin. "Long time no see. Have you met our new roomie?"

He tugs Deacon forward, and on instinct, I take a reflexive step back.

Gabriel all but growls beside me as he quickly tucks me behind his back.

"Shit, my bad." Felix offers me a chagrined grin. "I forgot about ..." He shrugs. "You know."

My aversion to strange men? Nearly all men, really. There are very few exceptions. Gabriel being one of them. I've gotten used to Julio and Felix, but only enough to be near them. Not to hug them or be any sort of touchy-feely with them. In a strictly platonic way, obviously. But you know what I mean. We've been friendly. But I don't know. I guess I really only count Gabriel as a friend.

Before, I mean. We're not friends now. We're not ... anything.

I swallow down the lump in my throat, reminding myself that it's fine. I'm fine. Felix is safe. And if this guy lives with

Gabriel, I'll assume they're friends, which means he's probably an alright guy.

Taking a deep breath, I force myself to take one cautious step forward, enough for me to see the new guy while still keeping myself shielded by Gabriel's back.

"No worries," I force out a smile, tamping down my anxiety. "New roommate?" I ask, my gaze flicking from Felix to Gabriel and then to the other guy. I take in his visible ink, both forearms decorated with intricate designs. He has light brown, almost hazel eyes framed with dark brows. Medium brown skin. Full lips.

There's a cross tattoo on the left side of his neck. A scroll design filled with script on the right. He's attractive, I guess. If you're into the whole athletically built, tattooed god sort of thing. But he's also ... imposing. A formidable player.

Is he on the soccer team? I don't remember seeing him on the field when I used to go to Gabriel's practices. And he's not the sort of guy you'd easily miss.

Gabriel likes to keep his circle tight.

I wonder how they know each other. And why I've never seen him around before.

"Yeah. Hey. I'm Deacon." The new guy shoots me a cocky smile, soft brown eyes scanning my face with interest. "Cecilia, right? Pretty name for a pretty girl."

Heat climbs up my neck, and not in a good way. I don't want him to notice me. To look at me like that. Like he finds me attractive. My breathing shutters, and Gabriel shifts abruptly, blocking me from Deacon's view. He glances over his shoulder once, looking down at me with concern flashing across his handsome face before turning back to the guys.

"You two should get to the field." His voice is hard. Cold. "Practice is going to be grueling today."

Felix's smile falters.

Silent communication passes between him and Gabriel before he nods, subtly drawing Deacon away. "Right. So, uh we'll see you out there. Later, Cecilia."

"Bye." I mutter, giving him a half-hearted wave.

I'm not sure he hears me.

As soon as they're gone from view, Gabriel turns halfway back towards me, then pauses, some of the tension seeming to drain from his broad shoulders.

He sucks on his teeth for a moment.

"You good?" His tone softens a fraction. This is Gabriel trying.

My chest squeezes and I nod. "Yeah. I'm good."

He nods his head, and the silence stretches between us again.

"Did you forget something in your car?"

My eyes snap up to his. "What?" The question slips out on autopilot before I put two and two together and correct my response. "Oh, no."

He tilts his head toward the doors. "You were heading to the parking lot ..." he trails off.

"My last class is canceled." I shrug. "Guess I'm all done for the day."

He dips his chin once before tilting his face up to the ceiling, almost like he's searching for the right words to say. Seconds tick past before he huffs out a sigh and god, I didn't know there could be so many words unsaid in a sound.

"I don't know where we go from here." There's defeat in his voice.

Neither do I, I want to tell him. But I don't know if that's the right thing to say or if I should say anything at all, so I stay quiet and wait for him to decide what to do. How we should move forward. I took Gabriel's choices away when I broke things off. This—allowing him to decide how we move forward—it's the least I can do.

"Do you want to come watch our practice?" Before I can respond, he adds, "I know the guys would like to see you. Julio asked about you this morning."

Oh. I find that hard to believe, and I don't really need the pity invite. He shouldn't have to see me at practice if he doesn't want to.

"No. That's okay. I ... uh ..." Julio is great. All the guys are. But they're not my friends, no matter how welcoming they've been to me. They're Gabriel's friends. His best friends.

And I'm the girl who broke their friend's heart.

I doubt any of them really want to be around me, though I appreciate that Felix was kind just now and said hello.

"You have other plans?" He knows I don't. I never do. I go to school. I go home. I hit the campus pool if I need a swim.

Rinse and repeat.

"Yeah." The lie rolls off my tongue. "I'll uh, see you around."

4
GABRIEL

"**I**'m going to murder him." I recount the moment I found Austin looming over Cecilia in the halls. How he was pressed up against her. How her eyes were wide and filled with tears. He's fucking terrorizing her.

That look of stark fear on her face. I don't ever want to see that look in her eyes again.

My blood boils, and my fingers curl into a fist. "Austin is a problem. One that needs to be dealt with."

Immediately. I'm sick of waiting around. I pulled back a little after Cecilia broke things off. I know she wants to fight her own battles, and with me out of the picture, it looked like Austin was laying off her, but fuck this. It's like the guy has a death wish.

"You can't retaliate," Julio says with a grimace. "We've gone over this before. He's provoking you for a reason. At his core, Austin is a bully. But he doesn't put himself in the line of fire.

He starts shit and lets his lackeys finish it. There's a reason he was goading you today."

"I know that," I snap. I've been trying for weeks now to find a way to get Holt kicked off the team and I've come up with nothing, but his stunt in the halls today reminded me of Coach's number one rule. No fighting off the field.

Best case scenario—if it's a minor infraction, a small tussle or some shoving—you're suspended from that week's game.

But players have gotten into more serious fights before and it's not uncommon in those situations for it to result in a player losing their spot on the team. Repeat offenders have even been expelled.

With my luck, my fate would be the latter.

Holt's rich-ass parents would storm the pitch and demand I be removed. With how much money they throw at the University, Coach would have no choice but to do what they wanted, and it'd be my future up in smoke. Not Holt's.

"I can't stand by and do nothing, either, J." From the moment Cecilia and I got together I've been trying to work out a solution, but short of her coming forward again and demanding some sort of justice—which there's no way in hell of her doing—there isn't anything we've been able to come up with.

Pursing his lips, he nods. "I know."

Felix shifts closer, his eyes straying to Deacon's who's casually leaning against our lockers, pretending not to hear our conversation. "Are we pulling him in?"

The man in question quirks a brow but remains silent, waiting for our decision. I like that about him.

Silent communication passes between Julio, Felix, and I. We've shielded Atticus from most of this. He's a freshman and his position on the field is goalie, so there's not a lot of opportunity for anyone on the team to target him. Thus far, Austin and his cronies have left him alone.

I'd like to keep it that way.

Deacon won't be so lucky, though. There's no way to hide the fact he lives with us, and to be honest, it's too much trouble to try. Holt, along with everyone else on the team, is going to get an introduction today. And it's not like we've been hiding him on campus. He's been kicking it with Felix all day. Austin will automatically mark him as an enemy the moment he lays his eyes on him. And with him open on the field ... *shit.*

"It's not something you should need to worry about," I tell him, feeling like an absolute dick for dragging him into this. "But we have problems with a few guys on the team. It doesn't mean you need to be involved in our problems, though." Living with our crew doesn't mean he has to take sides. He can try and stay out of it if he wants to. Keyword being try. "You're new here. There's no reason to rock the boat early on. But you should have a heads up because there's a chance you'll be targeted for living in the house. For being associated with us, whether you want to be involved or not." I tilt my chin toward Julio and Felix beside me. "Holt and his friends may not give you a choice."

Deacon's expression darkens. "Petty bullshit problems or real shit?" he asks, taking me a little by surprise.

"Real shit," Julio answers for me.

Deacon nods. "Alright. I'm taking sides. Pull me in."

I snort. "You can't make that decision without knowing what you're getting yourself into. And I can't give you all the details. Some shit isn't mine to share." Like what happened to Cecilia.

He shrugs. "Kasey and Dom vouched for you guys. That's enough for me. I don't need to play nice with anyone else. I'm here to play soccer. If people want to fuck with that, I know where my loyalty lies."

I level him with a considering gaze. "Just like that?"

He nods, hazel eyes determined. "Just like that."

Voices echo through the locker room as the door opens. We were the first ones here since most of us take morning classes, but it looks like the rest of our team has finally arrived.

"We'll fill you in and figure things out after practice." Julio says, shutting his locker and turning to me. "For now, focus. We don't need any distractions with Holt on the field, and we have a game coming up against the Crown Point University Hawks. They've had a killer season so far. We all need to have our heads on straight the moment we walk onto that field. Understood?"

We all mutter our agreements.

"Good. Now get dressed and get your asses on the pitch."

With that, Julio heads out, probably to go talk to Jameia—our assistant coach—and see what the plan is for today.

"You good?" Felix asks as soon as Julio is out of earshot.

"I will be," I tell him.

The corners of his mouth lift. "How are we playing today's practice?" he asks with a glint in his eyes.

I swear, the guy lives for this shit, so it's no surprise that his grin widens when I tell him, "Savage, my man. We wait for Holt to strike first," and he will. "And then we play fucking Savage."

BOTH MY SHINS ARE BLEEDING, BUT HOLT DOESN'T LOOK any better. He's got a bruise forming on his left cheek, and a trail of blood drips down his right elbow. He's been keeping that arm close to his side, too. A clear indication he doesn't want it jostled, so I know it hurts like a bitch.

Good.

We're halfway through practice, and shit is already ugly on the field. I can't take credit for the shiner. That one was all Deacon. He's been giving Holt a run for his money. From the moment Coach blew the whistle, Deacon's been on him.

I've got to hand it to the guy. For a freshman, he's a quick study.

Deacon Hunt analyzes the way each and every player plays, scrutinizing their position. How they move. Which direction they lean into when they move in for a steal or aim for a goal. It's fascinating to watch, and it's clear that no one on the field knows what to do with him.

The way his mind operates doesn't come as a surprise. Not when you really think about it.

Hunt was a quarterback for Suncrest U before his transfer to PacNorth. He's used to taking in the entire field, making note of everyone's position, the directions they're moving in. He's had to get comfortable with taking in massive amounts of information before making split-second decisions and that skill of his shows.

Deacon will make the starting lineup before the season's end. I have no doubt about it. Which is damn near unheard of for a freshman. This is only day one, and he's already performing at a high level. The only question now will be where to put him.

Soccer isn't like football. One player doesn't determine the play. But there are certain positions that can play to his strengths. Positions like mine. Not that I'm concerned.

We usually play 4-4-2 or 4-3-2-1 formations, so there are anywhere from three to four midfielders on the pitch at any given time. Watching the way Deacon's mind works, he'd be a killer attacking midfielder like myself. The only problem there is that an attacking midfielder provides support and opportunity for the striker to score, and right now, that person is Austin fucking Holt.

The division in the team is palpable, and I wish I could say it came from me, but Julio is right. We need our heads in the game if we're going to have any shot at beating CPU.

During practice at least, me and my boys are making an effort. I've passed that asshole the ball multiple times but Holt doesn't follow the play. He's aggressive, causing us to respond in kind as he takes cheap shots that interfere with advances that should be resulting in goals.

In short, he's turning practice into a mess, and Coach is pissed. We all are. The only thing improving my mood is that for every cheap shot Holt takes, I'm able to hit him back just as hard.

If he plays like this during our game, we're going to lose, and while he might not care given that soccer is just a pastime for him, the rest of us do. Even a couple of his frat buddies are starting to look visibly pissed off.

Coach blows his whistle in the middle of one of our plays.

"Reset," he shouts. "One-Two," he calls out our next play.

My gaze flickers to Deacon. "You good?"

His mouth twists, and I curse. He doesn't know this one. "I got it." I tell him, getting into position.

Deacon's rusty on the particulars of the game, and he'll need to spend time outside of practice memorizing plays, but he'll get there. All of that can be taught.

What comes naturally to the guy is his speed. He's fast as fuck and he's one hell of a good shot. He hasn't missed a single goal he's gone after. To say I'm impressed is putting it mildly.

"You gonna pull your fucking weight?" I yell at Holt. As the striker, that asshole is pivotal in a One-Two play.

"Fuck you," he shouts back.

Awesome. New plan. I put my hand up asking Coach to give us a minute and jog over to Deacon. Coach curses but gives me the time.

"A one-two is a give and go," I tell Deacon. "It's a two-player quick pass combination. You take possession of the ball and quickly get it to me, then run your ass up the field. We'll go back and forth until one of us is in position to score."

His brows draw forward.

"Hey," I snap my fingers in front of his face. "Quarterback," I say, trying to come up with a way for him to better understand this. "Take the snap. Go short and get it to me. As soon as I'm in possession, our roles reverse. You're the receiver. Go long. As soon as you take possession, you're QB again and I'll run up the field. Fast. Go long again. Rinse and repeat until we reach the goal. Got it?"

His mouth is still pinched, but he nods. Good enough.

We take our positions, and Coach blows his whistle, starting the play.

Deacon does exactly what I tell him, and since Coach called out the play, the other half of our team playing as our opponents are ready, but they expect Hunt to pass the ball to Holt and are taken by surprise when he gets the ball to me instead.

The play is on.

I race up the field, eyes tracking Deacon until he's in front of me, and I shoot it back over to him.

"What the fuck," Austin curses, racing after us. I block him out.

"Go, go!" Felix whoops, hanging back to play defense.

I sprint up the field, my cleats kicking up turf with each of my steps.

Deacon shoots the ball back to me, and I dribble forward, narrowly avoiding Austin's steal.

Asshole.

I pass back to Deacon.

We're two-thirds up the field. He's almost there when Deacon shoots me a look. He's not going to take the shot.

I spot the cross. Hunt's coming in from the wing. I get in front of him, just outside the penalty area and he snaps it back. The ball flies high through the air. I time my jump, connecting with it cleanly in mid-air. The satisfying thud of my foot meeting the ball echoes in my ears and I watch it sail toward the goal. Atticus leaps, arms outstretched but the ball goes high, sailing through the top corner of the net.

Goal.

"Holy shit, bro!" Atticus shouts after climbing back to his feet.

I chuckle, my euphoria riding high. "That was fucking magic," I tell Hunt.

He opens his mouth to respond, but before a single word leaves his mouth, Parker Benson plows right into him from behind.

Deacon doesn't have a chance to brace himself. His body goes careening forward, and he crashes into the field. Hard.

"What the fuck?" I snap, veering off in their direction. "The play was already over," I shout, throwing my arms in the air and shoving Benson back.

Not even bothering to apologize, Benson shrugs and jogs away.

Asshole.

I help Deacon to his feet, paying special attention to the way he moves. That fall didn't look good.

"You alright?" I ask.

He runs his tongue over his teeth, a dark expression crossing over his face. "Great."

Bullshit. The guy looks pissed.

"This the type of shit I should expect more of?" he asks. "I kinda thought it was just the one asshole."

My gaze sweeps over to where Holt is. Benson, Chambers, Pru, and a few others stand loose beside him, their gazes trained in our direction.

"Yeah," I tell him. "Holt doesn't like being outshined. He's pulling his boys in."

If Austin doesn't want to be cut out of a play, then he should get his head out of his ass and do the fucking play. The dick can't even fight his own battles. Not that I didn't see this coming. I knew he'd be pissed and find some way to retaliate. But what Benson did was a bitch move.

Deacon isn't the one who took Austin's position. I'm the one who slipped into his spot. The hit should have been directed at me.

Fuck them.

"Is it an us against them sort of thing?" Deacon asks. "I like to know where and how deep to draw my lines."

I nod. "It's looking that way."

The team knows there's a situation between Holt and me, and that's enough to draw some obvious lines, but so far, it's always been Austin against me. This is the first time another of our teammates has so blatantly gotten involved.

There's a divide between those players who are pledged to Zeta Pi, and those of us who aren't. The frat brothers are sticking together and following Holt like blind fucking sheep.

No surprise there.

But the rest of the team is loyal to Julio. He's our captain, so the team is used to following his lead. It feels natural, and if they've played with him for more than one season, then they know to trust his judgment.

Julio made it clear whose side he's on. Mine. And the rest of the team is either making their positions known or staying the fuck out of it. But until today, tensions have stayed strictly off-field, outside of the game. It's tense in the locker room. We don't all get along. But on the field, we keep our heads in the fucking game.

Deacon spits on the grass and grins. His saliva paints his teeth red, and between that and the gleam in his eyes, he's got one hell of a manic appearance. "Cool. So all the assholes over there are free game?" He rolls his neck from side to side, legs bouncing in place.

I nod. "Safe to say it's everyone who's pledged to Zeta Pi."

"Looks like I won't be joining any fraternities." His jaw ticks, but he doesn't drop his bloodstained grin.

I clap him on the shoulder. "Not unless you want to become besties with those twats." I nod toward Holt's entourage.

"Pass."

Figured as much.

Coach switches us to drills for the rest of the day. I think his plan is to wear us out so we can't keep taking our shit out on one another on the field. Despite how physical it's gotten, and how damn near everyone on the team is either bleeding or visibly bruised, he hasn't once yelled at us to knock it off.

Coach feels the pressure of our game against Crown Point University, too. And while he needs us all in one piece, it's to his benefit if we're pissed off during the game. That way, he can direct our anger.

When practice ends, we all make our way to the showers. My calves are on fire and an ache has settled into my lower back. In the locker room, I shed my clothes and grab a towel before heading for the stalls and making quick work of rinsing off the day's dirt, sweat, and blood. I have no intention of sticking around any longer than I need to. No need to chance another confrontation with Holt. Not when I'm as hot-headed as I am right now.

Done in the shower, I grab my clothes and get dressed before retrieving my things from my locker. Shouldering my bag, I linger a few minutes while the other guys finish up. Holt is talking nonsense a few rows away, and I tune his aggravating voice out.

We need to come up with a plan. One that actually has a shot of working, because on top of what Holt did to Cecilia, if today's practice is anything to go by, he's becoming a goddamn liability for the team.

Glancing at my phone, I fight the urge to text Cecilia. To see if she's okay.

She was visibly shaken after her encounter with Holt. But I know she wouldn't have accepted any comfort from me. She wants to stand on her own two feet. I get that. But there's nothing wrong with having a support system. With having people in your corner to watch your back. It's what I have

54

with Felix, Atticus, and Julio. Hell, after today, I feel confident enough to add Deacon into that mix.

Cecilia needs to know she has people. She has me.

I should message her.

I'm going to message her.

My thumb hovers over the keyboard and I type out a text only to delete it.

Fuck.

It's not complicated. We're not together, but we can still talk. Right? I mean, we haven't. Not for the past several weeks. But we could. There's no rule saying we can't be ... friends.

The word is bitter as I roll it around in my head.

I don't want to be her friend. The thoughts I have when it comes to Cecilia Russo aren't *friendly*. They're obsessive. Consuming. I want to know the girl inside and out. On an intimate level.

I want to know the girl she was before the assault. Know the survivor she's become. The fighter she is each and every day.

And I want to meet the amazing woman I know she'll be after she has time to heal. I want to know every version there is to know of Cecilia. And I want to lay claim to every goddamn one of them.

Fuck, I'm going to turn into a stalker or some shit with the way my thoughts are wandering, but I can't help it.

I want to own her. Mind, body, and soul. To strip her bare and memorize every inch of her sun-kissed skin. To get inside her head and know her innermost thoughts. Her secrets. Her fears.

Friends.

I barely manage to stifle a laugh and shake my head as I continue glowering down at my phone. No. I don't want to be her friend. But if soccer has taught me anything, it's that forward progress is never instant. I'm used to delayed gratification, and winning Cecilia back will be the sweetest form that there is.

Decision made, I type out a quick message.

> **Me: Hey.**

She has her messages set to show read, so I see the moment she opens my text.

Seconds tick by without a reply, and I consider typing out another one.

Am I that guy now? The one who sends a string of messages in some desperate bid to get a chick's attention?

There are no little bubbles. Nothing to indicate she has any intention of responding.

I rub the back of my neck. Fuck it. Guess I am that guy.

> **Me: Can we ta—**

I delete the text without sending it and try again.

> **Me: How are you—**

No. Shit. Why is this so hard? I delete my second attempt and take a deep breath. Just be casual. She won't want me checking in on her. Despite Austin being a fucking creep. I know asking how she's holding up is the last thing she wants to hear from me. It'll just make her throw more walls up.

Third time's the charm. I've got this.

> Me: We have a game against Crown Point University coming up. It's a home game. You should come.

I hit send and wait.

Fuck. Should I have worded that as a question? If I made it a question, she'd feel more obligated to respond. Damn. I should have—

Three little bubbles appear. She's typing a response.

Yes.

The hairs on the back of my neck raise, and I turn around to find Holt leering behind me, eyes locked on my phone. A cruel smile curls his mouth and he lets out a piercing whistle.

"Damn, Herrera. Who would have thought you'd be the one to turn pussy for a fucking cleat chaser?" He laughs and some of the Zeta Pi members join him.

Julio and Felix drop their shit and immediately step up to flank me. Out of the corner of my eye, I see Deacon rise from the bench beside his own locker, but Julio must wave him off because he sits back down, his expression calculating.

"Do you need something?" Julio asks, his voice steady.

Holt eyes him up and down with a sneer. "Not from you," he retorts. "Unless you plan on acting like our fucking captain for once and put your boy back in his place."

Silence.

The background noise in the locker room from the team's chatter, faucets being turned on and off, and other random sounds come to a halt as all eyes turn our way. The tension between us ratchets in the room.

Julio folds his arm over his chest and dips his chin. His eyes narrow into a cold glare. "You wanna run that by me again?" There's a warning in his voice, but judging by the smirk on Holt's face, he's not going to heed it.

Austin takes a menacing step forward. "Get your boy in line," he growls.

"Or what?" Julio deadpans. He doesn't need to raise his voice. To curse. Every guy in the room knows how serious Julio is right now.

"Or we're going to have problems," Austin snaps, but some of his earlier nerve is slipping away. His mouth dips, eyes now wary.

I laugh. I can't help it. One second it's so quiet you can hear a pin drop and the next I'm fucking cackling. "Or we're going to have problems," I repeat, my voice mocking. "You're such a fucking cliché. We already have problems, so why don't you back the fuck off? Or better yet, quit the team so we don't have to deal with your pretentious ass any longer."

Austin bares his teeth, but before things escalate further, Jamiea—our assistant coach—pokes her head into the locker room. "Everyone dressed?" she calls out. Her hand covers her eyes as she walks further into the room.

"All clear," Julio says, keeping his voice controlled.

She drops her hand and, almost as quickly, drops her smile. Her dark brown gaze flickers over each of us. "Everything alright?"

Austin takes a step back.

"All good," I tell her, not bothering to remove my gaze from Holt's.

"Just catching up with friends," he adds.

"Mm Hmm. I absolutely buy that." Sarcasm. Walking toward us, Jamiea inserts herself between us, forcing both Austin and I to take several steps back in order to give her enough room to pass for respectful.

Now, Deacon climbs to his feet. It looks like he's still got eyes for our assistant coach.

That's too bad. Jamiea won't cross that line. Not now that he's a student at PacNorth. She isn't much older than us. Twenty-five or twenty-six if I had to guess. And she's not a teacher. But she's still faculty and there are rules. Ones I know Jamiea well enough to know she won't break.

"Anyone want to explain what's going on?" She folds her arms and taps her foot, her impatience clear.

Holt and I glare at one another over the top of her curl-covered head, our eyes never leaving each other.

"It's all good," I tell her. "We were just heading out."

5
CECILIA

I go home after class, but the first thing out of my parents' mouths is to ask about Gabriel. I haven't told them we ended things. Not yet.

Life is finally going back to normal for me. They still hover. That's not going to change anytime soon. Not after the suicide attempt. But they've chilled with the fifth degree whenever I walk through the door.

Mom doesn't watch me like I'm a ticking time bomb she's waiting to see explode.

I don't want things to go back to that. So when my Dad asks why they haven't seen Gabriel around this past week, I lie. I tell him Gabe's doing extra training for an upcoming game and that I'm only here to drop off my school bag and grab some things before heading back to campus to watch his practice.

It kills me to lie to my parents, but what choice do I have?

Better a small white lie than breaking their hearts. I know they want what's best for me. They want me to be happy. But everyone needs to give me some breathing room so I can figure out what happiness looks like for myself. So I can sort out how to move on.

My phone buzzes, and I quickly glance at the screen.

"Speak of the devil," I tell my mom, flashing the screen in her direction long enough for her to read his name on the screen.

Her smile is wide when I tell her, "Gotta run."

"Alright, honey. Have fun."

I swipe across the screen to open the message.

> Gabriel: Hey.

Butterflies dance in my stomach as I stare down at the words. We're not really talking, but after today I guess we're not *not* talking.

But what am I supposed to say to that? Do I say "Hey," back? *Hey* doesn't really invite conversation.

Do I want to invite conversation?

I glance at the time on the screen and chew on my bottom lip. Gabriel should be at practice right now. Maybe the text was meant for someone else? Like a 'Hey, where are you?' if he was waiting on Julio or Felix to get there, maybe? That seems logical.

Exiting out of the screen, I decide not to respond. Mostly because I don't know what to say but it's fine. I'll see him tomorrow, along with every weekday this semester after that. Perks of us having classes together. If he has anything to say or talk to me about, he can do it then. I'll just act like I didn't see the message.

Since I'm not actually going to Gabriel's practice, I park beside the building that holds the campus pool. A good swim will help me to clear my head and should get me out of this funk. I feel like a jerk for not responding, but saying the wrong thing feels more detrimental than saying nothing.

When I step inside, I notice that the swim team is utilizing most of the fifty-meter lanes, but there's one on the far left that looks like it's available so I walk straight for it.

My phone buzzes again but I wait until I'm inside before digging it out of my pocket.

> Gabriel: We have a game against Crown Point University coming up. It's a home game. You should come.

I stare at the message, scrutinizing each individual word. Is he suggesting I come because he actually wants me to be there? Or is he just worried about me because of what happened with Austin today and he wants to keep an eye on me?

This is what he does, isn't it? He inserts himself into my life as a way of babysitting me. Making sure I'm okay. That I'm not going to do anything reckless. Austin is on the team, so it's not like he has to worry about where he'll be during their game.

Or is he thinking something worse?

We haven't been talking, so it's not like he knows how I'm doing. Shitty, by the way. Not that anyone's asking or that I'd volunteer that information out loud.

I'm anxious as usual. And if I'm honest, a little depressed. A breakup on top of what I'm already dealing with has royally sucked. But I get out of bed every day. I go to all my classes. I've lost more weight, but it's not super noticeable and hey, I look better in my swimsuit, so that's a plus.

The point I'm trying to make here is, I'm better than I have been.

Does Gabriel think I'll try and end my life again just because Austin decided to be his normal awful self today? Is that why he's all of a sudden messaging me after weeks of radio silence?

I hate thinking like this. It just reiterates why we can't be together. Gabriel always needs to fix things. To fix me. And I know I'm a wreck.

But anyone else in my position would be. What girl who'd been through what I've been through would do any better? No one. That's who.

I'm capable of standing on my own two feet. Gabriel needs to let me.

Urgh. I'm reading too much into this.

I consider ignoring this text as well, but that feels like an asshole move. I don't want him to think I'm ignoring him. I'm not. And he did follow up with more than 'Hey.'

I sigh, my fingers moving over my keyboard with what I hope is a safe enough response.

> Me: Maybe... I'll think about it.

I slipped my suit on beneath my clothes while I was home, so I quickly strip out of my oversized t-shirt and jeans and set my phone and other belongings on a chair before tucking my hair into a swim cap and putting on my goggles.

A whistle blows. "Come on, ladies. Push!"

I lift my gaze to the pool and a pang of longing stutters through my chest as I watch Coach Cho urge the girls to move faster. She looks down at her stopwatch, her expression pinched as her eyes flick from it to the nine swimmers racing through the lanes.

I considered going out for the swim team last year before the assault and everything that happened after it. I'm good enough to make the team. My fifty-meter freestyle is faster than Cate's—the team's fastest swimmer in freestyle for PacNorth. But I just … I don't know. I could never work up the nerve to go for it. I was on the cheer squad already, and at the time, I didn't want to rock the boat with my team.

Swimming has always been my stress reliever. I think I convinced myself that turning it into a competitive sport would take away my joy. Really, I think I was more concerned about upsetting my friends if I left the squad and chose swimming over cheer, but look how that turned out.

Joelle and Kim don't talk to me. And I'm not on the cheer squad anymore, nor did I join the swim team. I'm just … alone.

There's a part of me that misses being a part of something. Misses being on a team. But there's a bigger part of me that's terrified of joining one only to have the rug yanked out from under me all over again. Losing my friends after the assault was hard. Losing the team and everyone else I counted as part of my support system, that made everything that much harder.

It's too late for all of that now, though. The season has already started. Maybe next year I'll put myself out there. It'd make Mom and Dad happy. I sigh knowing how unlikely it is that I'll go through with it. But it's a nice thought. Something to be hopeful about, as Dr. Walker likes to remind me.

Hope is being able to see that there is, in fact, light despite all of the world's darkness.

I'm just over here still searching for it.

Pushing my thoughts aside, I make my way to the block and step onto it, getting myself into position. This is where I clear my thoughts. Where I let everything going on in my life go.

Curling my toes over the edge, I bend forward, keeping my face close to my knees as I grip the front of the diving block with my fingers.

Lifting my hips in the air, I take a deep breath and close my eyes. You've got this, I tell myself.

I hear the rustle of the other swimmers getting into position in the lanes beside me and wait for their coach to blow her whistle. I don't usually compete beside them like this. Not in such an obvious way. But today, I want to latch onto that hope.

My heart races with anticipation. The scent of chlorine fills the air, and for a second, I imagine what it would be like to race for PacNorth University. To hear the roar of a crowd. To know that everyone around me is cheering for me to succeed.

The only thing that matters in this moment is the water that stretches out before me. Not Austin's bullshit. Not the way things are between me and Gabriel. Not how my friends turned their backs on me. Or how all my parents seem to do is worry.

My anxiety doesn't matter. Depression doesn't matter.

None of it matters.

The world around me blurs, and my focus narrows to the clear blue lane ahead.

The seconds tick by and then I hear the sound I've been waiting for. "Take your marks!" Coach yells.

I'm not a part of the team, but screw it. For today, I'm going to pretend I am.

The whistle blows, announcing the start of the race, and I explode off the block. I don't know what stroke everyone else is doing but I also don't care. My body arches through the air. Water rushes up to meet me and for a split second, I'm weightless, suspended in the blue until I kick up and break the surface, slicing through the water like a knife.

I feel strong in this moment.

Brave.

My arms propel me forward, each stroke more powerful than the one before it.

There's this sense of urgency thrumming inside of me. I want to win. No. I need to win.

The water parts before me, a liquid highway that urges me to go faster.

The wall approaches, and I kick harder, my body driving toward the ledge. The seconds tick away, but time loses its meaning. All that matters is the final stretch.

With a surge of power, I reach out, my fingertips brushing the wall. I lift my head from the water and look around, counting the seconds until the next fastest swimmer reaches the wall.

One.

Two.

Three.

Four.

Holy shit.

Five.

Six.

Another girl touches the wall. She breaks the surface, a wide smile on her face until she sees me. She turns to her side, taking note of the other swimmers whose times she did beat. But she didn't beat mine.

Triumph floods through me.

I smile to myself and use the ledge of the pool to lift myself out of the water. That was ... exhilarating. I want to do it again.

Only my excitement is short-lived. As soon as I take off my goggles, I catch a familiar face pushing off from the wall across the room.

Parker Benson.

What is he doing here? I glance at the clock. Soccer practice must have just ended, but it doesn't explain why he's here. Or why he's heading straight for me.

His expression is dark. Angry. My stomach drops, and I quickly scan the room. No one seems to have noticed his arrival. Either that, or they don't care.

He's dressed in a pair of loose-fitting jeans and one of the University's navy blue hoodies. A wolf is outlined in white and neon green, with the school's crest taking up most of the center. His hair is damp. Freshly showered. Which means he came here immediately after leaving the locker room. But why?

What can he possibly want with me?

My breath catches in my throat, panic rising up inside me with each step that brings him closer. I try to get my legs to move, to run the opposite way, but they refuse to obey me.

Frozen in place, I hold my breath as Parker draws closer, his dark blue eyes locking onto mine.

His lips curl into a sinister sneer, and a shiver runs down my spine. A thousand questions swirl in my mind. What does he want? Why is he so angry? How do I get myself out of this?

Despite all of my questions, I have no answers.

My heart races, and my palms grow damp with sweat. My chest tightens, and all of a sudden I feel exposed in my conservative one-piece swimsuit. The urge to cover my body, to hide, sweeps through me, but worse is the desperate need to run fast and far away. Only, I can't. My feet refuse to move. It's like the wires have short-circuited inside my brain.

I feel like I'm drowning on dry land and any moment I'm going to black out and Parker will be free to do whatever he wants to me.

The memories of that night come rushing to the forefront of my mind. I can't escape them.

What. Does. He. Want?

As he approaches, his voice reaches my ears, a low and mocking tone that sends a fresh wave of fear down my spine. "For someone so small," he snarls, his words dripping with malice. "You're turning into a big fucking problem."

I open my mouth to respond, but nothing comes out. My voice abandons me, leaving me mute and defenseless. *Fuck. Fuck. Fuck.*

He steps even closer, his presence overwhelming. "You're fucking up soccer for me," he growls, circling me like a predator closing in on its prey. "You're messing with my future."

Every fiber of my being screams at me to run, to cry out for help, but I'm paralyzed. My fear has taken hold of me, rendering me powerless. All I can think about is when he and the others shoved me to my knees. How he shoved his cock into my mouth while Austin held my arms behind my back. How he violated me.

"Hey! Back the hell up," a woman bites out, and both Parker and I jerk in her direction. One of the team swimmers climbs out of the pool and approaches us, tearing her goggles and swim cap from her head.

"Are you deaf or some shit?" she snaps, her gaze trained on Parker. "Or are you just an asshole? I told you to back off. No girl wants you up in her personal space like this."

Parker scowls, but doesn't bother giving her his attention. "Walk away. This doesn't concern you."

She scoffs, "Pass," and moves closer until she's standing so close that if she takes one more step, she'll be smack dab between us. Her proximity forces him to pay attention to her now. "Back the fuck off, or we're going to have a problem." Her voice is even. Sure. She doesn't have to raise it to get her point across. You can hear the threat in her tone, or at least, I do.

My breathing becomes ragged. She shouldn't have said that. I don't know what Parker will do, but I can't imagine it'll be anything good.

With exaggerated slowness, Parker turns his face toward her. "Who the hell—"

Everything happens so fast. One second, Parker is towering over me. We're near the edge of the pool but a safe enough distance away that no one is going to accidentally fall in. Then the next second, he's tipping over the edge, exhaling a harsh note of surprise.

The girl shoves him hard and fast, seemingly out of nowhere.

Parker loses his balance and his body careens over the ledge, colliding with the surface of the pool at an awkward angle. The water sucks him under and rushes over his head.

Holy shit! I stand there frozen and wide-eyed, watching the water lap over him. Did she just—

I turn to look at her.

She stares down at the water, a satisfied smirk on her face.

Oh no. This is bad. Really bad.

Parker resurfaces and sputters out an angry curse. "You fucking bitch. You're going to pay for that."

He struggles in the water, his heavy clothes making it difficult to stay afloat as he swims toward us.

The girl folds her arms over her chest and glares at him, her expression lethal. "I told you to back off. You're the one who didn't listen." She turns her attention to me. "I don't like having to repeat myself, and men can be so fucking stupid sometimes."

My mouth opens and closes like a fish out of water. I have no idea what to say to that. Panic has stolen my words. What was she thinking? Parker is going to retaliate. Guys like him always do.

"You alright, there?" she asks, stepping closer to me. She waves a hand in front of my face.

My eyes flick between her and Parker. He's already hoisting himself out of the pool. His clothes are plastered to his body, wet hair dripping down his face. Shit, shit, shit. His jaw is tight. Nostrils flared. I've never been confronted by him before. It's always been Austin going out of his way to fuck with me. Parker Benson and Gregory Chambers—the other guys involved that night—they've always given me a wide berth. I sort of assumed they were just happy to get away with what they did to me and weren't going to chance it.

Austin doesn't work that way. He gets off on putting me in my place. On making me relive the fear and humiliation. I didn't think Parker was like that.

I guess I was wrong. I don't know why I ever could have thought that way. Parker was always sort of out of sight, out of mind. But that was stupid of me. He's always been a threat. Always been dangerous. They all are.

Something must have happened.

Think, Cecilia. Think.

He said I was ruining soccer for him, but what does that even mean? I stopped going to Gabriel's practices. I've never been to any of their games.

I'm not bothering anyone.

Fuck. The expression on his face is murderous as he climbs to his feet and makes a beeline right for me. Again.

We need to get out of here.

I grab the girl's arm, unwilling to leave her here to face Parker's wrath alone. Not when she defended me. She doesn't even know who I am. Why would she put herself at risk like that? Parker is pledged to the Zeta Pi fraternity. If one of those guys has it out for you, they all do.

This is bad. Really bad.

"Come on," I say, all but dragging her from the room by her forearm.

"What? Where are we—"

"Hurry!" I hiss and increase my steps.

Parker gets held up when some of the other swim team girls rush over, fawning over him and asking if they can help get him out of his wet clothes. One goes so far as to push the sopping wet material of his sweater up to his neck, exposing the hard lines of his abdomen.

Gag. But I don't stop to warm them away. Not when they're making it possible for the two of us to get out of here. I don't understand why women fall all over themselves for guys like him.

There is no amount of good genetics that will ever make Parker look like anything less than what he is.

A monster.

Quickening her steps, the girl follows me toward the exit. We're close. The door that will lead us outside is right there. I chance a quick look over my shoulder and our gazes collide.

"Cecilia!" Parker roars. "We're not done!"

The hell we aren't. If I never have to see Parker Benson again, it'll be too soon.

Ignoring his demand to stop, I break into a run.

"Come on!" My wet feet slap against the pavement. Quickly grabbing my things from the chair I'd dropped them on, I shove open the door and exhale a breath of relief as soon as I taste the crisp fall air. But we're not out of the woods yet.

"We need to put some distance between us and Benson," I tell the girl. "You can come back to grab your things from the locker room later."

Her brows furrow, but she nods, so I drop my hold on her arm, praying she'll continue following me.

We run between buildings, turning left when a small walkway between the commons and the library appears. Pressing myself to the rough stone wall, I strain my ears for any sign of Parker's pursuit.

I don't hear heavy footfalls on the pavement, and his furious voice never reaches my ears.

My chest heaves. I don't think he followed us. Which just means I'll need to be on the lookout for him whenever I'm on campus. I don't want him catching me off guard like that again.

I'm pissed at myself for just standing there like a frozen freaking fish. What would have happened if she didn't intervene? Yelled at me for sure, but what if he did more than that? What if he touched me or did something worse?

A shiver travels down my spine, and bile rises in my throat thinking about how Austin pressed himself into me. Would Parker have done something like that? Would he have tried to corner me? Maybe drag me off somewhere private? Would I have stayed so frozen in my fear that I would've allowed him to get me alone?

There's a chance I might have. But I don't let myself dwell on it right now.

"I think we're safe," I tell her, not believing my own words, but I need to say something. Bracing my hands on my knees, I force myself to slow my breathing. In through my nose. Out through my mouth.

The adrenaline is wearing off, and I'm beginning to feel lightheaded. I need to get somewhere quiet. Somewhere safe. I can't afford to break down and have a panic attack out here where I'm exposed. Parker or anyone else can stumble upon me.

If Parker is looking for me, there's a decent chance that Gregory or Austin are, too.

Birds of a feather ...

I shake my head. I've stayed quiet. I ended things with Gabriel. What more do they want from me?

"I'm Adriana," the girl says, sticking her hand out toward me.

I straighten, swallowing hard. "Cecilia." We shake hands, and I chew my bottom lip, trying to come up with some sort of explanation. I know she's going to want one. Any sane person would.

"You want to tell me what all that was about back there? Not sure what I walked into, but that guy—Benson, that's what you called him, right?"

And there it is. Explanation required.

"Parker Benson. But yeah, that's his name."

"He's a serious asshole. Is he your ex-boyfriend or something? If he is, you've got real shitty taste."

My lip curls. "Definitely not."

"Good." She nods. "But then, what's his deal?"

"I'm not really sure," I hedge. "He's never come at me like that." All true, though I leave out the part where he's one of three guys who assaulted me at a party this past summer. A lot of that night is a blur. I'm only able to remember bits and pieces.

Austin recounted the night's events in sickening detail, but I don't know if I believe him.

That's a lie.

I'm pretty sure I do believe him. I only wish I didn't.

Austin claims he was the only one to rape me. He's bragged about it actually. Like being the only one to fuck me while I'm unconscious is some prize.

Parker and Gregory fucked my face. I remember that part. Choking as Parker forced his cock into my mouth. Gagging when his cum hit the back of my throat.

He and Gregory took turns, and all three of them laughed as tears streamed down my face.

Whatever drugs they slipped into my drink that night kicked in shortly after that, so the last thing I really remember with any sort of clarity is when Austin lifted me onto the bed. I remember his weight pressing into me. The way he tore at my clothes and the feel of him groping my breast.

And then ... nothing.

I'm grateful for the nothing.

There's a recording of what happened. Austin taunts me with it often enough. He texted it to me the morning after. His way of threatening me to fall in line. He says the video makes it look like I'm an active participant. Like I wanted it to happen.

I didn't believe him, of course. But I watched the first minute or so of the recording. With the angle of the camera. You can't tell anyone is holding my hands behind my back. That I'm being restrained.

I threw up and stopped watching after that.

I don't remember everything they did to me, but I remember enough of what happened for it to break something inside of me. For that reason alone, I've never tried to watch it all the way through.

I want to forget what little I do remember, not add to it. How else am I supposed to move on?

"Are you okay? You look a little pale."

I wave her off and shove my dark memories back into their box. "All good," I tell her, blinking away the burning sensation in my eyes. "I just wasn't really expecting that. You know?"

Pursing her lips, she nods. Silence stretches between us. It's not uncomfortable per se. But I still have the urge to fill it.

"Thank you," I tell her. "I appreciate you stepping in like that. Though you should probably avoid Parker if you see him around campus. He's ..." I hesitate. "He can be dangerous." I'd never forgive myself if he targeted her next. She needs to be careful. "He's not someone you want to be caught alone with."

She ponders my warning. "Okay. I'll keep an eye out."

Good.

"He gives off major creep vibes."

She's not wrong.

"He does," I agree. Unraveling my clothes, I slip them on over my still wet swimsuit. "Maybe I'll uh, see you around."

"Hold up." She pulls her long, wet brown hair over her shoulder and gives me a considering look. "You're a competitive swimmer, right? Are you a part of a private team or something?"

I eye her PacNorth swimsuit again. She's probably freezing out here. I wasn't really thinking when I dragged her with me outside into the cold. It's fall in Richland so the sun is shining but there's enough of a breeze to make it chilly.

"No. I swim recreationally."

"Cool. Cool." Adriana mulls over her next words. There's something kind of, I don't know, off about her maybe. But not in a bad way.

Her voice is even with almost no inflection. I noticed that when she was telling Parker off. She never raised her voice. She didn't sound angry or scared. She was just to the point. Authoritative. There's something about the way Adriana speaks and holds herself that makes me feel like she's ... I don't know how to describe it. In charge, maybe? No. That doesn't feel right.

She's a predator. That word feels fitting. But not in the same way that Austin, Parker, and Gregory are predators. With Adriana it's more like she's confident of her place at the top of the food chain, not like she's going to use her position to hurt those beneath her.

It's a weird thing to wrap my head around, but being next to her now, I don't feel like prey. There's this innate understanding that I'm not as strong as she is. Not at her level. But I also feel sort of ... safe.

I roll my eyes. I'm not making any sense. Today has been a stressful day and my cracks are showing. That's all it is. I just need to go home, get a good night's rest, and forget all about today.

"Have you thought about going out for the team? One of our girls is injured and won't be back this season. We need to fill her place so Coach is opening up a last minute spot."

My ears perk up. Not because someone is injured. That's awful and I hope she recovers. But having a spot open mid-season is virtually unheard of.

"What's the stroke?" I ask while silently debating if I can do it. I thought about it earlier, being on a team again. But is it really something I want, or was it more just wishful thinking?

"Freestyle and butterfly."

I swallow hard. Freestyle is my jam. It's what I excel at. A small bubble of excitement blossoms in my chest. "I can do freestyle," I tell her.

Adriana smirks. "I know. I've seen you swim before."

Oh. That's ... cool. I guess. "My butterfly isn't great, though." Probably not as good as hers.

"It's better than Cate's was. You'll be fine."

Cate? There's only one Cate on the swim team that I know of. But she's their star. "Cate Carrington? She's out?"

Adriana smiles. "She is. And good riddance. Girl is a total diva." She's not wrong, but that doesn't mean I'll agree with her out loud.

Chewing my lower lip, I think about it. Like really think about it. I can join the team. I can compete. I ... I can do this.

"When are tryouts?"

"Technically, this Friday, but if I tell Coach you're interested, she'll probably cancel them. She's been watching you for a while now. You swim during our practices sometimes and she times you. You're faster than everyone else on the team in freestyle, butterfly, and breaststroke. The only one you struggle with is—"

"Backstroke," I finish for her. It's my least favorite.

She nods. "Yeah. But we don't need you for that. Not unless you want to do a medley."

And swim four strokes in the same race, not particularly.

"But like I was saying, if Coach knows you're interested, she's not going to make you try out. She'll just give you the spot with a smile and say welcome to the team."

I shake my head. "I don't want any special treatment. I want to earn my spot." I want to know that I got myself on that team. That I accomplished something.

"It's not special treatment when you're as fast in the water as you are. You totally smoked me today before that asshole showed up, and I'm the second faster swimmer on our team next to Cate. But I can respect that." She puts her hand out. "Let me see your phone."

I give it to her, and her fingers tap across the screen.

"There. I added my contact information. Tryouts are Friday at eleven."

"Okay," I tell her. "I'll be there."

6
GABRIEL

Cecilia is early to class this morning. Nothing out of the ordinary. But what sticks out to me is that she's texting on her phone. Taking her usual seat beside me, she keeps her head tucked low as her fingers fly over her phone's screen.

There's a tentative smile on her face. Whoever she's talking to, she likes them.

Jealousy digs angry claws into my chest.

Who is it? I need to know.

Cecilia doesn't have a circle. She talks to me. Or at least, she did. And then she has her parents. It's gotta be her mom or dad blowing up her phone right now. Except, normally when one of them messages her, she gets this pinched look on her face.

They worry about her. For good reason. I worry about her, too. But they've become helicopter parents and all their hovering just pushes Cecilia away. There's usually a touch of annoyance on her face whenever they check in on her at school. I'm sure it's annoying, but I wish my parents were more like hers. She doesn't know how lucky she is that her parents actually give a shit. Mine cut me out of their lives as soon as they could.

Watching her facial expressions now, she's not at all annoyed. She's ... happy.

Fuck, she's beautiful when she's like this. Hell, she's always beautiful, but seeing her smile. It's something special. Something she rarely shows the outside world. Which is why I'm so taken aback right now. I'm not used to seeing Cecilia like this. Not out in the open.

She likes to keep her emotions locked down. Her expression blank.

Before, she'd give me these small smiles when we were together. But I'm not on the receiving end of them anymore.

I wish I could break into that pretty little head of hers and rummage around. I don't like not knowing everything there is to know about her. Her reason for calling things off between us still doesn't make any sense. If I could get inside her head, maybe I'd find some answers.

I stare down at her phone, trying to read the name on her screen, but it's too small for me to make the letters out.

I need to know who she's talking to. The longer this back and forth messaging goes on, the more it sinks in that it is definitely not one of her parents. Is it a guy? Did she meet someone?

White hot fury courses through my veins. I swear to god if a dude is trying to move in on her ... I shake my head.

It's only been a few weeks. Weeks. Not months. And she didn't break things off with me to see other people. She said she needed time to figure her shit out. To heal. And for some bullshit reason, she couldn't do that and be in a relationship with me.

Fuck it. I need to know.

"Who are you talking to?" I ask, masking my irritation.

Her eyes flick toward me in surprise, like she hadn't realized I was here, but her fingers continue moving across the screen.

"Just someone from the swim team."

The swim team? Relief sweeps through me. Not another guy. Good.

"Are you thinking about trying out next season?" It'd be good for her. I don't know anything about swimming, but I've seen Cecilia in the water. She's fast.

"Umm ..." Her cheeks pink. "They have a last-minute spot this season. One of the girls is injured," she shrugs. "I'm thinking of trying out."

"Yeah?" I smile wide, and her blush deepens.

"Mm Hmm."

"When are tryouts?" I ask. It's none of my business, but she's talking to me and she hasn't put any walls up yet. I want to keep her talking. See what else she might share.

"This Friday."

Only a few days away.

"Hey, umm ..." she sets her phone down on her desk and shifts in her seat to face me. There's something she wants to ask me, but judging by the expression on her face, she doesn't know where to start.

"Yeah?"

Cecilia chews on her bottom lip, and I have to fight back the urge to press my thumb against her mouth, freeing the abused flesh. She chews on her lip when she's nervous.

What does she need to be nervous about?

"Did anything weird happen yesterday?"

My brows furrow together.

"During practice, I mean."

Is she worried Holt and I beat the shit out of each other on the field? We sort of did, but not in the way she'd be implying.

"No. Not really." I tell her. "Why? You worried about me?" The idea brings a smile to my face, but Cecilia doesn't match it. She wrings her hands in her lap. An anxious gesture that makes my hackles rise.

"What happened?"

She drops her gaze. Shit. That means something did happen. But Holt was on the field with me the entire time.

"Did Holt—"

"No," she cuts me off. "Nothing like that. It wasn't him." She purses her lips together and turns her head away. I get the feeling that last part, the bit about it not being *him*, she didn't mean to say that part out loud because it implies that it was someone.

Fuck.

"Cecilia—"

She shakes her head without looking at me. "It's nothing. Don't worry about it."

That's not going to happen. But before I can pry her for more information, our professor walks into the room.

"Good morning. Today we'll be discussing—"

I tune him out and pull my phone from my pocket, firing a text off to Felix.

> Me: Something happened with Cecilia yesterday. Can you ask around?

> Felix: *Thumbs up* emoji.

It'll have to do. Out of all of us, Felix is the most likely to find out. He talks to people outside of the team and our crew. He goes to the occasional party and likes to make new friends. People tell him things.

Cecilia pulls out her notebook and starts taking notes as Professor Arndt begins his lecture. He's picking up where we left off yesterday. Delving deeper into oppression within diversity.

"Oppression can be thought of as the social act of placing severe restrictions on an individual, a group or an institution. Can anyone list the restrictions Israel has placed on Palestinians residing within Gaza?"

A girl to my left raises her hand.

"Miss James?"

"They've restricted freedom of movement and access to water."

"Good. What else?"

Someone else raises their hand.

"Yes, Mr. Morel?"

"Aren't those restrictions justified?" he asks.

All eyes turn to look at the jackass who just spoke, our gazes mostly a mixture of disgust and disbelief.

"Care to elaborate?" our professor asks.

The guy who spoke—Morel, or whatever the fuck his name is—grins. The idiot has no idea he's already picked up the rope. Professor Arndt is giving him enough of it to hang himself with now.

"Israel's duty is to its people," he says. "The restrictions they've placed on Palestinians are there to protect their citizens from hostile terrorist groups since Hamas murdered Israeli citizens during the October 7th attack." He leans back in his seat, a satisfied smirk on his face.

I can only shake my head. "Something to add, Mr. Herrera?"

Not particularly, but since you asked, "Only that regardless of their bullshit reasoning, none of it justifies what Israel is doing now," I tell him. "Israel has been violently seizing Palestinian land while also creating an apartheid state. Hamas or no Hamas, you can't justify that."

"Israel has a right to defend itself," some asshole in the back chimes in.

"No, they don't. Not when it violates international law." The girl—James—retorts.

88

"Ah, I see we're getting somewhere," Professor Arndt interjects. "Which leads me to this week's assignment. You're to get into groups of two and put together a presentation regarding whether the United States and other world powers should intervene in the current conflict—"

"Genocide," I bite out.

He gives me a questioning look.

I lean forward on my desk. "It's important to use the right terminologies," I tell him. "It's not a conflict. And before anyone else chimes in, no, it doesn't constitute a war. The Palestinian people have no body of government. They have no military. What's happening in Gaza and in the West Bank is a genocide."

His eyes spark with approval.

I didn't speak up to earn his approval. I spoke up because most of the people in this room have never had to deal with being discriminated against. They've never had themselves or members of their family oppressed. Language matters. By definition, what is happening overseas right now is a fucking genocide. No one here is going to convince me otherwise. And yeah, the United States and world powers should be getting involved and they are. But they're helping out the wrong side. They're supporting the oppressors.

"Right you are, Mr. Herrera," he says. "And with that in mind, I want each group to take a position and justify your stance. Should the U.S. intervene in the genocide currently taking place or should they remain out of it? And if they intervene, what sort of action would you expect our government to take?"

"Regardless of which stance you choose to take in your assignment, you should be prepared to defend it with no less than four supporting arguments. I'll give you a few moments to find your partners."

My attention turns to Cecilia. "Me and you," I tell her, not giving her a choice in the matter.

She exhales a soft sigh. "Are you sure that's a good—"

"Idea?" I finish for her. "Yeah. I am." No way am I letting someone else in this class be her partner. There are maybe six other girls in the class, and from the looks of it, they're already paired up which leaves Cecilia with me or some other guy. This is a group assignment which means working together. Studying and shit. Yeah, her and some random dude, not happening.

"You'll need to work on the assignment outside of class," our professor says. "Presentations will be due at the beginning of class, not this Friday, but the following. We won't have time to go over everyone's presentations in class, so I'll be drawing three at random. Those individuals will be expected to present their arguments to the class. The rest will be graded during my office hours, but I expect everyone to arrive prepared. Any questions?"

Everyone shakes their heads. "Very well. You can have the remainder of class to get started and sort out a schedule for you and your partner to meet outside of class."

Reaching across the aisle, I muscle Cecilia's desk closer until it buts up against mine.

"Was that necessary?" There's a bite of annoyance in her tone.

"It was," I tell her, offering up a shit-eating grin. Doing research for a politically charged presentation isn't something I'd normally look forward to. But with this assignment, Cecilia has no choice but to spend time with me. That's one hell of a win.

Her phone buzzes on her desk and this time I'm able to see the name that flashes across the screen when she looks down to read the incoming text.

Adriana (Swim Team)

What the fuck?

With a narrowed gaze, I skim my eyes over the text and violate Cecilia's privacy. Ask me if I care.

> Adriana (Swim Team): Want to grab lunch after class today?

I watch Cecilia type out her response.

> Cecilia: Sure. Place?

> Adriana (Swim Team): The burger place on campus. The Wolf Den?

> Cecilia: See you there. *Heart emoji*

Heart emoji? Since when does Cecilia use emojis?

"Making plans?" My tone is casual, but I don't think I mask my interest enough because Cecilia darkens the screen on her phone and shoves it back into her bag.

"Just lunch."

I consider that and the person she's having it with. There's only one Adriana I know personally. It's not an uncommon name, so there's no reason for me to jump to conclusions, but I am. There's a good chance whoever Cecilia is talking to is someone I don't know, but the knot in my stomach is telling me otherwise. That her Adriana and mine are one and the same.

And if that's the case, Adriana Aguirre and I are going to have some words.

7
CECILIA

I don't know what I expected when I agreed to grab lunch with Adriana after class. Some part of me assumed it'd be awkward. Mostly because of me. But it hasn't been awkward. It's been ... nice.

"What year are you?" she asks, dipping a fry into some ketchup before popping it into her mouth.

"Junior. You?" I ask, taking a bite of my own food. I used to come here all the time. The Wolf Den was a popular hangout for the cheer squad and for most of the athletes at PacNorth. From the look of things, it still is.

The restaurant is packed with several students standing around their tables since there aren't enough chairs. Not that anyone really cares. The food is good and relatively cheap, and when you're a college student, you can't afford to be picky. Also, the bartender rarely cards. A perk if you're an underclassman and want a drink with friends. Not that I drink anymore.

"Same."

"Any plans after graduation?" I ask.

She pauses and thinks about it. "Not really," Adriana says. "Get a job, most likely. Maybe move out of Richland. I haven't given it much thought." She takes a bite of her burger and adds, "I'll probably move, though."

"Where will you go?" It feels weird to think about leaving Richland. It's always been my home. But I won't lie and say it doesn't have an appeal. If I lived somewhere else, I wouldn't have to worry about running into Austin. Not on campus and not around town. My parents would still be here, so of course I'd come and visit, but some separation could be good for us. Dad could focus more on work. Mom could host more of those charity functions she enjoys.

"I haven't really thought about it. But a move would be good for my parents." The way she phrases that. Good for her parents. It's weird. Wouldn't she be moving for herself? I know I would be.

"Do you have a good relationship with them?" I've always been close with mine. I don't tell them everything. Obviously. If they knew about this past year, it would destroy them. But I know they love me. That's never been a question.

Adriana shrugs. "It's not bad, but it can feel ... strained. They don't always know how to act around me." She shrugs again. "That's more of a *them* problem than a *me* one, but they love me the way parents should. It would make their lives easier if I moved away, so I guess I should plan on doing that after graduation. I'd like to make their lives easier if I can." Her smile is wistful but the way she says it, so matter of fact, like her parents would be happier with her gone, it makes me sad for her. Not that she seems upset at all while she's talking. Just very matter-of-fact.

"What about you? Do you and your parents get along?"

"Yeah. They hover, and that can be annoying. But for the most part, they're alright." Mom is a stay at home wife, so she was always there when I needed her growing up. Dad is in politics. He's Richland's Mayor, and he's always been the type to work long hours, but he'd drop everything if I called and said I needed him. They both would.

"Did they hover as much before the suicide attempt, or was it mostly just after?" she asks.

The hand with my burger freezes midway to my mouth, and my eyes widen as I register her words. Setting my food down, I stare at her with what I'm almost sure is a what-the-actual-fuck expression. Did she seriously just ask me that?

I swallow hard, trying to push past the lump in my throat. I've never had someone refer to what I did so ... casually.

My hand shakes as I reach for my water. Fuck. I put down my glass, steal my breath, and try again.

"I've made you upset," she says, tilting her head to the side as though to study me. "Why?"

She sounds genuinely curious, like she doesn't know why bringing up my previous suicide attempt would upset me.

"I don't like talking about what happened." I push my plate aside, my earlier appetite now gone.

"How are you supposed to move past it if you don't talk about it?"

"I do talk about it. It's just not something I casually bring up with people." Especially people I barely know.

Her eyes bore into mine until I fold and avert my gaze.

"You talk to your parents about it?"

Well, no. "Not really."

"Friends?"

I shake my head. Kinda hard when you don't have any of those.

"So, who do you talk to about it?"

Nobody.

My vision blurs. Urgh. Do not cry. Do. Not. Cry. I blink hard to clear my gaze and find a point on the wall across the room and stare at it. Hard.

"I guess I don't really talk to anyone about it," I admit. "But it's fine. I prefer it that way."

"Therapist?"

"No." I have one. Dr. Walker. But I don't talk to her about that. I sorta just sit there and wait for our hour to be over. I've been better these past few weeks about talking. I opened up a little about the suicide attempt. Meaning I've acknowledged it happened. But that's as far as I get. Seeing her every week checks a box. It's a step in the right direction, and I like leaving it at that.

"I get it," she tells me. "My parents made me see a shrink for years when I was a kid. I wouldn't tell any of them my secrets either."

I snap my attention back to her, but she isn't looking at me. Instead, she takes another bite of her burger, her expression blank, like admitting you had a therapist isn't a big deal, except that it is. College students don't walk around admitting things like that out loud. Mostly because our peers can be assholes, and no one wants to be ridiculed for needing a little help. But Adriana drops that bomb like she doesn't have a care in the world.

"Why did they make you see a therapist?" I ask, my curiosity getting the better of me. It's none of my business, and if she says as much I'll leave the subject alone, but I don't think I've offended her by prying. Granted, it's hard to tell with her. Adriana keeps her emotions locked up tight. It might just be because we don't know one another, but she's incredibly difficult to get a read on.

Adriana sets her burger down and grabs her napkin before wiping her mouth. "Do I seem different to you?" she asks.

My brows furrow. "Different in what way?" I mean, her bluntness is different, sure. But I don't think that's what she's asking.

She shrugs. "Like, am I abnormal to you?"

"I'm not sure any of us can really be considered normal," I tell her. "We all have shit and we all handle it in different ways."

The corners of her mouth curl into the ghost of a smile. "I like you, Cecilia Russo. You're different from most people."

"Uh, thanks."

"It's a compliment."

Alright. I'll take it as one.

"My parents made me see a shrink when I was younger because they thought there was something wrong with me."

Oh. I don't really know what to say to that. "I imagine that had to hurt."

She makes a face. "Not really. I knew where they were coming from. Like I said, my parents love me. It's just ... hard for them. Having a kid they think is different. I'm not what they expected."

"I don't get it." I feel like Adriana is trying to tell me something without coming out and saying it, but I'm having a hard time reading between the lines.

"I like you," she says again.

Okay. "I like you, too," I tell her.

"I would like us to be friends."

I mean, I was sort of hoping for that as well, so that's good. We're moving in the right direction.

"Alright. Let's be friends." It will take some time, getting to know one another to be real friends, the ride-or-die kind, but I'm game to try if she is.

"Good." Her smile widens, but it doesn't quite reach her eyes. "Friends are supposed to be honest with one another." Where is she going with this? "So I think it's important that I be honest with you."

Her eyes meet mine, and she holds my gaze, almost like she's trying to pass along some sort of silent communication.

"Okay?" I brace myself for whatever bomb she's about to drop, but what she says next isn't at all what I expected her to say.

"I don't think like you," she tells me. "After meeting with a therapist for close to a year, my parents were given a diagnosis."

"Alright." Where is she going with this? "Are you dangerous or something?" I mean it as a joke but she answers me seriously.

"No. Not really."

That's uh ... reassuring. I don't get the feeling that she's trying to scare me off, so I'm going to take her at her word. For now, at least.

I'm a firm believer in letting people show you who they are, and thus far, Adriana has been nothing but nice to me and she defended me when she had no reason to. Whatever diagnosis she received as a kid, it doesn't define her. She's still good people.

"Like I said, I want us to be friends. Unfortunately, I have a shitty track record at being a good one. It doesn't come naturally to me. But with you, I'd like to try. If you're open to that."

I feel sort of like I'm having a conversation with a female version of Sheldon Cooper from the Big Bang Theory, the way she talks to me so matter of fact and without any real emotion. It feels very similar to the character's speech patterns and mannerisms in the show.

"I mean, yeah. I'm down."

"Good." She picks her burger back up. "That settles it, then."

I guess it does.

"I might screw up," she tells me. "Not intentionally, of course, but you know," she waves a hand through the air, "the whole my brain not working like yours." Her lips purse in frustration. "Sometimes I slip up. I'm hoping that if I do, you'll give me a chance to fix it. That you won't—" she briefly looks away, "cut me off."

Oh. My stomach drops. Someone's done that to her before. I can relate. It sucks when your friends turn their backs on you. Whether it's your fault or not makes no difference. It still hurts.

"I won't make you any promises," I tell her. "We don't know each other well and I guess it would depend on the slip up." I shrug. Some things are forgivable. Others aren't. "But if something happens, I can try to hear you out at the very least. That's what friends do, right?"

Her expression relaxes, and she goes back to eating. "Thanks."

"Of course." I'd want the same thing. I wish Kim had been willing to hear me out after Austin lied to her. That she'd bothered to give me the benefit of the doubt instead of believing him when he said I wanted it. That I made it all up for attention because I was drunk and regretted my decisions. That because he didn't want a relationship with me after the fact, I was crying foul to retaliate.

She believed him right off the bat. I never even had a chance.

"Can I ask a question?"

Adriana's dark brown eyes flick to mine as she takes another bite. "You just did."

I roll my eyes. "A real one."

She shrugs and makes *a go* ahead motion with her burger.

"What do you mean by you have a shitty track record at being a good friend?" I've had my share of shitty friends, and while I'd like for Adriana and I to be friends, I don't want it to come back and bite me in the ass the way it did with Kim and Joelle.

I don't want to let someone in, only for them to stab me in the back. I'm not sure I can handle that sort of thing again. Not in my current state. I'd like to think I'm stronger now than I was a few months ago, but I'm not sure that's really true. I think I'm just finding better ways to cope. To survive.

Adriana takes her time chewing and swallowing her food before she answers. "In high school, I slept with my best friend's boyfriend."

Damn. That's ... rough. And definitely bad friend behavior.

"Why?"

"You want the real answer or what everyone else thinks?"

"The real one." Obviously.

She nods. "At the time, my friend had everything I thought I was missing. She was close with her mom in a way my parents and I never have been. In a way I don't believe we're capable of feeling for one another now. And she was happy. She smiled a lot. She laughed. She had this boyfriend who used to tell her how much he loved her every chance he got."

She pauses and mulls over her words. "I wasn't jealous. Not of him. It was never about the guy. But I wanted to know what that felt like. To be loved. Does that make sense?"

In a weird and sad kind of way, I guess it does. I picture Adriana as a teenager. A little bit lost and confused. She believes she isn't normal. That she doesn't think like everyone else. She mentioned a diagnosis, but she hasn't said what that diagnosis is. Regardless, being told you're different, it can feel isolating, and when we're teenagers, I don't know. Everything feels bigger. More heightened. I don't agree with her choice, but I guess I can sort of empathize, maybe.

"I was young. Seventeen. And still really naïve," she tells me. "I didn't understand that having sex didn't automatically equate to love. Some part of me thought I could have sex with him, feel what she'd felt, and move on. But—"

"It didn't feel like that?"

She shakes her head. "No. It wasn't anything like I imagined. It was rushed and painful and it left me with this feeling in my chest." She purses her lips. "It made me hollow." Adriana absently rubs a spot beneath her ribs. "I thought maybe I did it wrong. When my friend talked about sex, it was this intimate, beautiful thing. But that wasn't what I experienced, so I tried it again. After the third or fourth time, I realized it was never going to feel the way she'd described it for me. So, I stopped. Or at least, I wanted to stop."

She takes a sip of her water. "Her boyfriend wanted to keep sneaking around. I didn't. But he threatened to tell her I'd seduced him if I didn't keep sleeping with him. It took him saying that to me for me to realize what I did was wrong. And that finding out would hurt my friend." She shakes her head. "He knew from the start that she'd be upset and he did it anyway. I ... I didn't. I know it sounds like a cop out, and I guess it is." she sighs. "It just never really dawned on me, I guess. So when I realized my mistake, it was too late and there were no good choices. I took the path I thought would cause the least amount of harm and I let Ryker fuck me when he felt like it. I thought it was the better option at the time."

"Was it?" I ask, curious if her position has changed at all since then.

"No. She found out anyway and at the worst possible time. Her life was imploding and learning what I did only added to her pain, which was never my intention. She was an important person in my life. What I did, sleeping with her boyfriend, was a mistake. Not telling her what I did, not going to her and being accountable, that was also a mistake. And both of those things cost me. Rightfully so."

She regrets it. That's good at least.

"I don't make mistakes like that anymore," she tells me. "I learned from it as well as others enough to believe I'm capable of being a good friend now. I might still fuck up." She shrugs. "But not like that."

"So is being my friend sort of like an experiment?"

"Sure. Whether or not we're able to sustain a positive and mutually beneficial friendship can be considered an experiment. Neither of us knows how it will turn out. It makes sense to label it that way. But the same can be said for any relationship if you think about it."

I mean, she's not wrong.

"Are there any other questions you want to ask me?" she says, "This is probably a lot to take in. But I hope you're not reconsidering our friendship. That would suck." Her expression is blank when she says it, but I don't miss the flicker of worry in her eyes.

"What do you know about me?" I might as well start there. Adriana knew about the suicide attempt, so I'm curious what else she might know that I haven't told her myself.

She leans back in her chair, fingers drumming along the top of the table. "Your name. Age—twenty-one. You were assaulted at a fraternity party this summer. The fraternity members involved belong to Zeta Pi." She waves a hand through the air. "That's all public knowledge."

A rock sinks to the pit of my stomach. If you're a student at PacNorth and party at all, I guess it sort of is. Austin went on a pretty public smear campaign about me when I initially came forward, but it's been a couple of months since then. I was hoping the rumor mill had died down.

"You attempted suicide shortly after for reasons unknown, though I can make an educated assumption as to your reasons." Yeah. I guess she can.

"You were a cheerleader, but you quit after the assault. You mostly keep to yourself and seem to prefer isolation, though I haven't decided if that's entirely true. It might just be that you feel safer by yourself. That would make sense. Oh!" She snaps her fingers together. "And you were in a relationship with Gabriel Herrera. Or is that still ongoing? From outward appearances, it looks like one of you ended things. If so, I'm not sure which one of you decided to pull the plug, but I'd put my money on it being you. Gabriel doesn't get attached easily, but he was all in on you."

The blood leeches from my face. She ... wait. What? How the hell does she know so much about me? Is there some campus gossip blog I don't know about or is all of this standard information coming from the PacNorth rumor mill?

Oh god. If most of what she's said is public knowledge, how many people—I scan the packed restaurant, meeting the gazes of a handful of other students. Do all of them know?

I think I'm going to be sick.

"I should also mention that Gabe and I used to be friends. It seems like relevant information for you to be aware of."

"You were?" Knowing she was close to Gabriel is what my brain decides to latch on to. The rest I'll come to terms with later. "But you're not anymore?"

She shakes her head. "We had a falling out. My fault, of course. I slept with my best friend's boyfriend and Gabe and the rest of our mutual friends were closer with her. Sides had to be taken and they chose to continue their friendships with her over me." She shrugs. "I can't blame them for their decision, and I don't harbor any resentment. It's safe to assume most people would have made the same choice in their shoes."

Adriana tilts her head to the side. "Do you think you'll get back together with him?"

"What? N..n...no." I stammer my words. "No," I repeat, this time more forcefully.

Her eyes narrow, a small furrow forming between her sculpted brows. "I don't believe you."

"I can't control what you do or don't believe," I tell her defensively.

She nods. "True. But right now you're lying to me. Or to yourself. Either way, it's fine. It takes time to build trust in a relationship, but you should know that if you decide to be with Gabriel again, he won't approve of the two of us being friends. He might make you choose between us."

I don't know how to respond to that other than to say, "We're not getting back together."

She doesn't look convinced. "If you say so." Adriana takes one last bite of her burger before setting her plate aside. "If you do, I want you to know in advance that it's okay for you to choose Gabriel over me. A good friend would want you to be happy. So, you should choose him if he's able to do that. Make you happy, I mean. Besides—" her smile is wistful, "Gabriel's one of the good ones."

I swallow hard and try to wrap my head around everything she's told me. This get-together has been ... enlightening to say the least. I just have one more question.

"Who was the girl?" I ask. "The one who's boyfriend you slept with. What was her name?"

Her expression softens. "Allie."

8
CECILIA

Friday arrives faster than I expect it to. I survive the week without any further altercations and even manage to avoid seeing Austin again. A massive relief.

I still don't know what Parker was so angry with me about, but whatever it was, it looks like he's dropped it. No one else has stormed up to me, though I'm still worried enough not to drop my guard.

Adriana and I get together for coffee or lunch pretty much every day. And she was right about tryouts. As soon as I showed up at the pool this morning, Coach Cho kindly thanked everyone else for coming and excused them for the day before giving me Cate Carrington's former spot.

It's not how I wanted to get on the team, but when I tried to tell her I was happy to compete for the spot, she wouldn't hear it.

I'm using the locker room showers to rinse the chlorine out of my hair after today's practice when Adriana pops her head over the chest-height tile wall. "Plans this weekend?" she asks as she steps into the shower beside mine.

"Not really," I tell her. "I'm supposed to get together with Gabriel at some point to work on a class project but—"

"You're avoiding him?"

"Am I that obvious?"

She nods. "Yes. But it's okay. You're still not sure if you want to be in a relationship with him or not."

I flick water from the shower head at her. "I don't want a relationship," I remind her. "I just ... I don't know ..."

"You miss him?"

I shrug. "Sometimes," I admit. "But that doesn't mean I want to be in a relationship. Besides, it isn't fair to him. He has his entire future ahead of him. Gabriel is going to wind up on some professional soccer team, and the chances of him remaining local, let alone in the United States, are slim. I just ..." I huff out a sigh. Why am I even talking about this? "I don't want to be a burden. I want to figure my shit out and stop being afraid of everything, you know? It's like I need to relearn how to live my life."

Adriana purses her lips and gives me a considering look before saying, "You should go on a date."

My eyes bug out of my head. "Excuse me?" That came out of left field.

"Date." She shrugs like it's a perfectly reasonable suggestion. "You should go on a date."

"Didn't you hear me say I don't want to be in a relationship? Why the hell would I go on a date?" I shudder just thinking about it. The meaningless small talk. The awkward hesitation at the end of the night in front of your door. No, thank you.

"I did." She turns off her water and wraps a towel around herself. Wiping the water from my eyes, I do the same before following her toward our lockers. Since I'm on the team now, I've been assigned one for all of my things. "Dating doesn't have to equal a relationship." Adriana makes quick work of drying off before stepping into a pair of black leggings and a white crop top shirt that leaves her toned abdomen bare. "But putting yourself out there, exposing yourself to one-on-one conversations with guys you don't already know," she shrugs as she slips on a pair of socks and black Converse sneakers. "I think it could be good for you. It might help you to not be so afraid. You're really shifty."

"I'm not afraid," I argue. "And I'm not shifty."

She snorts. "You walk around campus like a scared bunny waiting for a fox to pounce."

Right. Okay, so I'm a little afraid. Rolling my eyes, I grab my clothes—a pair of high-waisted, distressed jeans, and a long-sleeved band shirt—and quickly put them on. "Nobody wants to date me. I'm ... damaged goods." I cringe at my own admission.

"You're not damaged goods," she says before closing her locker and throwing her bag over her shoulder.

"Maybe. Maybe not. But it doesn't change the fact that there isn't exactly a string of guys lining up to go out with me." And thank god for that. I'm humoring Adriana by even talking about this. I definitely have zero interest in going on a date.

"Just think about it. You weren't sure about joining the team either, but here you are." She shrugs. "Going on a date or two doesn't need to be this big thing. Besides, you might even have fun."

"Doubtful," I say, slipping my feet into my checkered Vans sneakers.

Neither of us talks while we finish getting ready. The sound of blow dryers makes it a little hard to hold a conversation, but I think about what she said.

I'm honestly not interested in being with anyone. I know where my heart is even if I won't admit it out loud. I just also know I can't be with him. Not when I'm still such a mess.

Going on a date might help me get over our—it feels weird to call it a breakup, but I guess that's what it is. A date might help me move on from that. From him.

Sooner or later, Gabriel is going to be with somebody else. He's a twenty-something year old college athlete. Girlfriend or not, it's not like he'd be celibate. What guy in his position would?

Has he slept with anyone else since we ... I swallow hard. Okay. So, a date. Not the worst idea. If I can muster up the courage to actually go. A shiver snakes down my spine. The thought of being alone with a guy I don't know is not my idea of a good time.

My heart races, and my palms get sweaty the longer I think about it.

Nope. I'm going to take it back. Going on a date isn't something I can do.

"Dating isn't in the cards for me," I tell her. "At least not anytime soon."

"That's fine," she says, unperturbed as she leads me outside to the parking lot. "But eventually, you're going to need to learn to live your life. The fear isn't going to go away. You have to accept it and do the scary thing anyway. That's the only way you'll get past it."

I really wish she was wrong.

9
GABRIEL

"**I**s she going to come inside?" Felix asks as he peers through the blinds of our front window.

"Get away from there." I snap, shoving him away from the window before Cecilia notices him and loses her nerve.

"Why is she standing on the sidewalk? Just go get her and bring her inside."

I fight the urge to smack him upside the head and instead say, "She'll come inside when she's ready." At least, I hope she does. Fuck. It's been a solid five minutes already, and she doesn't look any closer to climbing the porch steps than she did when she first arrived. I'm worried she'll change her mind about working on our project today. That she'll turn around and leave without bothering to come inside. It's aggravating. Especially since this time around, her reluctance isn't because of the rest of the guys living here. At least I don't think it is. This time, I'm pretty sure her hesitation is because of me.

I sigh.

"Who are you guys talking about?" Deacon asks as he jogs down the stairs, Atticus right beside him. Those two clicked right away, which is good. Maybe they can keep one another out of trouble. Not that Atticus is the rebellious type. Deacon, on the other hand, I guess we'll have to wait and see.

So far, since moving in, he's been on his best behavior. Shows up to practice on time, doesn't miss any classes. He cleans up after himself around the house and does dishes, even when not all of them are his. He's a model roommate. Until now.

"You two can't be down here," I tell them.

The four of us all together in a confined space is too much for her. Cecilia was only just starting to warm up to Felix and Julio prior to our split. With Deacon and Atticus added to that mix—

"Chill," Atticus says. "We're just grabbing drinks before we hole up in our rooms."

My shoulders relax.

"Even though we're starving," Deacon adds.

I wave them off. "Then grab a snack. What are you two, toddlers?"

"Take it easy," Felix says, peering out the window again. I can't help but look over his shoulder and— shit.

"Go. Go. Go. She's coming." I shove him toward the stairs.

"What's the big deal?" he complains. "Cecilia likes me."

"Good for you, *cabrón*." — *Fucker*—There's a knock at the door. "I need her to like me, not be distracted by you."

118

He grins. *Asshole.* "Not my fault I'm more popular with the ladies."

I growl and shove him toward the stairs again just as Atticus and Deacon return from the kitchen, a Jarritos and some chicharrónes in their hands. "Don't you guys have any regular food?" Deacon asks.

The knock sounds again.

"Bro, you live with three Mexicans," Atticus says with a shrug. "This is their normal. You'll get used to it."

The guys are finally out of sight, and I take a deep breath before opening the door.

"Hey, you made it." I force a smile into my voice, hoping she doesn't sense how nervous I am.

Her eyes flick up to meet mine before she quickly looks away. "Yeah. Hi." She steps inside and looks around. "Where is everyone? I saw a few motorcycles parked outside and there's another car in the driveway. Are your roommates home?"

Maybe I wasn't the reason for her reluctance to come inside. The thought brings a genuine smile to my lips.

"They're here." I tell her. Everyone aside from Julio, that is. Coach wanted him to stick around after practice. Something about strategies for our upcoming game. Who knows what they'll come up with, but it better be something good if we're going to have any chance at winning against CPU. The way practices have been going, we'll be lucky if we even get a point on the board. "They're just giving us some space to work on our project."

She nods and follows me as I lead her toward the kitchen. "Do you want anything to drink?"

Cecilia shakes her head and takes a seat against the back wall before pulling her laptop and a notebook from her bag. "I'm assuming we're going to argue for intervention, right?"

I snort. "Obviously."

She nods. "Cool. Just making sure we're on the same page."

I take the seat kitty corner to her, and my knee brushes against her thigh. She stiffens. But I don't pull it back, waiting to see if she'll shift away.

She does.

My stomach drops.

Scooting her chair in, she also uses the opportunity to scoot her chair a couple of inches away.

I grind my teeth together, hating those added inches between us, but there's nothing I can do about it. Not without giving myself away.

"Alright, let's get started." With any luck, once we get rolling on our project, Cecilia will loosen up and start to relax. I don't like the way she sits at the edge of her seat, spine ramrod straight. It's obvious she doesn't want to be here. I'm going to need to do something about that.

We've both compiled a stack of notes, research we've come across from reliable sources. So much of what Israel is claiming in the media is disinformation, so we decide to start our presentation off by showing documented sources where the IDF made claims against Hamas and the people of Palestine that have since been disproven.

The opposing side's biggest argument is that the Israeli government has a right to defend itself against outside attacks. Personally, whether a country has the right to defend itself and whether that same country has the right to commit genocide are two separate arguments, and under no circumstances is the latter ever true, but people don't want to hear it.

Arguing right and wrong isn't how you sway people. It's smarter for us to show a pattern of behavior that demonstrates how untrustworthy the IDF and the Israeli government are as sources. They lie. A lot. And for some reason, the hill that people want to die on is about them having the right to defend themselves. Discrediting their government will go further than trying to appeal to people's humanity. If history is anything to go by, the majority don't have any.

We spend the next thirty minutes with our heads bowed over our notes, and with each minute that passes, the knot of worry in my chest slowly unravels. Her arm brushes against mine, and unlike before, she doesn't immediately pull away.

"I think we should use this in our closing argument," she says, drawing my attention to an article printout. Shifting closer, I peer over her shoulder to read it, my breath ghosting along the side of her neck. I spot the goosebumps across her skin. The rapid pulse in her throat.

"Good idea," I tell her.

She turns, tilting her face up toward me. "Yeah?" she asks, her eyes meeting mine through a veil of dark lashes.

Our faces are impossibly close. If I lean in just a fraction of an inch ... my gaze drops to her mouth and Cecilia's tongue darts out to lick her lips. *Fuck.* Should I do it? I swallow hard, taking in her desire-laden gaze. Does she want me to kiss her?

Is that why she's looking at me like that? Or am I reading this wrong? What if she pushes me away?

Both of us are breathing hard, but neither one of us has moved. Her lips are parted, cheeks painted a captivating shade of pink. I dip my chin and am ready to say fuck it and lean in when there's a loud thump on the staircase, followed by a muttered curse. Cecilia goes rigid, her eyes suddenly wide like a kid caught doing something they weren't supposed to.

I swear to god I'm going to kill whichever one of my roommates is eavesdropping on the two of us right now.

"What was that?" Cecilia asks, using the distraction as a way to break whatever tension there is between us.

Desperation wraps thorn-covered vines around my chest, constricting my rib cage. "I'm sure it's nothing," I say, hoping she'll leave it alone and we can go back to what we were doing, or what I'm almost certain we were about to do.

There's another thump, followed quickly by one more. *MURDER.* I am going to murder whoever that is.

Pushing her chair back, Cecilia rises to her feet and goes to investigate before I'm able to come up with something to say that will stop her.

God dammit. I scrub my hand over my face. One hour. All I asked for was one fucking hour.

She was just starting to relax. I'm damn near certain she was going to let me kiss her. And would that have been a terrible idea? Maybe. But would I have enjoyed every second of it? Hell yes, I would have. Consequences be damned.

Shoving back in my seat, I move to follow her. There's got to be some sort of way for me to salvage this.

When I catch up, I find Cecilia standing at the bottom of the staircase, an amused grin on her face and any remnants of desire gone from her eyes. Felix is at the top, fighting with the iron banister that's currently imprisoning his leg.

"What did you do?" I wish I was more surprised.

Felix waves me off. "All good. Nothing to see here," he tells us. "Just slipped and well," he chuckles. "You guys go study. I'll be out of your hair in just a minute." I huff out a sigh. That seems unlikely.

"Do you need any—" Cecilia begins.

"No, no. I got it."

Obviously he doesn't. Cecilia must agree, because after a second of consideration, she climbs up the stairs and crouches down beside him, scrutinizing his leg. "How did you get your leg through here? The slats are so skinny."

He groans. "I know. This isn't something I'm proud of, and this freaking thing is cutting off my circulation." Felix kicks out with his leg, but all he manages to do is jiggle the banister.

"Can I try?" She makes a motion toward his leg, and I frown, annoyed by the very idea of her touching him.

"Uh—" Felix's eyes flick to mine. *'I'm going to kill you.'* I mouth while my eyes drill daggers into him.

His smile widens. "Yeah. Go for it." Hopping on one leg, he does his best to angle his body out of the way enough for Cecilia to get a firm grip on his calf and pull.

"Shit," he mutters.

"Did I hurt you?" she asks, throwing her hands in the air. "I'm sorry. I didn't mean—"

"No. You're good. Try again."

"Are you sure?"

He smiles down at her. "Absolutely." Felix reaches down for her hands and places them both on his leg. This fucker is flirting with her. You've got to be kidding me. As soon as she turns away, I make a slicing motion with my thumb across my throat.

Felix's eyes dance with mischief. I swear this asshole has a death wish.

Cecilia yanks on his leg again and this time with both of them pulling, they're able to dislodge his leg from the iron rails on the banister. Felix stumbles back into the wall before regaining his footing and as he does, two doors upstairs open and both Atticus and Deacon stick their heads out of their respective rooms.

"Everything okay down there?" Atticus asks. Green eyes scan the scene before him, and he grins. "Felix, what did you do?"

"I didn't do anything," he grumbles. "I was just walking up the stairs, minding my own business, when I tripped and somehow ended up with my leg stuck. I swear it's like the railing reached out and grabbed me." Right. He was innocently walking up the stairs. What he fails to mention is why he was downstairs to begin with.

Cecilia giggles and all four of our heads swing toward her. Her lips slam shut once she realizes she has our attention, and her cheeks heat, turning a beautiful shade of pink.

"Thankfully, this fine maiden saved me." Felix reaches down and offers her his hand. Hesitantly, she places her hand in his and allows him to pull her to her feet. "My savior," he croons.

Puh-leeze

"Yeah, yeah," I mutter, stepping up beside them. "Don't get stuck anywhere else tonight. We have a project to work on and you're turning into a distraction."

"Oh yeah?" he asks, like he doesn't already know about it. What's his angle here? "What's the project about?"

None of his business.

"We have to put together a presentation arguing our stance on whether or not world powers should intervene in the genocide being committed by Israel against the Palestinian people." Cecilia tells him.

"You're pro-intervention, right?"

She rolls her eyes. "Obviously."

"Cool. Want some help?" Felix asks her.

Absolutely the fuck not. This is supposed to be my time with Cecilia. I'm not fucking sharing it.

"Uh, yeah. Sure." Her eyes flick to me. "He can help, right?" she asks, biting on her full bottom lip. *Fuck.* Does this girl have any idea what she's doing to me?

"We can help too," Atticus says, stepping into the hall. Deacon follows suit, and the next thing I know, all three of these fuckers are following Cecilia and me as I usher her back into the dining room.

She eyes her original seat, gaze now assessing so before she says anything, I grab her books and the messenger bag she'd set on the table near the wall when she first came in.

"You three," I dip my chin toward my roommates, "sit over there." I indicate the side of the table that puts the wall at their backs.

Felix rolls his eyes, but no one questions the order as they shuffle one by one to the other side. Cecilia exhales a small sigh of relief, and I set her things out on the opposite side of the table. This leaves her back clear, so if she needs to get up quickly, she won't be sandwiched between anyone. She won't feel trapped.

I take the seat on her right, leaving the chair on her left open.

Cecilia's gotten more comfortable around the guys now that she's gotten to know some of them, but there are still moments when I can see the panic in her eyes. Like she feels the walls closing in.

She usually avoids leaving her back exposed. That's why she claimed one of the seats against the wall to begin with. But that was when it was just the two of us.

She likes to see if anyone is coming and doesn't like the idea of anyone sneaking up on her. With five of us here, her fear of being trapped outweighs her fear of being taken off guard.

"So, how far are you guys?" Felix asks, pulling Cecilia's notebook across the table and skimming her notes. We spend the next hour over the table, bouncing ideas off one another. At first, it's annoying. I don't like sharing Cecilia's time, let alone her attention.

How am I supposed to get her back with everyone else serving as a distraction?

But the longer we work together, the more she visibly relaxes. Felix teases her every time she scowls, flicking her nose and reminding her that's how she'll get wrinkles. And each time he says it, she laughs. Cecilia's only twenty-one. Wrinkles aren't something she cares about, but she admonishes him, nonetheless.

Atticus asks her all sorts of questions about our topic. He seems genuinely interested and does a good job playing Devil's Advocate, forcing us to think outside of the box to counter his arguments.

Deacon just watches us all at first. He's still settling into the soccer house, but he's comfortable enough. There've been a few times that I've caught him eyeing Cecilia with interest, but each time that he does, I make sure to catch his gaze and give him a warning look.

He dips his chin. An acknowledgment that she's off limits.

I get why he's interested. Any guy would be a fool not to be. She's fucking beautiful. Her dark brown hair reaches past her shoulders and is complimented by her equally dark brown eyes.

She's in great shape, thin but with a flare to her hips and the perfect sized tits. Not that Deacon would know that since Cecilia's typical outfit includes an oversized tee and ripped baggy jeans. Which is good. Because if I caught him ogling her in her swimsuit or if the fucker ever caught a glimpse of her naked, I'd need to gouge his eyes out.

Cecilia's thinner than what's considered healthy for someone her size, but not so thin that she looks malnourished. The weight loss is a result of her trauma. She forgets to eat, but I don't think it's intentional. At least, I hope it isn't. It's been a minute since I've really had to worry about her being depressed, but ... I don't know. Things changed.

Frowning, I take in her appearance, gauging whether or not there's a reason for me to be concerned. I should have paid closer attention since the split. Obviously it's had some sort of effect on her, even with her being the one to break things off.

How did I miss that?

I get up from my seat and pull out the bowl of *campechana*— a Mexican shrimp cocktail—Julio made the other day, along with some tortilla chips. The locally made kind where the salt and oil coats the tips of your fingers when you eat them and they come in a large clear bag. None of that Tostitos bullshit. Freaking Frito-Lay chips. They're not even a Mexican owned company.

If Cecilia is losing too much weight, there's an easy way to rectify that.

"Oh, sweet!" Atticus says as soon as I set the bowl in the middle of the table. "I thought you guys ate all of it last night."

Both Deacon and Cecilia eye the bowl curiously as Atticus uses a chip to scoop up some of the shrimp and vegetables.

"On a plate," I admonish as I grab a stack of paper plates and a serving spoon.

"My bad," he mumbles around a mouthful of food before releasing a groan. "So good."

Spooning a portion onto a plate, I set it in front of Cecilia before serving myself some.

"What is it?" she asks, leaning forward to take a small sniff.

"You've never had *campechana?*" Felix asks her.

She shakes her head. "No. I don't think so."

Felix whistles. "You've been missing out." He grins. "After you try Julio's *campechana*, you won't know how you survived without it in your life. The only one of us with better cooking skills than J is Gabriel but you'll have to come around more often if you want some of his cooking. The fucker is stingy and doesn't make meals for us often."

Reclaiming my seat beside her, I take a bite of my own food, hoping it'll encourage her to do the same. She takes a tentative taste and we all watch for her reaction.

"Oh, my God." We all grin at her response.

"Good, yeah?" Atticus asks as he elbows Deacon. "Bro, try it."

He doesn't look convinced, but after watching Cecilia take a few more bites, he shrugs and goes for it.

"Okay, this is hella good."

"Right!" Felix confirms. "Wait until you try Gabe's gorditas. They're to die for."

Rolling my eyes, I throw a napkin at his head. "You haven't had those in ages," I tell him.

"I know," he whines. "Which is all the more reason why you should step up to the plate and make them for us soon. Cecilia wants to try out your cooking skills, don't you, pequeñita?" *Little one.*

I grind my teeth, ignoring the nickname he uses for her. We'll discuss that later. And instead look at Cecilia, who's blush is now traveling down her neck.

"Yeah?" Felix encourages.

With a small smile, she nods. "Yeah, sure."

Throwing my arm over the back of her chair, I lean in, blocking everyone else from view. "You want me to cook for you?" I ask, dropping my voice low. My heart is all of a sudden thundering in my chest. Felix was right when he said I don't cook often, but I find myself wanting to cook for her.

"Mm Hmm," she shrugs. "If you want to."

My smile is wide as she tentatively matches my grin, and I sit back in my seat, leaving my arm draped over the back of her chair. She doesn't admonish me.

"Alright then," I tell her. "It's a date."

Out of the corner of my eye, I see Cecilia's lips part and her eyes widen at my casual use of the term *date* before she takes in the smiles on the guy's faces across from her. Felix cheers, making an unnecessary display of triumph that has the other guys laughing, but I don't pay them much attention, waiting to see how Cecilia responds.

Her lips close and despite knowing she wants to, she doesn't correct me. Instead, she offers me a barely perceptible nod.

Victory sweeps through me.

We eat our fill, and I make sure to add more to Cecilia's plate when I see that it's empty. The guys eventually wander off, finally leaving the two of us alone, but it's getting late, and I know any minute Cecilia is going to tell me she has to go.

I start clearing our mess, putting what remains of the *campechana* back in the fridge while Cecilia starts to collect her things.

"We made decent headway," she tells me.

"Yeah. Not too bad," I agree.

"So, I ... I guess—"

"Did you make a decision about tomorrow?" I ask. I know I should leave it alone. She agreed to dinner with me and the guys, and that alone is a win. But I can't help but push.

"What about it?" she asks, a small furrow between her brows. Did she already forget?

"The game against Crown Point?"

Recognition dawns on her. "Oh. So, umm ..."

"It would be cool if you came," I tell her before she has the chance to make up some kind of excuse. "Maybe bring some of the swim team with you if you've gotten to know any of them."

She chews her bottom lip. "I'll ask."

It's not a no, so for tonight, it will have to do.

10
CECILIA

Sunday is therapy day. Yay.

That's sarcasm, in case I wasn't clear.

My phone buzzes and since Dr. Walker hasn't come in yet, I take a quick glance at the screen.

> Adriana: Think of your therapist like a five-year-old child.

Weird. Why would I do that?

Before I can respond, another text comes in.

> Adriana: You'll be less likely to want to strangle her when she asks you invasive questions.

She's not wrong.

The door opens and Dr. Tabitha Walker steps inside. I type out a hasty "thanks" to Adriana and tuck my phone back into my pocket.

"Good morning," she says, taking a seat across from me.

"How's your week been?"

"Fine." I tell her, already hating this conversation, but that's not anything new.

"Anything you'd like to chat about today?"

"Nope."

She scowls before heaving a long, suffering sigh. "Cecilia, we've been seeing one another for a while now, wouldn't you agree?"

Four months, three weeks, and six days. But who's counting?

"Mm hmm."

"These sessions would be much more productive if you chose to confide in me. I'm here to help. You know that, right?"

I huff out a breath. "I know," I tell her. "But that doesn't make this any easier."

She smiles. "We'll start right there. What about speaking to someone like myself makes you uncomfortable?"

It's a struggle not to roll my eyes, but I manage it. "Everything about this is uncomfortable," I tell her. "I don't need to share my damage. No one wants to bring their trauma up to the surface. It's awkward, and it won't make me feel any better." It's hard enough keeping that shit buried deep down.

"How do you know unless you've tried?"

Trust me. I know.

"Let me ask you this," she says. "You go to an OBGYN for your annuals, yes?"

Interesting change of direction, but whatever. I nod.

"And you get nearly naked in front of a stranger, someone you see maybe once or twice a year, and allow them to invade your most intimate parts."

"I have." But that was before. I haven't been to my lady doctor since before the assault, and judging by my internal recoil at the mere mention of going, I doubt I'll be making a follow-up appointment anytime soon.

"Why is that? What reason do you give yourself to justify the personal invasion?"

I see where she's going with this. "It's beneficial for my health," I say, giving her the answer I know she's looking for.

A satisfied smile spreads across her face. "Exactly. Oftentimes throughout our lives, we have to endure uncomfortable situations for the benefit of our overall health. This is one of those moments, wouldn't you agree?"

"Sure." Not really.

"So for today, can we live in our discomfort? Just for the next hour. After that, if you want to go back to sitting in silence and riding the hour out, I won't pressure you."

I look out the window.

"Can we try?"

Without making eye contact, I let out a resigned sigh.

"Fine." I told Gabriel I needed to work on myself. That I don't want to be broken.

I can't rely on him to be the glue holding my cracks together. Joining the swim team is a start. And making a new friend is another step in the right direction.

Deep down, I know talking about everything that happened to me is something I can't avoid forever. Like Adriana said, how am I supposed to move past all this if I don't talk about it?

I might as well make today my day to try.

"But after today, if I want you to drop it, you will?"

She nods.

"Okay."

"Very good. Would you like to dive into the deep end or wade in the shallows for a bit?"

Turning my attention back to her, I consider the question. Wading in the shallows is only going to prolong the pain. I'd much rather rip off the band-aid and get this over with. So, I guess I'm diving in.

"You already know that I tried to unalive myself," I tell her and she nods. As far as she's aware, it's the sole reason for me being here. "Well, a little over a month before I slit my wrists ..." I swallow past the lump in my throat. Say it. You just have to say those three words out loud. Come on. You can do this.

I take in a shuddering breath.

"I was raped." There, I said it.

My confession takes Dr. Walker by surprise. I can see it in her eyes. The way she looks at me. There's so much unspoken apology in her softening gaze. I'm drowning beneath the weight of it. I can't look at her for more than a few seconds. Any longer and I'm going to lose my nerve.

Rip it off.

"It was at a frat party over summer break. Three guys were involved." She pales, but I ignore her reaction. I need to get all of it out on the table. If I stop or slow down, I'll choke on the words. "Two of them forced me to perform oral. The third raped me fully, but I was drugged, so I don't know the particulars of everything he did to me." I shrug. "After he put me on the bed is when it all sort of went black."

She swallows hard, probably trying to gather her words, but I'm not finished. Not yet.

"The next morning, I woke up in an unfamiliar bed with bruises on my body and cum between my legs. The third guy, the one who raped me, he came into the room shortly after I woke up when I was still trying to get my bearings." My laugh is hollow. "He suggested we get our stories straight." I clench my teeth, renewed anger coursing through my veins and I latch onto it. "I thought he was insane. He was so freaking sure of himself, and all I could think about was how I needed to get away from him. How I had to get out of that room."

I'm shaking now, struggling to keep it together.

"He let me go. Warned me to keep my mouth shut and then sent me on my way." I grimace. "Not that I listened. As soon as I got back to my dorm, I told one of my friends. She convinced me to go to my campus administration. It happened on campus grounds and we're both students at PacNorth University. I didn't want them to get away with it, but I also didn't want to draw a bunch of unwanted attention."

"Your father's election?" she pries.

A single tear slips past my defenses, and I hastily swipe it away. "Yeah. I'm sure you can imagine what the media is like when they get wind of something like that during an election year. It's never pretty." Not for people like me. "Going to admin, it wasn't ideal. I wanted them to get arrested. To go to jail. But I'm not stupid. I know the chances of that, so I figured, if they were kicked out of school, if they lost their positions on the soccer team, it'd be something." At the time, I convinced myself it would be enough.

"And what came of it?"

With my eyes closed, I whisper a single word. "Nothing."

She's quiet until I open my eyes. "There was no punishment for any of the boys?"

Baring my teeth in a grimace, I shake my head. "Not even a slap on the wrist."

She nods, scribbling something down on her notepad. "Have you told your parents?"

I shake my head. "No. Why would I? No one believed me," I tell her. "When the guys were brought in, they said I made it up. They said I was drunk. That I threw myself at them. Not once did any of them deny what they did to me. But they made it sound like I wanted it. Like I was only mad after the fact because I regretted my own decision."

I sniff. "Even my own friends turned their backs on me after that. So no, I never told my parents. I can't take the idea of them finding out and not believing me, too."

Dr. Walker jots something else down on her notepad before setting it aside.

"Was the assault your reason for attempting to take your own life?"

It's not that easy to explain. The rape was bad. What Austin, Parker, and Gregory did to me, it seriously fucked me up. But everything afterward—realizing no one believed me. That nobody cared—it made everything so much worse.

There was no justice. No closure. My entire life was shoved over on its axis and theirs didn't have so much as a bump in the road.

"That, plus everything that's happened since." It doesn't help that I still go to school with those guys. That I have to see one or more of them almost every day.

"I imagine things began to feel hopeless at the time."

Wiping my face, I nod. "Yeah. I guess so."

"Do you still feel the same sense of hopelessness now?"

"I—" I cut myself off and consider her question. Life isn't easy. It's really fucking hard. I'm still dealing with the nightmares, the panic attacks, and what is probably a case of PTSD, but ... I think about Gabriel. About joining the swim team. I think about the study session with Gabe's roommates and about making a new friend. "No," I tell her. "I don't feel hopeless like that." Not anymore.

Our time ends shortly after that. She offers to extend the hour, but I've had enough for one day. She schedules my next appointment for a week from today ,and I leave her office, not feeling any better than when I first stepped inside.

When I walk to my car, I'm greeted by an unexpected surprise, though not an unwelcome one.

"What are you doing here?" Adriana stands beside my Jeep, a disposable coffee cup in each of her hands.

"Providing moral support in the form of caffeine." She hands me one of the cups, and I bring it close to my chest. "It's a hazelnut latte," she tells me. "I don't know what your regular order is."

"This is perfect," I tell her, taking a sip. Warmth seeps into me and I close my eyes, relishing the feeling as I exhale a deep breath.

I stopped by the restroom on my way out and splashed some water on my face, but I'm sure Adriana can tell I've been crying. Thankfully though, she doesn't comment on it.

"We should do something fun this afternoon." She climbs into the passenger seat of my SUV when I unlock it. Walking around, I settle myself inside and take another drink of my latte.

"Where's your car?" I ask her.

"At home," she says. "I took a rideshare, so we didn't need to drive separately."

Makes sense. We talked earlier about hanging out sometime today. Not that I expected her to show up outside of my appointment. But I'm not complaining. Already some of the ache in my chest is subsiding. Looks like Adriana is just what the doctor ordered today.

"Anything in particular you want to do today?" she asks as we make our way out onto the main road.

"Gabe asked if I'd come to his game this afternoon." I don't know why I said that out loud. I'd already decided against going.

Adriana turns to look at me, her penetrating stare drilling holes into the side of my face. "Do you want to go to Gabriel's game?" she asks.

It feels like a trick question, so I shrug.

With a sigh, she slumps back in her seat. "That's a yes." I open my mouth to refute her statement, but she holds up a hand to stop me. "It's fine. We can go. I actually like soccer," she tells me. "I played a little as a kid, and it's been a while since I've gone to a game, so why not?"

She gives me another considering look. "How are you with crowds?"

"Not great," I admit.

Her sculpted brows are drawn together. "Okay. We'll park toward the back of the lot so we can get out of there fast if we need to. You do alright at school, so you'll probably be fine as long as we avoid the crush of bodies when everyone rushes to leave at the same time."

Sounds like a good idea.

"What time is the game?"

"Two," I tell her.

"Perfect. Enough time to eat and get ready."

11

GABRIEL

My eyes flick over the stands, searching for Cecilia. She never confirmed whether she'd show up to today's game or not, but a part of me is really hoping she does. Things have been good between us. Not great. But good.

They're steps in the right direction, even if they happen to be baby steps. Her showing up today would—

"Hey, man." Julio jogs up beside me and slaps a hand to my shoulder. "What's Cecilia doing hanging out with Adriana?"

"What?" I turn to him with a scowl. He points to a different section of the stands, and I follow his line of sight. Sure enough, I find her. My girl sits in the middle section of the stands on the end by the staircase. Beside her sits Adriana Aguirre, a former friend and fucking backstabber. "Shit. I wondered if that was the Adriana she was talking to."

Julio's dark brows pull together, and he rubs the back of his tattooed neck. "Do you think it's a coincidence?"

"Maybe. Maybe not." I shrug. "If she wanted to fuck with any of us, you'd be at the top of her list," I remind him. "It's been years since I've spoken to her. Adriana doesn't have any reason to mess with me." Not one that I know of, at least. And if she plans to use Cecilia as a means to get to us, I'll put a stop to that shit real fast.

Julio nods, but doesn't look convinced. Frankly, I'm not either.

No one in our crew walked away from Adriana on good terms. She fucked one of our friends over and the entire group was hurt by her betrayal. Allie took it the worst, but Julio was right up there with her. He and Adriana had a different relationship from the rest of us. Friendly, but also something more. He's always been tight-lipped about whether anything ever happened between the two of them.

I know about the time he got drunk and made out with her at a party last year, but according to J, it was a mistake, and not one he planned on ever repeating.

We gave him shit for it, anyway. Allie did too. But none of us really held it against him. He wasn't pursuing a relationship with Adriana or anything. He was hammered and made a mistake. We've all been there.

Mine was with a cleat chaser freshman year and it took me a full semester to shake her. I stopped going out and drinking at random parties after that.

I don't know what went down between Julio and Adriana after that night. It wasn't any of my business, and it's not like Julio is the type to bring it up.

Felix called him out on it when it happened, and that was that.

Seeing Adriana talking to Cecilia now, it doesn't feel right. Her expression is blank, but she's got her body turned toward my girl, a sign she's engaged in the conversation. Her spine is rigid and her eyes are trained on the field in our direction.

I'd put money on her gaze being locked on J.

Cecilia, meanwhile, looks to be having an okay time. There's a small smile on her face as she animatedly talks to Adriana. The longer I stare, the more I wish I could hear their conversation. Adriana must know we're looking because she raises her hand toward her head and gives me a quick salute.

Cecilia stops talking long enough to follow Adriana's line of vision. Her gaze washes over me, and she lifts her hand, giving me a hesitant wave. I return the gesture right as one of the refs blows a whistle, signaling that it's time to start the game.

It's half-time, and we're getting our asses handed to us. The score is three to one, with Crown Point University in the lead. If we don't get our heads out of our asses during the second half, we're going to lose, which will hurt our chances of being selected by the NCAA selection committee for the Championship at the end of the season. There's always a chance we'll get another shot against Crown Point during tournaments, but it's not how we want our season to go. It's always better to face a team in the tournaments that you've already won against.

It's a hard win when you walk onto the pitch, knowing they've already handed you a L.

In the locker room, Coach gives us his version of a pep talk. He reminds us that we've beaten the Hawks before, though he glosses over the number of years it's been since we managed it.

We played against CPU during the pre season but we didn't win. They didn't either. The score ended up one to one and after getting extra time, neither of us was able to score. It was a draw. This time around, the game is leaning in their favor.

"We're changing the line-up for the second half," Coach says. Julio stands beside him, his expression grim. I get the feeling that whatever changes Coach decided to make, Julio isn't a fan of them. Either that or he assumes the rest of the team won't be and he's bracing for the fallout.

"Holt, you're subbing the second half. Hunt, you're in. You'll play midfield and we'll see how it goes. Herrera?"

I rise to my feet.

"You play striker. You and Hunt had good chemistry during practice. I want to see that again on the field."

My eyes widen, and I look at Julio. He dips his head and gives me a sly grin.

"Yes, sir." This is what he stayed late to talk to Coach about. Fucking yes!

"Are you kidding me, Coach?" Holt demands, shoving to his feet. "This is bullshit."

"Don't take that tone with me. It's not bullshit, it's soccer. If you'd stop focusing on whatever problems you seem to have with Herrera and half of my goddamn team, and instead focus on the game, we might have a few more points on the board. As it is, you're making rookie mistakes to avoid working with members of your own team. I've had enough."

"You can't do this—"

"I'm in charge. I can do whatever the hell I want. Hunt, get your ass on the field."

"Yes, sir," Deacon says, and the rest of us follow him out.

The second half goes better than the first. Deacon and I find a rhythm Holt and I never could, and we race down the field, passing the ball back and forth to one another as we near the goal. The crowd's anticipation hangs heavy in the air, a pulsating energy that feeds our determination. We need a score.

As we get closer to CPU's penalty area, I feel their defenders closing in. The tension is palpable, but it's as if Deacon and I share an unspoken connection. We've spent countless hours on the field this past week and more in our backyard practicing together, going over plays. Living in the same house has always made Felix, Julio, and I more in sync with one another, and it looks like the same can be said with Deacon.

With a deft flick of his cleats, Deacon sends the ball back to me just as a CPU defender lunges in. I control it with a graceful touch and, without a second thought, pass it right back to Deacon. His eyes lock onto mine, and I see the glint of determination mirrored in them. We've got this. Right here, this is our moment to shine.

We're in perfect sync, two hearts beating as one on the pitch. The ball is stolen, but Hunt quickly recovers it and passes it back to me.

There's no hesitation. I strike the ball with a powerhouse outside kick and it soars toward the goal. Not anticipating the move, CPU's goalkeeper comes up short on his dive.

Time seems to slow as the ball finds the back of the net, and the crowd erupts with a deafening roar. The stands tremble with the collective joy of our fans, and my teammates rush me, Deacon damn near taking me off my feet in his excitement.

"Fuck, yes!"

A wide smile splits my face, and I fist-pump the air.

"Again!" I shout, and we all get back into position.

We score once more, bringing the score up from three to one to three to three. There are only six minutes left in the game, and it's our turn at the kickoff. None of us wants a draw against CPU again.

The pressure is on, but we're all determined to win this.

With every one of my heartbeats, I can feel the adrenaline surging through my veins. We have one last chance to claim victory. To take home the win. My gaze flicks toward the stands, spotting Cecilia. She's leaning forward, hands clasped together on her knees.

Does she feel it too? The energy that crackles in the air. Fuck. It's invigorating.

As the referee blows the whistle to restart the game, Deacon and I exchange a determined look and I signal him with my hand.

One-two. Just like we practiced.

The ball is in play, and we move forward as a team, pushing it relentlessly toward CPU's goal. The clock is ticking, and our fans are on the edge of their seats. Voices screaming through the air.

We navigate through the opposition's defense with precision passes, taking turns to run further down the field. Each sprint stretches longer and longer. We're almost there.

With just seconds left on the clock, I find myself with the ball at my feet, right on the edge of the penalty area. The defenders close in, but I see a gap, a small window of opportunity to take the shot.

I take a deep breath. This is it. The crowd falls into a hushed silence. It's like they can feel it too. Letting instinct take over, I unleash a perfectly placed shot towards the far corner of the goal.

The ball sails through the air, and it's a race against time. The CPU goalkeeper stretches to his limits, diving for the edge but he's a fraction of a second too late.

The ball kisses the back of the net, and the stadium erupts with a thunderous roar.

We did it! We scored with only seconds to spare. Fuck. "We won!" Julio grabs onto my shoulders. "We fucking won!"

"Fuck yeah, we did!"

My teammates rush to congratulate me, and I don't bother fighting the smile on my face. My eyes go back to Cecilia and pride washes over me when I find her on her feet, cheering on our win. I want to go to her. To lift her in my arms and taste her on my lips.

It's the adrenaline talking, but fuck that would be the cherry on top of today's victory.

Instead, I grab my things from our bench and sprint with the guys back toward the locker room, only to come up short when Felix elbows me in the side. "Do you see what I see?" he asks.

I follow his line of sight to find Holt looming over a girl on the far wall, almost but not entirely hidden from view.

"He stormed off as soon as he realized Coach wasn't going to put him back in," he tells me. "And went and found someone to occupy his time with." He raises his phone and snaps a pic.

"Is that—"

He nods. "Giana Paxton."

I eye the girl up and down. *"That's Gigi?"* No fucking way. She's the coach's daughter. A fucking high schooler at that and only just turned seventeen. Only she doesn't look like any seventeen-year-old I know. The freckle-faced girl who often acts as her father's shadow during summer break training is taking a hard stab at looking like a seductress.

"I need this image burned from my eyes," I mutter.

She's wearing a navy blue mini skirt that barely covers her ass and a white, skin-tight, v-neck tee that showcases her bright red bra underneath. If that wasn't bad enough, her tits are all but pouring out of her top as she leans in close to Holt.

He mirrors her movements with an arrogant grin. *Fucking hell.*

Giana's eyelids are smudged in black, and her lips are painted a deep shade of red. The makeup and outfit give her the appearance of someone older. *Much, much older.* Coach is going to kill her. But only after he fucking murders Holt.

Felix's expression is grim. "Remember when I mentioned he'd been poking around?"

Yeah, it was a while back when Cecilia and I were still ... we were still whatever we were. "It's escalated?"

"Yeah. Holt isn't just chasing after her anymore," he says. "Austin has her. He's fucking her in secret or some shit. I overheard him talking to some of the guys about it the other day, and Rion confirmed that she's stayed overnight multiple times at the Zeta Pi house, always in Holt's room."

Fucking hell. "What is she thinking?"

He grinds his teeth together. "She isn't. She's young and dumb and has stars in her eyes." I register the pure venom in his voice.

"Are we still sticking with the plan?"

He nods. "I've warned her off twice already. Until we have enough proof to bury Holt's ass, it's the best I can do."

I grimace. "I can try talking to her—" Giana's just a kid. She has no clue what kind of guy she's getting involved with. The kind of shit he's capable of. Holt messing around with her works in my favor. I need a reason for Coach to kick him off the team and this is as good as any. But even knowing that this gets me one step closer to my goal doesn't mean I'm alright with just throwing her to the wolves. I'll talk to her if Felix thinks it'll help. I know neither of us is okay with Giana turning into collateral damage.

He shakes his head. "It won't make a difference. Besides, they're not being particularly careful. I've got Rion Pru as my man on the inside. I'll have what we need and we can get rid of the asshole soon." It's a start. Taking soccer away from him is only the beginning. I won't be satisfied until Holt gets what he deserves.

"How'd you get Pru to turn?"

He chuckles. "Don't act so surprised. After what I told him before in the locker rooms, it wasn't all that hard. Dude's a follower, but he isn't all bad. He's got a heart, enough of one at least that he can't just stand by and do nothing while Holt takes advantage of a teenager. Not when he knows Holt's a repeat offender."

We join the rest of our team in the locker room, and I do my best to shake off my irritation. We just won against CPU. We should all be riding high. Instead, all I feel is a looming sensation of dread.

12

GABRIEL

Spotting Adriana in the halls as she exits her class Monday morning, I make a beeline straight for her. "What game are you playing at?" I call out as soon as I'm within hearing distance.

Dark brown eyes lift to meet mine. I'd almost forgotten how dark her gaze was. A shade of brown that's damn near black. "Hello, Adriana," she retorts. "How are you, Adriana? Long time no see, Adriana." There's a bite of annoyance in her words, but I'm not in the fucking mood.

"I'm serious, A." I snap, reverting to the nickname I used for her back when we were in high school. Pressing my arm against the wall, I block her exit when she moves to brush past me. "What's your angle with Cecilia? Why are you all of a sudden hanging out and being nice to her?" She fucked Allie over back when we were friends. I'm not going to stand by and watch her burn Cecilia, too.

"I am nice," she bites out, nostrils flaring.

Interesting. If I was less pissed, I'd take the time to analyze her reaction. Instead, I fold my arms over my chest and raise a brow. I don't have time to beat around the bush.

"Really? We must have different definitions of the word because fucking your best friend's boyfriend isn't something I'd consider *nice*."

Her jaw tightens, but beyond that small display, she's keeping her emotions locked tight. Typical Adriana. I swear, sometimes I wonder if the girl even has any. She's always been cold. Borderline frigid. Nothing ever seems to ruffle her feathers. Not unless Julio is involved, at least. Bro dodged a fucking bullet though, if you ask me.

"I fucked up. It was three years ago. You don't need to keep throwing it in my face. Move on."

Hold on. Is the ice queen taking responsibility for once? This is new. Back in high school, she was so fucking flippant about it. It's why everyone in our friend group took Allie's side and dropped her. There was no remorse. Not really. She didn't like that she'd been caught. But she wasn't sorry for hurting Alejandra. For being Ryker's side chick for who the hell knows how long.

Adriana pretended like she didn't understand why the rest of us were pissed on Allie's behalf. It was fucking infuriating for all of us. Julio most of all. He was the closest to her in our group. He's always been sorta like the girl's big brother. And Adriana's betrayal, it came out of left field.

We were ride or die. *Familia* to the bitter end. We would have forgiven her mistakes back then if she'd shown even an ounce of remorse. That's how important she was to our group. Our family.

But she made her choice. Too late to go back now.

"I'm not throwing anything in your face. I'm just reminding you of your proven track record and how un-nice you really are. Cecilia's been through a lot. She doesn't deserve whatever—"

She holds her hand up. "Enough. It's been years, Gabriel. Three long years. Get over it. Everyone else has."

Bullshit.

She shoulder-checks me and storms past, but I follow, my longer stride easily keeping pace with her. "I'm serious, A. You don't know the kind of shit Cecilia's been through. If you hurt her, Adriana, so help me—"

She stops abruptly and spins to face me. "You'll what?"

My jaw tightens, and I glare down at her pint-sized frame. "She's important to me," I admit. "I don't want to see her get hurt. So if you're using her to get back at me or—"

"And your feelings should matter to me, why?"

"Because we were like family before," I bite out.

Adriana throws her head back and laughs. But the sound is empty and unnatural. "Family? We were never family." She stabs her finger into my chest. "Families don't turn their backs on one another. That's what you always told me." She digs her finger deeper into me. "Family forgives. They have your back." She shakes her head. "So no, Gabe. I don't think so. You and I, we were never family."

I blink at the bite in her tone. For a second there, it almost sounds like she's ... *hurt.* But Adriana doesn't do hurt. Shit always just slides right off her back. "You and everyone else threw me away. I don't care if Cecilia is important to you. That's not why I'm being nice to her. You aren't even part of the equation."

"Then why—"

"Because I like her," she snaps. "It has nothing to do with you. I like her. I was a shitty friend to Allie. I admit that. But I'm being a better one to Cecilia. Or at least, I'm trying to. So back the fuck off. I'm not doing this to get back at you or hurt you or whatever bullshit reason you've dreamed up in your head. I'm doing this for me." She sucks on her teeth and stares over my shoulder, refusing to meet my gaze when she mutters, "When I saw her, she looked like someone who could use a friend. And if I'm being honest with myself, so can I. There isn't anything more to it. So, you can go away now, safe with the knowledge that I'm not going to fuck this up."

I search her expression, allowing her words to sink in. She's not wrong. Cecilia can use a friend, it's just ... I don't trust her.

What's to keep Adriana from turning her back on Cecilia if it suits her?

"You have her back?" I don't know how much her words are worth these days but I need to hear her say it out loud.

She nods. "I already shoved some asshole in the pool who was harassing her." She crosses her arms over her chest and flicks her narrow eyes back toward mine. "So yes. I have her back. You don't need to question that."

"What? Who the fuck was harassing her?"

She shakes her head. "It's handled. Leave it alone. I get the feeling Cecilia doesn't like you fighting her battles for her."

The corners of my mouth twitch. "She told you about that, huh?"

"We're friends," she reminds me.

"Alright, I'll back off," I tell her, taking a physical step back. "You can be her friend." For now. But if Adriana fucks up, we're going to have words again. I'm not going to stand by and let anyone hurt my girl. Not again, and not on my watch.

"I'm so glad to hear I have your approval," she says, rolling her eyes.

"I'm trying here, A. You and I have a lot of history, and it's not all good."

She huffs out a breath. "I'm not that person anymore, Gabe. Let it go already. We've both grown up. I'm not the same girl who screwed her friend's boyfriend. And you're not the same boy who was always stuck in his twin's shadow."

Her bringing Carlos up cuts fast and deep, and I wince. It'd hurt less if she punched me in the gut.

"Don't bring up my brother." My voice is a growl. Carlos has been gone for years now, but hearing people talk about him, having him brought up in casual conversation, it hurts the same every time. It never fucking lessens.

"Fine. But don't you think it's time for all of us to move on?"

I let the comment about my brother go. She didn't say it to get a rise out of me. She's just being matter-of-fact. But I'm not the one who gets to make that call. Who gets to decide when it's time to let this shit go.

"Have you talked to Allie?" I ask her. "Since everything that's happened?"

She snorts. "Are you kidding? Alejandra doesn't want to hear from me. She's happy. Has a steady guy, right? They're engaged, or getting engaged, last I heard." She shakes her head. "The best thing I can do for Allie is leave her alone to live her life. In no universe does she want to hear from me."

She's wrong. When Adriana went behind Allie's back and fucked Ryker, it destroyed her. She was already dealing with the loss of her mom and having to go to a new school. Being forced to move to a new town. Having to live with a bio-dad she'd never even met.

She was losing so much. Being forced to accept so many changes all at once.

And what Adriana did was the straw that broke the camel's back. Allie needed her best friend more than ever before with everything she was going through. And Adriana's betrayal was like a double-edged sword taking the boy Allie thought she loved out of her life, right along with her best friend.

"I disagree," I tell her. I could be wrong about this. But I don't think I am. Allie would welcome her back if she believed Adriana wanted a relationship with her again. If she was genuine about repairing their friendship. Allie's big on second chances, and while she isn't quick to forgive, she almost always comes around. "But I'll make you deal." An idea forms quickly in my mind.

Her eyes narrow. "I'm listening."

"You patch shit up with Allie, and all is forgiven. I won't bring up our past and I won't hold it against you. Clean slate." As far as I'm concerned, this is a win win.

She considers me for a moment. I can see the gears whirling in her head as she weighs the pros and cons of my offer. Despite how frigid she can be, I think there's a part of Adriana that misses being a part of our group. It might be a teeny tiny one. But it's there.

Her lips purse as I wait, making sure to keep my expression schooled so she can't see how badly I want this. If Adriana fixes shit with Allie, she'll have more of an incentive to be a real friend to Cecilia and it'll make it easier to keep an eye on her, especially if the rest of the guys are on board. Adriana might also decide to come kick it, maybe bring Cecilia with her.

My lips twitch as I fight back my smile. Yeah, I can work with this. It's no real hardship to be around Adriana if Cecilia comes as a part of that package. The more I think about it, the more I like the idea.

Scrutinizing her features—the minute changes to her facial expression as she considers my offer—I'm able to see the moment she decides to reject my offer.

A flicker of regret flashes across her gaze and disappointment washes over me.

I really thought she'd go for it.

Maybe she really didn't give a shit about us after all.

"Pass. I don't need your forgiveness. I'm getting along just fine. And if Cecilia and I remain friends for the long haul, it's you who will have to accept me. Not the other way around." She shrugs. "Either way, I'll be fine."

I grit my teeth. *Fine.* She'll be fine? I'm giving her a chance here. Why does she have to be so difficult?

I need to sweeten the deal. Adriana might not care if she has my forgiveness, but there is someone else's she's wanted for years now and she's never hidden that.

"What if I talked to Julio?" I ask. "I can smooth shit out between the two of you. Let him know you're turning over a new leaf. You know if the rest of us are on board with welcoming you back into the fold, he'll be good with it, too."

Her gaze snaps to mine. It's barely perceptible, but the change in her dark brown eyes is there. Hope. "Even if you and I were cool, it wouldn't matter. He'd never believe you."

"He would if you fixed shit with Allie. Actions speak louder than words, A. And you know how he feels about her. She's like a sister to him."

"I'm aware." She bites her lip, brows drawn together. "Allie is everyone's little sister. You all defend and protect her."

I chuckle, hearing the note of jealousy in her words. It's a new look for her. "Don't act like you've ever wanted Julio to look at you the way he does Allie. Sister isn't the position you've ever been after when it comes to him."

Her eyes darken, and her lips press into a thin line before she mutters a single word.

"Fine."

"Fine, what?"

"I'll reach out to Allie." She steps closer and juts her chin up in the air toward me. "But if she doesn't want anything to do with me, you still have to let shit go. And you have to tell him that I tried to make it right."

"Fair enough."

"Alright, then."

I expect Adriana to walk away after that but she doesn't. Instead, she lingers, pursing her lips like she has more to say.

When she opens her mouth, what she says is the last thing I expect her to say.

"Cecilia was raped," she says, her words pitched low so as not to carry. "Do you know who did it?"

"She told you?" That's ... unexpected. Friend or not, that isn't something Cecilia shares with people. Hell, her own parents don't even know.

Adriana shakes her head. "No. I already knew. But she knows that I know." I wonder how Cecilia feels about that.

"Her secrets aren't mine to share."

"But you know who it is?"

I nod. Adriana doesn't look pleased.

"I thought so." She seems to consider this. "Are you going to do something about it?" It's one thing to bring Julio and Felix in on my plans. Two people I trust implicitly. But it's another to tell Adriana, someone I most certainly do not trust. I don't need her telling Cecilia about what we're up to or worse, trying to interfere. She's not exactly predictable.

"Cecilia doesn't want me fighting her battles for her."

She scoffs, flipping her hair over her shoulder. "That's cute."

"I'm not trying to be cute."

Adriana gives me a patronizing look and starts walking backwards, her eyes still on mine. "You've always been true to your namesake, Gabriel," she says. "You're protective of the people you love and you love Cecilia. You may as well proclaim yourself her guardian angel. So, it's fine. Don't tell me. But whatever you have planned, make it hurt."

She flashes me a dark smile before she turns around, and then she's gone.

Some of the uneasiness in my stomach dissipates. I still don't trust her, but what she just said, it shows that at least some part of her cares. For now, it'll have to do.

13
CECILIA

My muscles burn as I rotate my shoulders. It's been over a week since I joined the swim team and the daily practices are kicking my butt into shape. "Looking good out there," Coach calls out as I dry off beside the pool.

"Thanks," I say. Wrapping my towel around my waist, I head over to where Adriana stands. We're all done for the day, and I, for one, need something to eat.

"All set?" I ask her.

She huffs out a breath. "I swam like shit today."

I bump my shoulder into hers. "No, you didn't." I'm not lying. Adriana is more of an endurance swimmer whereas I'm a sprinter. I'm fast in fifty and one hundred meter events, but once I pass two hundred meters, I noticeably slow down. Whereas with Adriana, once she hits the two hundred meter mark, she finds her stride. Anything over a four hundred meter event and she's an absolute machine.

"My time is three seconds off."

I snort. "In a four hundred meter medley after practicing relays with the girls for an hour first. What do you expect?"

She grumbles beside me, and we head for the locker room, making quick work of getting dressed.

"Have you given any more thought to the date?" she asks.

What? That kind of came out of nowhere.

I shake my head. "Not really. Why?"

She glances down at her phone and types out a quick text. "Willow's brother—Wyatt—is asking about you."

My brows pull together. "Who's Willow?" And who is her brother?

She laughs. "A freshman on the team."

Oh crap. I cringe. "I should probably try to get to know everyone, huh?" Or at least learn everyone's names. We did introductions that first day, but it's sort of been a whirlwind since then. There's so much to learn, and when you're spending most of your time face first in the water, you don't really have a lot of time to chat and get to know people.

"Maybe, but she's a freshman, so it's not like she expects you to know who she is."

Still— "Why is her brother asking about me?"

She shrugs. "He usually shows up at the end of our practices. Tall guy. Cute. Light brown hair. Athletic. He sits in one of the chairs by the door while he waits for Willow to finish. I think he takes her home after practices."

I vaguely remember seeing him, but I tried not to pay much attention. He wasn't someone I recognized, and he was in our space. The first time I saw him I cataloged his every move, but I don't know. I guess I sorta realized he never went far from his seat and the rest of the girls along with our Coach were here. No one seemed bothered by his presence, so after a day or two, I stopped paying him any mind and let it go.There wasn't a need to acknowledge him after that.

"I remember seeing him. But why would he ask about me?" It's not like I stand out from the crowd. I'm wearing the same unattractive navy blue one-piece everyone else wears with a high neck, thick straps, and razor back. Most of the girls hate them, but not me. The uglier, the better if you ask me.

Adriana huffs out a breath. "How should I know?" We grab our things and walk back outside. "He asked Willow if you were seeing anyone, but I guess she didn't know. She asked me the other day if you had a boyfriend, and I told her you didn't."

"Why would you do that?" I hiss.

"Because it's the truth." She lifts her chin toward my Jeep. "And it's given him the balls to stick around after practice a little longer so he can ask you out. Duh."

I whip my head around and my footsteps falter.

Wyatt stands beside my Jeep, his hands shoved into his pockets as he looks out at the soccer field to our right. I stare at him across the parking lot. He hasn't seen us yet. I can turn around and go back inside—

"Nope," Adriana says, looping her arm through mine and hauling me forward. "Deep breaths."

Tugging on my arm, I attempt to drag my feet, but Adriana isn't having it. "What are you doing? I do not want to talk to him," I whisper shout.

"Why not?" She whisper shouts back so Wyatt doesn't hear. "I already did some digging. He isn't known for random hook ups and seems like a nice guy. Willow says he's a good older brother. Doesn't bully her or her friends and he hasn't had a serious girlfriend in over a year, so he's not some asshole looking for a rebound."

"I don't—"

"Hey!" Adriana's cheerful call draws Wyatt's attention. *What is she doing?* His head swivels toward us, and I take in his nervous grin.

"Adriana—" I warn but does she listen? Of course not.

"You're Willow's brother, right?" she asks, striking up a conversation as soon as we're close.

"Yeah. I'm Wyatt."

Adriana nods her head. "Cool. I'm Adriana. This is Cecilia." She dips her head to me. "What can we do for you?"

"Uh ..." He's visibly taken off guard by the question. It's kind of adorable. She wasn't lying when she said he was tall. Or that he's cute. Not that I'm checking him out or anything. I just happen to have eyes. Wyatt's dressed in a pair of loose fitting jeans and a PacNorth hoodie. He has a ball cap covering his hair and casting shadows over his face. His eyes are blue, but not as piercing as Austin's. Wyatt's eyes are softer, with a hell of a lot more warmth.

Sensing that her question has thrown him off balance, Adriana gives me a sly look. "I'm gonna head out so Wyatt can ask you out, but I'll catch you later, okay?"

What? No. I cannot believe she just said that. My eyes widen in disbelief, and I shoot her a look that promises murder if she leaves me right now. Judging by the smirk on her face, she doesn't care. She gives me a thumbs-up and then a wave before she walks away to her own car.

Great. She abandoned me with him. A guy I don't even know.

Some friend. I grumble

"Sorry about that." I clear my throat, feeling a little self-conscious without Adriana here to play buffer. "She can be kinda ... forward."

Wyatt chuckles, his nervousness beginning to fade. "No worries. I appreciate a straightforward conversation."

"Cool." What am I supposed to say now? "Oh, and she was kidding," I tell him, stumbling over my words. "About you asking me out, I mean. She just says weird things sometimes. So please, ignore that. What she said, I mean."

God, I wish I could run away right now. Maybe find a hole to bury myself in.

He rubs the back of his neck. "I actually did want to ask you out. On a date. If you're open to it." The tops of his ears turn a bright shade of pink.

"You want to go on a date?" I ask. "With me?"

He nods, the top of his cheeks taking on the same pink hue. "Yeah. I do. You?"

Surprise flashes through me, and I blink at him. "Me?" I don't know why I asked that again. I just can't wrap my head around why he's even interested. I mean, have you met me? I don't exactly scream fun to hangout with.

Wyatt nods again, his gaze steady on mine. "Yes, you. I've seen you around, and I thought ... Well, I thought you might want to grab a burger or something sometime. I mean, if you're not too busy, of course. I just figured it would be nice to get to know each other."

His words are laced with a hint of awkwardness, but it only makes him more endearing. I don't get any strange vibes from him, and he seems relatively safe.

I'm tempted to say yes.

But I wasn't lying when I told Adriana I'm not looking for a relationship. Far from it, actually. But a date with Wyatt ... it might be nice.

Besides, it's just burgers, right?

I smile at him, ignoring the strange feeling in my chest. "I appreciate the offer, Wyatt. Burgers sound nice."

His face lights up with a mixture of surprise and delight, and I can't help but find his reaction contagious. "Yeah?"

I laugh and match his smile. "Yeah. Why not?"

We exchange numbers and decide on a date. Tomorrow night at seven.

As Wyatt waves goodbye and walks away, I watch him with a newfound sense of curiosity and, if I'm honest, a little anticipation. Maybe Adriana is right. Putting myself out there might be good for me.

14

CECILIA

"**I** don't think I can do this." Wringing my hands, I look at myself in the mirror.

"You'll be fine. It's one date. You can do it," Adriana says, coming up behind me. Her fingers comb through my hair, pulling it away from my face. "What do you think? Up or down?"

Biting on my lower lip, I shrug. "Does it matter? I think I'm going to cancel."

She sighs. "No, you're not." Then, "I'm braiding it. You always use your hair to hide. It'll be nice to get it out of your face."

"Do not."

She chuckles. "Yes. You do. And I'm picking out your outfit. None of this baggy shit. If you can wear a swimsuit, you'll survive wearing a dress."

Worry gnaws through me. Agreeing to a date might have been a mistake.

Adriana rummages through my closet in search of the perfect dress. Her fingers glide over the hangers, scanning the array of clothing I've collected over the years. Each piece carries a memory—a reminder of the girl I used to be. A summer dress I wore once to a spring fling. A red number that used to be my go to anytime Kim, Joelle, and I did a girls night out.

My mouth goes dry when Adriana pulls out a simple black dress, and I swallow hard. The fabric is delicate, clinging to its hanger. My heart races, and I curse. Of course she'd pick that one.

It's a short-sleeved, scoop-neck bodycon dress. And it is skin-freaking-tight.

It's been well over a year since I've worn it. Will it even fit? I mean, it should. If anything, I've lost weight since this summer. Not gained any. But what if it looks awful on me now?

Adriana turns around, holding up the black dress for me to see. Her eyes sparkle with encouragement. "What do you think about this one? Maybe with a cute heel or a knee-high black boot?"

I hesitate for a moment, then take a deep breath. "I like it. But no heels. I'm wearing sneakers." You know, in case I need to make a quick getaway or something.

Better safe than sorry.

Adriana rolls her eyes but smiles. "Fine. It'll still be cute." She rummages through my shoe collection and pulls out a pair of black-and-white checkered Vans. "These will add a touch of your personality while keeping it casual. Trust me, you're going to look amazing," she holds the items toward me.

The soft jersey fabric clings to my body as Adriana zips me up. Her low whistle as I pivot has a genuine laugh bubbling out of me until tears sting my eyes. Something I haven't heard from myself in ages.

When did laughing come so easily again?

Adriana works on my hair, her fingers deftly braiding it into two French braids that frame my face. As I catch my reflection in the mirror, I'm taken aback by the transformation. It's me, but it's a version of me I haven't seen in a long time. The illusion is almost perfect. This Cecilia looks lighter. Unbroken. Ready to take on the world in her sexy black dress and killer confidence.

If I straighten my spine and smile with enough wattage to light up the city, maybe I'll finally become her again instead of just pretending.

I slip on a few chunky bracelets from my vanity to hide the scars on my wrist and play with the charms on them while Adriana finishes with final touches to my hair, using a small amount of product to comb down and style my baby hairs.

Taking a step back, she admires her handiwork. "There. All done. You look incredible."

Tears threaten to well up in my eyes. I'm not sad, but maybe a little overwhelmed. "Thanks."

She hugs me tightly from behind, her words warm and reassuring. "You deserve to feel beautiful, Cecilia. And don't forget, going on this date doesn't have to mean anything. There's no pressure."

I study my reflection again and immediately wonder what Gabriel would think of the outfit. Guilt settles low in my gut. "This still feels wrong," I mutter, voicing my concerns. "It feels like I'm cheating or—"

"But you're not," she assures me. "You don't owe Gabriel anything. You've been through enough, and it's time to put yourself first. He would understand."

Something tells me he really wouldn't.

I take a deep breath, the weight of my past relationship gradually easing off my shoulders. Adriana is right. This date isn't about Gabriel. It's about me rediscovering my self-worth and having the courage to put myself out there. I can do this. It's just one date.

AT SIX FIFTY-FIVE, THE DOORBELL CHIMES A STACCATO beat that matches my fluttering pulse.

"I got it!" I call out, rushing down the staircase. Adriana left maybe ten minutes earlier. She offered to stick around until Wyatt showed up, but I'd rather not have the audience. My parents are bad enough.

"Cecilia, do you—"

"Mom, go." I make a shooing motion toward my mother when she steps into the entryway. "I told you, I got it."

Her eyes flick up to mine, and a small gasp slips free from her lips. "Oh my," she exclaims. "You're beautiful." Her eyes gloss over, and I try to ignore the fact that I'm pretty sure my mom is two seconds away from crying.

"Thanks, Mom." The doorbell rings again. "I have to go."

"Is Gabe—"

"No," I nudge her back toward the doorway that leads into our living room. "Another friend. I'll see you later."

Before she can say anything else, I open the door and step out onto the porch, closing it swiftly behind me. Pressing my body against the door, I meet Wyatt's kind smile with one of my own. "Hi."

Wyatt's wind-tousled brown hair hangs over warm eyes that trace my body in shy approval. "Wow. You look ... just ... wow, Cecilia."

My nerves settle at his gentle tone and the way his hands stay clasped behind his back, not reaching to touch without permission. He clears his throat, color staining his sharp cheekbones before his gaze flicks to my left. I turn to see my mother, who is very obviously spying on us through the curtains.

He waves at her.

She waves back.

Covering my face, I try, and fail, to stifle my groan.

"Please ignore her."

His grin widens. "Why? She seems nice."

Shaking my head, I hop down the steps from my porch, hoping Wyatt will follow. "If you look in her direction for too long, she's going to take it as an invitation to come outside and the next thing you know, you'll be having dinner with my parents instead of the two of us going out."

Wyatt chuckles, falling into step beside me. "Good to know. Though for the record, dinner with you and your parents sounds like a pretty good time."

I look up at him, expecting to find a mocking smile or some other indication that he's kidding, but instead, I find a genuine grin. He really wouldn't mind having dinner with my parents. Huh, that's interesting. Most guys see parents and want to bolt.

I hesitate by his car—an all-black Ford truck—and try to quell my sudden uneasiness. "Do you, uh, want to drive separately? I can follow you to The Wolf Den in my Jeep." I didn't really think the whole, picking me up for our date thing through, and I won't lie, being in an enclosed space with him sounds mildly terrifying right now. "You know, that way you don't have to bring me all the way home afterwards." Win, win. Right? Please say yes.

Wyatt gives me a perplexed look as he unlocks and opens the passenger side door. "That's okay," he says, stepping to the side. "We can use the ride over to talk and get to know each other. Besides—" Worrying my bottom lip, I reluctantly climb in. "Pretty sure I'd lose points with your mom if I wasn't an absolute gentleman." He throws a thumb over his shoulder, so I look.

Oh, my god. She's still watching us.

With a groan, I cover my face. "You win."

He chuckles and closes my door before jogging around to the other side. I fiddle with the heater while he gets himself settled, and then we're on our way. When he's not looking, I plug The Wolf Den into my maps app on my phone and discreetly track our progress. I'm not worried we'll get lost or anything. But it feels prudent to make sure we don't take any unplanned detours. You know, safety first.

When we arrive, Wyatt is quick to hop out, rushing to my side to open my door before I even have the chance to unbuckle my seatbelt.

"Thank you," I tell him.

His smile is wide, and he reaches a hand out to help me out of the truck. Placing my hand in his, I ignore the boulder that rolls in my stomach and accept his help jumping down from the vehicle.

"Gentleman, remember?" he says with a wink.

Tugging on my hand, Wyatt leads me inside. His touch is unnerving, though not entirely unwelcome. He doesn't make my skin crawl or anything like that, but my hand quickly grows sweaty in his hold. I focus on the surrounding people, taking in the boisterous music and rowdy crowd. My heart races, and I flex my fingers, wishing he'd let go of me.

Yeah, so maybe it is a little unwelcome.

Damn.

A hostess directs us to a table, and we take our seats. Wyatt finally releases me to slide into the booth seat across from me, and I exhale a breath of relief. Rubbing my hands on my thighs, I reach for my menu and skim over the options.

"Do you come here a lot?" Not my best opening line, but I've never claimed to be good at small talk.

"Yeah. Once a week or better," he says. "Most Friday nights after a game."

"A game?" I didn't realize he played a sport. Or maybe he just means after watching one?

"Yeah. I'm on the football team, and the guys and I like to grab a drink and some food afterward. Have you been to any of our games?"

"Not this year, but," I shrug, "I used to go watch a lot of the games last season." When I was in cheer, it was sort of a requirement.

"The season's almost over," he tells me. "You'll have to come to a game before it ends. We're crushing it this year."

I make a noncommittal sound. "Maybe."

Our waitress arrives at our table then and offers to take our orders before whisking our menus away and promising to return soon with our drinks. Conversation moves smoothly after that. Nothing too deep. Wyatt's a Sophomore at PacNorth working on a degree in structural engineering. He's a grade level below me, but we're the same age—twenty-one.

He took a year off after high school to sort out what he wanted to do. Something I secretly wish I'd considered. He plays football, obviously. Running back, which is kinda cool. It makes sense why he's in such good shape. Not that I've really noticed. He just has broad shoulders, I mean.

He has one brother and one sister. Both are younger. His brother is still in high school and his sister—Willow—is a freshman on the swim team. We haven't really talked much since I joined the team, but she seems nice. Quiet. She's like me and mostly keeps to herself. Hopefully, she doesn't mind that her brother and I are on a date. I probably should have felt her out about that before agreeing. What if she is vehemently opposed to her teammates going out with her brother? Not that we're like *going out,* or *going steady.* Whatever people call it these days. It's just one date. We're not like *dating.*

Exhaling a sigh, I pick at my napkin, tearing off small pieces until I'm left with a small pile of shreds.

I'm making this too complicated.

It's just that dating a teammate's brother or ex, that sort of thing, can get messy. I doubt Wyatt and I will go out again, so it shouldn't be a problem, but yeah. I mean, maybe I'll check in with Willow tomorrow or something. Make sure everything is okay.

No. That's dumb. We've never even talked before, and she is the one that asked Adriana if I was seeing anyone. It's fine. Why am I spiraling over this?

Thankfully, Wyatt doesn't seem to notice my mini freak out. He's easy to talk to. Mostly because he does the majority of the talking, but I don't mind. He has a nice voice, and he keeps his attention focused on me despite the dozens of other girls walking around the restaurant.

"So, what are you studying?" he asks before taking a drink of his Coke.

"Public relations," I tell him.

"Oh, cool. What got you into that?" He's so animated with the way he talks. Like he's genuinely interested. It's sweet.

"My Dad. He's our uh ..." This part is always a little weird. "He's Richland's mayor."

He coughs, choking on his Coke as his eyes go wide. "No shit?" he asks after pounding on his chest. He reaches for a napkin to wipe his face and coughs again to clear his throat.

Heat rises in my face. "Don't make it weird." I wince, realizing I said that out loud, and Wyatt's face splits into a grin.

"Not weird," he assures me. He takes another drink of his Coke, this time without issue. "Just took me by surprise, but that's cool. Really cool," he says. "So public relations. Do you have your eyes set on politics too, or is that so you can maybe help him out on his campaigns and stuff?"

"No politics for me." I shrug. "But yeah. I guess so, I can help him out. I'm still not one hundred percent sold on it, but I was undeclared last year and public relations makes sense, so I just rolled with it."

Our food arrives, and our conversation takes a momentary pause while we both focus on eating. My attention is pulled toward the televisions above the bar, and I catch myself watching highlights of one of PacNorth's previous football games.

"Last week," Wyatt says, and I flick my gaze toward him. "The game."

"Oh, yeah. Which one are you?" He points to one of the guys on the screen. "Number sixty-seven."

We finish our meal and watch the game, and all in all, I decide to count this date as a win. We've been here for almost an hour. I haven't had a panic attack, and Wyatt's been ... nice. If tonight's date is a test, I'm passing with flying colors.

A wave of relief sweeps through me. Yeah. This was good.

Now if I can just figure out a way to call an end to the night before I do something embarrassing, I'll be set. "So, this was fun." I smile, picking at the last of my fries.

"Yeah. It was." His eyes crinkle at the corners, and he offers me a toothy smile. "I had a really great time."

He reaches a hand across the table and places it on top of mine. His eyes stare into my own, searching.

Oh no. He wants to do this again.

Is he going to ask me out? Like, here? I thought there was a three day rule or something like that.

Swallowing hard, I tug my hand free and place it in my lap. "I did too." All true. I did have a good time. But I'm just dipping my toes back in the water here. Proving to myself that I can do it. You know, be normal again. I'm not actually interested in dating, or you know, like having a boyfriend or anything. Does he want that?

No. I'm getting ahead of myself. Breathe, Cecilia. I try to suck in a lungful of air, but my throat feels tight. I can't get enough air into my lungs. Shit. Now I decide to panic? Seriously?

"We should—"

"Yeah. So, um ..." I say at the same time.

He laughs, and I force myself to follow suit but it's choppy and breathless. Hopefully, he doesn't notice.

"Sorry."

"No. You go ahead."

I really don't want to. I don't want to mess everything up. Licking my lips, I try not to hunch my shoulders as I remind myself that I'm jumping the gun here. Wyatt hasn't asked for a second date and there's a chance that he won't. While we were talking, he mentioned he was swamped with school and football. That's why he hasn't done a lot of dating this year. He'll probably want to keep this casual, too. Be friends, maybe. Friends would be nice. I could use more of those.

A phone rings, interrupting my train of thought, and I exhale a sigh of relief.

"Sorry." Wyatt pats his jean pockets, shoving his hand into one and retrieving his phone. He glances down at his screen, a small frown on his face when he sees who's calling.

Whoever they are, they obviously need to talk to him. It's the third call he's gotten since we arrived at The Wolf Den. I didn't miss the calls before that he just silenced in his pocket without looking.

"Is it alright— "

"Of course. Yes. I mean, you should answer that. It might be important."

Some of the tension on his face eases, and he nods.

Good.

Maybe the interruption will give me time to think of something to say. I'm so awkward at these sorts of things now, and I hate it. I was never like this before.

But Wyatt seems nice. He *is* nice. Different from the kind of guys I used to date. Though I guess he and Gabriel do have some similarities. They're both athletes, both outgoing, but not overly arrogant.

So maybe he is my type. Wait. No. Gabriel was a one-off, right? Is he my type or were all the guys I dated before him my type? I don't really know. Not that any of it matters. I don't even know why I'm thinking about Gabriel right now.

"Thanks." Wyatt offers me a sheepish grin and brings his phone to his ear, answering the call. "Hey, man. I'm on a date, so make it quick."

He listens to the speaker for a moment, a small furrow forming between his brows. Reaching for my glass, I take a sip of water and survey the room.

"No. I can't." Wyatt huffs out a breath. "Dude, this is not the time."

His mouth twists into a grimace, and he glances over at me in question, though I'm not sure what sort of response he expects from me.

"Fine." Another pause. "Okay. I'll swing by on my way home." He grunts. "Whatever."

Ending the call, he shoves his phone back in his pocket.

"Everything okay?" I ask, toying with my bracelet.

Taking a deep breath, he nods. "Yeah."

"You sure?" He doesn't seem like everything is okay.

Plastering a smile back on his face, he pulls out his wallet and throws several twenties down on the table. "All good. Are you ready?"

Oh. "Mm Hmm." That's one way to call an end to the date.

Wyatt leads me outside, holding the door open for me as we exit the restaurant. I follow him over to his truck where he once again opens the passenger side door for me, waiting until I'm buckled to close it and jog around to the other side.

"Sorry about the phone call," he says, steering the truck onto the road.

"It's fine, really." I try to reassure him.

"No, it's not." He sighs and runs a hand through his light brown hair. "This isn't how I wanted our date to end, with me rushing you home. It—" He shakes his head and keeps his eyes on the road.

Not how he wanted the date to end? What did he think was going to happen after dinner? It was just a dinner date, right? I mean, I didn't plan on there being anything else after that. But if he did—

He probably just meant he planned to order dessert or something.

"It's okay. We both had fun. That's all that matters."

"Yeah." He sighs and glances at the clock on the dash. "Would it be okay ..." He trails off, and I turn to face him in my seat.

"What?"

With a grimace he adds, "My buddy was calling because he left his bag in my car." He tilts his chin, and I peer in the backseat, spotting the dark red backpack in question. "He has a chemistry exam in the morning and needs his books to study. His place is on the way. Could we maybe ..."

"You want to drop it off on the way?"

Relief flickers across his face. "Yeah. Would that be okay?"

"Of course," I tell him. No big deal.

15

GABRIEL

I sink into the leather sectional, my mind racing with a million thoughts. Felix and Deacon sit on either side of me, their bodies taut with tension as we huddle together in our living room. The soft glow of the flatscreen TV casts an eerie light, but none of us pay any attention to the game footage playing on the screen.

Felix reaches into a worn manila folder, the excitement dancing in his dark eyes undeniable. He pulls out a stack of photographs, each one more damning than the last. He fans them out on the coffee table before us like a winning hand in a high-stakes poker game, and for a moment, we're all acutely aware of the gravity of our situation.

"Okay, guys," Felix begins, his voice laced with determination. "I think we have enough." He gestures at the photos of Austin and our coach's underage daughter, Giana, caught in various compromising positions. "Now we just need to figure out how to get this to Coach."

"Fuck, this is—" I don't like this.

Deacon picks up one particularly damning photo. Before today, all Felix had were close-ups. Austin looming over Gigi. Maybe kissing her neck. They were inappropriate, sure, given the age difference. But not illegal, per se.

But this...

"We shouldn't have these," Deacon mutters, his gaze fixed on the photo. "This is ... wrong." He throws the photo back on the table. You can't see her intimate parts. Thank fuck for that. But you can tell the girl is naked. Austin is similarly undressed and settled between her legs. The photo is taken from a window, the image a little blurry but clear enough to reveal the intimate nature of the scene within. To know exactly what's happening in that room.

"If you think this is bad," Felix shakes his head. "This is just what we have proof of. If what Rion Pru told me can be believed, it's just the tip of the iceberg."

Deacon's jaw tightens. "Fuck guys like this."

Yeah. My thoughts exactly.

I run a hand through my hair. "We can't just go to Coach with these. He already thinks we have it out for Austin." My history with Holt is shitty at best, and growing worse day by day. Coach made it official after our last game and gave me Holt's spot on the team as the striker, leaving him in reserves. If shit was ugly before, it's gotten way uglier.

"Coach is going to want to know how we got these. And then what? What do we say?" I can't imagine how he'd react if he knew we resorted to stalking the sonovabitch.

My phone rings, and I check the caller I.D. 'Pops' flashes across the screen. I silence the call, ignoring the flash of irritation I feel at seeing his name illuminate my screen.

Deacon rubs a hand over the intricate scroll design tattooed on his neck, his expression troubled. "We should have someone else give him the photographs. Someone Coach trusts implicitly."

Felix leans forward, resting his elbows on his knees as he ponders the idea. "So, who do we know that can handle this?"

Julio is the obvious suggestion since he's Captain on the team, but Coach will still ask questions. Questions none of us want to be responsible for answering.

"What about Jameia?" Felix asks.

Deacon's eyes light up at the suggestion. "Our assistant Coach?"

"You know any other Jameias?" Felix deadpans. The gears in my head start whirling. This could work. She's close to Coach, and she's a hell of a lot easier to talk to about stuff like this than he is."

Deacon grins, his hazel eyes sparkling with mischief. "I like it. I volunteer as tribute. It's the perfect excuse to talk to her about something other than soccer." He scratches the back of his neck. "I swear that woman avoids me every chance she gets."

I can't help but chuckle at Deacon's optimism, shaking my head. "Bro, she's not going to date you. Or do whatever else you want her to do with your ass. That's why she avoids you."

He snorts. "Doesn't mean I can't try."

"Your funeral," I tell him, rolling my eyes.

My phone rings again. Why is my Dad calling me? We're not exactly on speaking terms. Hitting the silence button, I send him to voicemail. If it's so important he can leave one.

"But seriously, though. Do we think Jameia would be willing to help? No questions asked?" Felix asks.

I shrug, my gaze distant. "It's worth a shot. Jameia's not the type to turn a blind eye to something like this, and the photos will carry more weight coming from her than from us. Coach won't have any reason to question information that comes from her."

Deacon nods in agreement. "Tomorrow after practice?" We all nod, and Deacon leans back on the couch, a satisfied expression on his face. "Cool. I got this."

As we continue discussing everything that comes next, Felix mentions his plan to attend the Zeta Pi party tonight. I don't know why he bothers. We have what we need. But I leave it alone. No point in objecting. I want Cecilia to be safe. Getting Holt removed from the team is little more than a baby step in the right direction, but it's something, and right now, something is all I need because it's a hell of a lot more than nothing.

Cecilia's doing her own thing. Putting herself back together and all that shit. Without me. I hate it, and I feel fucking useless but this ... we can take care of this. And who knows, maybe Felix will stumble across something else.

16
CECILIA

"**I**'ll wait in the car," I tell Wyatt as he turns left, detouring to his friend's place.

"You don't have to do that," he says. "You can come in. Say hi, maybe?"

"It's fine. Really. I'll just dink around on my phone while you do your thing."

His shoulders dip in relief. "I appreciate how cool you're being about this," he says. "But no way am I leaving you in the car. Spencer's place can be crazy, and I don't want anyone to bother you while I'm inside."

Why would anyone bother me? I'll just be alone in the car. I'm assuming Wyatt will park in the driveway. Maybe on the side street. Does his friend live in a shady neighborhood or something?

He takes another left, and my heart starts to pound as we pass a series of familiar houses.

"Where did you say your friend lives again?" Shit. This is not good.

"Greek Row." He slows, driving well below the speed limit as we approach the— "He lives there." Wyatt points toward a large two-story house, fully illuminated with loud music coming from it and the lawn littered with PacNorth students.

"The Zeta Pi house?" The blood drains from my face. This is a dream. It has to be.

Wyatt nods, confirming my worst fear. Dread sits like a lead weight in the pit of my stomach.

Scratch that. Tonight is a fucking nightmare.

"Yeah. Have you been to one of their parties before? They're dope."

"Not in a long time," I mutter. *"Never again,"* I whisper to myself.

Unaware of the sheer horror flooding me, Wyatt brings the truck to a stop at the curb. Killing the engine, he reaches into the backseat and grabs his friend's bag before getting out. But me, I'm frozen in my seat. I can't be here. I can't—No. Just no.

There's a knock on my window.

"You coming?" Wyatt asks, his voice muffled through the glass.

"I think I'll just wait for you here."

He shakes his head and opens my door. I consider grabbing the handle to hold it shut but he's faster than my frozen fingers are. The music is louder now. A heavy thrum that hits me square in the chest.

"No way. These parties get crazy. My mother would kill me if she knew I left a girl out in the car at one of these things."

He reaches for my hand and, with a mind of their own, my legs move to follow him.

With our fingers laced, Wyatt climbs the front steps of the house with me close at his side. Instinctively, I tuck myself closer to him. "Please don't be here," I whisper under my breath. Please.

I don't miss the curious looks from some of the partygoers. There are a few faces I recognize and plenty of people who seem to recognize me. As we step inside, the noise grows louder, but Wyatt doesn't hesitate as he weaves through the crowd, effectively dragging me along with him.

He heads to the kitchen, saying hello to the occasional person here and there. Adriana said he wasn't in any of the fraternities, so why do so many people here know him? Is this his crowd? His usual scene?

"Wyatt!" a voice shouts, and Wyatt drops my hand to wave.

"Hey, man."

"You made it! I didn't think you'd show." The guy approaches. Tall. Wide. Corded with muscle. He has a lopsided smile on his face as he nears, but that can easily change. He holds his hand out and Wyatt takes it, the two pulling one another into one of those guy handshake hug things.

"Sorry to disappoint," Wyatt says. "I was on a date when Spence called, whining about needing his books." He lifts the book bag off his shoulder.

"A date—?"

His gaze finally flicks toward, me and the newcomer eyes me with open curiosity.

"I'm Terrance," he offers.

I open my mouth to speak, but nothing comes out. With a quizzical look, he turns to Wyatt as if to ask *what's wrong with her?* But Wyatt brushes the silent question off. That's good. I don't think I can talk right now. It's hard enough just to breathe.

"This is Cecilia," he tells him.

I'm in the Zeta Pi house. Austin's house. Is he here? Of course he is. Austin never misses a party, let alone one his own frat throws. I scan the room, looking for any signs of the boy who's been hell-bent on tormenting me, but I don't catch sight of him.

Okay, good. If we can do what Wyatt said, just get in and out, it'll be okay.

I can do this.

I can be here for a few minutes. Not see Austin. Not talk to people. Leave.

I suck in a breath. Then another.

I'm fine.

Is it hot in here? I tug on the neckline of my dress.

"Have you seen Spencer?" Wyatt asks his friend. "I can't stay long—"

"Yeah. He's upstairs in his room trying to study."

"With all this racket?" Wyatt asks.

I focus on their conversation, using it to block out the noise and intrusive thoughts swirling around inside my head. I've got this. Deep breath.

Terrance shrugs. "You know how he is. Kid's allergic to social activity."

Can't say that I blame the guy. I'm pretty allergic to people right about now, too.

Wyatt chuckles. "Cool." He jerks his chin toward the staircase and steps that way. "We'll head up and drop this off."

Wait. Up?

Wyatt reaches for me, and on instinct, I step back.

Brows furrowed, he gives me a bewildered look.

"I'll uh ... I'm going to wait down here." Yep. That's what I'm going to do. I'll stay right where I am. Wyatt can go drop off the bag and then we can get the hell out of here.

"You sure?" Wyatt asks, his blue eyes warm and concerned.

I eye the staircase warily and try to tamp down on the fear flooding through my system.

Scenes from that night flicker across my vision.

Austin's smile. Him offering to help me find my friends. Me following him upstairs. That was my first mistake. He led me into a bedroom he swore he'd seen Kim go into, and I believed him. God, I was so naive.

The moment I realized my friend wasn't inside the room, that it was his friends in there instead ... I should have bolted. But

Austin was fast. He didn't give me time to think before closing the door and leaning against it, intentionally blocking my escape.

All of it comes rushing at me, and suddenly I'm drowning. Hyperventilating where I stand.

"Cecilia?" Wyatt's voice is laced with concern.

I can't do this. I can't be here. My head turns left and then right, my eyes frantically searching for the exit, but the crowd is thick, and my feet are frozen in place.

"Dude, what is going on with your—"

Someone touches my shoulder. I scream. "Don't touch me!"

"Whoa. Hey. It's just me—" Wyatt's voice. It's just Wyatt. But what do I really know about this guy? He's friends with people in Zeta Pi. This could have all been some elaborate plan to get me here. He could be friends with Austin. What if he brought me here so they could hurt me again? What if Austin put him up to this? To asking me out?

I bring my arms together and curl into myself. If I hold myself tight enough, maybe I can keep myself together. But I can't — breathe.

"Just Wyatt." I whisper to myself. Adriana vouched for him. He's a nice guy. Don't jump to conclusions. Nothing happened yet. That word—yet. That's what worries me.

I need to get out of here.

"Cecilia?" He tries again, stepping closer and invading my space.

My heart races, and there is this ringing in my ears. My vision narrows.

No. No. No.

"What is happening right now?" he asks, but I don't think he's talking to me.

"Move!" someone else shouts. "Get the fuck out of my way!"

There's a commotion behind Wyatt, and a few seconds later, Felix is there, pushing his way through the crowd, swearing at people to back up and get out of his way.

My eyes track his progress, a flicker of relief trickling through me. I know him. It's going to be okay, I tell myself.

With my lips parted, I suck in a shaky breath.

It's not enough.

"Hey man, we're sorta dealing with something here ..." Wyatt starts.

Felix wedges himself between us and shoves Wyatt hard in the chest. "Back the fuck off!" he roars.

I catch Wyatt's startled expression over Felix's shoulder. He doesn't strike me as the confrontational type—despite being on the football team—but the same can't be said for his friend Terrance.

"What the hell is your problem?" Terrance snaps and takes two steps forward.

I shrink back.

"You," Felix challenges. "Why the hell are you two up in her space?" With every word, he pushes forward, putting more space between the two of us while simultaneously forcing the surrounding people to take several steps back. He's giving me breathing room and god, am I grateful for it.

"Look man," Wyatt tries, his tone nothing but reasonable. "I don't know what you think is happening here, but we were on a date and—"

"A date?" There's doubt in his voice.

Wyatt nods just as Felix turns, peering over his shoulder to look at me. He raises a brow in question, and I give him a small nod.

His lips quirk, and there's a spark of mischief in his eyes. "You've got some explaining to do, pequeñita." What is that? *Little girl*, I think.

I should probably be worried, but there's no bite to his words. He's teasing me. Something about Felix doing that, here and now, it eases some of the panic clawing at my chest.

Wordlessly, I nod.

"Did they hurt you?" he asks with genuine concern, ignoring Wyatt when he answers for me, assuring Felix that they didn't do anything to me. That they don't know why I'm all of a sudden freaking out.

Through all of it, Felix keeps his dark brown eyes locked on mine, waiting until I answer him.

I don't have the right words. My initial panic drains out of me with him near. Felix is safe. He's ... not *my* friend. He's Gabriel's. But I trust him in a weird sort of way. I know he won't hurt me. He isn't an unknown. He's never been anything but friendly.

Swallowing hard, I shake my head. It's the best I can do right now to assure him that I'm okay.

It's enough.

Felix turns his attention back to Wyatt and Terrance, and though I can't see the expression on his face, I can hear the clear authority in his voice. "Here's what's going to happen," he says to them. "I'm going to take Cecilia home."

Wyatt opens his mouth, but Felix cuts him off.

"Your date is over. If you weren't a complete asshole, maybe she'll call you." He shrugs. "But I wouldn't hold my breath because you, my friend, you fucked up."

I guess it's a good thing I wasn't hoping for a second date after this.

Wyatt's brows draw together, and the corners of his mouth dip down into a frown, but Felix saves him from asking the question that's clearly written across his face.

"You brought her here. To Zeta Pi."

My stomach tightens. He wouldn't say anything. Would he?

Wyatt looks even more confused now than he did before, and I silently pray he stays that way. It's bad enough with the number of people who do know what happened to me. I'm not in any rush to add to that list.

"Look, man—" Terrance interjects.

"No. You look." Felix's voice takes on a menacing quality. "This is your house." Felix spreads his arms wide. "These are your brothers. Right?" He waves at the crowd hovering around us. Most of them are pretending not to eavesdrop, and thankfully, the music is loud enough that they'd have to strain to hear our words. But there are a few people openly gawking. I can only imagine what they think of this right now.

Felix draws a lot of attention, even when he's not trying to. And right now, he's damn near putting on a show.

"Yeah, what of it?" Terrance says.

"You need to clean house." There's an edge in Felix's voice. One that feels a lot like a warning.

"What the hell are you talking about?" Wyatt asks, but Felix keeps his gaze trained on Terrance. Stabbing a finger in his direction, he adds, "You know what went down here this past summer. What happened to her. This is your house. There's no way you don't know."

An oily feeling slicks down my spine. No. Please no. Why is Felix saying all of this? Why can't we just leave? I don't want to be here for this.

Terrance looks at me in question, and I see the second recognition slams into him. His eyes go wide and he curses right before his jaw hardens.

He wasn't in the room. Wasn't one of the guys who—I can't even think of it. It hurts too much.

But he wasn't there.

He lives with them, though. He belongs to the frat and was probably here that night. At the party. If not, I'm sure he heard the stories. The rumors. Austin would have made sure of it. He was proactive when it happened and made sure everyone knew his version of the story.

Felix is right. Looking at him now, it's obvious Terrance knows. Because Austin did what he set out to do. He painted me as the villain. The liar. The fraud. And it's just as obvious that Terrance doesn't believe my side of what happened to me.

"Nah," Terrance shakes his head. "You got it all wrong—"

My back stiffens even though I knew this was coming.

"No." Felix barks. "I don't."

Terrance doesn't look convinced, and a part of me hates that. I don't even have to voice the words to know he'd never believe me. I'm just a cleat chaser to him. A floozy. As far as he's concerned, I got exactly what I wanted that night.

Felix makes a sound of disgust at the back of his throat and shakes his head. "¡Que te jodan, cabrón!" *Fuck you, asshole.* "Does her behavior line up with someone making shit up?"

He doesn't give Terrance the chance to answer, but I can see that he's thinking about it now. Probably replaying whatever stories he's been told and trying to match them up with whatever he thinks he sees in me now.

Meanwhile, Wyatt's gaze is flipping back and forth from me to Terrance to Felix and then back to me. I'm not sure if he heard the rumors or not.

He doesn't look surprised like his friend. He just looks confused. Not that it matters.

This date is a disaster, and it's obvious it won't be happening again.

Felix turns his back on them, and warm brown eyes settle on mine in apology. "Lo siento, pequeñita." *I'm sorry, little one.* "Te puedo llevar a casa?" *Can I take you home?*

I want to say yes, but suddenly, my throat is filled with broken glass and my limbs are locked. All I can seem to do is stare at Austin through Felix's chest because even with him in the way, I know Austin is there. It takes every ounce of my being just to breathe.

17
GABRIEL

My eyes dart over the words, and my heart jumps into my throat. What the hell did Felix get himself into this time?

> Felix: Get to Zeta Pi. Now.

"Julio!" I call out, knowing he'll hear me from his room.

I quickly type out a message in response to Felix's cryptic text.

> Me: All hands on deck?

"What?" Julio's voice echoes from his room. Before I can answer him, Felix's reply comes through.

> Felix: No. But you need to come get your girl. Zeta Pi house. Now.

Fuck.

My heart pounds harder, and panic grips my chest like a vise. I rush to the kitchen and grab the keys to my motorcycle off the hook.

"Where's the fire?" Julio asks as he sees me scrambling to shove my feet into my boots.

What the hell is she doing there?

"Cecilia's at the Zeta Pi house," I blurt out, my mind racing with a thousand different scenarios. None of them good.

"Fuck," he curses.

My thoughts exactly. Grabbing my helmet, I sprint out the door. The need to get to her thrums through me. If anything happens to her, I don't know what I'll do.

Why is she there? We had a plan. Deacon is going to get the pictures to Jameia tomorrow.

Julio calls out at my back. "Want back up?"

"I got it!" I shout back, my voice firm. Felix didn't say it was an all-hands-on-deck situation, which means between him and me, we can handle it. No sense in dragging Julio into the fray.

I throw my leg over my bike and back it out of the driveway.

As soon as I'm on the street, I flip the ignition and shift my bike into gear, barreling down the street at breakneck speed. Less than ten minutes pass before I make it to Greek Row. As soon as I'm in front of Zeta Pi, I kill my engine and get off my bike. Sprinting for the front door, I tear off my helmet.

My eyes scan the room as soon as I step inside, my gaze sweeping for Cecilia. The scene inside is pure chaos. Girls are dancing, guys are grinding behind them, and everyone seems to be in full party mode.

My heart pounds, and I scan each cluster of people, looking for any sign of Cecilia's dark brown hair and delicate frame. She's too damn tiny and hard to find in this sea of people.

Some unfamiliar chick sidles up to me. "Hey," she says. "You killed it at this week's game against CPU."

I grunt, hardly spare her a glance, and brush past her, but the girl is persistent.

"So uh, do you come to these parties a lot?"

I ignore the question, still scanning the crowd.

There.

My eyes latch onto what I know is the back of Felix's head, and I shove my way toward him, ignoring the girl when she calls out my name.

"Gabriel! Wait up."

Not happening. I'm not here for some cleat chaser's attention. I'm here to get my girl.

"Where is she?" I demand as soon as I'm within earshot.

Felix looks up at the sound of my voice, relief washing over his features.

He steps aside, revealing Cecilia.

Her skin is pale, her brown eyes wide and filled with fear. Her hair is pulled back into twin braids, exposing the column of her neck, and I can see the rapid thrum of her pulse. But what my eyes get stuck on is what she's wearing.

Cecilia's in a dress.

I can't help but do a double-take. Holy shit. That's some dress —black and figure-hugging, short, resting on the tops of her thighs.

It's a sight I can't quite wrap my head around. Don't get me wrong, she looks good. Better than good. She looks amazing. But still, my brows furrow in confusion.

Why is she dressed like this?

There's a guy talking to her, but it doesn't look like she's paying him any attention, and Felix doesn't let him get too close.

Good.

I give the guy a quick once-over. He's not familiar, not someone I know.

"That was fast," Felix comments, a hint of humor in his voice.

Fucker.

I shoot him a glare. Like he didn't expect me to ride over here like a bat out of hell after that text he sent me. When Felix turns his attention to me, the guy trying to talk to Cecilia manages to shift closer, reaching out to touch her arm. My eyes sharpen, and my blood boils with barely tempered rage.

Why is this asshole touching her?

Cecilia flinches away from his touch, and my anger intensifies.

"What did you do?" I growl, my voice like gravel.

The guy jerks his eyes toward me. "I've got this," he says to me with misplaced confidence.

214

Cecilia offers no response. Her eyes are locked on something in the distance, and I follow her gaze to see Austin Holt standing on the other side of the room, near the kitchen's back door. He offers me a smug grin and raises his beer in a mocking salute.

Son of a bitch.

I position myself to block him from Cecilia's view and move closer to her.

"Cecilia," I pitch my voice low, "Hey, baby girl, look at me."

But there's no response from her. Tears well up in her eyes, and she trembles on her feet. That guy is still fucking touching her, but to her, it's like he's not even there. None of us are.

All she can see is Austin.

"Hey, man. I said I got this," the guy tells me. "We're good."

Is he fucking kidding me right now? "No, you're not good. She's having a panic attack, and you're in my way."

His expression darkens. "Look, I don't know who you—"

I ignore him, taking another step closer to her. "Cecilia. Look at me."

Nothing.

"Bro, seriously. Who the hell are you?"

I do not have time for this shit. "Who the fuck are you, man? And why the fuck are you touching her?"

He startles, taken aback by the fury in my voice, but seems to recover when he steps forward, getting in my face. "I'm Wyatt, her date. Who the fuck are you?"

My vision goes red hearing him refer to himself as her date. But I don't have time for this asshole's bullshit.

My gaze snaps to Felix, my jaw tight with anger. "Her date?" I seethe, the word leaving a bitter taste in my mouth.

He nods. "Dumbass stopped here on his way to take her home."

My head falls back and for a second, I stare up at the ceiling. Did I do some fucked up shit in a past life or something to make me deserving of this? Fucking hell. Can't a guy get a break?

"Look, I didn't know," the guy starts to explain.

Oh, and now he does?

Good for him.

"You got this?" I ask Felix, indicating the douchebag beside me.

"Yeah," Felix says, his voice laced with irritation. "I got it."

With that settled, I shove the guy out of my way and into Felix's grip. He wraps his arms around the guy—Wyatt or whatever the fuck his name is—trapping his arms at his sides, while I turn back to Cecilia.

As long as we're here, in this fucking house, she won't be able to pull out of this.

Getting her out of here needs to be objective number one. We can talk and sort everything else out after that.

Dipping low, I wrap my arms around her knees and hoist her over my shoulder. She doesn't even object to the contact, just exhales a shaky breath.

"What the hell!" Wyatt shouts at Felix. "Dude, let go." Then he turns to me. "Where the hell are you taking her?"

"Chill the fuck out," Felix snaps. "And you—" He glares daggers at the fucker's friend. "Don't even think about it. Let my boy handle this."

"You can't just—"

I don't stick around long enough for Wyatt to finish his sentence.

I carry Cecilia outside, ignoring the weight of Holt's gaze on my back as I head straight for my bike. The evening breeze whips around us and sends goosebumps along my skin. Cecilia's got to be cold.

Setting her on her feet, I cup her face in my hands and force her dark brown gaze up to mine.

"Cecilia?" Tears well up in her eyes. I thumb the moisture away, stroking her cheeks. "I've got you," I tell her. "I've got you." Pulling her into my embrace, I give her what little comfort I can before reminding myself that we need to get out of here.

Tugging my helmet onto her head, I buckle the chin strap and help her onto the back of my bike. She's still a little out of it, but she's responding to my directions, even if it isn't with words.

"Don't let go," I tell her as I pull her arms snugly around my waist. Her tiny hands curl into the material of my shirt, and I kick myself for not remembering to grab my coat on my way out. She's going to freeze to death on the ride home. In that dress—*shit*.

I still can't wrap my head around seeing her out like this. And on a date.

There's a whole mess of feelings swirling around my head, but anger is the one punching hardest through the noise.

She's out with some random guy when it's only been a handful of weeks since she broke things off. What the hell is going on? Does she want a relationship now?

Jesus—fuck.

Is she seriously considering being with someone who isn't me?

Just the thought of her with another guy, letting him touch her. It's like a volcano erupting inside me. I can't wrap my head around why she would do this to me. *To us.*

18
CECILIA

Gabriel's entrance into his house is like a sudden clap of thunder, his voice a crackling lightning bolt of fury. "What the hell were you thinking?" he snaps, barely allowing me a moment to breathe.

"Why are we here?" I counter, looking around the room. "Why didn't you take me home?" The remnants of my panic dissipated on the ride over to be replaced by a potent cocktail of equal parts humiliation and irritation.

I feel exposed, vulnerable, as if every wall I've carefully built around myself has crumbled to dust.

I can't believe I completely locked down like that.

I was making progress. Things were getting better.

Dammit.

One look at Austin in that house, and suddenly, I couldn't breathe. I couldn't think. If I'm honest, I was losing my shit even before that. Seeing him just made things worse.

When fear hits you like that, you're supposed to go into fight or flight. But all I did was freeze, and he watched me. Wordlessly drinking his beer like I was his favorite fucking show.

Gabriel bares his teeth at me, his body vibrating with anger as the door slams behind him.

I jump, and he immediately curses.

"Fuck. I'm sorry." He huffs out a breath and visibly pulls himself together, reining in some of his anger.

"Why are we here?" I repeat the question, my words echoing in the tension-laden air.

Gabriel's gaze bores into me, stripping away any semblance of defensiveness. His silence is a palpable force, pressing down on me like a suffocating weight.

"Gabriel?" I prompt again, my voice laced with uncertainty.

"Because you're being reckless," he finally responds, his tone edged with frustration. "And obviously need somebody to talk some sense into you. What the hell were you thinking going to Zeta Pi tonight? Do you have any idea what could have happened to you?"

My spine stiffens, my breath catching in my throat. "Of course I know what can happen," I retort, my voice rising in defiance. "It's already happened before!"

"Then why were you there?" he shouts back, his voice cutting through the air like a blade. This isn't the Gabriel I know, the one who never raises his voice, never loses cool.

Not with me.

Part of me recoils at the sight of him like this, his anger a raw, unfamiliar presence. But another part—the part that craves his attention, his intensity—revels in it. In knowing that I'm the reason he's like this, and that for once, he isn't treating me like a fragile piece of glass, ready to shatter at any moment.

Gabriel only ever yelled at me once—when we first met, before he knew everything that's happened to me. I was afraid of him then. But I'm not afraid of him now.

I stand my ground, meeting Gabriel's fiery gaze with my own defiant stare. The air between us crackles with tension, thick with unspoken words and unresolved emotions.

"Why were you there?" he repeats, his voice softer this time, but no less intense.

"It was an accident, okay?" I retort, frustration lacing my tone. "It's not like I planned on being there tonight. I—" Screw this. I bite my tongue, my patience wearing thin, and make a beeline for the door.

He's not my keeper. I don't owe him any explanations. I'm not some child. I'm twenty-one years old. I don't need to answer him.

"Where the hell do you think you're going?" he snaps, his hand gripping my arm and yanking me back around to face him.

"Home," I reply curtly, my jaw set as I stare down at his hand on me and ignore the electricity racing up my arm.

"You don't have your Jeep," he reminds me, his grip tightening slightly. He doesn't hurt me. No. Gabriel would never do that. But his hold is firm. Unyielding.

"I don't care. I'll walk." I jerk free from his hold and reach for the door. But before I can open it, his hand slams down on it, blocking my exit.

"Move."

"Cecilia—" his voice rumbles, sending shivers down my spine. The warmth of his body envelops me, making my stomach tighten with a mixture of nerves and something else I refuse to name. He leans forward, dipping low until his lips brush the shell of my ear. "You're not leaving," he growls.

My thighs clench, and I hate the way my body responds to him.

I turn around to face him. My hands press against his chest, a feeble attempt to create some space between us, but his arm remains firmly braced over my shoulder, trapping me against the door.

He's so close. *Too close.*

His scent, a tantalizing mix of musk and spice, fills my senses, clouding my thoughts.

Why does he smell so good? Glaring at a spot on his chest, I push at him again, desperate to break free from this invisible hold he has on me, but he doesn't budge.

Frustration simmers beneath my skin, mingling with the heat radiating from his body. Why won't he just step back? Why does he insist on invading my personal space like this?

We need boundaries. We're not together anymore. He can't just force himself into my life whenever he sees fit.

"You can't keep me here," I protest, my heart hammering in my chest.

"I can, and I will," he counters, his voice firm and unwavering. "At least until I know you're not going to be a danger to yourself—"

Before I can even process his words, my hand moves of its own accord, the sound of the slap echoing in the tense silence that follows.

My eyes widen in shock as I watch the red mark bloom on Gabriel's cheek, the realization of what I've done hitting me like a ton of bricks.

"Oh my god," I whisper, horror washing over me. I've never lashed out at someone like this before. Guilt threatens to consume me. But even as I recoil from my actions, I can't bring myself to apologize to him. Not after what he just insinuated.

How could he?

I can't believe he crossed that line and while I am absolutely mortified with my reaction, I refuse to let him make me feel small. Not about this.

"I am not going to kill myself just because I had a shitty ending to my date." My voice trembles.

His jaw ticks and almost in slow motion, he drags his gaze back to mine.

"That isn't what I was saying—" Gabriel starts, but his words cut off abruptly, and I realize my mistake too late.

"Your date?" His tone is sharp, his eyes narrowing with calculation.

Panic claws at my chest.

Shit. Fuck.

"It's been a long night," I offer weakly, attempting to diffuse the tension that crackles between us like electricity. "I shouldn't have hit you," I tell him. "But you were out of line."

Gabriel doesn't back down. Instead, he looms over me, closing the distance until there's barely an inch separating our faces. The intensity of his gaze makes my heart race, and I struggle to maintain my composure.

"I don't give a shit," he says. "I wasn't insinuating anything, but fuck it. We'll skip over that for right now. You're not walking home, and you're going to explain this date," he insists, his voice firm and unwavering.

"Absolutely not." I counter, desperation creeping into my tone. "I'm leaving. You can get out of my way, or you can drive me yourself. Your pick. But I'm going." Riding on the back of Gabriel's motorcycle isn't my idea of a perfect solution, but it's better than being stuck here with him.

"No," he snaps, using that one word as a complete sentence. Damn him and his stubbornness.

"You're being unreasonable," I argue, my frustration boiling over.

He barks out a humorless laugh. "You haven't seen me unreasonable yet."

Our gazes lock in a staring contest, neither of us willing to blink and give in. I forgot what it was like. Sparing with him like this. Going toe to toe with anyone really.

Seconds pass, turning into minutes, and neither one of us budges.

"What now?" I ask, breaking the silence.

Gabriel's jaw tightens. "Tell me about your date."

Pass. That sounds like a terrible idea.

I shake my head vehemently, already dreading this conversation. "It was just one date. There's nothing to tell," I say, hoping he'll drop it.

Gabriel's eyes darken with suspicion. "I want to know why you were on a date to begin with. What happened to needing space? What about all that bullshit you fed me about needing to fix whatever the fuck you think is broken inside you on your own?"

Venom drips from each of his words, and I flinch. But despite being faced with his anger, I don't miss the emotion that flickers over his gaze when he voices the questions.

Hurt.

Guilt churns in the pit of my stomach as I meet his hard gaze. "It was just one date," I repeat, my voice softening because despite the ass he's being right now, I don't want to hurt Gabriel. That's never been my intention. "I wanted to see if I could do it. If I could go out like a normal college girl." I sigh and tug at one of my braids. "I'm not planning to see Wyatt again. It was just *one* date." I offer the explanation almost as a peace offering, hoping to ease the tension between us.

What I do in my free time is none of his business, but it doesn't cost me anything to give him this.

Gabriel pushes away from the door and paces the length of the living room, his frustration palpable. It's clear he doesn't like my answer.

"So tonight was what, a test?" he demands, his tone sharp.

I nod slowly. "Yeah," I admit, the weight of failure heavy on my shoulders. "Adriana and I thought—"

The sound he makes is mocking. "Of course, this was her idea."

My brows knit together in confusion, but before I can question him further, he demands, "Why?"

Despite my better judgment, I move closer to him, unable to bear the sight of him hurting like this. "Why what?" I ask softly, my voice barely above a whisper.

I know I should leave it alone. I should take this opportunity to open the door and slip away, but for whatever reason, I can't.

My body is drawn to Gabriel like a moth to a flame. Sooner or later, I know I'll get burned, but I move closer to him anyway.

"Why what?" I try again.

"Why him?" His question hangs heavy in the air, unspoken implications lingering just beneath the surface. I hear the question Gabriel doesn't bother to voice out loud.

What does Wyatt have that he doesn't?

The truth is, nothing. There's nothing Wyatt has that Gabriel doesn't. Not anything I'm looking for, at least.

"He asked," I explain. "His sister is on the swim team, and—" I shrug, "I don't know. He seemed nice enough, and he just happened to be the first guy to ask. I'm not trying to get into a relationship here. It was just a date. Nothing more."

Gabriel's jaw tightens as he absorbs my words. "Were you planning to sleep with him?" he asks. I don't miss the accusation in his tone..

"Excuse me?" I rear back and fold my arms defensively across my chest.

Gabriel stops pacing and faces me fully. "If the date had gone well, were you planning on fucking him?"

What the hell is wrong with him? Indignation rises inside of me. "No, of course not. Do you seriously think I'd do something like that? Do you think I'm that easy?"

Gabriel's gaze remains steady on mine, and I can sense something brewing beneath the surface. The tension between us crackles.

He curses. "I didn't say you were easy."

"No, you just implied it."

Gabriel curses. "Fine," he concedes, his voice low and intense. "My bad. I'm sorry. But you went on a date to test your boundaries. Is that it?"

I nod cautiously, wary of where this conversation is heading.

It feels like a trap.

"And you're planning to go on other dates," he continues, his tone probing. "See how things go with other guys?"

I shift uncomfortably, uncertainty gnawing at me. "I don't know. Maybe," I confess, the weight of my own words sinking in. I hadn't really thought about anything beyond getting through tonight, but yes. Eventually, there will be other dates. Tonight was a disaster. I won't be going on any more dates anytime soon, but damn. I was so close. I made it through dinner. The car ride. Being alone with Wyatt in a confined space. Things only went sideways after he got that call from his friend. If he'd just taken me home—

"And then what?" Gabriel steps closer, his presence overwhelming as he invades my personal space. "After the dates. We'll say you go on five, maybe ten. What's the next part of your little test, hmm?"

I swallow hard, feeling the weight of his words pressing down on me. "I ..." I falter, unsure of how to respond.

"If things go well, are you going to let one of these guys kiss you?" His question hangs in the air, accusing and loaded with implications.

But there are no other guys. This is all hypothetical.

Before I can protest, Gabriel's hand cups my jaw, sending a jolt of electricity through me. My breath catches in my throat as he draws me closer, his touch setting my nerves ablaze.

My stomach does a somersault.

"And if you don't freak out after that kiss, what comes next? Are you going to let one of them touch you?" His other hand moves to cup my breast, and I freeze, my heart pounding in my chest.

"Gabe—" I begin, but my words falter as his hands guide me backward until my back meets the solid wall of the living room.

I'm trapped, pinned beneath his intense gaze.

My heart races, thundering against my ribcage.

Neither of us speaks, but the silence is deafening, broken only by the sound of my shallow breaths. I feel exposed, vulnerable, and achingly aware of every inch of his body touching mine.

My eyes are wide as I stare up at Gabriel in the dimly lit room, his hand still on my breast.

The atmosphere is thick with anticipation.

I should push him away. Make him stop. But I don't do either of those things. Because Gabriel is touching me and fuck, I missed this.

"Is that the end goal?" he asks, his fingers flexing around my breast and grazing my sensitive nipple. My back arches into his touch. "To be touched?"

I struggle to find my voice, my mind racing with conflicting emotions. "I—" But before I can respond, he presses into me, his touch sending sparks flying, and I can't help but tremble beneath him.

"No one else is going to make you feel like this." he says, not waiting for a response. "I have a proposition," Gabriel murmurs, his voice sending shivers down my spine as he presses closer, his hand now kneading my breast.

My lashes flutter as pleasure sparks through me, a low moan threatening to escape my lips.

Fuck.

Gabriel angles my head upward, his honey-brown eyes locking with mine, holding me captive.

"Are you listening, baby?" he asks, his gaze intense as he watches my every move.

I wet my lips nervously, feeling his eyes follow the movement, sending heat pooling low in my belly.

"You don't want a relationship, is that right?" His words are a whisper against my ear. His body presses firmly against mine, his hips pinning me to the wall.

"That's right," I manage to breathe out over the roaring sound in my ears.

"But you want to be physical with someone. You're working up to eventually being kissed. Touched. To being fucked." His words hang heavy in the air, and I can't help but shiver at the raw desire in his voice.

He doesn't phrase it as a question and it's obvious he isn't expecting a response.

Instead, he continues, his tone growing more and more heated with each word. "What you did tonight was reckless," he growls. "Irresponsible. If Felix hadn't called me, if he hadn't been there—" A shadow passes over his face.

"If you want to get physical, you want someone to touch this body—" He trails off, his hand sliding down from my breast and over my stomach. My breath hitches when he moves lower.

Lower still. Until it reaches the apex of my thighs beneath my dress.

He boldly cups my sex, his touch igniting a fire within me. "You come to me."

My lips part on a gasp.

The thin lace of my panties is hardly any kind of barrier as he presses the heel of his palm into me.

It takes close to a minute for me to register his words.

"You want ..."

"Yes." His eyes bore into mine. "It's not a relationship," he continues, his eyes never leaving mine as he creates small circles against my core with the heel of his hand. "You don't want one, so that's not what I'm offering. There are no strings attached with this."

"You want us to be—" My voice falters, uncertainty muddling my thoughts. What exactly is he proposing? "Friends with benefits?"

"Call it whatever you want. I'm going to look at it as an escape. A way to let off some steam." Gabriel's voice is low, husky, sending shivers down my spine as he continues to toy with me, my body coiling tighter and tighter.

I suck in a breath, overwhelmed by the pleasure coursing through me. God, that feels good.

"But you want to push boundaries, don't you, sweetheart? You want to get comfortable fucking and being fucked. So that's what we'll do."

"We've already done that," I manage to stutter, my words barely coherent as his touch sends electric pulses through me. His hand between my legs makes it impossible to think.

My hips jerk forward of their own accord, seeking more of his touch, more of that delicious friction.

Gabriel chuckles, the sound sending a wave of heat rushing through me. His breath ghosts over my lips, teasingly close.

If I lift up on my toes just a fraction of an inch, we'll be kissing.

I want him to close that distance. To press his mouth against mine.

I shouldn't want that. I know I shouldn't. But—

Oh god. His touch intensifies, sending waves of pleasure crashing over me. *Yes. Fuck. Right there.*

"No, baby girl. We've had sex. We most certainly haven't fucked." His voice is like gravel, rough and intoxicating.

Goosebumps break out over my skin.

"It's a bad idea," I protest weakly, my words breathless. "Things between us are ... complicated." But my body betrays me, craving his touch despite the turmoil in my mind.

He dips his head to trail open-mouthed kisses along my neck, and I shudder in response.

So close...

"Then we'll uncomplicate them," he murmurs. His words send a thrill of anticipation through me. With a deliberate motion, he pushes aside my panties before swiping two fingers between my folds, and I moan unabashedly at the sensation.

Gabriel groans against the sensitive skin of my neck, his hot breath sending shivers down my spine. "So fucking wet," he murmurs, his fingers slick with my arousal as he circles my clit.

I jolt in his arms, electricity rushing through my veins.

"All I need you to do is say yes," he whispers, his voice rough with desire.

He's just as turned on as I am right now, and I'm not even touching him.

Gabriel pulls back enough to look at me as his fingers quicken their pace between my legs, driving me closer to the edge. I'm right there, teetering on the brink of ecstasy, my legs trembling beneath me as white spots dance behind my closed eyelids.

"Yes," I moan and my orgasm crashes over me, taking with it the final threads of my sanity and my self-control.

Gabriel's mouth crashes into mine, our kiss a fierce collision of tongues and teeth. I'm breathless, lost in the intensity of his touch. This kiss is nothing like before—It isn't gentle or patient. There's no tenderness or hesitancy—it's raw, primal, consuming.

I can't breathe.

Gabriel devours my mouth, his one hand tangling in my hair as he angles my head, deepening the kiss even further. With a swift motion, he unravels the elastic bands securing my braids, allowing my hair to tumble freely around us.

God, he feels so good.

Before I can catch my breath, he lifts me effortlessly into his arms, his hands gripping the backs of my thighs as he demands, "Wrap your legs around my waist."

I comply without hesitation and am rewarded with the undeniable press of his arousal against my core.

"Fuck," I gasp as he grinds against me.

"Say it again, baby girl." His fingers flex on my thighs, and he carries me out of the room. "Tell me that you want me to fuck you."

19
GABRIEL

Cecilia moans against my mouth as I blindly make my way into the kitchen. The need to claim her, to bury myself inside of her body and mark her as mine rips through me. I dig my fingers into her skin, pulling her harder against me. I know I'm being rough, but I can't fucking control myself. She was on a date. A fucking date. I swear to god as soon as I find out who that asshole is—

Wyatt. I have his first name.

"Say it," I demand, my voice rough with need as I lower her onto the kitchen island. The surface is the perfect height, positioning her just right for what I have planned. Her legs fall from around my waist, her fingers clutching at the material of my shirt.

There are too many layers between us. With an impatient growl, I rip off my shirt, tossing it aside before shedding my jeans and briefs in one swift motion.

Cecilia is next. I lift her dress up and over her head before discarding it on the tiled floor. I want to take my time with her. To go slow and savor every inch of her body. But the urgency pulsing through me demands otherwise.

I'm incapable of going slow right now. I'm so fucking desperate for this girl.

My eyes lock onto her tits. She isn't wearing a bra. *Fuck me.* Unable to resist, I capture one of her dusky nipples between my lips, reveling in the way she melts beneath me.

Her spine arches, and she throws her head back, letting out a soft groan.

That sound ... it goes straight to my dick.

"Look at me," I command, my voice sharp as I meet her startled gaze. Her chest rises and falls with each ragged breath, her arousal palpable in the air between us.

I lean forward and capture her nipple between my teeth again, tugging on the sensitive nub and kneading her flesh until she's writhing beneath me. Simultaneously begging me to stop and asking me for more.

Reaching down, I hook my fingers on either side of her panties and slide the scrap of lace down her legs. She raises her hips, helping me get them the rest of the way off.

Then I take her in. Pressing her thighs open, I drink in the blush on her cheeks, the heavy rise and fall of her chest. My eyes dip lower to the flutter of her belly until I reach her bare and glistening cunt. She's so fucking perfect.

"Say it," I demand, watching as she squirms beneath my penetrating gaze. Her hesitation only fuels my desire, driving me to push her further. "You want me to fuck you? Give me the words."

Her hooded eyes meet mine, her thighs trembling as she attempts to close them, but I won't allow it. I push them apart, exposing her dripping cunt to my hungry gaze.

"Now isn't the time to be shy," I tell her, my voice thick with need. "You trust me to make you feel good, right?"

She nods, her desire evident in the way she meets my gaze.

"I need to trust that you'll tell me what you need," I continue. "And if it's too much, that you'll tell me to stop."

"I don't want you to stop," she whispers, lust heavy in her gaze.

"Good girl," I growl, capturing her mouth in a fierce kiss. "Tell me what you need."

Her whimper ignites something primal within me.

"I want..." she begins, her voice tinged with desperation. "I want you to fuck me. Please."

Yes. Fisting my cock, I position myself at her entrance, her wet heat inviting me in. She's soaked for me, and I momentarily close my eyes, savoring the feel of my swollen head pressing between her folds.

Anticipation grips me tight, but before I can move, her delicate hand grips my wrist.

I tear my gaze from where our bodies connect to look at her face. Her dark brown eyes pierce mine and I wait, a flicker of determination flashing across her beautiful face.

"Not just sex," she says, her voice breathy. It's taking every ounce of my self-control not to slam into her right now as my brain struggles to interpret her words. "I want more than that. We've had sex before, but you said we've never fucked. I want that. I need you to fuck me like you know I won't break."

Done.

With a single, hard thrust, I bury my cock inside her, claiming her in a way that goes beyond mere physicality.

"Fuck," she hisses.

I give her no reprieve, no time to adjust to the sensation of me filling her so completely before I withdraw and thrust back in, harder this time than before.

Desperate need surges through me, a primal hunger that demands satisfaction. And judging by the way Cecilia responds to me, she craves this feeling just as much.

A shudder runs through her body, her features contorting momentarily with discomfort before softening with pleasure. I set a relentless pace, her body rocking hard and fast against mine as I relish the way she clenches around my dick.

She feels perfect, so tight around me it's almost unbearable.

"Touch yourself," I tell her, watching as she startles before hesitantly obeying my command.

Her hand finds its way between us, fingers circling her clit as she heeds my order. Her hips buck forward, and her pussy squeezes my cock. *That's it.* A moan of pleasure falls from her lips, and I lean forward to capture the sound.

The scent of her arousal fills the room, driving me wild.

I need to feel her come on my cock. To see her lose herself to me fully.

Cecilia's tits bounce with each one of my thrusts, stealing my attention. Her nipples harden. It's like her body was made for mine, every curve fitting perfectly against me.

"Don't stop," she pleads, her voice laced with desperation.

As if I ever could. I've been deprived of this woman for far too long. Desperate and aching for her. Nothing, not even the roof collapsing on top of us, could make me stop now.

Not when I have her right where I want her.

Her breaths grow shorter, her movements more frantic as she approaches the edge.

"Are you close?" I ask, my own desire nearing its peak.

"Yes," she gasps, her eyes fluttering shut in ecstasy as her fingers circle her clit even faster.

"Eyes on me," I demand, needing to see her pleasure reflected in her gaze.

She complies and dips her chin forward. Her lust-filled eyes meet mine as I continue to drive her towards release.

I feel it building within her, the tension in her body reaching its breaking point. "Oh God," she moans. She's right there. I see it in the look in her eyes. The desperation on her face.

Nah. Fuck that. "God isn't the one fucking you. I am." I bite at her bottom lip. "The only name you cry out when I'm inside of you is mine, understood?"

She nods eagerly, her voice barely above a whisper as she says, "Yes."

"Look at how greedy your pussy is," I rasp, watching her gaze drop to where our bodies are joined. "You want me to fill this tight little cunt with my cum, don't you?"

She whimpers.

"No one else can make you feel like this." I replace her hand with my own, my thumb rubbing tight circles over her sensitive nub while I continue to thrust ruthlessly between her thighs.

"Look at me, baby girl. Look at me as you come on my cock. Show me how good only I can make you feel."

She keeps her eyes on mine, and something about the connection makes what we're doing intimate as fuck. She can't hide from me like this. She can't mask what she's feeling.

Her legs shake, and her pussy clenches around me as I feel the first ripples of her orgasm.

"Yes," I hiss as her mouth falls open, a cry of release escaping her lips. "Come for me, baby. Just like that."

So fucking good.

I'm only a few seconds behind her, the sight of her shattering helping to throw me over the edge. My balls tighten, and I thrust deep as my orgasm crashes over me, every muscle in my body tensing with pleasure. Bracing my hands on either side of her, I fuck Cecilia through my release, my movements sharp and shallow as she milks every last drop from me.

My breath is heavy, and I'm dripping with sweat when I finally stop, basking in the aftermath of our combined orgasm. I feel like I just ran a fucking marathon, and already I want to do it again. Pushing my hair out of my eyes, I look down at her.

Her cheeks flush a bright shade of red.

Fucking adorable. I will never get enough of this girl.

I capture her lips in a kiss, and she melts into me, her body boneless and satisfied.

She smiles against my mouth. "That was ..."

"Yeah," I murmur as I withdraw from her, my cock still half-hard. "We're definitely doing that again."

Cecilia presses up on her hands, but I'm crowding her, not allowing her to rise to a seated position. Her brows furrow, but I ignore her confusion and steal another kiss.

Bringing my hand up between us, I catch the cum that's started dripping out of her pussy and press it back inside of her, burying my fingers deep.

"What are you—" she gasps as I finger fuck my cum back inside her.

"I'm not finished with you yet." I don't want a single drop of my cum to go to waste. I need all of it inside her.

Her breath hitches, and she shudders beneath my touch. "Gabriel, I ..." Her mouth falls open.

That's it. Give me another one.

I need to see her shatter all over again.

I add another finger, stretching her further. She's so fucking tight. Even after being freshly fucked her pussy grips my fingers like a vise.

My thumb circles her clit, and she cries out, her skin still sensitive.

"I can't."

"Yes, you can." I growl. "Come for me again."

Her head thrashes back and forth, and she makes these desperate, needy sounds that go straight to my dick.

"I ...I ..." Her mouth makes this little O right before she shatters, and fuck, it's a beautiful thing to behold.

Her head falls back, her eyes squeeze shut, and the sounds she makes—*fuck*.

When she finally comes down, I slip my hand free from her folds and pull her flush against me. Her arms wrap around my waist, face pressed tight to my bare chest.

We stay like that for a few minutes before I draw back and help her to her feet.

I pull my jeans back on while I wait for Cecilia to clean up in the bathroom and fight the urge to barge in there and join her.

When she comes back out, I scowl, not liking what I see.

"I uh ... I should go."

Absolutely not.

"You should stay," I insist, not liking the distance she's putting between us.

She shakes her head, arms crossed defensively over her chest. "No. This was a—"

I close the distance between us, my tone firm. "If you say this was a mistake, we're going to have a problem. Nothing about what we just did—" I gesture to the counter, still gleaming with our combined juices. I'll need to clean that up before my roommates come home. "—was a mistake."

Her cheeks flush, and she avoids my gaze.

I refuse to let her retreat. Cupping her jaw, I force her attention back to me. "Nothing about that," I growl, "was a mistake. Do you hear me?"

"That's not—" She swallows hard and shakes her head. "I wasn't going to call it a mistake."

My shoulders relax. Good. Because it wasn't one. "Then what's wrong?" She's acting cagey, already trying to put up walls between us.

Cecilia bites her lip and takes a step away. My hand falls back to my side. "We need to set boundaries," she says. "Things are already complicated between us. We need to create guidelines for whatever this is going to be. We're not ... together, right? I'm not ready for that, and you said no strings."

My jaw tightens. I don't want there to be any boundaries between us, but I get what she's saying. This is supposed to be casual, even though nothing about what I feel for this woman is casual in the least.

"Alright. Lay them on me." If Cecilia needs to establish a few rules, so be it. I'll agree to damn near anything if it means I can have her.

Relief flickers across her face. She expected me to be difficult about this, but see? I'm full of surprises today.

"I don't think we should do sleepovers."

That's dumb. We should absolutely do sleepovers. Then I can fuck her morning, noon, and night, but it's fine. I'll work them in later. I can be patient.

Sort of.

Well, I can try.

"Okay. What else?"

She licks her lips. "No cuddling."

Also dumb, but fine.

For now.

"Alright. Any other rules I should be aware of?"

Cecilia takes a deep breath, and I can see the nerves running through her like a live wire. She's anxious about laying down these rules and she's waiting for me to reject them.

There's an intriguing mix of vulnerability and determination in her eyes.

I like seeing this side of her. She's more animated. More alive.

"Um ..." She hesitates, searching for the words. "I think we should keep this between us. No telling anyone that we're ..." She waves toward the counter. "You know."

It's not an unreasonable request, but it still stings a little. I want everyone to know that she's mine, even if only in private, but I'll play along.

"That means no holding hands. No PDA. Our relationship outside of this, when we're on campus, is the same that it has been."

"I won't lie to my roommates. I won't offer up any information unless they ask about you, but if they do ask, I'm not going to lie about what we're doing."

Her lips purse, but I'm not finished. "And when you're here, I'm not going to sneak around and hide you. We're both adults," I respond, my voice steady, though I can't help the pang of disappointment knowing she'd prefer no one know. "But outside of my place, we'll keep things on the down low. Agreed?"

She chews on her bottom lip, a nervous habit that I find inexplicably sexy. "I can live with that."

Good.

"Anything else?"

She nods. "Yeah. Umm... Let's agree to not get too...attached. Emotionally, you know? This is purely physical, right? We both know what we're getting into here."

Her words hit me like a cold shower, and it's hard to hide the hurt that flickers across my face. I want all of her—body, heart, and soul—but I'll settle for what I can get. This was my suggestion, after all, so yeah, no getting emotionally attached. Noted.

"Yeah, of course," I reply, my voice devoid of any emotion, even though her words are a punch in the gut. "I don't like dealing with cleat chasers during the season. They're annoying as shit, but you know," I shrug. "I'm no saint, and I'm not looking to be celibate. So, this is a win-win."

Cecilia glances at me, her eyes searching mine as if she's trying to read into my words.

"So you're okay with all of this?" she asks, her vulnerability peeking through.

I put on my best poker face and offer her a carefree smile. "Absolutely. These are your rules, and I'll respect them." She sighs, and I can see the tension ease from her shoulders. "But I have one of my own."

"You do?" Her expression turns from relieved to cautious.

Reaching out to cup her cheek, my thumb brushes over her lips. I need her to know how serious I am about my rule because this one, for me, is non-negotiable.

"I don't share when I'm with a woman. When I'm fucking her." Her cheeks heat at my vulgar words. "We're not in a relationship. I don't own you." Yet. We'll get to that. "But while we're messing around," I press my thumb against the seam of her lips, and her mouth parts for me. I press inside. "I own this mouth." With my other hand, I cup her core. "I own this pussy." Her breath hitches, and want fills her eyes, even as she tries to hide it.

I drag my finger free from her lips and grip both her hips, pulling her into mine.

"This shit between us, it's exclusive. Understand?"

She swallows hard but nods.

Good. I'll play by her rules, but I'm not going to stop pursuing her. She's welcome to set up as many boundaries and rules as she likes. One by one, when she's least expecting it, I'll tear them all down.

20
GABRIEL

Dropping Cecilia off at her parents' house leaves a bitter taste in my mouth, a sensation that lingers despite the cool night air. What I really want to do is drag her back to my place and make her fall apart all over again. But there are *rules*.

My upper lip curls just thinking about them.

"So uh ..." Cecilia stammers, her voice breaking the silence as we stand on her doorstep.

Without hesitation, I reach out, tucking a stray strand of hair behind her ear. My fingers linger, tracing the curve of her jaw before finding their place on her hip, pulling her closer. Leaning in, I capture her lips in a kiss, silencing whatever words were about to spill from her mouth. She sighs into the kiss, her hands finding purchase on my chest. When her lips part, I resist the urge to deepen the kiss, instead pulling away, keeping it chaste.

Confusion clouds her features, her brows furrowing.

"Don't overthink shit," I murmur against her forehead, planting a gentle kiss there. "There's no reason to make this weird. Let it be what it is." While I turn it into what it isn't.

Her cheeks flush, nodding in agreement. "Right. Yeah. Okay."

God, she's fucking adorable when she blushes like that. I can't help but chuckle. "See you tomorrow, Cecilia."

Not waiting for a response, I climb back onto my bike as she unlocks her front door. She pauses just inside the threshold and looks back at me over her shoulder. Her cheeks are still pink. Yeah, she's going to go to bed thinking about me. Smiling to myself, I pretend not to notice as I secure the strap on my full-face helmet, waiting just long enough for her to slip safely inside.

I don't like that I have to drop her off. That I can't pull her into my side and fall asleep with her lying beside me in my bed. But for now, it's okay. I'm able to breathe my first real breath since she broke things off.

I'm back in the game. And I'm a hell of a lot closer to getting my girl back. For good.

I take another deep breath, relishing in the contentedness I feel as I head back to the soccer house. I'm not at all surprised when I find all four of my roommates in the living room despite the late hour.

What surprises me more is that they stayed out of the house as long as they did, giving Cecilia and I some much needed privacy, but now that she's gone and they're home, did the fuckers really need to wait up for me?

Felix is the first to jump to his feet, leaping over the back of the sofa as soon as I walk through the door. His grin is wide with anticipation. "So?" he prompts eagerly.

I raise a skeptical eyebrow. "So, what?" I'm beat and would much rather catch some Z's than have whatever conversation he's hoping for tonight.

Felix groans. "Don't play dumb, cabrón." *Fucker*. "How'd it go? Is she—"

"She's fine," I cut him off, not wanting to discuss the details. The less they know, the better. "We talked. She's okay now. I took her home." I can't say the same for the asshole she was on a date with. That fucker and I are going to have some words. But Cecilia—I grin, thinking about what we did— yeah, she's good.

Felix waggles his eyebrows suggestively. "And ...?" He eyes me up and down, giving me an expectant look.

"Come on, bro. Don't leave us hanging," Atticus chimes in.

"There's nothing else to tell," I deflect, hiding the truth behind a facade of nonchalance. "We're good. But we have an early start tomorrow, remember? So stop pestering me about my personal life and go to bed."

Keeping our arrangement on the down low is another of her rules, and while I'd like to shout from the rooftops exactly what we did and where we stand, a gentleman is never supposed to kiss and tell.

Scrubbing a hand over my face, I stifle my chuckle. I'd hardly consider myself a gentleman. Not with the ideas swirling around in my head. The things I plan to do the next time I have Cecilia alone in a room.

Fuck. I'm getting hard just thinking about it, which means I need to get the hell out of here and into my room. Maybe rub one out before bed.

"Please tell me you're kidding?" Felix whines, "You swooped in and saved the fucking day. How do you not get the girl after a knight in shining armor moment like that?"

I shrug, brushing off the question, and notice that Julio still hasn't moved from his seat on the couch. When my eyes meet his, the look on his face calls me a liar.

So what if I am?

Julio doesn't want me with Cecilia, anyway, and it's not like I need his sour mood bringing me down.

"It's fine. We're cool now. Stop harassing me about my love life and go to bed. I'm not going to go easy on any of you fuckers in the gym tomorrow. You know J won't either," I say, dipping my head toward the broody fucker.

Felix grumbles but makes his way upstairs, Atticus following close behind him.

Julio is slower to get up, and right before he passes me, he stops.

I know he has something to say, and I already know I'm not going to like whatever it is.

"Spit it out," I tell him, bracing myself. The guy can never just leave well enough alone. I know he doesn't approve of me pursuing Cecilia. That he thinks both of us should work on our shit. But I'm happy right now.

Can't the guy give me a break, just this once, and let me bask in the afterglow for a little while?

Julio's mouth pulls into a frown, and he shakes his head. "You're a grown man," he tells me. "You can make your own decisions."

I grunt. "Glad we're on the same page."

Disapproval radiates from his gaze, but he keeps his mouth shut after that, heading for the stairs. Thank fuck for that.

Deacon is the last to get up, taking his time as he gathers his things from the end table. A glass and plate, his phone, and some weird stuffed plush thing. He drops his dishes in the dishwasher while I put away my jacket and helmet. I expect him to head upstairs when he's done, but instead, he walks back over, his expression thoughtful as he approaches me.

"You need something?"

He rubs the back of his neck, choosing his words carefully.

"Is she the girl you've been messed up about?"

I nod, surprised by his perceptiveness. "Yeah."

I haven't told Deacon about Cecilia. They've met, obviously. But it isn't like we've sat down and I've given him the 411. Though I wouldn't be surprised if Felix or one of the other guys gave him a quick rundown when he moved in.

I'd been so out of it that day.

But I have the rest of my roommates up in my business twenty-four-seven as it is. I'm not looking to add to the mother hen crew.

"What about her?" There's a bite in my voice I hadn't intended, but Deacon catches it.

His brows lift, hazel eyes taking me in.

"Look, I'm not trying to be an ass," I tell him. "But if you're going to suggest I cut my losses and move on or some shit, I don't want to hear it. I won't meddle in your shit," I assure him. "And I'd appreciate it if you stayed out of mine."

"I wasn't going to suggest anything," he reassures me, sensing my defensiveness.

Good.

"All I was going to say is, if she means that much to you, don't let anyone else influence your decisions," he tells me, taking me by surprise. "I know he's your boy but—" He hesitates, seeming to choose his words carefully. "Look, I'm not trying to start anything between you two."

"Then don't." I shrug, eager to end the conversation.

Julio's been my best friend since grade school. There isn't anything Deacon can say to cause problems between us. Not real ones, at least. J's always coming from a good place.

When it comes to Cecilia, he's a little one-sided. But he'll come around. The guy worries about me. That's all it is.

"You know how he feels about your girl?"

Nodding, I tell him, "I do."

"If you care about her, like if she's the one—" He pauses for me to confirm my feelings one way or the other, but I do neither and wait him out instead. He sighs. "Don't let anyone else get in your head. If she's it for you, then go all in. Make sure that girl knows what she means to you."

"She does," I assure him, though doubt creeps in. Have I made my feelings clear enough? I poured my heart out to her once already. Nothing's changed for me where she's concerned, so I don't think I need to do that again. Hell, with where we stand now, repeating myself will only scare her away.

But I appreciate where the guy is coming from.

"Good," Deacon nods, a weight lifted off his shoulders. "And sorry if I'm overstepping. I just ..." he purses his lips. "I'm watching in slow motion as one of my boys back in Sun Valley loses his girl. You think they know how you feel and then poof." He shrugs. "Words need to be said. That's all I wanted to say."

"Thanks, man," I clap him on the shoulder, grateful for his insight. "Cecilia and I, we're good for now."

He nods, satisfied, and we each head to our rooms.

Lying in bed, images of Cecilia consume my thoughts like a drug, her essence intertwining with every fiber of my being. It's more than just being "good for now." It's about fighting tooth and nail for her, for us, until she's mine in every way possible.

21
CECILIA

I find Adriana on campus the next day and spill everything that happened the night before. "I don't know what I'm doing," I confess, feeling overwhelmed.

"You're getting laid," she tells me with a smirk. "That's what's happening. Why do you sound so torn up about it?"

I groan, rubbing a hand over my face. "This is bad." Right? Of course it's bad. How can a friend with benefits situation-ship with Gabriel be a good thing?

Shit.

What was I thinking?

"I don't see what you're so upset about," she says. "The way you described last night, it sounds like you had a good time. What's the problem, here?"

"Oh, I don't know," I say, my voice dripping with sarcasm. "Maybe it's the fact that I went on a date, had a panic attack, got in a fight with my ex, and then we screwed each other's brains out, all while agreeing to continue screwing one another's brains out as friends with benefits. None of those things belong together."

"If you say so," she says with a shrug. "But I still don't see a problem with this. The date is whatever," she waves a hand through the air. "You weren't interested in him anyway, right? Like romantically."

"Well, no." He was nice, but I'm not looking for a relationship here. A second date would be misleading. Not that he ever got around to asking with everything that happened.

"Okay, so that settles that one. The panic attack ..." Her lips purse together. "It could have been worse. You overcame one of your fears and are here talking about it today. I'd call that progress."

Swallowing hard, I nod. Yeah, I guess you can say that. It sucked in the moment. Royally. But it is what it is. The best thing I can do now is put it behind me and pray it doesn't happen again.

I shudder. Fuck Austin. And Fuck the Zeta Pi house. They do not get to win.

"What about the Gabe thing?" I ask, my anxiety spiking as I trail after her toward my next class. That's what I'm most worried about here.

"What about it?" she counters.

"You don't think it's a massive mistake?" I ask. "The more I think about it, the more I realize that no matter how we do this, one of us is going to get hurt. I've already hurt him once before. I don't want to do that again. He deserves so much better. But I also—"

"You want him?" she asks.

"Obviously," I mutter. "But it's more than that. Last night was … different. It was intense, and I don't know if I can do casual with him." The way he makes me feel, I don't know how to describe it. Last night was … it was something and everything all wrapped into one. We've had sex before. Sweet, romantic, cautious sex. But never anything like that. Never where Gabriel drops the reins and just fucks me like an animal.

And don't get me wrong, I liked what we did before. And I appreciated how careful he was with me, but …

I chew on my bottom lip.

Adriana smirks knowingly. "So what I'm hearing is that Gabriel's dick is that good?"

"Shut up." I smack her arm.

"Oh my god. It is! I can't believe Gabriel Herrera's dick is that revolutionary." She chuckles. "Who would have known he had it in him?"

My face burns with embarrassment. "Yes, okay? It was amazing." I loop my arm through hers and all but drag her down the hallway. "Now stop talking about it."

I can't believe I just admitted that out loud, but I mean, it was really good. Like the best sex of my life good.

"No way." Her eyes twinkle with mischief. "If the dick is that good, you need to enjoy it. Have fun and stop overthinking everything."

"But what if it all goes wrong and blows up in my face later?" I protest.

"You can't predict the future," she says. "But you can definitely enjoy the present. You both want the same thing. Don't let something like a little fear hold you back from having the best sex of your life. It's okay to be a little selfish." She wiggles her brows, and I can't help but roll my eyes.

"Yeah, maybe."

"Yo! Cecilia!" Gabriel's voice pulls me from my thoughts, and I spot him waiting outside our classroom door, a cocky grin on his lips. "You coming?"

He dips his head toward Adriana in greeting, and she mirrors his nod.

I exhale a breath of relief when I don't spot any animosity in either of their gazes. I know they have history, but maybe enough time has passed that they've both moved on?

I glance at Adriana, who gives me an encouraging nod. "Go on," she murmurs. "Have fun with your man."

"He is not my man," I protest, but there's a smile on my face as I practically skip down the hallway toward Gabriel.

"Hey," I say as I reach him.

"Hey, yourself." His eyes dart around, ensuring we're alone before he pulls me close.

"What are you doing?" I hiss.

His head dips forward, and my eyes fall to his lips. "Gabriel —" Any protest dies on my lips as he kisses me. This kiss is nothing like the one he gave me on my porch last night—this one is all-consuming.

My arms instinctively find their way around his shoulders, and I press myself against his chest.

His hand presses to the side of my neck, thumb tracing my pulse, as he angles my head the way he wants it and deepens the kiss.

There is no way we can stop doing this.

His lips on mine feel like a wildfire, burning away my doubts and fears. His mouth devours mine as though I'm the air he needs to breathe.

I am in so much trouble.

When we finally break apart, both of us are breathless. "We should get to class," I whisper, my lips tingling from the kiss.

I need to move. To walk away. Because if I don't, we're going to do that again and we're too exposed. Someone is bound to see us.

"We should," he agrees, his grin suggesting he's not done with me yet.

Right. "Okay," I say, forcing myself to step back and walk through the doorway. Gabriel follows close behind, and we take our seats.

"What are your plans tonight?" he asks.

"Swim," I tell him. "I don't really know after that. Why?"

He shrugs, his gaze intense as he shifts in his chair. I can't help but notice the way his legs spread, and the very obvious bulge between them.

He chuckles, and I quickly look away when I realize I've been staring.

Cecilia. Get it together.

"Come over afterward. I'll make dinner," he suggests, catching me off guard.

My brows pull together. We already completed our project and turned it in. Ours wasn't one of the ones chosen at random by Professor Arndt, so we don't need to go over how to present it or anything.

"What for?"

His eyes drink me in slowly, and I don't miss the heat in his gaze. Right. That.

My skin prickles under his intense stare, and I'm acutely aware of the heat emanating from him.

It's like he's undressing me with his eyes.

Clearing my throat, I nod. "Yeah. Umm ... " All of a sudden, I feel both exposed and turned on by my reaction to him. Slightly embarrassed too, if I'm honest with myself.

We agreed to sex with no strings, so of course he's cashing in. And I mean, I want him to, right?

When his gaze meets mine again, the fire in them licks through me and shoots a bolt of need straight into my core.

Yes. I definitely do.

But is it too soon?

"I promised the guys I'd make gorditas, remember?" Gabriel adds, sensing my hesitation.

Right. "What time?" I manage to ask, my voice betraying my growing anticipation.

A smirk tugs at the corners of his lips, triumph evident in his expression. "What time are you done with practice?"

"Four PM."

"Can you come straight over afterwards, or do you need to go home first?"

Butterflies swarm in my belly, and I shake my head. "I don't need to go home first," I tell him.

"It's settled then."

As our teacher walks in, we fall silent, but Gabriel and the anticipation of what awaits us later today consume my thoughts for the rest of the day.

22
CECILIA

"**T**hey're going to hear us," I pant out between ragged breaths.

Gabriel lifts his head from between my legs, a dark scowl on his face. "I don't give a fuck who hears us." Pushing up on my elbows, I shove at his shoulder and draw my legs together.

He growls, pressing his palms firmly down on the inside of my thighs until they're flat, leaving me spread wide open. "And neither should you," he snaps before diving back in.

"Fuck," I hiss, my back arching involuntarily as pleasure courses through me. "We had a deal," I remind him, though the memory of our agreement fades under the intensity of what he's doing to me right now.

His tongue dances over my clit, sending sparks of ecstasy shooting through me.

"I'm aware" he murmurs, his fingers sliding inside me, adding to the intoxicating pressure.

I moan, my head spinning with pleasure.

"Gabriel," I whimper, unable to form coherent thoughts. "Oh —Right there."

He chuckles darkly between my thighs, the sound vibrating against my sensitive clit. His fingers work expertly, driving me to the brink of ecstasy. "Yes. Please—" I plead, my hips bucking against his touch, seeking release.

My fingers twist in his sheets. I'm so close. His mouth latches onto my clit and he sucks. Hard.

"Oh fu—" My hips jerk forward, chasing some measure of relief, but Gabriel's grip on me is iron-tight. "Please. Please. Oh—" I'm begging now and I don't even know what I'm begging for. For him to stop? For me to come? I'm lost in a sea of sensation and can't find my way out.

The crown of my head presses into his headboard, and I'm right there, but Gabriel releases my clit and draws his fingers back.

No! I was so close. I'm breathing heavily, my body crashing hard from an unfulfilled high. *Dammit.*

"Look at me," he demands, his voice firm.

Dropping my chin, his heavy-laden gaze collides with mine. My breath hitches as our eyes lock.

"You only come when your eyes are on mine, got it?"

This again? Swallowing hard, I nod. No way in hell am I about to complain. Not when I need him to do that thing with his tongue again.

"Good girl," he says, thrusting his fingers back inside me. His thumb draws circles over my clit, and his dark gaze holds mine, keeping me ensnared. "You want to come?" he asks, his voice dripping with promise.

"Yes," I pant. "Please."

An arrogant smirk tugs at his lips right before he curls his fingers, finding that hidden spot deep inside of me. Stars explode behind my eyes, but I only have seconds to relish in the pleasure crashing over me before Gabriel flips me onto my belly, his fingers never leaving my clit as his free hand yanks my hips back to his groin.

He draws out my release, leaving me trembling and breathless as small whimpers are torn from my throat.

"You doing okay, baby girl?" he asks, his voice tender.

I nod weakly, unable to form words as he rubs his cock against me. My shoulders sink into the mattress. I can barely breathe. It's too much, yet still, I arch my back, my body silently begging for more.

He glides his dick between my folds, teasing me with the head.

So good. Shifting my weight, I press myself against him.

"Are you still worried about someone hearing us?"

"No," I gasp, still struggling to catch my breath.

Gabriel continues with these slow, leisurely strokes, never sinking inside of me.

My brows pull together, and a small frustrated sound slips past my lips.

"You want more, baby girl?"

"Mmm."

Gabriel chuckles, "Words, baby. I want to hear the words."

"Yes," I tell him. "More. Give me more."

He sinks into me, his grip on my hips firm as he fills me completely. I cry out at the sensation, lost in the overwhelming pleasure.

"Beg me to fuck you," he commands, his voice rough with need.

Without hesitation, I comply. "Fuck me," I plead, my voice a desperate whisper. "Please, fuck me."

Drawing back, Gabriel slams his hips forward, sending shockwaves through my body. Pressing one hand over my head, I brace myself against his headboard.

"Holy—" His voice catches as he drives into me again, his movements becoming faster, deeper, more demanding. He's pushing me, testing my limits, and I welcome it, craving the intensity. "Fuck."

He goes faster. Deeper. Gabriel pushes me to take all of him. And I do. Happily. He groans behind me and my toes curl, feeling my body coil tight once again.

His fingers flex against my skin, holding me in place as if afraid to let go.

Frustration has me biting my lip. He's holding back. I can't have that.

With a surge of boldness, I push up onto my hands and knees, arching my back, inviting him to take control. "More," I demand, my voice dripping with need. "Gabriel, give me more."

He growls in response, his fingers tangling in my hair, pulling my head back and exposing my neck. He twists the long strands of my hair around his fist.

The sensation sends shivers down my spine, a mix of pleasure and pain that ignites something primal within me.

He tugs harder and my scalp smarts, tears forming in the corners of my eyes.

The mix of bone-deep pleasure and that small stab of pain pushes me closer to the edge. I've never felt anything like this.

He pistons in and out of me, his thrusts deep and relentless. My stomach clenches, and my pussy spasms. I'm going to come again.

Gabriel curses under his breath. It's like he can feel it when it happens.

Somewhere in the back of my mind, I realize we're not using a condom.

Again.

We didn't use a condom last night. In fact, I don't think we've ever used one, and that's ... not good.

Panic flares within me, but I push it aside, consumed by the intensity of the moment. I'm on the pill, so there's that. But having sex without a condom is reckless.

Fuck, he feels so good like this, though.

Skin on skin. His body looming over mine.

The hand still gripping my hip shifts and his palm covers one cheek of my ass, his fingers digging in.

I hiss.

"Do you like that?" he asks, dominance lacing his voice.

Incoherent words of pleasure tumble past my lips, and Gabriel chuckles.

"Yeah. You like that."

His hand falls away only to return with a *crack!*

I freeze, a sharp gasp escapes me, and a spear of pleasure zings through my clit.

Holy fuck. Did he just spank me?

His hand massages my ass, soothing the sting away before he pulls back and does it again.

Crack!

His hand connects with my skin, sending a jolt of pleasure coursing through me. I cry out, though from pain or pleasure, I'm not entirely sure.

Before I can gather my thoughts, he strikes me again. "Oh, fuck."

The sensation is overwhelming, sending me spiraling into a whirlwind of pleasure.

"You strangle my cock every time I smack this beautiful ass," he tells me. "My girl likes a little pain."

"I—" My lips part, but no words come out. It's a good thing it wasn't really a question.

Crack! He does it again.

"Fuck." I curse, and the next thing I know, I'm flying.

I tighten around him, and he groans in response. "Fuck, baby." He slows his thrusts but keeps them deep while he curls his body over mine. His lips skim my shoulder, teeth scraping against my skin. "That's it," he murmurs, his breath hot against my skin. "Milk my cock. Just like that." His words send a shiver down my spine, and I cling to him, riding the waves of my release. My head falls back on his shoulder, and one of his hands comes up to cup my breast, fingers pinching and rolling my nipple.

"Don't stop," I plead, my voice barely a whisper. "I need you."

He curses, and his teeth bite into my shoulder, eliciting a sharp stab of pain. I cry out, feeling the skin break, but he doesn't let go. Gabriel lets out a guttural groan, the sound muffled against my skin.

Hot spurts of his release shoot inside me, and my entire body shudders. His release seems to go on forever, and my arms shake as I struggle to hold myself up.

When he draws back, I collapse. My shoulders hit the comforter and my face mashes into the pillows. A string of unintelligible words spill out of my mouth, but he gets the gist of it and falls onto the bed beside me.

"Yeah," he agrees. "It was good."

Gabriel rolls me onto my side, pulling me close against his chest. His muscular body easily envelopes mine, and his fingers trace lazy circles on my skin.

He lingers on the tender spot he left on my shoulder, his finger gently pressing against the abused skin.

"I left a mark," he murmurs, pressing his lips to the bruise. I shiver at the sensation, his reaction comforting.

"I'm not surprised."

He hums in response, his fingers trailing down my spine.

"You seem oddly pleased about that," I tell him.

Gabriel chuckles. "Maybe I am."

I roll over to face him, my eyes searching his. "You could sound less smug about it," I say, wincing when the mark rubs against the sheets.

He grins before kissing the tip of my nose. "I could, but where's the fun in that?"

Rolling my eyes, I smack his chest, ignoring the pang in my own.

Reaching for the sheet, I tug it up to cover my body and pull myself into a seated position.

Gabriel frowns, but I ignore him as my eyes scan the floor in search of my clothes. They sort of went flying after dinner when we finally made it to his room.

"What are you doing?" he asks, confusion evident in his voice as I crawl over him to reach the edge of the bed.

I gesture to my scattered clothes. "I'm getting dressed."

He sits up, his scowl deepening, but I'm having a hard time looking at his face with the rest of him on display.

His sweatpants catch my eye, and I toss them onto his lap. "Put those on," I tell him.

His frown morphs into a grin. "Better idea," he counters, rising to his feet. His dick is already half hard again. Is he supposed to be ready to go again this fast? I mean, that's not normal, right? "Let's both stay naked and get back in the bed."

My eyes travel over his body, taking in the deep V at his waist and the way his stomach flexes when he moves. I try, and fail, not to stare at his dick, licking my lips because god, nobody should have a body this perfect.

"Can't," I tell him, my voice suddenly breathless.

Gabriel crowds me, tugging the sheet from my hands. "Bullshit," he says. "There's nothing stopping us from doing exactly that."

"Rules, remember?"

Looking down at me, he grins. "The rules say no sleepovers, and trust me ..." He leans down and trails his lips along my jaw. "What I have planned doesn't include any sleeping."

I shiver but manage to remain strong. "The rules also say no cuddling." Brushing past him, I find a shirt—his, not mine, but fuck it—and pull it on.

The material falls to my mid-thigh, and I shrug. It will do.

Gabriel's gaze flicks over me hungrily. "I like you in my clothes," he says, his expression darkening.

My heart leaps into my throat. I don't know which one of us moves first, but the next thing I know, his lips are on mine. My fingers grip his shoulders, and his hands tangle in the long strands of my hair.

Being with him, feeling Gabriel like this, it wakes up every nerve ending in my body. I don't want this feeling to end.

Without breaking the kiss, Gabriel lifts me into his arms. My legs lock around his waist, my hands holding fast to the back of his neck. The way he kisses me has me rocking against him, chasing some sort of friction. He groans into my mouth, and I nip at his full bottom lip.

When we come up for air, we're both breathing heavily, but there's a wide grin on Gabriel's face.

"You're relentless," I tell him.

"Guilty." He presses another kiss to my lips.

"Arrogant."

"That too."

I sigh but kiss him again, despite knowing that I need to make him put me down.

"I need to get dressed."

Gabriel presses his forehead to mine and tightens his grip on my thighs.

"No clothing allowed when you're in my room," he says. "I want that rule added to the list."

A breathy laugh escapes me.

"You can't just add new rules whenever it suits you," I tell him.

Walking us back, he drops down on the bed, my legs coming down to rest on either side of him. His erection presses into me, and without thinking, I glide myself over his length.

He hisses right before he tears his shirt up and over my head.

"Right now," he tells me, leaning forward to trail kisses along my breasts. "I'm pretty sure I can get away with whatever I want."

23

GABRIEL

The locker room buzzes with energy as we unwind from our morning training session. The familiar scent of sweat and Icy Hot hangs thick in the air, mingling with the sounds of conversation and the clatter of equipment being stowed away.

I lean back against the cool metal of my locker, relishing the sense of accomplishment that comes from a solid morning workout. Closing my eyes, I let out a sigh of contentment, the tension of the morning melting away like ice under the sun.

Cecilia didn't stay the night like I wanted her to, but she did stay late, finally dragging herself from my bed well after 2 AM.

It's progress, if you ask me, and the memory of seeing her leave in my shirt brings a satisfied smile to my lips.

"What's got you grinning like a fool?" Felix's voice breaks through my reverie, his tone filled with playful curiosity. "I'm dead tired, about to fall over on my feet, and you're over here looking like you just won the lottery."

I crack open an eye, glancing at him with amusement. "No reason," I reply casually, not bothering to hide my grin.

"Our boy got lucky. That's why he's walking on cloud nine," Deacon chimes in, his voice carrying a hint of amusement.

I shoot him a mock glare, brushing off his comment with a wave of my hand. There are some things better left unsaid and Cecilia becoming locker room talk is one of them.

"No shit?" Felix's eyebrows shoot up in surprise.

"Dude, how did you not hear them banging like a pair of rabbits last night?" Atticus adds with a smirk, mischief dancing in his eyes. "Your room is right next to his."

"Bro, I sleep like the dead as soon as my head hits the pillow," Felix tells him with a shrug. "But—"

"Before you ask, I'm not spilling any tea," I cut him off, raising a brow.

Cecilia's rules about discretion are already grating on my nerves, but I'll honor her wishes. I refuse to treat our relationship like some dirty little secret, but I'll respect her boundaries by keeping it low-key around the guys.

"Yeah, man. You are. You were with Cecilia, right?" There's a hint of worry in Felix's voice. "I mean, if you're into someone else that's cool, just—"

"I'm not," I cut him off firmly. "But it's also none of your business. Understand?"

"Fine. Whatever," Felix mutters, clearly disappointed.

Julio's voice breaks through the chatter, his tone serious. "This is going to end badly," he says, his words casting a shadow over the lighthearted atmosphere.

I shoot him a warning look, shaking my head slightly. "Don't," I say firmly, holding up a hand. "Let me enjoy this." I've been waiting for things to fall into place, and now that they finally are, I refuse to let anyone spoil it.

He grunts in response, wisely choosing to drop the subject.

"You guys about wrapped up?" I ask, eager to change the subject and move on from Julio's ominous comment.

On top of a great night with Cecilia, Holt didn't show up to train this morning. Guy must still be pissed about Coach giving me his spot on the field. Sucks to be him.

But as relieved as I am about that, my mind can't help but drift to the photographs we gave Deacon the other day.

"Did Jameia tell you her plan?" I ask him, my voice pitched low with concern as we collectively head for the door.

He shakes his head, his expression troubled. "No. She was taken off guard by the whole thing and wanted a few days to go over it, I think." He shrugs. "She was pretty upset when she saw them, though. I can't see her sitting on the pictures for long."

A knot forms in my stomach at the thought. "Ok. Good," I murmur, trying to push aside my uneasy feeling.

If she doesn't give them to Coach, it's not the end of the world. We made copies.

But the anticipation of not knowing when the other shoe is going to drop is enough to stress all of us out. Or at least it's stressful for me.

Deacon claps me on the shoulder, offering a reassuring smile. "Hey, we did what we had to do," he says. "Whatever happens next, we'll deal with it. And you, my friend, should enjoy your girl before all this shit hits the fan."

He's right—we've done what we can, and now it's time to savor the calm before the storm. "Thanks, man." I can't seem to shake the knot of unease in my stomach. When Coach finally finds out what Holt's been up to with his daughter, things are going to get messy.

So long as Cecilia doesn't come into the line of fire when it all goes down, we'll be good. But there's this nagging feeling I can't seem to shake that has me worried. What happens if Holt comes after her? If he blames her yet again for something I did?

I don't like the possibilities my mind throws at me, and worse, I don't like the fear I feel wondering whether Cecilia will forgive me if she learns I'm fighting her battles again.

It's too late to change my mind now. What's done is done.

Now, we wait.

WALKING UP TO THE DOOR OF MY FIRST CLASS, MY EYES scan the room, zeroing in on the back of Cecilia already in her seat. I take a step toward her when a hushed call of my name breaks through the quiet hum of the hallway.

Turning, I spot Adriana waiting for me, her presence unexpected.

She waves me over, and with a reluctant sigh, I pivot and make my way toward her.

"What's up?" I ask, stealing a glance at the clock on the wall. Time is ticking, and my class is about to start. She's going to have to make this quick.

"Here." Holding her hand out, she offers her phone to me.

I accept it, puzzled. "Why are you giving me this?"

Fidgeting with the straps of her backpack, she shrugs. "Figured you wouldn't believe me unless I offered you proof."

With a furrowed brow, I swipe my thumb over the screen, finding an already open text conversation.

> Adriana: I don't really know how to start. A lot of time has passed but I wanted to apologize for what I did in high school. It was never my intention to hurt you, and I'm sorry that I did. I don't need your forgiveness. I know I don't deserve it. But I thought you should know I truly am sorry for my part in everything. I fucked up, and I hate what I did to you. xx A

My eyes widen at the words, and I glance up at her in disbelief. "You really sent this?"

She purses her lips and nods. "Keep scrolling."

Returning my attention to the screen, I do exactly that.

> Adriana: Also, I heard you were engaged. Congratulations. I'm really happy for you.

Both messages are time-stamped two days ago, with an incoming reply from Allie marked just one day later.

> Allie: Thank you. I appreciate that.

Short. Sweet. Leave it to Allie not to give anything away.

> Adriana: It's the least I could do. Wishing the best for you. xx A

There's another response from Allie, this one from earlier today.

> Allie: Can I ask you something?

> Adriana: Anything.

> Allie: Did you love him? Is that why you went behind my back?

> Allie: Sorry, I shouldn't have asked that. Ignore me. None of it matters now, anyway.

> Adriana: I didn't. And you can ask me anything. You deserve whatever answers you need.

> Adriana: I wanted to feel loved. It's not an excuse. I can't justify what I did and I won't try to. But I guess I thought if I slept with him, he'd love me the way he loved you. I'm sorry. I fucked up and it was wrong.

> Allie: Oh A. I'm so sorry.

> Adriana: You don't have any reason to apologize to me. Don't be sorry. This is all on me.

> Allie: I know what things were like for you ...

My mouth dips into a frown as I read, confusion settling in. Was there something going on with Adriana back then that we didn't know about?

I continue scanning the messages.

> Allie: I wish you told me that before. When it all happened. Why didn't you? I was sorta waiting for you to reach out and when you didn't *shrugging emoji*

> Adriana: Your entire world was on fire. I knew I fucked up. The best thing I could do for you then was leave you alone.

Shit. Adriana's really laying it all out there. I won't lie, I didn't really expect her to follow through. But based on Allie's reaction, I'm glad she did.

> Allie: I'm running late to work. Can we talk later? I'll call you, maybe. If that's okay?

> Adriana: Okay.

I hand Adriana's phone back to her after that, and she hastily shoves it in her back pocket.

"Happy now?" she asks, still biting her lip.

"Are you?" I ask, genuinely curious.

Her eyes look everywhere but at me, and her blinks come fast and hard.

"Yeah," she says, her voice catching slightly.

"I told you she wanted to hear from you," I tease, a small smirk playing at my lips.

"You always have to be right, don't you?"

I shrug. "What can I say? When you know, you know."

Rolling her eyes, she sniffs again before rubbing at her eyes with the backs of her hands. "Whatever. Are we good?"

My smile drops. "Was this just a transaction for you?" I ask, my tone serious. "Are you still going to talk to her after all that?"

Her eyes narrow, and she bristles at my question. "Of course I am. Are you serious right now? Allie is being a freaking saint about this. I'm not going to throw her kindness back in her face by ghosting her like that."

Good. Satisfied with her response, I nod. "Needed to be sure."

Adriana scoffs. "Whatever. You don't trust me. Thanks for the reminder Gabriel, you've made your position loud and clear."

Guilt churns in my stomach, and I rub the back of my neck. "I don't mean it like that," I tell her, my voice softer now.

"Yes, you do," she shoots back. "And it's fine. I've earned that from you. But you promised if I fixed this, you'd clean the slate. This was your proof. I'm fixing it. So the next time we talk, try not to be such a dick."

With that, she storms away, leaving me feeling like a complete ass.

Fuck.

The bell rings, and I realize I'm officially late.

Great. There goes the epic start to my day.

24
CECILIA

I make it four days before I'm no longer able to avoid Wyatt.

I'm honestly surprised I made it that long.

Willow casually asks me about the date at practice, and while the question is innocent enough, it feels like she's phishing. Oh well. At least now I can put a face to her name.

I tell her it went fine but that I'm still dealing with some stuff in my past and am not really ready to see anyone in any sort of ongoing capacity. I gloss over my mini freak out in case her brother didn't give her all the gory details. Fingers crossed there.

But I assure her that Wyatt was really nice and that we had a good time. I'm not harboring any bad feelings toward him, regardless of how the night ended. None of it was really his fault.

Willow seems to accept my response, not digging any further than what I willingly offer. I figure she'll probably pass my responses on to her brother and that will be that.

I was wrong.

Wyatt shows up at our practices just like before, but he's always gone by the time I get out of the locker room. I might linger for an extra couple of minutes while gathering my things, but it's not specifically to avoid him.

Gabriel's practice usually ends around the same time as mine, and lately, we've been indulging in ... extracurricular activities together.

My cheeks heat just thinking about the things we did this morning. It might be getting out of hand. But damn, I can't help it. This friends with benefits thing is almost a week in and I'm not finding any downside. Not yet, at least.

"You ready for our meet this weekend?" Adriana asks as we head out the door.

"Definitely," I tell her. It'll be my first competition, and the anticipation is killing me. We're traveling to Sun Valley to compete against Suncrest U, and I couldn't be more excited. "You?"

The question has barely left my mouth when my feet come to a sudden stop.

"Wyatt?"

Pushing off of his truck, his long strides eat up the space between us until he's standing right in front of me. My eyes flick to the truck again, spotting Willow in the front.

She gives me an apologetic shrug before turning around in her seat.

"Damn," Adriana murmurs, "We took our sweet ass time. He must really want to talk to you." She rocks back on her feet.

"You're not helping," I hiss, feeling my cheeks heat up.

Swallowing hard, I turn back to Wyatt. Pretty sure he caught all of that.

"Um, hi."

"Hey," he says, raising his hand in a small wave.

We stand there in the parking lot, neither one of us saying anything else.

"Well, this isn't awkward," Adriana adds.

I glare at her. "Not helping," I repeat.

Her lips twitch, and her eyes look out toward the field. "Incoming," she offers, and I follow her gaze.

Gabriel spots us and starts cutting across the field. Panic grips me. "Shit," I mutter under my breath. My stomach jumps into my throat.

"So, um, what's up?" I ask, trying to keep my voice steady.

Wyatt offers me a small grin, oblivious to my rising anxiety. "I just thought we should talk. I feel kinda shitty about how things ended on our date."

"It's fine," I tell him, needing him to say his piece and go fast and far away. "I had a good time."

"Yeah?" His expression brightens with hope.

Uh oh. That isn't my intention, but I'm also not trying to be a bitch.

"Yeah," I confirm. "I think it's just too soon for me to do the whole dating thing, obviously." I let out a self-deprecating laugh, my cheeks burning with embarrassment.

His expression softens, and I see a look of pity on his face. "Yeah, I'm sorry. I didn't know about that. If I did, I never—"

"Time's up," Adriana interjects.

"Is there a problem?" The sound of Gabriel's gravelly voice sends shivers racing down my spine.

Wyatt's head snaps toward him, and I don't need to look over my shoulder to know Gabriel is standing right behind me. I can feel the heat radiating from him, seeping into my back.

"Hey man, can we have a minute?" Wyatt asks, unaware of the situation he's stumbled into.

With a grimace, I wait for Gabriel's reaction. He doesn't disappoint.

"No, man. You can't. So why don't you—" He steps forward but I reach out, my fingers latching onto his hand.

"Gabriel," I whisper, shaking my head. "Just a minute?"

His jaw clenches. "No."

So much for that. Pursing my lips, I try not to get angry. Gabriel's just looking out for me. He's being overprotective right now, but I know it comes from a good place.

Unsure of what to do, I look at Adriana, but she shrugs. "Don't look at me. I've never been able to get Gabe to listen."

Wonderful.

I pinch the bridge of my nose, sighing heavily.

"I appreciate you coming to talk to me," I tell Wyatt, giving him my full attention. "But we're good. You don't have anything to worry about."

"Is he—" Wyatt's eyes dart between us.

"A friend," I assure him, answering his unspoken question. "A very protective, sometimes hot-headed *friend*." I emphasize the last word, and Gabriel growls behind me.

Lovely.

"Okay, I guess I'll ..." Wyatt gestures toward his truck.

"Yeah. I'll see you around."

"No, she will not," Gabriel snaps, pulling me away.

"What are you doing?" I hiss.

Looking over my shoulder, I spot Adriana smiling as she goes to her own car.

"You're not going to help a girl out?" I call out to her.

She shakes her head as I stumble forward, Gabriel's hand on my hip steadying me.

"You're in good hands," she chuckles.

"Are you good?" Gabriel gives me all of a second to catch my bearings before tugging me over to the bleachers.

"Fine, thanks for asking," I mutter. "Where are you taking me?"

We don't climb the bleachers like I expect. Instead, Gabriel tugs me behind them, shielding us both from the bright sun.

Dropping my hand, he moves aside, his steps harsh and angry.

"Are you upset with me?" I ask, unsure of where his anger is coming from. I search his face for any hint of what can possibly be bothering him, but I find nothing.

He remains silent, staring ahead.

"Gabriel?"

His jaw ticks.

I approach him cautiously, as if dealing with a wild animal. "What is it?"

He grabs my wrist and spins me around, pressing my front against the cold steel of the bleachers.

"I told you I don't share," he snarls, his lips brushing against my ear.

I twist in his arms, but he refuses to allow me to face him. "You're being ridiculous," I tell him. "Wyatt just wanted to talk. You know, clear the air."

His hands grip my waist, pressing me forward. With my hands braced on the metal frame, I crane my neck to look over my shoulder.

"What are you doing?" My heart races in my chest. Is he—

His eyes don't look at my face, instead they're trained somewhere on the small of my back, his gaze unfocused.

"I'm not sharing you," he repeats.

"I'm not asking you to," I stammer, trying to get through to him. If he would just let me turn around.

Coming to some sort of decision, Gabriel grits his teeth. His index fingers hook onto both sides of my leggings and he starts to pull down.

"Don't you dare," I warn him.

His eyes snap to mine, a challenge burning in their depths.

"Or what?"

Shit. I don't know what to say to that, not that he gives me much time to formulate a response.

He drags my leggings over my hips, his fingers hooking into the material of my panties and tugging them to my knees at the same time.

The cool autumn air kisses my backside, and heat burns through my chest.

"Gabriel Herrera, you are not screwing me outside behind the bleachers of our freaking university!"

His hands squeeze my bare ass, his hooded eyes never leaving mine. "Watch me."

Panic courses through me, and I struggle in his arms. "Absolutely not," I hiss, twisting free, but with my leggings still around my legs, I stumble forward onto my knees.

"This works too," Gabriel chuckles darkly as he follows me to the ground.

"Gabe," I blow my hair out of my face.

I hear the sound of his zipper and look back to see him pulling the hard length of his cock free.

"We are not doing this," I tell him, my thighs clenching at the sight of him.

"Is this a hard line for you?" he asks, pressing the swollen head against my folds.

My brain short circuits, my breaths coming shorter and faster now.

Gabriel pushes an inch inside of me.

My mouth falls open. "Gabe—" My fingers curl into the soft grass, nails digging into the dirt.

"Is this a hard line for you, Cecilia? Tell me now."

"I—" Fuck. I don't know. It's wrong, yet some part of me wants this. "We shouldn't—"

"I don't give a shit about what we should or shouldn't do," he interrupts, his voice laced with anger. "I care about the fact that some asshole you went on a date with is trying to get back into something with you."

"That's not—"

He doesn't let me finish.

"And because you don't seem to understand the seriousness of it, I plan on burying my dick so far up inside of you that the next time some asshole tries hitting on you, you'll remember exactly who this pussy belongs to. Am I making myself clear?"

This is a volatile side of Gabriel that I should be wary of.

A possessive, division-one athlete side of him that refuses to lose no matter the game.

"Yes," I force out, my voice breathless.

"Good. Now answer my fucking question. Is this a hard line for you?"

He's mad. I can see it in his eyes and hear it in his voice. My core clenches, heat pooling between my thighs. And I don't know what to make of it. I'm embarrassed by the desire I feel in this compromising position.

Without any real thought to what I'm doing, I press my hips back into him.

"No," I admit, uncertain if any hard lines exist where Gabriel is concerned.

Anyone could stumble across us. All they'd have to do is walk over to this side of the field and they'd get an eyeful. But despite knowing that, it doesn't stop me from giving in to him.

"Good," he grunts.

A tendril of excitement and fear shoots through me. As much as I crave Gabriel's touch, I don't know what to expect when he's like this. This is an entirely new side of Gabe. One he's never shown me before.

I know I should be wary, but the reckless part of me that's only recently started to emerge is intrigued. Hell, I'm excited.

"Brace yourself," he says right as he thrusts hard and fast, filling every available space inside me.

My mouth falls open on a gasp.

Gabriel grabs my ass cheeks harshly. "I'm going to fuck you until you can barely move," he tells me. "Maybe then you'll remember that this body is mine."

Holy shit.

I stifle a moan. Something tells me if I give in to what Gabriel says, if he knows how badly I want this, he'll take full advantage, consuming me until there's nothing left.

I can't give myself over to him like that. This has to stay casual. Only sex. But the tightness in my chest warns that it's already become more than that.

Gabriel shoves my top up my back, not stopping until the material is pushed over my chest. One of his hands tugs down the lace of my bra, fingers brushing over my hard nipple.

"Were you going to give him a second chance?" he demands. His thumb and forefinger pinch my nipple, twisting and tugging hard until a sharp cry falls free from my lips. "No."

"You don't date other guys," he says, thrusting in and out of me. "You don't talk to them. You don't look at them. You don't give them the time of day. Am I making myself clear?"

I press my lips together, desperate to hold in my response.

"Answer me," he snarls. Jerking my arms out from under me, he slams me up against his chest, his hard length finding a new angle that utterly destroys me.

"Fuck," I moan.

One arm bands my waist, holding me firmly against him while his other hand falls between my thighs. His fingers expertly locate my clit and stroke the sensitive bundle of nerves until I shatter into a puddle beneath him.

"Are we on the same page?" Gabriel's voice breaks through the haze of pleasure.

I manage to choke out a shaky yes, my hands reflexively holding onto him wherever his body touches mine.

It takes me a moment to catch my bearings, but when I do, the soft murmur of approaching voices reaches my ears.

"Gabriel–"

He pauses and silences me by moving the hand between my legs up to my mouth.

He hears them, too.

The smell of my own arousal fills my nose as his fingers dig into my cheeks. He resumes his thrusts, his palm muffling my cries.

"Shhh ..." he whispers low in my ear. "Don't make a sound."

The sound of our skin slapping together echoes in the hidden space, and I strain my ears for any hint of the voices getting closer.

Fear and anticipation trickle through me. What if we get caught? What do we do?

As we listen, I realize the voices are drifting away, not getting closer.

I let out a muffled sigh of relief. Thank god for small favors.

"Looks like the coast is clear," he tells me. His hand falls from my mouth to my throat, his fingers wrapping around my neck. "Hope you're ready for me."

Gabriel quickens his pace, his thrusts becoming punishing. I jerk with each motion, relying on his grip to hold me up.

My lungs are burning but it's not because he cuts off my airway. I belatedly realize I'm holding my breath. I open my mouth, sucking in a lungful of air as anticipation swirls low in my belly.

"Who does this pussy belong to?" he demands.

"You," I tell him breathlessly. "It's yours."

His lips latch onto the sensitive skin between my shoulder and neck, his mouth finding the previous mark he left on my skin. He sucks on the tender flesh, hard, marking me in a visible way once again.

"All of it," he rasps. "Every inch of this body is mine."

Releasing my throat, he presses me forward. My hands meet the cool grass once more, but he doesn't stop when I'm on my hands and knees. Instead, his palm presses between my shoulder blades, pushing me down until my cheek kisses the earth.

He slaps my ass, the sting reverberating through me.

Fuck. That one hurt.

"Stay still," he commands, his hands gripping my ass. His cock continues its relentless assault while his fingers spread me open.

"Gabriel ..." I try to coax him down from whatever ledge he's on. I don't know how much more my body can take. I'm soaking wet, my arousal dripping between my thighs as he pounds into me. He feels so good, but I'm utterly spent.

He wasn't kidding when he said I wouldn't be able to move. At the rate we're going, he'll have to carry me home when he finally finishes.

"Slow down."

His fingers dig into my skin.

"No."

He hits that spot deep inside of me, and I whimper. I can't. I don't have it in me to orgasm again.

I pant and claw at the grass, my body no longer feeling like it's my own.

Gabriel doesn't stop. He doesn't slow down.

His ruthless pace goes on, and on, and on.

"I can't," I plead with him.

Another orgasm tears into me, ripping my sanity into shreds. I'm so fucking sensitive, my nerve endings made hyper-aware.

"Good girl," he praises. "One more."

There's no fucking way. He can't seriously expect a third orgasm out of me. It's not possible.

"C-come inside me," I whimper, hoping the allure of his release is enough to throw him over the edge. "I want you to come inside me, Gabriel."

"Fuck," he curses. "Not yet."

He spreads my ass cheeks apart once more, only this time, he doesn't stop there. One hand dips between us, gathering moisture from between my thighs.

"W-what are you doing?"

"It's okay," he tells me. "Relax."

My breath stutters in my chest as he presses a wet finger to my other hole. Oh my god. What is he — He presses the digit inside of me, his cock relentless as he pounds into my pussy.

The different sensations, the pressure and stretch he elicits inside of me, it's too much yet not enough.

"Have you ever taken a cock here?" he asks as his finger starts a slow and steady thrust in and out of me.

I shake my head, whimpering.

"Don't worry," he chuckles. "I'm not fucking your ass."

Thank fuck.

"Not today, at least."

He's joking, right? He has to be. Would he actually want to do that? To claim me there?

Swallowing hard, I push away my thoughts. His fingers and cock work inside me, driving me wild. He finds a rhythm where at all times, some part of him is in one of my holes.

My vision blurs, and all I can manage are these desire-laden incoherent sounds.

"I think taking your ass is something we should work up to," he says, his voice tightening. "Fuck. You're so tight back here," he groans. "I can picture how good your ass will feel—"

He's close. Wiggling my backside, I urge him on. There's not much more I can take. I'm dripping with sweat, my hair plastered to my face.

He presses a second finger into me.

"Oh. Fuck," I cry out as he releases a guttural groan.

"Yes." His cock jerks and pulses inside me, filling me with his release.

My heart beats fast in my chest, my lungs heaving with the effort to draw in air.

Slowly, Gabriel pulls out of me, drawing his fingers free at the same time. I collapse onto my side, uncaring that my leggings are still wrapped around my ankles or that my shirt is caught on the top of my bra, leaving my stomach bare.

I need a minute to catch my breath.

Tucking himself back into his pants, Gabriel rights his clothing, looking just as good and put together as he did before we ran this marathon of sex.

Meanwhile, I'm lying over here like a puddle of goo in the dirt.

"I hate you," I tell him.

His lips curl into a grin, and he leans forward, pressing a kiss to the tip of my nose. "Hate you too, baby girl."

My brows pull together. "Liar," I tell him.

He chuckles. "Only when you lie too."

25
GABRIEL

"**A**nything?" I ask.

Julio shakes his head. "Not that I'm aware of."

I mutter a curse and scrub my hands over my face. "What's taking so long?"

"Should we deliver them ourselves?" Felix asks.

"No," Julio answers. "Let's give it a few more days."

A couple of days is all he's going to get. Holt has been a complete asshole at practice, not giving a shit about any of our upcoming games. He's turned into a cancer for the team. His piss-poor attitude soaking into the other players in his fraternity like a disease.

"He's ruining morale," I say.

Julio's expression is grim. "I know. Coach does too. But there's not much we can do. He lost his spot, but until Jameia delivers the photos, that's as much as we're going to get. Not gonna lie," he tells me. "I'm surprised you've managed to hold the position."

"What the hell is that supposed to mean?" I ask, irritation lacing my voice. "Do you honestly think that asshole is a better striker than me?"

He shakes his head. "No, you asshole. Calm down."

Mollified, I grind my teeth and let him speak.

"Holt's parents made at least two visits to Coach's office that I know of."

What the hell?

Julio raises a hand, halting all of our comments. "There's always yelling. Threats. Once there was an offer of more money," he shrugs. "But Coach is holding his ground. For now."

It's the, *for now*, that worries me.

Grabbing my phone, I shoot Cecilia a quick text. We saw one another earlier in the day, but that was only during our classes. It's been close to twenty-four hours since I was inside of her, and I think my dick is going through withdrawals.

> Me: My place tonight?

Her response is quick.

> Cecilia: Can't.

I scowl down at her reply.

"Who pissed in your cheerios?" Felix asks, dropping down onto the seat beside me.

"What?" I glare up at him. "Go away."

He spoons some of a Duvalín into his mouth, eyes dancing. "Nah. I think I'm good. What's our girl saying?"

My expression darkens. "She's not our girl," I snap at him. She's mine. What the hell is wrong with people these days? I've made it really fucking clear that when it comes to Cecilia, I'm not fucking sharing.

Felix leans back in his seat, pulling out his own phone. His fingers flutter over the screen. "You sure about that?" he asks.

The phone chimes with an incoming message, and he flashes me a grin before showing me the screen. My eyes scan both his original message and the response.

> Felix: Hola pequeñita. You going to come hang out with us today?

I'm really starting to hate that fucking nickname. She's not his little one. Cecilia isn't his anything.

> Cecilia: Can't. We have a swim meet in Sun Valley and the team is getting a hotel for the weekend. Raincheck?

My eyes narrow, and I reach for the phone, but Felix pulls it back, fingers flying as he types out another response.

"What did you say?"

It chimes again with her response.

"What did she say?" I ask, leaning into his space.

Felix hugs his phone to his chest. "Relax," he says. "I'm just making plans to—"

To hell with that. Grabbing the phone from his hands, I rise to my feet. My eyes scan over the messages before Felix has a chance to steal the device back.

> Felix: Suncrest U! I'm coming. I know how badly you want to see my handsome face cheering for you in the stands. And Deacon is excited to visit his home turf.

My head lifts, eyes seeking Deacon out. "You're in on this?" I ask, waving Felix's phone in the air.

His mouth twists in confusion. "In on what?" he asks.

"Going to Sun Valley for Cecilia's swim meet at Suncrest U? When the hell did you and Felix talk about this?"

Deacon shrugs his shoulders. "Yeah. I'm down. I don't have anything else planned this weekend. You?"

Hold up. "Is this a prearranged thing or are you just agreeing on the fly?" I ask.

Felix snickers, his ass still seated and relaxed as can be on the couch.

"First, I'm hearing of it," Deacon says. "But I'm still down."

I turn to Felix and throw the phone at his chest. "You're an asshole," I tell him.

His phone chimes again, and his smirk spreads into a wide grin. "Take that back or I'll tell Cecilia you don't want to come with us. She's asking about you."

"She is?" I lunge for his phone again, but this time, he holds it out, keeping it away from me.

"Yeah, cabrón, she is. So what's it going to be? You coming or not?"

"Obviously. You're not going to my girl's meet without me."

"Ooooh!" He drags out the sound. "It's like that now, huh? You're calling Cecilia your girl."

"You know what I mean," I snap, punching him in the spot I know will give him a dead arm.

"Sonova—"

"Don't pretend you didn't deserve that."

Felix sputters, eyes flicking around the room in search of allies. "Don't look at me," Julio tells him. "I'm with Gabe. You had that coming."

Felix pushes out his bottom lip, pouting like a freaking toddler.

"You just wait," he grumbles. "When Cecilia's around, she'll make you assholes be nice to me."

Flipping him off, I level Felix with a glare. "Keep pushing," I tell him. "See where it gets you. Cecilia's off limits and I'm only going to warn you once. I don't play around when it comes to her. Got it? No jokes. No funny business. Keep it in check. She's not a game."

Felix must hear in my voice how serious I am because all humor falls from his face and he nods. "Yeah. Alright. I'll back off."

"Good."

"But we're still going to her meet," he tells me. "She deserves our support."

With a nod, I exhale a loud sigh. "Fine." Because he's right. She deserves that and more.

THE ROAR OF MY BIKE SWEEPS THROUGH THE AIR AS WE pull onto Suncrest U's campus. The ride over gave me a lot of time to think. To really mull things over between Cecilia and me.

My plan's always been to get her back. But I'm starting to question if I'm going about things the wrong way.

We've been screwing like rabbits. No complaints about that. But Cecilia and her stupid rules make it harder to go any deeper than that. She's keeping me at arm's length, and no matter how thoroughly I pleasure her body, her heart and mind are still a million miles away.

Pulling into a parking spot, I kill the engine as Julio, in his car, pulls into the spot beside me. He drove the rest of the guys over, aside from Atticus, who needed to stay behind and study for some big test he has on Monday for one of his classes.

Eyeing the large brick building marked Aquatics, we fall into step with one another.

"Are we late?" Felix asks.

I glance at my phone and shake my head. "Shouldn't be," I tell him. "Start time is in ten minutes."

"Sweet," he whistles. "Right on time."

Deacon surveys the scene, his eyes quickly cataloging the surrounding faces. "Looking for someone?" I ask.

He nods, but before he can speak, a tiny blond comes barreling toward him. "You're here!" she screams, throwing herself into his arms. He lifts her up without effort and her legs wrap around his waist before he gently places her back on her feet.

She punches him in the arm, and I wince.

"I missed you, you jerk."

Finally getting a good look at her, my lips split into a wide grin. "Damn, Kasey. No love for me?"

She rolls her baby-blue eyes but offers me a smirk. "You," she says, shaking her finger at me, "Are trouble. No hugs for you."

I chuckle. "I don't know what you're talking about?"

"Mmm Hmm," she mutters, folding her arms over her chest. "You mean you never intentionally antagonized Dominique with me just to get a rise out of him?"

"I don't know what you're talking about."

She quirks one blond brow. "Really? A certain birthday barbeque seems to come to mind."

I raise both hands in mock surrender. "Okay, okay. You got me. But in my defense, that asshole had it coming."

Deacon grumbles beside me. "That asshole is my brother," he says, and all three of our collective gazes snap to him.

"No shit?" Felix asks.

He nods, expression grim. Poor guy. I'd be a little grim if that broody fucker was related to me too.

"Stop it," Kasey admonishes. "Dom's not all bad."

Deacon quirks a brow. "You two better?"

Her face falls and something that looks a lot like pain flickers across her face. "Of course," she shrugs, brushing Deacon's question off. "It's just a rough patch. We're fine."

He scrutinizes her. "If you say so."

The two share a couple of minutes of small talk, Julio and Felix joining in, but my attention keeps wandering. I can't help but look around in the hopes of catching a glimpse of my girl before her competition.

Felix told her we'd be here, but still, I want her to see us. To know we showed up for her big day. Every athlete wants to know they have people behind them, cheering them on. And we—me and the guys—we're her people.

I've never been to a swim meet before, and I'm intrigued by the energy in the air. It's much more charged than I anticipated for this kind of thing. The pool area is bustling with activity, swimmers stretching beside the lanes, coaches giving last-minute pep talks, and spectators slowly filling up the stands.

Cecilia arrived earlier in Sun Valley with her team—catching the team bus—while we left later in the day. I'd have met her sooner, maybe explored the town a bit with her if I'd known about the meet in advance.

An oversight I plan to rectify in the future.

Scanning the crowd, my heart pounds with anticipation. I spot Cecilia near the pool, chatting with her teammates, her eyes focused and determined. I swallow hard, gaze trailing from the top of her swim cap covered head down to the tips of her bare toes.

She looks good. Better than good.

"Come on," Julio says, drawing my attention. "We should grab our seats."

Nodding, I keep an eye on Cecilia as I follow J and the others to the bleachers. We find seats to the left in the fourth row, and I brace my hands on my knees, shoulders forward as I give Cecilia my full attention.

She still hasn't seen us yet, but as the whistle is blown and the swimmers are called to attention, her eyes glance one last time over the crowd.

"Yes!" Felix shouts, "Let's go!"

Cecilia's eyes jump over him, a small smile on her face before her gaze finally settles onto mine.

Her lips part, and I swear I see the tops of her cheeks turn a bright shade of pink. Licking my lips, I lift my hand in a wave.

She grins, her eyes lingering on mine for a second longer before she turns to her lane, her graceful legs stepping up onto the block.

"She looks good," Deacon says.

My eyes narrow. "Don't look at her."

He rolls his eyes, and Kasey snickers beside him. "I didn't mean it like that," he tells me. "I just meant that she looks good, like her head is in the game. She looks ready."

I grunt. That better be all that he meant.

The race begins, and I feel a surge of pride watching Cecilia dive into the water. She swims with confidence, her strokes smooth and powerful as her arms cut through the water.

In the 50-meter race, she takes an early lead and never looks back, finishing first with a time that leaves the competition in her wake.

The crowd erupts into cheers as Cecilia touches the wall, her smile radiant as she climbs out of the pool. I can't help but grin as I watch her, feeling a swell of pride in my chest. She's amazing.

A couple more races follow before Cecilia is up again.

In the 100-meter, she once again dominates, her determination shining through as she powers through the water. The crowd cheers her on, their voices blending into a chorus of support. And when she touches the wall, I know she's done it again, taking first place with ease.

"Holy shit," Felix mutters. "She smoked them."

"I know." I can't help but grin. "Cecilia's a beast."

"Damn right, she is. Remind me never to challenge her to a race."

"Noted."

As Cecilia emerges from the water, I make my way down to the edge of the pool where other friends and family wait for their girls. My heart pounds with excitement, and when Cecilia sees me, her face splits into a shit-eating grin.

"Did you see that?"

I reach out to her, pulling her into a tight embrace, not caring that she's soaking the entire front of my shirt.

"You were incredible," I murmur, pressing a kiss to her forehead. "I'm so fucking proud of you."

"Hey," she admonishes but without any real heat. "No PDA."

I ignore the reminder, taking in her smile. The way she looks up at me, her eyes shining with a mixture of happiness and relief.

"Relax. I was being friendly."

She rolls her eyes.

"But really," I tell her. "You killed it."

"Thank you," she whispers, her voice thick with emotion. "I'm glad you were here."

"Always," I tell her. "No matter what. I'll always be right here, cheering you on."

She wraps her arms around me, squeezing tight.

"Any more races for the day?" I ask, and she pulls back to peer up at me.

"Nope, all done."

"Go grab your things. I'm taking you out."

"I—" Her brows furrow like she plans to argue, but before she can say anything, another small body comes barreling into her from behind.

"Holy shit, you were amazing!" Adriana hugs Cecilia from behind, lifting her off her feet and twirling her around.

Cecilia laughs, the sound rich and carefree.

Adriana puts her down and Cecilia turns to face her.

"Me? What about you? You destroyed that four hundred meter."

She rolls her eyes. "I won by less than a second, but you," she raises a brow. "You took not one but two wins and both by a landslide. We need to celebrate! Come on, the girls are all trying to decide where to go."

Cecilia's eyes meet mine, and I can feel my smile as it falls from my face.

"Uh—"

"Go," I tell her. "You should celebrate."

She hesitates, and I swallow hard, bracing myself for disappointment. But it's fine. She just accomplished something big, and she deserves to go out and celebrate that, even if it isn't with me. I want this for her. Truly.

"I just ..." I notice the tops of her ears turn pink when she tucks a wet tendril of hair behind her ear. "I was looking forward to seeing you," she confesses.

My chest swells. "Yeah?"

Bobbing her head, she nods. "Yeah."

Schooling my features, I tamp down on the sheer excitement thrumming through me right now. Hell fucking yes. My girl wants to spend time with me.

"You wanna go out with your team and meet up with us later?" I ask. "We grabbed a few rooms at the same hotel," I tell her. "Or ..."

Her eyes brighten. "Or?"

My lips curl into a grin. "Or you can get changed and come with us now."

Her eyes flick to Adriana, and I already know where her mind is heading. "Adriana, too," I suggest, and I can see that I've taken Adriana by surprise.

"What do you say?" Cecilia asks her, her expression earnest.

"Uh, sure. We can do that."

"Yay!" Cecilia jumps and wraps Adriana in a fierce hug. "Thank you." Pulling back, she looks at me and says, "We'll be right back." Then she drags Adriana to the locker rooms, presumably to get dressed.

Julio steps up beside me, his mood like a dark cloud hanging over him. "Did you just invite Adriana Aguirre to hang out with us?"

"I did."

He curses under his breath. "Care to explain why?"

I shrug my shoulders, "Nope."

26
CECILIA

As we step into the Sun Valley's neon signs and lights museum, a wave of color and light washes over me, enveloping me in a mesmerizing kaleidoscope of vibrant hues against the backdrop of the darkened night sky.

The neon signs shimmer and dance, casting their iridescent glow onto our faces, igniting a sense of wonder and awe within me.

"Holy shit," Felix murmurs, taking in the illuminated space.

"I know, right?" Kasey says, bouncing on the balls of her feet. "This place is pretty great."

The atmosphere crackles with anticipation, each neon light pulsating with energy and life, creating an electric symphony that resonates through the air. The hum of the electric lights is a soothing melody, blending seamlessly with the buzz of conversation and laughter as we step deeper into our neon-lit adventure.

"This place is amazing," I exclaim, my eyes darting from one sign to the next, taking in the intricate designs and vibrant colors. The glowing bulbs and attention to detail in each one of the works.

Gabriel nods in agreement, a playful smile tugging at his lips. "I've never seen anything like it. How did you find this place?"

Kasey leads us past the gates. "Dominique brought me here once," she shrugs. "Since then, it's kind of become one of my favorite places."

"I can see why," I tell her as we wander through the maze of neon signs, the rest of our group trailing behind us.

There's excitement dancing in everyone's gazes as one by one, we take in the displays.

Gabriel adjusts his pace to match mine, ensuring I don't have to struggle to keep up with his longer strides. "Look at that one." His voice cuts through the vibrant chaos, drawing my attention to a particular sign hanging high on the wall overhead.

It's a large heart, glowing with a fiery red hue, surrounded by intricate neon filigree. The heart pulsates with an otherworldly glow, casting a warm, comforting light that seems to beckon to us from across the room.

"That's a Milagro," Gabriel says, his voice tinged with reverence as he gestures toward the sign.

"A what?" I ask, curiosity piqued by the unfamiliar term.

"A Mexican heart," he says. His smile is warm when he looks down at me and adds, "Milagros are little miracles. They're symbols of hope and promises of things to come in my culture. Seeing one is a good omen."

I can't help but be captivated by the sign's beauty and the meaning behind it. The intricate details of the neon heart seem to shimmer and dance in the soft glow of the surrounding lights, casting whimsical patterns on the surrounding walls.

"You should make a wish," he tells me. "Seeing a Milagro is a lot like seeing a shooting star. Don't waste the opportunity."

As he gazes at the sign, I can't help but stare at him, my heart fluttering with emotions I struggle to put into words. Swallowing hard, I try to conjure up a wish, but the longer I look at him, the more I realize that what—no, who—I truly want is standing right in front of me.

As I stand here, mesmerized by the Milagro, a sense of reverence washes over me. I have a newfound appreciation for the beauty and significance of all the blessings in my life. All of my tiny miracles.

I can't help but feel grateful to be where I am right now, sharing this experience with Gabriel. With our friends.

I glance over my shoulder to see Julio and Adriana wandering off, their heads tilted toward one another in hushed conversation.

Meanwhile, Felix, Kasey, and Deacon head in another direction, leaving Gabriel and me to explore on our own.

Gabriel shifts his weight, the back of his hand brushing against mine.

I hold my breath.

His skin grazes mine again, the barest of touches before he turns. "Come on," he says. "Let's look over here."

My fingers curl into a fist, and I ignore the disappointment sweeping through me. We have rules, I remind myself. No PDA, which means we definitely cannot hold hands.

So why do I want him to reach for mine so badly?

As we weave through the neon lights, I can't help but feel a twinge in my chest, the feeling unsettling. This, spending time together even if it's with a group of friends, there's something intimate about it. It feels deeper than just casual fun.

Shaking myself, I push the thought aside, focusing on the bright colors and playful atmosphere.

"Hey, look at this one," Gabriel says, pointing to a particularly obnoxious sign. "Now that is a work of art."

I cover my mouth to stifle my laugh. "The oversized goose wearing hot pink cowboy boots and a cowboy hat is a work of art?"

He grins, his eyes dancing with mirth. "I never said it was good art."

I nod in agreement, but my smile slips. I can't shake the feeling that maybe, just maybe, my feelings for Gabriel are growing beyond what we agreed upon. And that worries me because when it comes to Gabriel, I always seem to be in way over my head.

"Hey," he says, his voice pulling me out of my thoughts. "Are you okay?"

I force a smile, trying to push away my concerns. "Yeah, I'm fine. Just taking in all the lights."

Gabriel's gaze is searching, his eyes not fully convinced. "You sure?"

I nod, but the words catch in my throat. I want to tell him how I'm feeling, but we made a deal. And despite what Gabriel said before, feelings change. Just because I'm feeling this way doesn't mean he is. Gabriel seems content with our arrangement. No sense in disrupting that.

I plaster on a smile and grab his arm, pulling him toward another neon sign. "Come on, let's check out this one."

Gabriel follows, his hand brushing against my thigh.

I really wish he could touch me.

27

GABRIEL

Irritation coils in my gut like a restless serpent as I glance at my buzzing phone, silencing yet another call from my father. It's the fifth time this week, and not once does the man leave a message

Yet he keeps calling.

What the hell does he want?

I push aside thoughts of him, focusing instead on Cecilia. Tonight is supposed to be about her. About her big win. Seeing the lights illuminate her face as she smiles wide, her gaze filled with wonder as she takes it all in, leaves me breathless.

She's so fucking beautiful.

We spend a little over an hour at the museum before hunger gnaws at all of us and we decide to grab a bite at the Sun Valley Station—a local twenty-four-hour diner.

Despite the lively atmosphere, a heavy tension lingers, suffocating the air around me after seeing my father's call. But it's just me. Everyone else seems to be having a good time.

Conversation flows freely between friends. Everyone's smiles are genuine, their laughter infectious.

But I can't shake this feeling that another shoe is going to drop.

Why does he keep calling?

I manage to make it through the meal, keeping mostly to myself when our waitress drops off the bill. Everyone reaches into their wallets to grab some cash, enough to cover their portion. But when Julio retrieves his wallet from his back pocket, a small envelope lands beside it.

He mutters a curse under his breath as he tosses a twenty onto the table, sliding the envelope over to me. "Sorry, meant to give this to you earlier," he says, his expression troubled. "It slipped my mind."

I reach for it, my fingers tracing over the thick paper to read the calligraphy style gold lettering. There's no return address, but the envelope is heavy. The paper is a thicker quality than your run-of-the-mill mail.

I rip the top and tug the card free from inside.

A whoosh of air slips past my lips followed quickly by a curse.

Fuck this.

I barely get a glimpse of the first line before the words make my blood run cold and I throw it back to the table as if the fucking thing bites.

"What is it?" Cecilia asks, her hand reaching for the card.

You are cordially invited to the wedding of ...

"It's nothing," I snap, my frustration bubbling over as I rise from the table.

I toss a few bills onto the table, enough to cover the tab, and head for the door. Cecilia calls after me, but I don't bother to respond.

Stepping outside into the chilly night air, I close my eyes and try to steady my racing thoughts.

The others follow suit, their expressions grim as they join me outside. Kasey asks about our plans for the night, but my mind is elsewhere. Driving back to Richland now would be reckless—it's late and I'm not in a good headspace. But the thought of spending another moment in this heavy silence is unbearable.

I see the way Julio and Felix are looking at me.

As everyone says their goodbyes, I linger beside my bike, feeling the weight of the evening pressing down on me. Cecilia's gentle touch breaks through my reverie, her concern evident in her voice.

I try to brush off her questions, but her persistence softens my resolve.

"Are you okay?" she asks, her eyes searching mine.

"Fine," I manage, my tone softer now. Taking a deep breath, I try to push aside the turmoil churning inside me. "I'm fine," I repeat, more to convince myself than her.

She sinks her teeth into her bottom lip.

"So, uh ..." She swallows hard. "Your mom is getting remarried?"

"Looks like it."

She nods. "It's none of my business—"

"Then leave it alone," I cut her off. "My mother isn't something I want to talk about right now."

Her brows pull together, and I know she wants to argue, but with a sigh, she folds her arms over her chest and lets it go.

"Here." I hold out my extra helmet for her and help her secure it. "Let's get you back."

After we arrive back at the hotel, we all take the elevator and head to our respective rooms. We got two, each with two queen beds, but the thought of going back to mine sends a spear of dread into my stomach. I hesitate beside the door for Cecilia's. She and Adriana are sharing one, and I've never been more envious of the girl in my life.

"I'll see you in the morning," I tell them both, dropping a quick kiss to Cecilia's forehead.

Adriana huffs out a breath, her tone irritated when she holds out her hand. "Give me your room key," she demands.

I scowl at her. "Why would I do that?"

Her eyes flick from me to Cecilia. "Because weird shit is going on with you two. You're getting stuck in your head and she—" she points a thumb in Cecilia's direction, "is going to stay up all night worrying about you. I, for one, would like to get some sleep. Give me your key, and I'll take your bed. You can have mine," she snorts. "Though I doubt you'll use it."

Rolling my eyes, I pull out the thin electric card and hand it to her. "You sure that's the only reason you want to swap?" I ask her. "You know I'm rooming with J, right?"

She shrugs. "He'll get over it. Let me just grab a few things."

We all three step inside Cecilia's room while Adriana grabs some pajamas and heads into the attached bathroom, presumably to change.

She comes back out in a pair of sleep shorts and an oversized shirt with a small toiletry bag in her hands.

"See you two in the morning," she says, heading for the door without so much as a backward glance.

Cecilia is the first to break the silence now that it's just the two of us in her room.

Her voice is hesitant as she speaks. "Gabriel, about the invitation ..."

I tense, the mention of the wedding an unwelcome intrusion into my thoughts. "I don't want to talk about it. There are far more interesting things we could be doing in this room than discussing my mother's wedding." My gaze drifts to the bed, a silent invitation lingering in the air.

Cecilia's breath hitches at my insinuation, her eyes flickering with a mixture of uncertainty and desire. She takes a small step closer, and I meet her halfway, closing the distance between us. "Gabriel, I—"

"No more talking." I silence her words with my lips and walk her closer to the bed.

"Wait," she gasps, tearing her lips free.

I ignore her, trailing kisses down her neck as my fingers work to unbutton her jeans.

"Gabriel, stop." I freeze, my hand halfway into her pants, fingertips grazing the lace of her panties.

"Why?" Drawing back, I stare down at her.

Her chest is heaving. Her pupils are already dilated. She wants this. So what gives?

"I'm not sleeping with you," she says.

My frown deepens. "Why not?"

She laughs, smacking my chest lightly before she pulls my hand free and re-buttons her pants.

"It's my time of the month." A pink blush stains her cheeks. "I just started this morning."

I'm not seeing the problem here.

"Are you in pain?" I ask.

Her face twists in confusion? "What? Oh, no. Not really. I'm uh ..." Her blush deepens. "My cycle isn't usually that bad. The cramps, I mean."

Alright. "Then what's the problem?"

"I'm bleeding." She waves a hand down toward her crotch. Has no one ever fucked this girl on her period? I thought chicks were hornier around this time. What gives?

"As you've already said," I tell her. "But if you're not in any pain, why does a little blood need to ruin our night?"

Her mouth drops open. "You're kidding, right?"

Nope. And if a little blood is her only objection, I'm not about to let that slow me down. Crowding her space, I grip the backs of her thighs and hoist her into my arms. She braces her hands on my shoulders to steady herself, and instead of the bed, I make a beeline for the attached bathroom.

"What are you doing?" she hisses.

I nip at her full bottom lip. "I'm going to fuck you."

"Absolutely not." She wiggles in my hold, and I have to tighten my grip so I don't drop her.

"What is the problem?" I ask again. "Do you dislike sex during your period? Does it hurt?"

"No, it's just ..." She trails off. "Messy."

I grin, using my foot to kick the bathroom door open. "Problem solved," I tell her as we step inside the brightly lit tiled room. "Shower sex, it is."

28

CECILIA

Setting me on the bathroom counter, Gabriel releases me to tug my shirt over my head.

"Wait—"

"No," he says again, his hands moving to my jeans. He unbuttons them quickly, tugs the zipper down, and shimmies them down my hips and past my legs with little help from me.

Unclasping my bra, he tosses it aside before dipping low to kiss my collarbone. "So fucking beautiful," he murmurs.

I shiver when his hand comes up, thumb stroking over my sensitive nipple.

"I—" I should say something. An objection or—I don't know.

"Stop thinking," he tells me.

Stepping away, he turns on the shower, taking a few extra seconds to adjust the water temperature until he gets it just right.

Turning back to me, he strips out of his own clothes until his body is gloriously bare, his cock already hard and jutting out from his body. My eyes greedily drink him in, and he smirks, mouth curled into an arrogant grin.

When he reaches for me again, he pulls me to my feet and hooks his fingers into the lace of my panties. There's no hesitation as he pushes them down to pool at my feet.

"A string?" he asks, and instinctively, I clench my legs.

"Umm ..."

He kisses me, his tongue and lips serving as a distraction as his free hand trails down past my tummy. He presses between my legs, and I'm about to object when he tugs on the string between my thighs, effectively pulling my tampon free.

I gasp, and he swallows the sound, discarding the tampon in the waste bin without ever pulling away.

"There," he murmurs against my lips. "Problem solved."

He nudges me toward the shower enclosure, his lips and hands never leaving my body as we step in. Swallowing hard, I step under the warm cascade of water.

Gabriel steps into the shower right behind me, his presence immediately overwhelming me in the small and enclosed space. A jolt of anticipation spears through me, and a twinge of self-consciousness gnaws at my gut.

Gabriel's arms wrap around me, pulling me flush against his chest. I can't help but tense slightly, worry lingering in the back of my mind. But his touch is gentle, his lips finding the curve of my neck with a tender hunger that melts away some of the insecurities I have.

"You're perfect," he murmurs against my skin, his words a balm to my doubts.

His hands roam over my body, igniting a fire inside me that eclipses any concerns I may have. With each caress, each kiss, he shows me just how much he craves me, period or not.

I arch into him, and he reaches down, drawing one of my legs up and over his hip.

Water cascades over our heads, and Gabriel's dark strands stick to his forehead as he says, "You ready for me, baby?"

I nod, and he slowly guides himself into my core.

My mouth drops open as slips inside, his length stretching me more than what I'm used to.

Fuck," he mutters, his head falling to my shoulder. "So good," he says. "So fucking tight."

I hiss at the intrusion, my body more sensitive than usual.

When he's fully seated inside me, he flexes his hips, going impossibly deeper.

"Gabriel."His name falls from my lips. A plea for him to move.

"I've got you," he says.

Drawing his hips back, we both stare down at where our bodies connect. My blood stains his cock, and my eyes flick up to his face, but I don't find disgust there like I expect. All I see is adoration in his eyes before he slides back inside me, his thrust achingly slow and gaze now locked on mine.

"Oh—" My body trembles and he does it again, drawing out each one of his thrusts.

I've never felt so desperate before. So needy. The way he takes me, his eyes boring into mine, his hands reverently holding my body, leaves me breathless and filled with wonder.

"That's it, baby. Fuck," he curses. "You take me so good."

He kisses my lips, and I moan into his mouth. One calloused hand keeps hold of my thigh, the other grasps the side of my neck.

"More," I plead. "Faster."

He chuckles and shakes his head. "Nah. Tonight, I'm going to take you nice and slow," he tells me, thrusting back inside. "Just like this."

I don't know how much more of this I can take.

My chest rises and falls, breasts heaving with each of my breaths. A sly grin slips past Gabriel's lips as he pulls back, far enough to stare into my eyes. The connection is intimate, his hold unwavering as he continues to thrust in and out of me.

His cock hits that secret spot deep inside of me, and my leg shakes. I avert my gaze. It's too much. He's too much.

"There it is," he says, amusement lighting up his eyes. "Look at me," he demands. "I want to watch you come on my cock." Gabriel grunts. "I want to see the moment fireworks go off in your eyes."

His fingers dig into my thigh as I squeeze his biceps, desperate to stay standing, but I'm not sure how much longer I'll make it.

"Come on, Cecilia," he encourages.

My hips jerk forward to meet his, the friction sending waves of pleasure coursing through me. I slide my hands to Gabriel's shoulders, my nails digging into his skin as I teeter on the edge of ecstasy.

"Come on my cock, baby." His words, his touch, his relentless rhythm all push me closer to the brink. With each thrust, the tension builds, my body coiling tighter and tighter until I'm on the precipice of release.

And then it hits me.

A surge of pleasure crashes over me. My back arches, and my mouth falls open in a silent scream as waves of pleasure consume me from head to toe.

Gabriel's eyes never leave mine, capturing the raw intensity of the moment as my body trembles with my release.

His own breaths come ragged and heavy, matching the erratic pace of my heartbeat.

"Oh, fuck."

As the fireworks explode behind my closed eyelids, Gabriel's arms wrap around me, holding me close as I ride out the storm.

When I come down, he quickens his pace. His movements become more urgent as he chases his own release, and I watch him intently through hooded eyes.

My breath catches in my throat, and I get lost in the raw intensity in his gaze. The sheer possessiveness he doesn't bother to mask.

Gabriel's brows furrow in concentration, his lips parting slightly.

I lean forward and kiss him. My teeth tugging at his full bottom lip.

He groans into my mouth.

I can feel the tension building in his muscles. His body coils like a tightly wound spring on the verge of snapping.

His rhythm becomes more erratic as he inches closer to the edge. I wrap my arms around him, pulling him closer, urging him on as I revel in the feeling of his slick body against mine.

"Fuck." With a guttural groan, Gabriel finds his release, his body shuddering against mine as he empties himself inside me.

I hold him close, feeling the warmth of his breath against my skin.

The water continues to fall around us, the enclosure thick with steam. After several long seconds, Gabriel releases my thigh, lowering my leg until it touches the warm tile and I'm able to stand on my own two feet.

In this moment, it's as if time stands still. All that exists is the two of us, lost in our own blissful oblivion.

But there's a warning in the back of my mind reminding me that like all good things, this too will eventually come to an end.

Only, I realize, I don't want it to.

29
GABRIEL

Cecilia puts on a clean pair of panties and reaches in her bag for a sleep shirt, but before she has the chance to pull it on, I pluck the offending fabric from her fingertips and replace it with my own.

"Here," I tell her.

Smirking while cocking her head to the side, she doesn't comment as she tugs my shirt over her head. The hem falls to the tops of her thighs, and I can't help but feel a surge of possessiveness seeing her wear my shirt.

Almost like she isn't aware she's doing it, I catch Cecilia tugging up on the collar, scenting my shirt. Her breath is deep, her sigh content.

A smile tugs at the corners of my lips. "Do you like how I smell?" I tease, catching her off guard.

Her cheeks flush a delicate pink, and she quickly drops her hand, attempting to play it off. "I was just—"

But before she can finish her sentence, I pull her close, pressing my lips to hers in a heated kiss, effectively distracting her from any further explanation.

"I like you in my clothes," I tell her. "And I like my scent on your skin."

It's yet another way of marking her as mine. Maybe I can convince her to take one of my sweatshirts when we get back to Richland.

Pulling away, I note the exhaustion evident in her expression and lead her over to the bed. She needs rest. It's been a long day for her, and while I'd love nothing more than to strip her bare all over again, I know Cecilia needs a good night's sleep.

After pulling on my discarded boxer briefs, I drop onto the bed and tug her down beside me. Pulling her body flush against mine, her back to my front, I breathe in the coconut scent of her shampoo. A wave of contentment sweeps through me.

This is how we're supposed to be.

The warmth of her body against mine is exactly what I need, and I squeeze her small frame tighter to my chest.

"You're breaking the rules," she whispers, her voice soft but playful. An admonishment without any real heat.

I chuckle, nuzzling into the crook of her neck. "Rules were made to be broken, weren't they?" I whisper, trailing kisses along her neck.

"Mmm," she murmurs and settles into me.

"Relax," I tell her. "It's only one night. Or would you rather I go to my room and send Adriana back here instead?"

"No. You can't do that." She huffs out a breath. "They're probably both asleep already, anyway."

"Then it's settled."

She sighs. "One night."

"One night." I let the lie fall from my lips.

"Then we follow the rules again," she says.

Unlikely. After having her in my arms and holding her through the night, I know there won't be any going back for me. But she needs the lie in order to relax, so I give it to her.

As exhaustion begins to claim me, I feel myself drifting off. The steady rhythm of Cecilia's breathing lulls me into a state of relaxation until her near-silent words have me opening my eyes again.

"I think you should go to the wedding," she says quietly, rolling over in my arms to face me. Her gaze searches mine. "I know it hurts you not having a relationship with your family." I stiffen at her words, and she places her hand on my bare chest. "This can be your chance to fix things with your mom." I open my mouth to argue, but she brushes her fingertips along my lips. "Treat it as an olive branch, Gabriel. Because I think that's what that invitation is. Don't miss out on that opportunity because you're scared of being hurt again."

Her words hang in the air, heavy with some other unspoken meaning. Is she also talking about us? Is she afraid of missing out on this, on what we have, because she's worried about getting hurt?

I try, and fail, not to read into it. I'm hearing what I want to hear instead of listening to what she actually says. There's genuine concern in her eyes, and a part of me knows she's right.

But the idea of facing my family, of confronting the painful memories that come with that, fills me with apprehension. It might be an olive branch, but if it isn't ... if it was a mistake ...

"I don't think—" I begin.

"Please," she murmurs, leaning forward to kiss the corner of my mouth. "I really think it can be good for you."

How the hell am I supposed to deny this woman?

Reluctantly, I nod, knowing deep down that this might be a mistake. "Okay," I concede. "I'll go."

But I have a condition, one that breaks yet another of our rules. "But only if you come with me," I add, my voice barely above a whisper. "You have to be my date."

Her eyes widen in surprise, and hesitation flickers across her features. It would be a public outing, a breach of our carefully constructed boundaries. But as she meets my gaze, I see the resolve in her eyes.

After a moment of contemplation, she nods, her lips forming a small smile. "Okay," she agrees softly. "I'll go as your date."

CECILIA LEAVES BRIGHT AND EARLY ON THE BUS WITH the rest of her team. I try to convince her to ride back with me on my bike, but she declines.

I know what she's doing. I'm not blind.

She's trying to put space between us after we spent the night with one another, and I don't like it. But I decide not to push her. Not today.

I'll let her have her space. For now. But she's delusional if she thinks she'll be spending the night tonight anywhere but in my bed.

Since practice isn't until later in the day, the rest of us decide to burn some time and visit an old friend.

We meet up with Allie and her fiancé, Roman, for breakfast.

As I walk into the Sun Valley Station, the nostalgic vibes of the place hit me like a wave, transporting me back to a time of poodle skirts and slicked-back hair. I'd been too distracted the night before to really take it in, but today I'm seeing it with new, much less exhausted, eyes.

Sun Valley station is a vintage-styled diner straight out of Grease, complete with neon signs and checkerboard floors.

Allie is the first to spot us, her face lighting up with a smile as she rushes over to greet our crew. "Gabriel!" she exclaims, enveloping me in a warm hug. "It's been too long."

"Yeah, it has," I reply, returning the hug before she moves on to Julio, Felix, and Deacon, hugging each of them in turn. I can't help but notice the protective aura that surrounds her fiancé, Roman, as he watches her interact with us. He grumbles when she hugs us, but he's decent enough to shake each of our hands, even if he tugs Allie back to his side at the first opportunity.

There was a time when an innocent hug would have sent Allie over the edge. She's come a long way and worked through a lot of her past trauma. We all have this broody fucker to thank for that. Not that I'll ever admit it out loud. Pretty sure J won't either. But regardless, we're grateful.

Roman keeps Allie close, a possessive hand resting on her thigh as we join them at their table.

It's a subtle gesture, but it speaks volumes about their relationship.

I can't help but feel a twinge of jealousy as I watch them together, knowing I'd be the same way with Cecilia if she'd let me.

We settle into the booth, the atmosphere buzzing with conversation as we catch up on each other's lives. Allie fills us in on her latest welding adventures and talks about watching Roman play football while he sits beside her, his arm now wrapped around her waist in a protective embrace.

He's a junior at Suncrest U. Their star receiver. If he wasn't such a dick sometimes to anyone who isn't Allie, I might actually be impressed. But Roman's never been one for making new friends. He's only here for her. And that's just fine. The way he looks at her, his eyes filled with adoration and love, it's clear she's his entire world.

The two of them, they're exactly as they should be. Content in their relationship.

It's a stark contrast to the tumultuous emotions swirling inside me, but I push them aside, focusing on enjoying the morning with friends.

30

GABRIEL

I cut a path across the parking lot toward the locker room with Julio at my side, our steps hurried, knowing we're fucking late.

Coach is going to have our asses.

Deacon and Felix left our place ten minutes before we did in Deacon's car. Julio and I decided to ride our bikes over but it looks like that ten minutes is going to make a difference.

"Shit," I mutter, glancing at Julio. "We're screwed."

He grimaces. "Maybe not."

With any luck, we can slip in unnoticed, but I won't hold my breath.

Shoving the door open, I step inside, bracing myself for Coach's reprimand, except he's nowhere to be found. Tension hangs thick in the air, and the team is scattered about, everyone trying to get ready while the muffled shouts from Coach's office penetrate through the closed door.

I exchange a glance with Julio, both of us silently acknowledging the storm brewing there.

"Damn, what's going on?" Julio mutters under his breath, his eyes darting towards the closed office door.

Deacon walks toward us. "It's done," he mutters.

My gaze jerks toward him. "It's Holt in there?"

He nods, and a surge of satisfaction washes over me.

"Finally."

With a smile curling my lips, we grab our gear. It's obvious the team is trying to block out the escalating confrontation behind the door.

But the yelling grows louder, more volatile, making it impossible to ignore.

All eyes are on the door now.

My grip tightens on my duffel bag, muscles tense as I exchange uneasy glances with the guys around me. This is what I wanted, but why is Coach dragging the conversation out? Kick Holt off the team and be done with it. What the hell is there to still talk about?

With a suddenness that startles us all, the door bursts open, slamming against the wall with a reverberating crack.

Austin storms out, fury etched into every line of his face.

Before I can react, he shoves me hard, the impact sending me careening into the unforgiving metal of the lockers.

"What the hell, man?" I push myself up, muscles coiling with adrenaline and ready to retaliate, but Parker Benson is already between us, holding Austin back.

"Chill, man! It's not worth it!" Benson's voice is firm, but there's an underlying tremor.

Chambers comes up beside them and asks, "What happened?"

"This isn't over," Holt seethes, shaking off his friend's hold. "You're going to regret fucking with my life."

"I didn't do anything, asshole." I glare at him. "So you can take your temper tantrum to someone else."

"You got me kicked off the fucking team!" he shouts.

"What the fuck?" Parker and Chambers say in unison.

"No fucking way," Parker says, shaking his head. "That's bullshit. They can't—"

The unease in my gut twists into something darker. There's no way for him to know the photos came from us. Coach doesn't even know that. But it's obvious Holt suspects me, and he's not wrong.

"Come on, man. Let's go cool off," Gregory says, pulling Austin away. "This isn't over. You can fight this."

Holt's nostrils flare, and with one last glare in my direction, Austin relents, allowing his friends to lead him out of the locker room. The tension eases slightly, but the unease remains, a nagging feeling at the back of my mind.

Before I can dwell on it further, Coach emerges from his office, his face flushed with anger. "Alright, everyone! Get your asses on the field, now!"

We scramble to comply, the chaos of the locker room fading into the background as we focus on the task at hand. But the unease lingers, a shadow over what should have been just another practice.

As I jog onto the field, I can't shake the feeling that something is going to happen. Another shoe is going to drop. I grab my phone and type out a quick text.

"Herrera, put that away or you'll be running laps the rest of practice," Coach warns.

> Me: Are you on campus?

I STARE AT THE SCREEN, EARNING MORE OF COACH'S IRE, but I waste precious seconds waiting on a response that doesn't come.

"Herrera!"

"On it, Coach." I hastily comply—putting my phone away—but Cecilia's silence weighs heavily on my mind. I'm probably overreacting, but the way Austin looked when he left, I don't like it. And I don't trust the fucker.

The last time he was pissed with me, he took it out on Cecilia.

What if he tries shit like that again?

Fuck.

I should have thought this through. Had a plan in place for watching over her, at least until the dust settled. She's been back for a few hours now, so with any luck, she's already tucked away safely at home for the day.

She doesn't have practice today. It's supposed to be a recovery day for her and the rest of the team after the meet, so she shouldn't even be on campus right now.

I exhale a breath. I'm letting Holt get in my head, and I need to shake it off. That asshole doesn't get to mess with me anymore.

"Come on," Julio says, sensing my unease. "Let's just get through today."

Nodding, I concede, telling myself I'll go to Cecilia's place and check on her as soon as practice is over.

Coach puts us through a series of drills for the next thirty minutes that leave me dripping in sweat, but despite the physical exertion, I can't shake the feeling that something is wrong.

Cecilia still hasn't responded to my message despite the two additional texts I sent, and worry is gnawing at my gut.

I don't like this.

"Something's wrong," I tell Julio, wiping the sweat from my forehead with the hem of my shirt.

"Obviously. Coach is pissed and taking his anger out on us."

"Not that," I tell him. "Cecilia isn't responding to my messages."

Felix jogs up beside us. "Bro, if you don't get back on—"

"I need to go." There's no reason for me to think something has happened to Cecilia, but I know it in my gut. Something is wrong. I got what I wanted. Holt's off the team. But my girl still isn't safe. I know how he operates. Holt always retaliates.

Fuck. This was a mistake.

"You can't just walk out in the middle of practice," Julio says.

"Watch me."

"Gabe—" I wave him off, but he falls into step, jogging beside me.

"What are you doing?" I ask.

"You're not going alone," Julio says, his voice resigned. "We're coming with you."

Felix nods in agreement, his expression determined. "Yeah, man, we got your back. We'll deal with the fallout with Coach after we find your girl."

Relief sweeps through me right as Deacon joins us, his usually calm demeanor replaced by a steely resolve. "I'm coming, too," he says.

I open my mouth to argue. Coach is going to lose his shit if we all walk out right now, especially with a game coming up.

"We're a team, remember?" Deacon says, cutting off my argument. "We stick together."

I hesitate, torn between my urgency to find Cecilia and the risk of involving my teammates in what might turn out to be nothing. But their unwavering support bolsters my resolve, and I nod, gratitude swelling in my chest.

"Alright," I tell them. "Let's go."

31
CECILIA

I slice through the water, arms pumping as I near the wall. Flipping underwater, I kick hard, hurtling myself forward. I slap the tile, pausing to see my time on the overhead clock. A smile stretches my lips. A personal best, even exhausted.

Adriana would be proud. She was right to convince me to join the team. I love this. I love the competitive nature of the sport, even when I'm only competing with myself, and today more so than most, I need the distraction.

My head's been a mess since we got back from Sun Valley this morning. I thought the bus ride home would give me time to think, but all it's really done is give me more time to drum up questions I don't have the answers to.

Things are changing with Gabriel and I. After last night, I don't know, it's like something has shifted, and I can't figure out whether or not that's a good thing. Hence, being here at the pool despite not having practice today.

I hoped the extra time to myself would help me sort through some things, but aside from pushing myself to the point of physical exhaustion, I haven't accomplished much else.

Reaching for the edge, I push myself half out of the pool when a blur of motion catches my eye.

Cruel fingers twist into my hair, dragging me back, and I cry out only for my shriek to die as my cheek slams into the concrete.

Pain explodes across my face.

Someone wrenches my head back, and I thrash in their grip. My eyes water, making it hard to see, but I blink through the pain, and little by little, Austin's twisted face comes into view.

I open my mouth to scream, but right as I do, he forces me under water, choking off my cry for help.

Bubbles race past my face while I scream before clamping my mouth shut.

I writhe, panic and the need for air battling within me. Darkness swarms my vision.

How long can I hold my breath? Two minutes. Maybe three if I'm lucky. I haven't really tested it in a while.

Austin releases me, and I explode upwards, gulping air in ragged gasps.

Relief washes over me, but it's short-lived when my eyes rise and lock with Austin's. "Miss me?"

His fingers twist in my hair and he shoves me back under.

My struggles are weak, terror and adrenaline filling my veins. I kick with everything I have, but it's the end of the day. I've been here for over an hour, and my body is tired. I have little fuel left in my tank.

Panic grips my chest, making my movements erratic and with no real direction.

I can't breathe.

My lungs burn as I struggle to fight the overwhelming urge to take a breath. I'll drown if I do. I know I will.

But as each second passes, the urge to breathe hammers into me.

The back of my throat burns. I claw at Austin's hand on my head, my short nails digging into his skin. Despite my efforts, all it seems to do is piss him off more, enough to shove me down harder.

He's going to kill me. He's really going to kill me.

Changing up my tactic, I stop trying to reach the surface and instead, dive downward, aiming for the darkened bottom of the pool. But Austin knows what I'm trying to do because his fingers tighten their grip on my hair, keeping me from moving out of reach.

He has complete control over me, and again, I am powerless to stop him. Powerless to keep him from hurting me.

Angry tears sting the backs of my eyes to mix with the chlorinated water.

It's not fucking fair. Why is this happening to me? What did I ever do in my life to deserve this?

Austin drags me closer to the edge, making sure to keep my head firmly beneath the water. His entire forearm is in the water now. The rolled sleeves of his shirt soaking wet.

My side scrapes the pool's wall, and I twist in his hold, reaching for the ledge. My fingers scrape along the concrete lip, but I can't get enough leverage to drag myself up.

He's too strong.

My fingers slip down the smooth tiled surface, and I hear the muffled sound of Austin's laugh.

He's enjoying this. This asshole is going to kill me, and he's going to do it with a freaking smile on his face.

Anger begins to override my logic. My lungs burn. Ache. They demand I take my next breath. But as soon as I do, it's game over. I won't let him win. He's taken enough from me. He can't have this. He can't have my life.

I slam my fist into his forearm. I rake my nails down his skin.

Fuck!

My vision darkens at the edges. I swipe at the hair tangled around my face before reaching up and feeling my way across my head to Austin's hand again. Digging my fingers beneath his, I try in vain to pry his hand open. When that doesn't work, I sink my short nails into his skin again, giving the task everything I've got until his laugh cuts off and he curses above me.

Fuck you, Austin Holt. Fuck. You.

The weight above me vanishes, and I swim for the surface. As soon as I break it, I gulp down a lungful of air. Coughing and gasping through each breath. My hair sticks to my face, making it impossible to see, but all I can think about is getting as much air into my lungs as possible.

"Bro, we need to leave," someone says.

"Relax and go watch the door," Austin responds.

Less than a handful of seconds pass before fingers tangle into the dark strands of my hair again.

"No!" My eyes latch onto Parker's—who's standing across the room, watching the door like Austin ordered—for less than a second when a hard strike slams into my already injured cheek. If it wasn't for Austin's grip in my hair, I know I'd go crashing back beneath the surface.

I cry out, the sharp stab of pain making my head spin.

Don't pass out. Do not pass out.

"You think you can hurt me?" he screams, jerking me close. Half my body hovers out of the water as I kick furiously to get away. "You think your pointless struggles can help you get away?" Austin shakes me like a rag doll, and my heart leaps into my throat.

Come on Cecilia. Think.

"Don't do this." He likes it when I beg. When I break. I just have to give him what he wants and maybe he'll let go. Or at least give me the opportunity to get away. "Please. Austin. I didn't mean—"

He stops shaking me and pulls me closer, my upper half now out of the water and over the pool's concrete edge. I try to get my leg over the lip, but his hold won't let me.

With an almost gentle touch, he pushes my hair out of my face with his free hand, and I blink back my tears.

Cruel blue eyes meet mine.

"Are you sorry?" he asks.

"Yes." I swallow hard and choke out my words. "I'm sorry," I tell him. "I'm really really sorry." I'll say whatever he wants to hear if it means getting out of here alive. "To both of you." I direct my words toward Parker, too. If I can't get through to Austin, maybe I can get through to him.

The door opening reaches my ears, and I crane my head, hoping the sound means someone will help me, but instead of help arriving, it's Gregory Chambers who steps into the room.

No. Dread fills my gut, but I refuse to give up.

My eyes flick toward the clock. Pool hours are almost over. The janitor should be by within the next half hour to lock up. Only, I don't have half an hour. I have minutes at best. I need to buy myself enough time for help to show up.

With shaking fingers, I bring my hand toward his face. Austin latches on to my wrist before I'm able to make contact. I wince when he squeezes, my bones grinding into one another, but I school my expression. "I wasn't going to hit you," I tell him. His eyes are guarded. "I'm done fighting you. I don't ..." I hiccup on a sob. "I don't want to fight with you anymore. I don't want to fight with any of you."

He watches me carefully through narrowed eyes but releases my wrist.

Parker shifts on his feet. "Holt, we need to—"

362

"Shut up," Austin snaps, his eyes never leaving mine.

Stealing my breath, I press my hand against Austin's smooth cheek, keeping my expression blank of the emotions I'm feeling as I say, "I'm truly sorry. I didn't mean to ..." What? Shit. Think of something.

I wet my lips and try a different tactic. "I don't like that you're mad at me."

It sounds weak, but my words seem to do the trick. Some of the anger leaves Austin's gaze, and the corners of his mouth quirk into an arrogant smirk.

He eyes me curiously but doesn't shove my hand away when I stroke his jaw. Swallowing hard, I decide to push my luck a little bit more. I need him to let me out of the pool. If I can just get on my own two feet, I can make a run for it. I'll have to get past Parker and Gregory, but I'll figure out how to do that after I'm out of the water.

"We don't need to be at war with one another," I tell him. My voice is soft. Whispered, "Nobody needs to know about this. You can let me go and we'll just pretend it never happened. I promise. I won't say anything to anyone. You have my word."

"She's lying," Gregory says.

"I'm not. I swear," I tell them, my voice pleading.

Austin considers me for a moment. His expression is amused, but I don't know if it's in a good or a bad way. Then he chuckles to himself, and for a moment, I think he's going to release me.

He extends his arm away from his body, pushing me further over the edge of the pool.

No. *No!* "Austin, please!"

"It's too late for apologies, Cece. You should have kept your mouth shut before. I lost my spot on the team because of you. I won't make the mistake of believing that lying mouth of yours and let you take anything else from me."

"Please. Austin, I don't know what happened with the team," I tell him. "But I can help you fix it. Let me help. I won't tell anyone!" Tears fall down my face. He's going to kill me. This isn't just some sick game to mess with me. He's actually going to go through with it, and for the first time in months, I realize I don't want to die.

With almost measured slowness, Austin lowers me back to the surface of the pool, his cruel eyes never leaving mine. "Austin. Please." I beg, kicking with everything I have. I'm desperate to stay afloat.

"Goodbye, Cecilia."

"No!"

I take one last breath before my head is pressed beneath the surface, and like before, I kick and twist, desperate to get free. But unlike before, only a handful of seconds pass before the hand holding me down is gone.

My heart clenches, knowing this is probably my last chance. Without missing a beat, I dive deeper and swim for the other end of the pool. I have to get there before Austin does. I have to reach the other side first.

My chest squeezes, lungs burning, but I'm almost there.

A body crashes into the water above me and strong arms wrap around my waist, pulling me tight against a hard chest.

"No!" I scream, the word muffled underwater.

I was so close.

I flail in his hold, tugging at the material of his shirt to get him to release me, but his grip on me tightens. I let loose another scream of frustration and air bubbles fan out in front of me.

Keeping me in his arms, he kicks his powerful legs and pushes us toward the surface. It only takes a moment for me to realize Austin isn't dragging me deeper. That we're getting closer and closer to the light up above. I still in his arms, letting myself be dragged to the surface as I try to slow my racing mind and think. Austin isn't wearing a short-sleeved shirt like whoever is holding me. He's wearing a long-sleeved polo with the sleeves shoved up to his elbows.

I twist to look behind me, but my hair floating around me obscures my vision. Whoever has me now isn't Austin. Heart soaring, I begin to kick alongside him, propelling my body forward. Our heads break the surface, and he lifts me up, shoving me into the arms of another guy who waits by the edge of the pool.

I'm dragged over the ledge, my thighs scraping across the concrete floor, but I hardly notice. I choke and sputter, coughing out the water in my lungs. "Are you alright?" Despite the familiar voice, I shy away from his touch when he reaches for my shoulder and turn to look back at the water.

Felix lifts himself from the pool before tearing his waterlogged shirt off and tossing it to the side.

"I've got her," Julio says beside me. "Go help them."

I follow their line of sight to see Gabriel straddling Austin's chest as he delivers punch after punch to Austin's face. I

365

flinch with each hit Gabriel lands, a part of me wishing he'd stop. Deacon is only a few steps away, squaring off with Parker and Gregory and blocking their path to the exit.

"On it," Felix says, sprinting into the fray.

"You okay?" Julio asks, concern coloring his voice. He pulls out his phone and dials a number.

"There's been an attack," he says into the receiver. "PacNorth University. Campus pool. A girl was almost drowned."

He pauses to listen.

"Yes— His name is Austin Holt."

Another pause.

"Six three, white male. Blond. Blue eyes. Two accomplices. Yes."

He grimaces. "Parker Benson and Gregory Chambers."

A bang sounds behind us and my stomach drops when I see Gabriel lift Austin from the ground only to slam him back into the concrete.

"Fuck," Julio curses. "Just get someone down here." He hangs up and drops his phone beside me. "Are you good?" he asks me again. "Cecilia, I need an answer. Do you need me to rush you to the hospital? Are you okay?" He curses again. "He's going to kill him."

Wide-eyed, I nod my head, chest still heaving. "I'm good," I tell him. "Go. Don't let him kill him. He can't—" As much as I'd like to see Austin dead for all the things he's done to me, I don't want Gabriel going to prison because of it.

Julio doesn't hesitate, rushing for his friend. I look away and take the opportunity to catch my breath, taking stock of myself. My head is dizzy, heart still racing, but I don't feel like I'm going to pass out anymore.

Julio rips Gabriel away from Austin and shoves him back, keeping him away from Austin's unmoving body.

Shit. Is he too late?

"Enough!" Julio roars, shoving Gabriel again. "He's down. You have to stop."

Gabriel doesn't look like he wants to listen.

I contemplate getting up but decide against it. I don't think my shaking legs can hold me right now. There's more shouting and commotion as campus security comes in, followed quickly by two officers.

They assess the scene and decide Austin is the first person to approach. One of the officers checks for a pulse while the other talks to Deacon, and then everything happens so fast.

Parker and Gregory are arrested.

Paramedics arrive a few minutes later, and Austin is carted out on a stretcher. He groans as they move him, so he's still alive.

Part of me is relieved, but another part of me is wholly disappointed.

Felix and Julio manage to keep Gabriel in place while the officers and paramedics move around to work.

Seeing Gabriel like this, all riled up and angry on my behalf, it twists something inside of me. Makes emotions bubble up inside my chest that I don't want to examine too closely.

My fingers gently probe at my cheek, and I wince. The skin is split and blood stains my fingertips.

A paramedic crouches down in front of me, and I stumble back on my hands and knees.

"Whoa. It's okay. I just want to check you out," he says.

Shaking my head, I flinch when he reaches toward me again, and the next thing I know, Gabriel is beside me.

"Give her some space," he snaps.

"Hey man, I'm just doing my job."

Gabriel ignores him, his honey-brown eyes finding mine.

"She'll get checked out later," he says, his eyes never leaving mine.

"Sir, that's not—"

Gabriel turns to face him. "You're not touching her. Not right now. Back off, and when she's ready, she'll get checked out."

The paramedic raises both hands. "Fine. But make sure—"

"I got it," Gabriel snarls and turns his back to him again.

Moving forward, Gabriel sits on the wet concrete beside me, and with bloodied hands, he pulls my wet and shaking body into his arms.

"I almost lost you," he murmurs against my hair, and I cling to him, clutching the fabric of his shirt and curling into his chest. His arms encircle me, and the next thing I know, he's lifting me from the ground and heading for the doors.

"The police are going to want a statement," Julio reminds him as soon as he's within earshot.

Gabriel stops but doesn't turn around. His eyes remain on mine as he says, "They can have one in the morning. I've got more important shit to worry about right now than giving the 5-0 a statement. The center has cameras. Tell them to look at them."

My eyes widen at the reminder, and a small smirk curls the corners of Gabriel's mouth. "Let's see Holt worm his way out of this." To Julio he adds, "I need keys." Julio nods, rushes over to say something to Deacon, and then returns with a pair of keys in hand. He and Gabriel swap sets before Gabriel starts walking again. As soon as the cold air outside hits my damp skin, I shiver.

"Where are we going?" I ask, curling my face into his shoulder.

"I'm taking you home," he tells me.

I don't want to go home. I'm not ready to face my parents. They'll want to know what happened. And they'll ask questions. Questions I'm not ready to give them the answers to. But before I can open my mouth to object, he adds, "My home. I want to take care of you. If you'll let me."

With a sigh, I nod against his chest, wrapping my arms tighter around his neck. "Okay."

Some of the tension drains from his shoulders, and when we reach what I assume is Deacon's car, Gabe carefully opens the door and helps me into the front seat. Taking a blanket from the back, he wraps it around my body before helping me to secure my seatbelt.

"I should probably take you to the hospital," he says, but I shake my head in a definitive no.

"I'm fine," I assure him. "I don't want to go to the hospital. I just ..." I swallow past the lump in my throat. "I just want to go home with you."

32
CECILIA

As we drive, Gabriel's hand rests gently on my thigh, a silent reassurance amidst the chaos swirling in my mind. I watch the passing scenery through the car window, my tender cheek pressed against the cool glass.

I lost my spot on the team because of you. I won't make the mistake of believing that lying mouth of yours and let you take anything else from me.

What did he mean by that?

"Did something happen today?" I ask as we pull into Gabriel's driveway. "When you got back from Sun Valley?"

He doesn't answer.

Coming around the car, Gabriel opens the passenger door and scoops me into his arms, carrying me inside.

"I can walk," I tell him, but my argument is weak as I wrap my arms tighter around his neck.

"You're not wearing any shoes," he reminds me.

Right.

Gabriel carries me up the stairs and into his room before depositing me on the bed. He disappears for a few seconds into the bathroom, and I hear the shower turn on before he returns with a large fluffy towel and an extra pair of clothes.

"Come on," he says. "I'll help you—"

"I got it," I tell him, accepting the clothes and towel. "I need a couple of minutes."

Jaw tight, he nods. "I'll be right here if you need anything."

Turning away from Gabriel, I close the door behind me, needing a moment to collect myself. The harsh fluorescent light of the bathroom casts stark shadows across my bruised and battered body as I strip out of my swimsuit and stand before the mirror.

With trembling hands, I reach up to touch my cheek, wincing at the tenderness beneath my fingertips. The split in my skin is angry and red, a stark reminder of what I endured. My left eye is close to being swollen shut, the bruise already beginning to darken, painting my face in shades of purple and blue.

Turning slightly, I take in the raw scrapes on the side of my thigh and shoulder. The skin is tender to the touch, my body aching with every movement now that the adrenaline has worn off.

But it's not just the physical wounds that haunt me. It's that feeling of helplessness. Of being overpowered all over again.

Tears blur my vision as I struggle to make sense of it all, to reconcile the image in the mirror with the person I am. The one who was healing. Recovering. Dammit. I was finally starting to put my life back together and then this happens—

Taking a deep breath, I force myself to focus, to push aside the tide of emotions threatening to consume me. I turn away from the mirror and step into the warm shower Gabriel started for me.

The water cascades over me, washing away some of the pain and blood, but it does little to ease the ache in my heart. I close my eyes, desperate for the warmth of the shower's spray to seep into my bones, but the next thing I know, I'm crying and I can't seem to stop.

These loud shaky sounds explode from my chest, and I press the back of my hand to my mouth to smother my sobs.

I can't do this. Not again. There will be questions. The police were there. There's no way to keep this quiet, and I just know it's going to blow up in my face.

I'm sure Austin will come up with some sort of story or excuse again, and then what?

Gabriel said there were cameras, but will that be enough? What am I going to do if he gets away with hurting me all over again?

I can't ... I suck in a labored breath.

Defeat wraps around my shoulders. I can't handle another altercation with Austin or his family again. Every time I go up against him, I lose.

I brace myself against the tile wall, wishing I could make sense of today.

Something had to set Austin off, but what was it?

Closing my eyes, I replay what happened and try to recall Austin's words.

He blamed me for losing his spot on the team, but why? I didn't even know he'd been kicked off the soccer team until he screamed it at me.

I'm not trying to ruin Austin's life here.

All I've ever wanted is to stay out of his way. Out of sight so he leaves me alone.

This doesn't make any sense.

When I emerge from the shower, Gabriel is leaning against the bathroom counter waiting with the towel, his expression tight and etched with concern. He takes one look at me and holds the towel out in his arms. "Come here, baby," he says, and I step into his arms, too tired to care about the ugly marks and bruises on my naked body.

Gabriel wraps me in the towel, his touch gentle yet possessive, as if he's afraid I might slip away if he lets go.

His hands are clean of blood. He must have washed up while I was in the shower. He changed his clothes too, exchanging his torn and blood-stained practice shirt for a clean black T. Breathing him in, I sink into his embrace, the weight of the day finally catching up to me.

Gabriel holds me close, his heartbeat a steady rhythm against my ear. For a moment, I allow myself to believe that everything will be okay, but reality comes crashing back as Gabriel pulls away, his eyes filled with regret.

"I'm sorry," he whispers, his voice heavy with guilt. "I never should have put you in danger. This is all my fault."

His words cut through me like a knife, reopening wounds I thought had healed. "What happened?" I ask, my voice trembling. "Why did Austin attack me?" *How was this your fault?*

Gabriel's gaze flickers away, a haunted look in his eyes. "I ... I found out about his relationship with my Coach's daughter," he confesses, his voice barely above a whisper. "I thought if I exposed him, he'd get kicked off the team and he was." He hangs his head. "I thought I was doing the right thing. After what he did to you, I wanted him to—" He shakes his head. "I fucked up. I wanted Austin to get what he deserved, but I didn't think that he'd go after you for it."

The pieces fall into place, the truth hitting me like a sucker punch to the gut.

Gabriel's betrayal cuts deeper than any physical wound. "You had no right," I choke out. "I told you not to fight my battles, and you went behind my back, anyway. Even after I asked you to let it go?"

I push away from him, anger and betrayal coursing through me like a raging inferno.

This is why we don't work. This is why I had to push him away to begin with. Why can Gabriel never leave well enough alone?

"I trusted you," I whisper, my voice raw. "You promised you'd back off. But you lied to me."

Gabriel reaches for me, his eyes pleading. "Baby, I know. I fucked up and I'm sorry," he says, his voice cracking with desperation. "I thought I was doing what was best for you. I never meant for shit to blow up like this. For you to get hurt."

Shaking my head, I back further away from him, clutching the towel tighter against my chest.

His words ring hollow. The damage is already done.

"You don't get to decide what's best for me," I say, my voice trembling with anger. "You don't get to play the hero and expect me to be grateful when you're the reason I was in harm's way in the first place."

I push past him, my heart suddenly heavy. "I can't be here right now," I tell him. I'm so pissed. This— I shake my head. I didn't deserve this.

"Cecilia, baby. Wait."

I grab the clothes he set out for me and hastily throw them on, shoving my legs into the sweatpants and pulling on one of Gabriel's oversized shirts.

Voices can be heard downstairs, the guys just now making it home.

I step into the hallway and jog down the stairs.

"Cecilia—"

I don't slow my steps. My head is a mess. My heart is even more twisted and confused. After last night and then this morning, I thought things were different. In a good way, I think. We were moving in a different direction. Toward something more. But how do we move forward from this?

I can't even look at him right now.

I told Gabriel not to fight my battles. He wasn't helping. And every time he pissed off Austin, he made things worse.

I could have died today. Austin very well may have killed me. And for what? Because Gabriel needed to deliver some twisted brand of justice on my behalf? A justice I never even asked for?

"Can you drive me home?" I ask Julio as soon as I step into the living room. He looks past me to Gabriel, who's made up ground and stands close behind me.

"You sure you don't want to stay?" he asks. "Just for tonight?" The question is directed toward me, but his eyes stay locked on Gabriel's, almost like he's asking permission.

Folding my arms over my chest, I keep my voice firm. "I want to go home," I tell him. "You can take me or I'll find another way."

Gabriel clears his throat behind me. "Cecilia, just let me explain. Please."

I ignore him and walk toward the door.

"Are you coming?" I ask Julio.

His eyes flick between us before he curses. "I'm sorry," he says, and for a second, I think he's talking to Gabriel, but then he levels apologetic eyes on me. "You're upset and that's understandable but I don't think you should be alone after what just happened. Whatever is going on with you two, talk it out. Let Gabriel be there for you."

He swipes his keys from the entryway table and dips his head toward Deacon and Felix who cautiously loiter near the living room, looking everywhere but at us. "We'll go grab some food and give you two some privacy to work things out."

With that, all three of them leave, filing out one after the other. I'm tempted to follow them and force my way into Julio's car, but I don't have it in me. I can't keep fighting like this. I'm tired. So fucking tired. I just need all of this to end.

33
GABRIEL

"**F**uck this," Cecilia mutters, tugging at her wet hair. She lets out this angry sound as she whirls around to face me where I still stand frozen at the bottom of the stairs. "I just want to go home!" she screams, her eyes red-rimmed and brimming with tears. "I—URGH!" Her voice cracks and she swipes angrily at the tears now slipping down her face.

The ache in my chest intensifies, a heavy weight pressing down on me as I watch her unravel before me. I want to go to her, to pull her into my arms and make everything okay. But I know it's never that simple.

Not after what's happened today.

Hearing her breakdown in the shower, it fucking gutted me. I've never heard her cry like that before. Cecilia's always been so strong. But she's breaking apart right in front of me, and the thought that I played a part in her pain .... It's unbearable.

How do I fix this?

My mind races, desperately grasping for the right words to say, but I keep coming up fucking empty.

"Why don't we—"

"No!" she snaps, holding a hand out defensively when I step closer. "We aren't doing anything. I want to go home. If you won't take me, then ..." She trails off, her voice breaking as she fights back tears. "Then something. I don't know. I don't have my phone. But dammit, I've been through enough today. Please. Just take me home."

Screw this.

Drawing closer, I gently pull Cecilia into my arms. She resists at first, pushing against my chest, but I refuse to let her push me away. Not this time.

My girl is hurting, and I'll be damned if she won't allow me to alleviate at least some of her pain. She can demand to go home all she likes, but deep down, I know that's not what she really wants. And it sure as hell isn't what she needs.

Wrapping both arms around her small frame, I press her tight to my chest. "I'm sorry," I mutter against her hair. Tucking her head beneath my chin, I hug her with every ounce of my being, praying for some of my strength to seep into her fragile bones.

Cecilia doesn't need to be home or alone right now. She needs to know she has people. That I'm here for her, no matter what. That she's safe now. Holt can't get to her. I beat that pinche cabrón—*fucking bastard*—to within an inch of his life.

I should have killed him. I wish I had. Maybe then Cecilia would finally feel some peace.

But with any luck, Holt won't be leaving the hospital anytime soon, and when he does, it'll be straight to a concrete prison cell.

"You're sorry?" she mutters, her voice dripping with bitterness. "Sorry doesn't cut it, Gabriel. You knew what Austin was capable of, and you still went behind my back. You promised you'd let me fight my own battles." She pounds her fist against my chest, her frustration palpable. "You lied to me. You said we don't lie to each other, and then ..." She hiccups, her voice breaking. "You lied."

"I thought I was doing what was best for you," I argue, desperation creeping into my tone. I get that she's scared and angry. She has every right to be. But can't she see what this means? Holt was arrested. What he did to Cecilia, it's all on video. PacNorth has security cameras everywhere. He can't lie his way out of trouble this time.

"I never imagined he'd go after you like this," I tell her. "If I did ..." I shake my head, unable to finish the thought. Would I have walked away? *No.* I might have tried something different. Made sure to have a contingency plan in place and ensured Cecilia was safe at my side when it all went down, but no, I still would have gone through with it. That bastard deserves to lose everything—fucking everything—that he cares about. "I would have made sure you were safe," I tell her.

"But look at the bright side." I know it's hard for her right now, but in a messed up sort of way, what Holt did, it was a good thing. "Holt can't get to you anymore. He's going to go down for this. There will be jail time. Gregory and Parker were arrested, too. You're safe now." None of those bastards will ever be able to get to her again. Not after this.

"Well, congratulations," she mutters, her sullen tone laced with sarcasm. "Looks like your plan worked out perfectly."

"I didn't plan for any of this," I insist, my frustration evident.

I'm not dismissing what happened. What she went through. Today was a complete fucking mess, but it wasn't all for nothing.

"I just wanted him to face the consequences of his actions," I admit. "And now, he will." It's hard to see it now, but something good did come out of this.

"And what about the consequences for me?" Cecilia counters, her voice trembling. "Have I not been through enough?" She hastily swipes at her cheeks with the back of her hands. "*Urgh!*"

I open my mouth to respond, but she cuts me off before I can utter a word.

"You have no idea what it feels like to be attacked like that. To be helpless and afraid. And not for the first time." She tries to push me away again, but I hang on. "All because you couldn't leave well enough alone. You couldn't trust me to know what *I* needed. But let me tell you, it wasn't this."

"I'm sorry," I say for the hundredth time. "I never wanted you to get hurt."

"Well, I did," she says, her voice raw. "And I don't know if I can forgive you for that."

My stomach jumps into my throat. She doesn't mean it. She can't. Cecilia is running on fumes. Her emotions are high, and she's crashing from the adrenaline in her system. She doesn't mean what she's saying. She's tired, and she needs rest. She's just lashing out in her pain.

Tomorrow, once she's had time to rest and recover, she'll understand.

She'll forgive me. She has to.

"I'll make it right," I tell her. "I'll fix this."

She shakes her head against my chest. "You can't, Gabriel." Her voice is soft. Defeated. "You can't."

I refuse to believe that, but I don't argue. Instead, I hold her close, feeling her tremble against me as silent sobs wrack her body. Her tears soak through the material of my shirt, but I don't care. All that matters is that she knows she's not alone.

The fight drains out of her after that, and despite her earlier anger, she allows me to hold her close, her hands now clinging to me as she continues to shake.

Fuck.

This girl is killing me.

"Don't cry," I tell her, holding her impossibly tighter. "I've got you. We're going to get through this." I walk her back toward the couch and pull her into my lap. Thankfully, she doesn't fight me this time. Her soft weight settles against me, and Cecilia curls into me like a cat, tucking her legs close to her chest.

"I've got you," I murmur, pressing a gentle kiss to her forehead. "No matter what, I've always got you."

Rubbing her back, I do the only thing I can, and wait for Cecilia to tire herself out.

It doesn't take long. Ten, maybe fifteen minutes tops.

Her cries cease, and her tears dry on her cheeks. Looking down at her, I can see the exhaustion in her eyes as her lashes slowly begin to flutter closed.

As she drifts off to sleep, her breathing slow and steady, I hold her close, vowing to do whatever it takes to fix this. To make things right.

34
CECILIA

My mouth is dry and my head aches when I wake up the next morning. Sun filters in through the windows and I squeeze my eyes shut against the bright rays.

Where—? Realization dawns on me. Everything that happened. Austin trying to drown me. Parker and Gregory standing guard close by and ... letting him.

Bile rises in the back of my throat.

Not a dream.

Fuck.

Shifting, the body beneath me lets out a soft groan.

What?

Oh.

I'm still in Gabriel's lap. His arms cage me in, his head thrown back against the sofa and lips slightly parted. I can't believe he fell asleep sitting up like this. That can't be comfortable.

Carefully, so as not to disturb him, I climb out of his lap, stifling a groan of my own as my body screams at me in protest. Fuck, just moving hurts. My entire body feels like one giant bruise.

A floorboard creaks, and my head jerks up to find Julio beside the stairs.

"Morning," he says, his voice soft as he brings a mug of coffee to his lips.

"Hi. Umm ... Morning."

He tilts his head, a silent suggestion to follow him, so I do. Julio leads me into the kitchen where he pours a second cup of coffee before handing it to me. "Milk and sugar are on the counter," he says.

"Thanks." I curl my fingers around the cup, the warmth seeping into my skin. "What time is it?" I ask.

"Just after seven. Everyone else is still asleep."

I nod.

Adding milk to my coffee, I slip onto one of the bar stools and try not to think about what Gabriel and I did on this counter. God, I hope he disinfected it.

A blush steals over my cheeks, and I duck my head. Now isn't the time for those kinds of thoughts.

I wonder what's going to happen now.

"Do you know—" I cut myself off, too afraid of the answer to voice the question. But Julio must know what I was about to say because he answers me anyway.

"Holt's at PacNorth medical," he says, and I stiffen. "Under guard, so not as a free citizen." That's a relief. "He's been arrested, and from the sounds of it, he's being charged with attempted murder, assault, attempted manslaughter, and reckless endangerment. When the hospital discharges him, he'll be transferred into police custody. After he's booked, the judge will schedule an arraignment and we'll go from there."

Swallowing hard, I nod. "How long do you think until ..."

"I don't know," he says, rubbing the back of his tattooed neck. "The hospital isn't going to disclose his injuries to just anyone, and I doubt his parents feel like sharing." He shrugs. "Could be a few days. Could be longer. Gabe did a number on him, but for all we know, his injuries could all be superficial. Bruises and swelling. Or it could be more serious. Broken ribs. Some internal bleeding." Another shrug. "There's no real way for us to know."

Taking it all in, I try to tell myself this is a good thing. As long as Austin is recovering, he won't have time to worry about me.

Only I don't believe that. Austin tried drowning me all because he lost his position on the soccer team. What will he do to me now that I'm the reason he's been arrested?

Fear sinks its claws into my skin, its icy tendrils creeping up my spine and constricting around my heart.

If he gets away with this ... I swallow hard. No. I can't think about that.

But fuck. It's all my mind wants to think about.

"I have a friend who works at the hospital. He can't give me details, HIPPA and all that, but he'll give us a heads up when they get ready to discharge him."

"Okay. That's ... that's good."

"Yeah." Julio rubs the back of his neck again, a nervous gesture. "So, uh, your parents have been calling. A lot."

I freeze with my coffee cup halfway to my mouth. "What?"

His smile is apologetic. "Your dad's the mayor," he says. "Someone down at the precinct let him know his daughter was assaulted yesterday. When he couldn't get a hold of you, he started blowing up Gabriel's phone."

The mention of my parents' attempts to reach me sends a pang of guilt coursing through me.

"Shit." I groan. "I left my phone on campus." They must be so worried. I didn't even think about letting them know about what happened. Hell, I didn't even bother to text Mom that I wouldn't be home last night.

Stupid. That was so freaking stupid.

Julio pulls a slim black phone out of his back pocket. "Adriana helped me out by grabbing your things from your locker when I went back last night. I turned it off," he apologizes. "You were asleep and you needed the rest. But I spoke to your pops. He knows you're here with Gabe and that you're okay."

With a mix of gratitude and trepidation, I accept my phone from Julio, its screen dark and silent, a stark contrast to the cacophony of missed calls and messages that are undoubtedly waiting for me.

"And my dad was okay with that?"

He sighs. "He wasn't happy about it. I had to talk him out of coming here to get you, but ..." he hesitates. "Your parents love you. They know you've been through a lot and this, it's scary for them. But I promised them you were okay, and when I told them you were sleeping, your father agreed it was best to let you rest and recover. Though I'm sure he's expecting a call this morning now that you're up."

"Thank you," I tell him. "You didn't have to do that."

"It was no problem."

A comfortable silence stretches between us and we each drink our coffee. I contemplate powering on my phone, but something tells me it'll only push me into motion, and I'm not ready for my day to start just yet.

Mom and Dad can wait. As can the rest of the world. I still need time to wrap my head around all of this.

Finishing my cup, I rinse it in the sink before loading it into the dishwasher. I'm about to return to the living room and see if Gabriel is awake, but Julio's soft voice stops me.

"He really cares about you," he says, voice pitched low.

"I know," I tell him, not sure of what else to say.

The scrape of his chair on the floor has me turning back around to face him. Julio rises to his feet, dark eyes troubled as he refills his mug. "I don't want to see him hurt. After the first time—" He shakes his head and, without looking at me, takes a drink of his coffee. "If you're leading him on—"

"I'm not," I assure him.

"Then what is it?" he asks. "You two aren't back together, are you?"

I shake my head.

"Then what are you doing? Because you're acting like you are, and Gabriel isn't capable of casual. Not when it comes to you."

Ducking my head, I avert my gaze. I know that. At least, I do now. But—

"I don't know," I tell him, my voice little more than a whisper. "I thought we ..." I shake my head. "I don't know what I thought."

"And now?" he asks.

I tuck my hair behind my ear, hating the direction of this conversation. "What do you mean?"

"Has anything changed?" he asks. "Do you want to be with him now?"

Swallowing hard, I shake my head. "I'm not ready for that." And after what happened yesterday, I don't know if I'll ever be. I thought what we were doing, that it was okay. It worked for both of us. But he lied to me. He went behind my back when he knew how I felt about him being involved. I don't trust him. And I can't be with someone I don't trust.

"Then let him go, Cecilia." Tears prick the backs of my eyes. "If you care about him at all, let him go."

35

CECILIA

Julio offers to drive me home and I let him, not waking Gabriel up before I go. A sliver of guilt worms its way into my chest, but it's better this way, I think. I need to talk to my parents and I can't do that with Gabriel there, hovering.

If I woke him to say goodbye, I know he'd want to come with me. But I also know how he gets. Overprotective and overbearing. I'll have enough of that coming from my parents. I don't need it from him, too.

As I step through the front door of my house, the familiar scent of home envelops me, offering a fleeting moment of solace amidst the anxious energy that's consumed my morning.

But even as I take refuge in the familiar surroundings, I'm not looking forward to the conversation I'm about to have.

I'm not ready.

My parents are waiting for me in the living room, their faces etched with worry and concern. And beside them stands a police officer, his presence a stark reminder of the events that unfolded less than twenty-four hours ago.

"Sweetheart, are you alright?" My mother's voice trembles with emotion as she rushes to my side, enveloping me in a tight embrace. "I've been so worried. They said you were attacked—" she chokes on a sob. "Oh, my god. What did he do to you?"

"I'm okay, Mom," I manage to tell her. "I'm fine." Lie. "I'm okay." She clings to me the way she did in the hospital. *Before*. Only this time, I didn't try to take my own life. Someone else did.

I wince as her hold on me tightens, but I don't have it in me to ask her to let go.

After more tears and whispered words, she finally releases me and reclaims her seat beside my father. She pats the space next to her, a silent encouragement to join them.

I don't think I can have this conversation and look at them, so instead, I take the armchair kitty corner to the couch.

Thankfully, Mom doesn't comment on my choice, but she doesn't look happy about it. Her eyes are glued to my face, horror spreading across her features as she takes in each splotch of blue and purple she can find. It's a good thing Gabriel's sweats and oversized sweater hide the rest of my body from view. With the way Mom is looking at me, I'm surprised she hasn't insisted we go to the hospital.

Dad remains stoic, his gaze fixed on me with unwavering intensity. He's trying to keep it together. This is his politician persona. But I can see the pain lurking beneath the surface, the silent anguish of a father who would do anything to protect his daughter.

For his benefit, I force out a small smile.

I hate this.

That I've inadvertently caused my parents more grief.

"Ms. Russo," the officer begins. "Would you mind answering a few questions?"

"Sure," I tell him, tucking my legs beneath me.

"Would you prefer to go somewhere more private—"

"She's fine speaking here," my dad interjects. There's a knock on the door and my mom rushes to answer it. "And she won't be answering any questions until her counsel has arrived."

Mom ushers a man into the room. He's vaguely familiar. Tall, mid-forties. His tan skin contracts nicely against his well-cut navy-blue suit.

I've met him before. Though only briefly. He works for Dad. I've seen him around on the campaign trail. "Cecilia, this is Mr. Ayala." To him, Mom adds, "Thank you so much for coming on such short notice."

My manners and the expectant looks on my parents' faces force me to stand up and shake Mr. Ayala's hand before he moves on to shake the hand of the officer, handing him one of his business cards.

"Where are we?" Mr. Ayala asks, taking the last available seat.

The officer clears his throat. "There seems to be a misunderstanding," he says. "Ms. Russo isn't under arrest. I'm just here to ask her a few questions. A lawyer isn't needed for this conversation."

"Officer—?" Mr. Ayala starts to interject.

"Koch," the officer supplies.

"Ah, yes. Officer Koch," Mr. Ayala acknowledges. "While I'm aware Ms. Russo isn't under arrest, it would be prudent that she has adequate representation." He turns to me, his expression softening. "Cecilia, it's just a precaution. Your parents want to make sure you're protected and that your rights are respected throughout this process."

That's uh, nice.

Officer Koch doesn't agree, judging by his sigh. "Very well," he says. "Is anyone else joining us today?"

"This is everyone," Dad says.

He nods. "Alright then, we'll begin."

Taking a deep breath, I steel myself for what I know will be a difficult conversation.

"In your own words, can you explain the events of yesterday afternoon, starting with the moment you arrived at the PacNorth campus pool?"

Opening my mouth, I answer his questions, doing my best to block out the tear-stained expression on my mother's face as she processes my words. I try to keep my emotions in a box as I recount yesterday's events.

How Austin grabbed me by the hair and held me underwater when tried to come up for air. That I hadn't even known he was there until it was too late.

I mentioned Gregory Chambers and Parker Benson. How I saw them during the brief moments I was able to get some air. I stick close to the facts, leaving out what I was feeling. The terrified thoughts that'd run through my head.

And then I get to the moment help arrived. I tell him about being pulled out of the pool. About the guys saving me. I gloss over Gabriel beating Austin to a pulp, telling the officer I was too focused on catching my breath after being rescued to know what was going on around me. Gabriel and the others will have their own questions to answer. I won't let my words contradict their story in any way.

"And what reason would Mr. Holt have for attacking you the way he did?"

I shake my head. "I don't know."

"Is it possible that you may have inadvertently provoked—"

"I'd like to remind you, Officer Koch, that my client, Ms. Russo, was attacked. She is the victim here, not the aggressor. To suggest otherwise, that she provoked her attacker in some way, is inappropriate and beyond uncalled for."

"I didn't mean—" Officer Koch clears his throat. "My apologies. I was only asking if there was something else that occurred prior to the assault that might help to explain why Austin Holt attacked you? We're trying to uncover the young man's motive for the assault and are experiencing some ... difficulty."

"I didn't do anything," I tell him. "I never did anything to Austin. Nothing to justify—" I wave a hand through the air. "All this."

"Are you sure?" he pushes. "Have you had any prior altercations with him, or either of the other two men involved?"

Chewing my bottom lip, I hesitate. "Nothing related to—"

He cuts me off. "Austin's family has implied that you're fixated on ruining their son's reputation. They claim false allegations have been made—"

"Stop!" I tell him. My heart pounds a rapid staccato in my chest. How does he know? He shouldn't— No one else is supposed to know about that night.

My eyes snap to my parents, but all I see is confusion etched across their faces.

"I'm not trying to ruin Austin's life," I tell him. "I've never made false allegations against him."

He flips through his notebook. "I have it here that allegations were made to PacNorth University's—"

"It wasn't false," I cut him off, my chest heaving.

Thankfully, Mr. Ayala interjects. "I'd like a moment alone with my client."

"That won't be—" Officer Koch begins, but Mr. Ayala doesn't let him finish.

"I'll have to insist." He pushes to his feet. "Ms. Russo, would you join me?"

Numbly, I follow him past our living room and down the hallway into my father's study.

Sweat beads on my forehead, my palms clammy and slick. I feel dizzy, disoriented, as if the ground beneath me could give way at any moment.

Mr. Ayala closes the door behind us and my eyes snap to it. "Open," I snap. Taking a breath, I try again. "Sorry," I mutter. "But can we leave the door open?"

He scrutinizes me before cracking the door a fraction of an inch. Then he moves to the opposite side of the room, leaving a clear path for me to leave should I want to.

"Is this better?" he asks.

I nod. "Yes. Thank you."

He leans against my dad's desk, bracing himself on the edge. "I can't adequately protect you if I don't know the full story, so I need you to be honest with me. Can you do that?"

I'm not sure I have much of a choice, so I nod.

"Can you give me the short version of what Officer Koch was alluding to in there?"

"Austin, Parker, and Gregory raped me at a frat party last summer."

He blinks. I've taken him by surprise.

"And you disclosed this information to ..."

"PacNorth's Administration," I tell him. "I reported it in the Title Nine office."

He nods. "And what came of it?"

Bitterness coats the back of my throat. "Nothing. They didn't believe me."

"And the police?"

I shake my head. "I didn't go to them," I tell him. "If the school didn't believe me, I assumed no one else would."

"Are your parents aware?"

I shake my head again. "No. I—" I swallow past the lump in my throat. "I don't want them to know. It would break my mom."

A flicker of sympathy softens the lines of his face. "You're aware this information is bound to come out? There's no way to keep this information secret given the recent assault against you. The police are looking for a motive and won't stop digging until they have one. Austin's defense will also use this information if they feel it can help their case. There's no keeping it quiet now. Do you understand?"

A stone sinks to the pit of my stomach. I think I knew that already, but a part of me had hoped ...

"Yeah," I mutter. "I understand."

"I'm going to need you to go back out there and tell Officer Koch about the first assault, in detail. Along with any other altercations that have occurred between then and what transpired yesterday. Can you do that?"

"Do I have a choice?" I mutter.

"Unfortunately, no," he says. "Not if we intend for the charges to stick. I can request a few hours. At most, maybe a day. But you'll need to make a statement, and it's likely that you'll be interviewed more than once by multiple officers."

Swallowing hard, I nod. "Is there any way to do that without my parents around?"

"There is," he says. "But in times like these, it's often best to have a support system at your side. Your parents love you very much—"

"I know," I tell him. "It's just ..." I chew on my bottom lip. "They've been through so much already. I don't want to cause them any more pain."

"Let them be there for you," he suggests. "It would cause more pain to be pushed away than to know everything that's happened. And forgive me for overstepping, but ..." he tugs at his tie and purses his lips, almost like he's struggling to find the right words to say, "I've been by your father's side for several years now. I know him pretty well and consider him a true friend."

I wait for him to continue.

"Your father was distraught when he learned you tried to kill yourself."

My eyes water, and I quickly look away.

"He blames himself," he tells me.

"He shouldn't," I whisper.

Mr. Ayala shrugs. "That may be. But parents often do. Especially when they can't make sense of something. When they don't have the full picture."

I nod, understanding what he means.

"Alright," I tell him. "They can stay."

Mr. Ayala leads me back to the living room, and for the next hour, I tell Officer Koch and my parents everything that happened. Everything that's been happening these past few months. I spill all my secrets. Even those I still believe are too painful for my parents to bear.

36

GABRIEL

She's not answering her phone and Cecilia hasn't shown up to school for three days now.

I'm losing it.

I've taken to getting updates on her well-being from Adriana, of all people, since Cecilia is still taking *her* calls.

It's infuriating. I need to see her. To talk to her and make sure she's okay.

I'm pissed that she snuck out of my place, but I understand that she's hurting and overwhelmed. I just wish she'd let me be there for her.

But even her parents—who happen to love me—are helping her dodge my calls, and every time I show up on their porch, they make up some excuse about her resting and turn me away.

Cecilia's staying safely tucked away—like Rapunzel in her tower—and despite my best efforts, I've yet to be granted entry.

My phone buzzes in my pocket, and I jump to answer it. "Cecilia?" I answer, not bothering to check the caller ID.

Silence.

"Is that you?" I try again.

A man clears his throat. "It's me," he says, and I stiffen.

"What do you want?" I ask, recognizing my father's voice.

"Mijo,"—*son*— he says. "Podemos hablar?" *Can we talk?* "Is now a good time?"

"No. It isn't," I tell him and hang up my phone.

He calls again, and this time I ignore his call.

I haven't had anything to say to my father since he and my mother signed over my trust, effectively cutting me out of their lives. He wants something. It's the only reason he can have for calling, and these days, when it comes to my parents, I'm not in a giving mood.

"Everything okay?" Julio asks, stepping into the room and seeing my expression.

"Peachy," I tell him.

"Give her some time," he suggests. "You're worried, and that's fair, but give her some space. After what she's been through, that girl needs it."

My jaw tightens. I'm getting really sick of Julio suggesting I back off. When is he going to get it through his thick head that I'm not going to give up, not when it comes to her? His bullshit is getting real old.

"My dad called," I tell him, eager to change the subject.

His eyes widen. "Yeah? What'd he want."

"Don't know. I hung up on him."

Julio sighs and scrubs a hand over his face. "Seriously?"

I cut him with a glare. "Yes. Seriously. What the fuck would you have me do?"

"Talk to the man," he says, throwing his hands in the air.

"When hell freezes over," I tell him. "As far as I'm concerned, my father died months ago. So did my mother."

Julio grunts. "I take it you're not going to her wedding, then?"

I snort, prepared to tell him I'm not, when an idea slips into my mind.

Desperate times call for desperate measures.

Glancing at my phone, I consider messaging Cecilia now but the wedding is still a few weeks away, and Julio was right when he said she has a lot on her plate. I'm not trying to add to it.

Giving Cecilia space feels like the right thing to do, but it's eating away at me. Still, if she needs time, I'll respect that.

For now.

Maybe.

Hopefully.

I fucking hate this.

I can't shake the feeling of helplessness that gnaws at me. It's like being stuck in a nightmare, unable to reach the person I care about most.

Depending on how long she plans to avoid me, I can use my mother's wedding as an excuse to reach out to Cecilia later. To spend time with her and see how she's doing.

It feels manipulative. Wrong. But at this stage in our relationship, I'm not above it.

That should bother me, but it doesn't. And I should feel ashamed about that, but I don't.

I turn to Julio, my brows drawn together. "I'm going to the wedding."

He raises an eyebrow, clearly surprised by my sudden change of heart. "You sure about that?" he asks cautiously.

I nod, not at all confident in my decision, but what other choice do I have? "Yeah. I already told Cecilia I'd go," I say, my voice firm. "Maybe she'll still come with me. You know," I shrug. "After the dust settles."

Julio studies me for a moment, his expression not at all pleased. "If you think it's a good idea—" he hedges.

"I do," I assure him, feeling my shoulders relax now that I have some semblance of a plan. I pull out my phone, ready to mark the wedding date on my calendar. It may be a long shot, but if there's even a chance of Cecilia going with me, of spending time with me again, I'll take it.

And maybe, just maybe, this can be the first step towards putting things between us back together.

I won't let our relationship splinter apart. Not over an asshole like Austin Holt. He doesn't get to take her from me.

37
CECILIA

"**H**e asked about you today," Adriana says.

"You've mentioned that before," I tell her with a sigh.

"He asks about you every day."

Using my concealer and a beauty blender, I gingerly press over the purplish skin around my eyes and the bruises marking my jawline. It does little to hide the state of my face, but there isn't much more I can do.

"I know," I tell her. "I keep meaning to call him back."

Adriana drops down on my bed. "When, Cecilia? When are you really going to call him? Because that man is falling apart at the seams with worry over you." She huffs out a breath. "It's annoying. This sad and mopey Gabriel is so different from the version of him I know."

Shame washes over me. "I know," I tell her. And I do. I read all of Gabriel's messages. I listen to each and every one of his voicemails. I know he's worried about me, but I'm just ... "I'm so angry with him," I admit. "And it's like I get angrier with every passing day."

She nods, understanding reflected in her eyes. "He broke your trust."

"Yeah."

"He went behind your back. Blew up your life. And now you're stuck dealing with the mess."

"Pretty much," I tell her. It's been a week since the assault, and in that time I've withdrawn from one of my classes and switched the other two to online only. My parents have assured me it's for the best. That I can go back to in-person classes next semester. But it still feels like a loss. Like Austin is taking more away from me.

Mr. Ayala wasn't wrong when he said I'd be interviewed more than once. I've had to recount my story four times already and I'm dreading the day I'll have to do it again in court. I don't know where things are going to go from here.

The media caught wind of the story and reporters have been on our doorstep every day. The house phone never stops ringing, and I can see how the stress of all this is getting to my parents.

I'm happy Austin was arrested. He deserves to go to jail for what he's done to me and with any luck, he will. But if Gabriel had just left things alone ... I hang my head. I wouldn't have to go through any of this. I wouldn't be putting my parents through this either.

"Then be pissed at him," Adriana tells me. "Yell and scream at him. Tell him he's an asshole. But you need to get it out.

Bottling everything up inside isn't going to do either one of you any good. If this is too big a thing for you to get over, Gabriel needs to know that. And you need the chance to tell him how you feel. To rip him a new one for breaking your trust. You deserve the opportunity to show him your anger."

Swallowing hard, I nod. "Maybe."

Adriana snorts. "No maybe. Call him." She holds my phone out to me. "It's been a week, Cecilia."

Shoulders slumping, I accept the phone. "Okay," I tell her. "But ..." I hesitate. "Maybe I'll start with a text."

Rolling her eyes, she grins. "Fine. Whatever. Start with a text."

Opening my message app, I pull up the chat with Gabriel, my eyes briefly skimming over his earlier messages. He sends me a *good morning* text every day before his classes begin and a *goodnight* text at the end of every night. There are more in between. Sometimes he asks me about my day. Other times he says he misses me and tells me about his.

I've only gotten the *good morning* message so far today.

> Me: Hey.

His response is immediate.

> Gabriel: Hey. Are you okay?

> Me: Yeah. I'm okay.

"I don't know what to say to him," I tell Adriana, glancing up from the screen.

She shrugs. "Be honest with him. Tell him you're angry and see if maybe he wants to get together to talk."

"Is that a good idea?" My stomach does a summersault at the thought of seeing Gabriel in person. Am I ready to face him?

"It's not a bad one," she says.

I guess I'll have to be.

> **Me:** Do you think we can talk?

> **Gabriel:** I can pick you up ...

> **Me:** No. I'd rather drive.

> **Gabriel:** My place? The guys are out of the house right now. We'll have some privacy for a couple of hours if you're free now.

Swallowing hard, I force myself to thumb out a response.

> **Me:** Okay. I'll see you in thirty.

> **Gabriel:** See you then.

38
GABRIEL

I lied when I told Cecilia the guys were out.

Not a big deal.

I kicked all of their asses out as soon as she said she was on her way and I've been pacing the entryway ever since.

Hearing her Jeep pull into the driveway, I don't hesitate to open the front door.

I refuse to give Cecilia a chance to change her mind about this. It's been a week of her avoiding me and I've had enough.

If she hadn't messaged me today, I was getting ready to storm her house and demand her parents allow me to see her. I doubt I would have succeeded, but I'm desperate and out of ideas.

Cecilia drags her feet getting out of her car, and it takes everything in me to keep myself rooted on the porch. To not rush over to her and pull her out of the damn thing myself.

"Hi," she says, lingering beside the driver's side door.

"You coming in?" I ask, trying to keep my tone casual despite the uncertainty swirling inside me.

Cecilia hesitates for a moment before nodding, her movements stiff as she walks towards the porch. I step back to give her space, my hands clenching into fists at my sides. I'm over the fucking moon that she's here, that she finally reached out to me. But I don't know what to expect right now. I can tell she's nervous, but Cecilia should never feel like that around me.

As she reaches the porch, I hold the door open for her, trying to ignore the tension crackling between us. She brushes past me without a word, and I swallow down the lump forming in my throat as my eyes greedily drink her in.

She's wearing loose-fitting jeans and my hoodie. Was that intentional, or did she just throw it on without thinking? Either way, she looks good in my clothes. The marks on her face are another story. She's tried covering them with makeup, but the dark marks and swelling around her eye are still visible despite her efforts. Is that why she's been hiding? Is she ashamed of how she looks?

She shouldn't be. Cecilia's never been anything but beautiful.

Inside, the atmosphere feels heavy with unspoken words, and I struggle to find the right thing to say.

"How are you?" I finally ask, my voice coming out more strained than I intended.

She shrugs, her gaze flickering away from mine. "Fine," she mutters, her tone clipped.

I resist the urge to reach out and touch her, knowing she won't welcome the move. Instead, I shove my hands into my pockets, feeling the weight of the silence pressing down on us.

"You said you wanted to talk," I start, my voice cautious as I try to broach the chasm that's only seemed to grow between us this past week.

Her eyes flick to mine, and I get a glimpse of anger buried beneath the surface. "Yeah, I do," she says, her voice sharp.

Alright. Anger. I can work with this.

I take a step closer. "I need to understand what happened," I say, fighting to keep my tone even. She's not the only one upset. "You took off without so much as a goodbye and then ghosted me for a week."

"What happened?" Cecilia scoffs, her eyes flashing with emotion. "You happened, Gabriel. You went after Austin without even talking to me about it, and now everything's a mess."

My chest tightens at her words. I thought we hashed this out already. "I was just trying to protect you," I argue, desperation creeping into my voice.

"But you didn't," she says. "You managed to make everything worse."

"I didn't mean—"

She holds her hand out, and I snap my lips together.

"I know," she tells me. "You didn't mean to. You had good intentions. You didn't think Austin would go after me. I know." She pushes her hair out of her face. "I know, but even knowing, it doesn't make any of this better. You still lied to me. I thought I could trust you but—"

"You can," I interject. "You know you can."

Shaking her head, she takes a few steps back. "No. I can't. I thought I could, but you proved me wrong when you went behind my back."

Is she being serious right now?

The irritation bubbling inside me reaches a boiling point, and before I can stop myself, I'm closing the distance between us, my hands gripping her hips tightly and pulling her toward me. "You think I wanted this?" I demand, my voice raw and angry. "You think I enjoyed seeing you in pain?"

Cecilia meets my gaze, her dark brown eyes blazing with defiance. "You don't get to play the hero, Gabriel," she spits, her words cutting deep. "You had no right meddling in my life. Not after I told you to back off."

"So your solution is to ghost me? Real fucking mature, Cecilia."

"Ghost you?" she snaps, "What did you expect? I can barely look at you without feeling like I'm being stabbed all over again, only this time in the chest."

I open my mouth to respond, but she cuts me off with a bitter laugh. "You betrayed me," she accuses, her voice trembling with emotion. "Don't you get that? You broke your promise to let me fight my own battles. Regardless of your intent, you stabbed me in the back and my life is imploding because of it."

The weight of her words hits me like a punch to the gut, and guilt consumes me. "I'm sorry," I whisper, my voice barely audible above the pounding of my heart. "I'll say it a thousand times if that's what it takes for you to believe me. I'm so fucking sorry."

But Cecilia doesn't want my apologies, and before I can say another word, she's pushing me away, her hands shoving against my chest with surprising force. "I don't accept your apology," she hisses, her eyes blazing with anger.

I stumble backwards, my chest aching with the force of her rejection. But despite the pain, I can't tear my gaze away from her. There's something raw and vulnerable in her eyes, something that draws me to her like a moth to a flame.

Her chest is heaving with each of her labored breaths. Before I can stop myself, I'm closing the distance between us once again, my lips crashing against hers in a desperate, angry kiss.

The anger and frustration that's been building between us explodes in a wave of passion and desire, and I lose myself in the heat of the moment, the world fading away until there's nothing but Cecilia and the burning need that consumes us both.

After the initial shock, I expect her to shove me away, but she surprises me when instead her arms wrap around my neck and she pulls me closer to her.

Our tongues and teeth clash against one another, and she bites at my lips, her teeth breaking the skin.

I hiss into her mouth, the taste of my blood mixing with the flavor of her kiss.

"I hate you," she says when she finally tears her mouth from me. "And I don't forgive you," she says again.

"Then hate me," I tell her.

Hoisting Cecilia into my arms, she wraps her legs around my waist and I carry her up the stairs and into my bedroom. "Hate me. Curse me. Yell at me." I press her against my bedroom wall, grinding my length against her center. "But stop pushing me away."

"We can't do this," she protests weakly, her voice breathless as I trail kisses along her jaw, mindful of the bruises on her skin.

"Yes, we can," I insist, my desire for her clouding all reason and doubt.

Dropping her onto the bed, I tear my shirt over my head. Her gaze drinks me in and she licks her lips, lust flaring in her eyes.

I grin.

My fingers fumble with the buckle on my belt, and then I'm shoving my jeans over my legs and kicking them off my feet.

Reaching for her, I help Cecilia out of my hoodie before pressing her back to the bed and making quick work of removing her pants. When we're both naked, I climb over her, settling myself between her legs.

Cupping her jaw, I pull her eyes toward me.

"This is a mistake," she whispers.

"No, baby girl," I tell her, "Nothing between you and me can ever be a mistake."

Dipping forward, I claim her lips once again, my cock sliding into her hot, wet center. A perfect fit. I groan into the kiss, my hips thrusting forward to fill every inch of her.

"Gabe!" she cries out.

"I've got you," I tell her. "Eyes on me."

Her lashes flutter open to lock onto mine, and unlike before, I don't fuck her with abandon. I make love to my girl, showing her with my body what my words have failed to.

As our bodies move together in a rhythm as old as time, I pour every ounce of love and remorse into our embrace. With each thrust, I tell her that I'm sorry. With each caress, I promise never to hurt her again.

Cecilia's breath hitches in her throat as I whisper words of devotion against her skin, my lips tracing the curve of her neck with reverence.

I bury myself deep inside her, losing myself in the feel of her beneath me.

"What are you doing to me?" she mutters.

Pressing my lips to each of her breasts, I dip my hand between us and begin stroking her clit. "Showing you I'm sorry," I tell her.

Cecilia's back arches as she reaches the edge at breakneck speed.

"Taking care of you in a way that only I can."

She shudders beneath me, her release crashing over her in languid waves. "Gabriel," she sighs my name with her release, and I lean forward, stealing the word from her lips.

My own release is quick to follow, and it only takes a few more pumps inside of her before I'm emptying myself between her thighs.

Collapsing beside her, I pull Cecilia close, her heartbeat echoing against mine.

Her leg hooks over my hip and I press myself back against her core, feeling the warmth of my release dripping out of her.

Something dark and possessive sweeps through me, and for a moment, I'm tempted to shove my cock back inside her, if only to hold my cum in.

Perspiration dots her skin, and I press a kiss to her shoulder.

"We can't keep doing that," she says, her breath fanning over my chest.

"Yes, we can." My arms around her tighten. "You can be angry. You have every right to be," I tell her. "But don't …" My voice grows thick. "Don't push me away."

Cecilia pulls back. Lifting her chin, her dark brown eyes meet mine as she bites on her bottom lip. "I don't think I can get past this," she whispers.

Her confession breaks something inside of me, but I refuse to allow her words to take root.

"Then don't," I tell her, shoving my emotions in a box and tucking them away. If I've learned one thing in dealing with all the rejection from my own family, it's that I'm great at compartmentalizing. "Don't get over it. Don't forgive me." I press a kiss to her forehead. "Hate me if that's what you need to do," I tell her, and I mean it. I'll take her anger and hatred. I'll accept whatever she decides to throw at me. "Just don't push me away."

39
CECILIA

I'm honest enough with myself to know I'm avoiding Gabriel, but I no longer ignore his calls and texts.

We fall into a pattern of sorts over the next two weeks.

We talk on the phone almost daily. He keeps it short and sweet. Casual check-ins and hellos. But I avoid him beyond that.

Sleeping with Gabriel again was a mistake. I know that, and I think he does, too. It's why I haven't allowed myself to go to him again.

There've been plenty of opportunities.

He invites me over or asks to come see me virtually every other day. And every now and then, I catch sight of him outside my bedroom window, leaning against his motorcycle across the street. He never lingers for long, but he always parks somewhere where he knows I can see him. It's his way of telling me he's not giving up on me. That he'll always be there.

It's sweet, but despite his efforts and pleas for me not to push him away, it's exactly what I do.

I don't know how else to get around it.

If I allow myself to see him, I'll sleep with him again. My willpower is only so strong and right now, Gabriel is the only person able to grant me even a molecule of solace.

But at what cost?

It doesn't matter if I tell Gabriel I can't be with him. That it's only sex and nothing more. That's what we agreed to, but what goes on between us doesn't feel like just sex.

It never has.

I wish I could lie to myself a little longer and convince myself it'll all be okay, but I don't think I can.

Julio was right. It's not fair to him.

And despite my anger, despite feeling betrayed, I won't do that to Gabriel. I won't use him.

So I brush his efforts off instead.

We're still dealing with reporters and Dad is knee-deep in his attempts to salvage his re-election campaign. What happened with Austin doesn't only affect my life. It affects my entire family. And I'm trying to be there for them as much as they're trying to be there for me.

I'm back to therapy twice a week. For right now, at least.

I agreed to the increase mostly because it gave me another reason to tell Gabriel I was busy, but it's been helping. Now that everything's out in the open and I don't have any more secrets to hide, things are ... not easier, per se.

But they're different. In a good way.

I don't know how else to describe it. Some of the weight's been lifted off my chest, I suppose.

Austin is being released from the hospital tomorrow afternoon, and Mr. Ayala has assured me he'll be taken into custody immediately.

Parker and Gregory were released on bail last week. No surprise there. But I have a restraining order against them in place and Mr. Ayala assures me I'm safe. If either of them violate the restraining order, they'll go back to jail until their trials, and he's confident neither man will risk it when they're facing less severe charges than Austin is.

He prepared me for the possibility of one or both of them being offered a plea deal, and I think I've finally come to terms with that.

Austin won't be given the same opportunity. His charges are more severe. Attempted murder. Assault. He won't be offered bail, and he's looking at a long time behind bars. A serious relief.

All three men have also been expelled from PacNorth and kicked out of Zeta Pi. Regardless of what happens in court, they don't have a future at PacNorth, and I won't have to see them again.

Not on campus, at least.

"Cecilia," my mother calls from downstairs. "Are you hungry?"

"I'm fine," I call back, not bothering to look up from my book. My teachers were able to accommodate my request to transition to online only and the reading load has been intense, but I'm grateful for the distraction and even more grateful that I didn't have to drop out completely. I wouldn't have minded so much before, but with the swim team, I'm not willing to give my spot up.

I missed practice that first week after the assault, but I've been there every day since.

It's the one place where I feel a little bit normal.

Mom is back to hovering again, the way she did after my suicide attempt. If I thought it was bad before, it's nothing like this.

She barely leaves the house, and when she does, it's only ever if my dad happens to be home. He's taken to working more from his home office, likely at her request. They know everything that's happened now and I guess I thought it would help, and in some ways, it did. But it's also made them worry more. If Mr. Ayala delivers bad news, like when he told me Parker and Gregory made bail, my parents started watching me like I was a ticking time bomb.

I wish I could reassure them I'm going to be okay. That I'm not going to do anything reckless. But my words hold little weight when they've seen me lose myself before.

Sometimes when Mom thinks she's alone, I find her crying in her room or sniffling in the kitchen. She's having a hard time digesting everything that's happened, and she and Dad both keep apologizing as if what Austin did to me could possibly be their fault.

I've tried to tell them it isn't. That I don't blame them at all. But Mom insists a mother is supposed to know when something is amiss. She blames herself for not realizing there was more to my suicide attempt. For assuming I was overwhelmed with college or merely depressed. I don't know how to make her pain go away.

"Are you sure?" she tries again. "I can make some lasagna. Your favorite."

"I'm not hungry," I assure her. "But thank you."

I can hear her sigh all the way from the living room. She's trying, and I'm grateful for that.

But sometimes, I just need to be alone.

40
CECILIA

It's getting late when the sound of murmured voices from downstairs trickles into my room. Glancing at the clock, my brows furrow together, taking note of the time before I pad down the hallway.

Leaning over the banister, I peer downstairs, the dim light casting long shadows across the foyer below. Lately, it's become a familiar routine, these late-night visits from Dad's campaign manager, Mr. Ayala, or Officer Koch.

They seem to be the three recurring presences these past couple of weeks.

"Thank you," Gabriel's voice floats up the stairs, his tone tinged with a sense of urgency. "I promise, I'll be quick."

The familiar sound of his voice catches me off guard, my breath catching in my throat as I strain to hear whatever he says next.

My heart skips a beat, the mere sound of his presence sending a jolt of anticipation through me.

What is he doing here?

Seconds later, his steps are pounding up the stairs, the rhythm of his stride echoing in the quiet of the house. My pulse quickens, a flutter of nerves dancing in my chest as I stand frozen at the top of the stairs, dumbfounded by his unexpected appearance.

Gabriel clears the last step, his figure looming large in the dim light, his honey-brown eyes drinking me in like a man dying of thirst. The intensity of his gaze sends a shiver down my spine, and I swallow hard, trying to steady my racing heart as he moves closer.

His presence, so close, ignites a flurry of conflicting emotions inside of me—longing, uncertainty, and a flicker of desire.

But I push them aside, steeling myself against the pull he exerts on me. *Play it cool.* I remind myself.

"What are you doing here?" I manage to ask, my voice coming out more breathless than I intend it to. It's only been a few weeks, but god, I've missed him.

"I wanted to talk," he says, his voice soft. "Can we go in your room?"

My mind races, searching for an excuse to avoid being alone with him, but I know that I can't keep avoiding him like this. Reluctantly, I nod, leading him to my room where we can speak without Mom and Dad listening in.

As we settle into the quiet space, the tension between us is palpable. I can feel his gaze on me, probing and searching, but I refuse to meet it, focusing instead on a spot on the floor.

"Why didn't you just call or send me a text?" I finally ask, unable to contain the question any longer. "It's late. Don't you have practice early tomorrow?"

Gabriel shifts uncomfortably, his expression pained. "I wanted to talk to you in person," he admits. "I know things are ... complicated."

I offer him a small nod, a silent acknowledgment of his words. *You can say that again.*

"I just ... I miss you, Cecilia. More than I thought possible." The vulnerability in his voice cracks through my defenses, stirring something deep within me. But I can't let myself be swayed by his words, not when I've worked so hard to rebuild the walls around my heart.

"I miss you too," I admit, my voice barely a whisper. "But that doesn't change what happened."

Gabriel nods, his expression pained. "I know. Which is why I know I have no right asking this of you, it's just ..." He hesitates.

Swallowing past the lump in my throat, I peer up at him through the veil of my lashes. "What is it?" I ask, my voice barely above a whisper, my heart pounding in my chest.

"I was hoping I could ask a favor," he begins, his voice hesitant. "If it's too much, just say the word. I don't have any expectations here. It's just ..." He trails off again, his eyes searching mine.

"What's the favor?" I prompt, my curiosity piqued despite my reservations.

"Tomorrow is my Mom's wedding." Oh. I'd completely forgotten about that. "And I know you're busy. You have a lot going on so the timing is absolute shit but, I was hoping you'd maybe hang out with me for the day."

His words catch me off guard, but as I meet his gaze, I see the raw vulnerability in his eyes, the unspoken plea for me to do this. My answer is almost immediate. Despite the uncertainty between us, I could never deny him this. Gabriel may have hurt me, but he's hurting too. I won't abandon him when he needs me most. I still care about him.

"Of course," I nod, offering him a small, tentative smile. "But aren't you going to the wedding?"

He shakes his head. "Nah. It's a bad idea no matter how I look at it. But just knowing what's happening tomorrow," he shrugs. "It's hard. I don't need to be there to know she's moving on with her life and I really don't want to spend my day stuck in my head about it."

I get it, but I still think he should go. His mom getting married is no small thing.

"Any chance I can get you to reconsider?" I ask.

Pursing his lips, he considers me. "She doesn't want me there." I can hear the little boy in his voice, the one who's been hurt by his mom, but who desperately craves her love and acceptance.

"She sent you an invitation," I remind him. "I'd say that's a pretty big indication that she does."

Gabriel shakes his head, unconvinced. "Trust me, she doesn't. Me going wouldn't end well."

"I'll still be your date," I tell him. "If you go." Clearing my throat, I add, "I'll spend the afternoon with you regardless, but I think we should go to the wedding. I'd like to meet the woman who helped make you."

Gabriel's expression goes slack. "You want to meet my mom?" he asks, his voice filled with disbelief.

"Why not?" I tell him. "You've met mine."

His mouth twists into a grimace. "That's different," he mutters. "Yours loves you."

My heart breaks at his words.

"She loves you," I assure him. "Besides, I promised I'd go with you before and I'd like to keep that promise. We should go to the wedding. Trust me. This will be good for you. For your mom, too."

"It will blow up in our faces."

Rolling my eyes, I laugh. "It won't. Trust me. Please."

"You don't need to convince me out of some misguided obligation," he says, and I can see he's grasping at straws, searching for a way out of this. "You're not responsible for fixing shit between me and my family."

"It's not like that," I say, my tone gentle. "We're friends, and this is what friends do, right? They're there for one another. Let's go to the wedding. Let me be there for you. I promise nothing bad is going to happen."

Gabriel nods, his expression pained. "Friends. Right," he says, his tone guarded all of a sudden.

I feel a pang in my chest, a flicker of sadness washing over me. But I remind myself I can't keep leading him on. If we're going to remain in each other's lives—something I'd very much like for us to do—then we need to redefine our relationship. That means being friends, and only friends.

Nothing less and nothing more. We can't tread water in the gray area anymore.

"Alright," he says. "We'll go to the wedding."

Really? Good.

Relief sweeps through me. I know he has his reservations, but this is going to be so good for him. If I've learned anything from my therapist these past couple of weeks, it's that the deepest wounds require us to experience the most discomfort in order to heal from them.

Going to his mom's wedding isn't something Gabriel wants to do, but it's something he has to do if he's ever going to put their issues behind him and move on.

"What time do I need to be ready?"

Drawing closer, Gabriel cups the back of my neck and pulls me to him. I hold back the urge to melt against his chest, keeping my back stiff as his lips press against my forehead and he whispers against my skin.

"I'll be here at four to pick you up," he murmurs, his words sending a shiver down my spine. "Thank you for this."

His touch lingers on my skin, searing me with an intensity I'm desperate to ignore. But as he pulls away, I force myself to meet his gaze, to keep my emotions in check despite the butterflies dancing inside my stomach.

"I'll be ready," I reply, my voice steady despite my nerves.

Gabriel offers me a small, grateful smile before turning to leave, his footsteps echoing down the hallway as he descends the stairs. Left alone in the quiet of my room, I give myself a moment to exhale, to release the tension coiled tight inside my chest.

It's just a wedding. I remind myself. *What's the worst that can happen?*

41
GABRIEL

Cecilia steals my breath the next day when I arrive at her place to pick her up for my Mother's wedding.

She greets me at her door in a pale blue dress that falls to the ground in soft gauzy waves. The dress is sleeveless, the neckline scalloped in a way that accentuates the column of her neck.

Her hair is styled in loose waves around her face and she's wearing more makeup than usual. A mask to cover the lingering discoloration on her skin, but she's just as beautiful as ever.

"You look stunning." I tell her and offer her my arm.

She accepts my arm and follows me outside. "Thanks."

I lead her to my bike only to hesitate as I take in her dress once again.

"I didn't really think—"

"I wore shorts underneath," she says with a grin.

Perfect.

Helping her adjust her helmet, I guide her onto my bike and we set off for the wedding.

We're a few minutes late when we arrive, so I slip in the back, taking a seat in one of the last pews of the church. Cecilia slides in beside me, her hand immediately finding mine. "You doing okay?" She squeezes, a subtle sign of reassurance.

"I'm good," I tell her and squeeze her hand back, only to release it to rub my hands over my slacks.

I'm fucking nervous. I still can't seem to get over the fact that I was invited, but maybe Cecilia's right. Maybe this is Mom's way of extending an olive branch after everything that's happened since Carlos's death.

Mom's already made her way down the aisle and stands front and center with her soon-to-be husband before the priest. Her dress is white, with long lace sleeves and a full skirt. It's both simple and elegant.

She smiles at the man standing before her as he holds her hands and smiles back.

She looks ... happy.

I haven't seen her smile like that in years. There are people on either side of them—bridesmaids and groomsmen. No one that I recognize. The two boys beside the groom are young, close to my age. They beam at the happy couple. One even swipes a tear from his eye but maintains the smile plastered across his face.

The priest asks for the rings, and then my mother speaks her vows. I hear the love in her words, the adoration. It's hard to listen to, knowing how long it's been since I was on the receiving end of her affections, but there's a part of me, a really small fucking part, that's happy for her.

Losing Carlos broke both of my parents. His death tore our entire family apart. And while I doubt I will ever forgive her for the way that she handled things, I still want her to be happy.

She's my mom.

The ceremony ends, and the priest pronounces them husband and wife. They kiss, and the crowd claps and cheers, everyone clamoring back to their feet. The happy couple makes their way back down the aisle, and each of them smiles and waves to their family and friends.

When Mom reaches the end, her eyes find mine.

Shock widens them, and her smile dims, but only for a second before she turns her gaze away from me.

What the hell was that?

We follow everyone outside to the reception. Tables have been arranged across the lawn with elaborate centerpieces on display.

Cecilia loops her hand through my arm, and I lead her across the lawn toward the back. We take our seats, but I can't shake the unease that's settled into my gut. Cecilia senses it too, her eyes searching mine for a hint of what's bothering me.

"Still doing okay?" she asks again.

"She wasn't happy to see me," I say, voicing my fears out loud.

Cecilia places a hand on my shoulder. "That's not true," she tells me. "She looked surprised, that's all. She probably didn't expect you to show up with how things are between the two of you. Relax."

I run a hand through my hair, my fingers trembling ever so slightly. "I don't belong here," I murmur, my voice barely above a whisper. "This is a bad idea."

She frowns, concern knitting her brows. "What do you mean?"

I gesture vaguely to the boisterous celebration around us. "All of this ... it's not me. I don't know these people, and I'm not sure I want to." My mother's marrying into a whole new family, connected to people I've never even met. What sort of parent does that?

Cecilia's lips part like she wants to say something, but instead, rests a reassuring hand on my arm, her touch a lifeline in this sea of strangers.

"It's okay to be nervous," she tells me. "It's normal. But try and enjoy the reception. Everything is so beautiful." There's a wistful note in her voice. I thought being here—spending time with Cecilia today—would be a good thing. Hell, I wanted this. Anything to put her by my side, but I wasn't at all prepared for the nauseous feelings rolling around in my gut.

"We should go." I push to my feet.

Cecilia rises with me but quickly steps in my way. Her hands come up to capture my face. "We can leave if you want. It's okay." Good. Because that's exactly what I plan to do. This was a terrible idea. "But you should at least tell your mother congratulations and say goodbye. I think she'd be hurt if you left without saying anything."

Fuck. She's right. I swallow hard before taking a deep breath. "Okay." I can do this. "We'll congratulate the happy couple and then go."

Cecilia smiles, her eyes filled with compassion. "Alright. Let's go find her."

As we make our way through the crowd, my discomfort gnaws at me like a relentless itch. People eye me curiously, and I can't shake the feeling that I'm not welcome here.

When we reach my mother, she's talking to a small circle of guests. The groom and one of his groomsmen stand close beside her.

"Hi," I offer as we approach. I lean in and press a kiss to her cheek. "Congratulations, Mom." I turn and offer her new husband my hand. He shakes it. "I'm Gabriel. Her son. It's nice to meet you." He looks at me with a mixture of shock and confusion before dropping my hand.

"Justin," he supplies before turning to my mother. "Bernadina?" There's a question in his voice.

My mother's face contorts in disbelief. "What are you doing here, Gabriel?" She whispers my name as if it's a curse.

I step back, realization digging knives into my chest. "You sent me an invitation. I ... I thought you wanted me to come?"

Her new husband—Justin—looks taken aback, clearly not at all aware that his new wife has a son.

He clears his throat awkwardly. "It's nice to meet you," he says. "I didn't know Bernadina had a surviving son." So she told him about Carlos, but she didn't bother mentioning me?

451

Sharp talons sink into my chest, twisting and yanking until it becomes difficult to breathe.

My mother tries to regain her composure, her voice strained. "This wasn't supposed to happen. There must have been an oversight. I didn't mean for you to be here. I—"

The words sting more than I expect, and anger bubbles up within me. "An oversight? Really, Mom?" There's a bite in my voice that I don't intend to be there, but *fuck*—is she for real right now?

The younger of the groomsmen steps forward. "I'm the one who sent the invitation," he says, and all eyes turn in his direction. "I found your contact information in Bernadina's address book. I didn't know who you were. I thought you were family, given the last name. I'm sorry. I was just trying to help with the wedding." He ducks his head and mumbles another apology.

"It's alright, son," Justin tells him. "We'll get this sorted out." I can see it now. The resemblance between the two of them. I flick my gaze between him and another of the groomsman, who's now making his way toward us.

"Hey." He smiles wide as soon as he's close and offers me his hand. "I'm Asher. Have we met?"

They've got to be no more than a year or two apart. Close to my age. Brothers. A spear of jealousy hits me square in the chest.

Cecilia's fingers wrap around my biceps. "Gabriel?" she says, and I realize the groomsman—Asher— is still waiting for me to shake his hand.

Fuck. My jaw clenches.

Asher drops his hand once he realizes I'm not going to take it. He looks around at the faces in our circle, taking note of the tension that hangs thick in the air. "What's going on?" The question is directed at his brother. "Adam?"

"You replaced us," I say to my mother. "One for Dad—" I indicate Justin, her new husband. "One for Carlos." I turn to Adam. "And one for me." My eyes meet Asher's dark brown and confused gaze. He's the closest in age to me. Hell, for all I know, he's also twenty-two. A stepbrother. Carlos is dead, and this guy is now my stepbrother.

The surrealness of the situation slams into me and I bark out a laugh. It's jagged and hollow even to my own ears, but fuck if I care.

My mother winces.

What she's doing, it's a slap in the face. She's built an entirely new life with a new husband and new children, one where there's no room left for me.

I can't contain my emotions any longer. "I'm sorry for intruding on your perfect day," I snap, my voice dripping with sarcasm. "Congratulations on your new family. I hope you give a shit about this one more than you did your last."

I turn my back on them and storm away. Cecilia rushes after me, struggling to keep pace in her heels. I know I need to slow my steps, let her catch up to me, but I can't. All I want to do is put as much distance as possible between me and my mother.

Fuck her and fuck her new family.

"Gabriel, wait!" Cecilia calls out.

I ignore her. I can't ... fuck. The walls are closing in on me. I can't breathe. My chest squeezes like a vice cutting off my airflow. I can't do this right now. I need—my eyes dart around, searching for an escape— a way out of this nightmare.

I shove my way through the crowd, ignoring the bewildered looks from my mother's guests. Cecilia's cries fall on deaf ears, drowned out by the storm of emotions raging inside me.

She just ... she fucking replaced me. And worse, she erased me. Her new husband didn't know who I was. Didn't know she had a son. That I was a part of her life. That I existed. She told him about Carlos. About the son she lost. But she didn't tell him about me.

Why?

I stumble past the entrance gates, my fingers fumbling for my phone. Typing out a quick message to Felix, I head for the sidewalk. I need some air. I need—I don't know what the fuck I need. Air, space—anything to make sense of the chaos in my head.

Fuck.

I just need a minute. A goddamn minute to think. Or ...

A delicate hand wraps around my bicep. "Gabriel," Cecilia says, her voice cautious. She moves to stand in front of me, dark brown eyes lifted up to look at my face. "Are you okay?"

"Are you kidding me?" I bite out, jerking my arm away. "Do I look okay to you?"

Hurt flashes across her expression. "I'm sorry," she stammers. Pity and sympathy cloud her gaze, but I have no need for either emotion. "I didn't know this would happen. That your mom would—" She sniffs. "I thought seeing her would be good for you. That maybe you two could patch things up. That you could find closure."

She had no idea it would be like this. I scoff.

Bullshit.

I warned her. I told her this was a bad idea. I might have glossed over my reasons, but she knew I was against this. That I didn't want to be here. I knew coming here would blow up in my face. I fucking knew it.

Cecilia's eyes plead with me, asking for something I can't give. "Gabriel–"

I lift up my hand. "Just leave me alone." I can't talk about this. Not now. Not with her. Nor with anyone else for that matter. Not in the state of mind I'm in right now. I'm too close to the edge. My control on the verge of snapping. I need her to walk away before I say something I can't take back.

"I'm only trying to—"

A surge of anger rises inside my chest. "Why?" I grip my hair in frustration. "You had no right before. And you have no right now. Why can't you just leave this alone?"

She drops her gaze. But the dam has broken and I'm no longer able to halt my words. They steamroll right out of my mouth. "We could have just left. That's what I wanted. I wanted to leave. But you—" I point an accusatory finger at her. "You said we needed to congratulate them. That she'd be hurt if I didn't at least say goodbye."

I throw my hands in the air. "Are you satisfied?" I ask. "It wasn't enough that you convinced me to come here in the first place. I told you it was a mistake. Fuck! Cecilia. Why?"

She flinches, recoiling beneath the shroud of my anger. "I—"

"No," I cut her off, my voice dripping with frustration. "I don't want to hear it. I don't want anything from you. No apologies. No bullshit platitudes. Just leave me the hell alone. I can't even look at you right now." I'm lashing out. Even as I say the words, I know what I'm doing is wrong. Blaming her. I'm just so pissed off, I don't know how to stop.

A single tear escapes her defenses, tracing a path down her cheek.

I look away, hating myself for what I'm doing.

This isn't her fault. This is on me. I knew this was a bad idea. I knew it would hurt. That something would go wrong. But she asked it of me and I caved because I wanted to be with her. I gave Cecilia this power over me when I handed her my heart. This ability to bend me to her ways.

"I didn't mean—" she starts. Stops. Swallows hard and then tries again. "I was only trying to help," she whispers.

"Yeah, well, I never asked for your help."

"I know. And I'm sorry it's just that—"

A car pulls up on the sidewalk beside us and Felix gets out of the driver's seat. "You good?" he asks, the engine still running as he leans against the hood.

Cecilia's brows twist in confusion.

"Yeah. Thanks for coming," I tell him.

Felix nods. "I got you," he says to me before turning his attention to Cecilia. He opens the passenger door for her. "Come on. I'll take you home."

Cecilia's gaze flicks between us, her mouth tight with confusion. "But—"

I turn away and start walking in the opposite direction. I'm done with this conversation. Felix will handle things now. He'll make sure she gets home safe.

"Gabriel!" she calls out.

"Let him go. He needs time to—" I don't hear the rest of Felix's words, but I feel Cecilia's hand on me again, tugging at my dress shirt, her fingers pressing against my skin.

"Where are you going?" she asks, a thread of desperation in her voice.

I shake my head, refusing to look at her. I can't answer her question because the truth is, I don't fucking know. All I know is that I need to get away from here. From my mother. From Cecilia. From everyone.

"Just talk to me. I'm sorry, okay? I didn't mean for this—"

Something inside of me snaps and a coldness I've never felt before settles into my bones.

I grab her by both arms and press her against the side wall of the church.

A startled gasp slips free from her lips.

"You told me once to back off. That I couldn't save you. Remember that?" She flinches before offering me a barely perceptible nod. I'm being a dick and I know I need to stop. I need to rein myself in, but I can't seem to stop myself from voicing my next words. The ones I know will finally be enough to get her to leave me the hell alone. To push her away.

"Then stop trying to save me. I don't want or need your help. Got it? You're making shit worse."

"But—"

"All I need is to be left the fuck alone, Cecilia. Get that through your head."

"You don't mean that."

I laugh, the sound dark and brittle before I crowd into her space. "Yeah, I fucking do. And in case there is any confusion about where we stand, it's over. I'm done." I tear my gaze away from her. "I don't want to be your fucking friend."

My chest heaves with the effort it takes to move away from her. I don't want to see the hurt on her face.

What the hell is wrong with me? Why am I doing this?

I can't even answer the questions for myself.

"Gabe, please—" There's a plea in her voice.

"You were right to let me go," I tell her. "To push me away. I never would've had the strength to walk away from you on my own before." Shaking my head, I let out a harsh laugh. "But it looks like today, I am."

42
CECILIA

I don't know what's happening. How did we go from working things out between us, to being friends, and then to it all falling apart in less than a day?

Gabriel's words slice through my heart like a blade, and I feel my world shatter into a thousand tiny pieces.

"What?" I manage to whisper, my voice shaking.

Gabriel's confession leaves me breathless, and I'm drowning in a sea of confusion and pain. What does he mean? He can't really mean that, can he? He doesn't even want us to be friends?

He's just upset, right?

Everything is going to be okay.

Desperation climbs up my throat. He can't walk away. Not like this.

"I know I messed up," I tell him. "I made a mistake." I close the distance between us again. Gabriel's angry and hurt. He's

461

not thinking straight. If I can just get through to him. Show him that I'm not going anywhere. He has me. I'm right here and I'm not letting go. Not in his time of need.

I reach for his face and turn it toward me. His eyes refuse to meet mine, but that's okay.

I trace his jawline with my fingers, caress the stubble on his skin. "Today is really shitty," I whisper. His mouth hovers only a few inches away from mine. "But it's going to be okay. I'm right here. I'm not leaving you—"

Gabriel's eye finally lock on mine, offering me a window into the turmoil inside of him. His touch is agonizingly tender as he reaches up to thumb away a tear from my cheek.

"You were right before" he says, his voice thick with emotion.

Relief sweeps through me. He's listening. We're going to be okay. "We're just two broken people, and broken people can't fix anyone else. They need to fix themselves."

No. No. No.

I reach up and press my lips against his, hoping it makes him feel something. Anything. It's fucked up and not okay. I keep telling myself to make up my mind. That I can't continue leading him on like this. But what do I do the moment he threatens to walk away?

I kiss him.

I don't know what else to do. All I know is this desperate achy feeling spreading through my chest, screaming at me not to let him walk away. I can't lose Gabriel. Not like this.

Gabriel doesn't kiss me back.

His body is rigid. His hands keep me firmly in place. I fall back to my feet and tear my eyes away.

It hurts. Seeing him closed off like this. I open my mouth to protest, to deny his words and the chasm I feel opening up between us, but nothing comes out.

My words catch in my throat like thorns, and I'm left speechless, suffocating from the pain that steadily builds inside of me.

I've really lost him. This is it. The final nail in the coffin.

Tears blur my vision, and I try to blink them away, but they overflow, trailing down my face in rivulets that I know are ruining my makeup. I can't find it in me to care. My chest feels like it's breaking, like my ribs are being cracked open and my heart is being shredded within its depths.

Gabriel's thumb gently brushes against my cheek, and his touch is both a comfort and a torment. I ... I don't want to lose him.

Why did it take this very moment for me to realize that?

"I think I will always love you, Cecilia Russo," he whispers, and my heart splinters more. "But—"

"No!" I choke out, my voice raw with anguish. "No." My lungs heave with each of my breaths. "I was wrong. I—" I was so wrong. He can't agree with me. He just can't. Things will get better. We'll be better. He can't—

Choking on a sob, I find myself wrapped in Gabriel's arms, held close against his chest, my cries resonating against him. The fabric of his dress shirt soaks up my tears as if it can absorb the pain I feel.

My fingers clutch at him, desperate to hold on, to keep him from slipping away.

"You weren't wrong," he murmurs against my hair. His voice is steady, but his hold on me tightens. "We can't keep pretending that we can fix each other. That being together alone can make either one of us whole. And I can't pretend I'm okay only being your friend. I'm not. I don't want this."

"We can try," I cry harder into his chest. "You said that you loved me. Why won't you try being my friend?"

It's on the tip of my tongue to offer him more. To beg for him to take me back, but it wouldn't be right. Not like this.

Gabriel tilts my chin up, forcing me to look into his eyes. The anger has receded, leaving only tenderness and regret in his gaze. "Love isn't enough, baby girl," he says, his voice heavy with remorse. "I wish it was, but it just isn't. And we ..." He hesitates. "We need to heal. We need space." He throws my own words from before back at me.

I collapse into his embrace, the weight of his words crushing me. The realization that we're breaking apart tears me in two, leaving behind a hollow ache in my chest.

"I don't think I can be whole without you," I whisper, clinging to him as if his strength is the only thing keeping me from falling. "I tried. I thought I could do it on my own before, but I can't." Telling him this is selfish and wrong, but I need him in my life.

I was wrong before. I never should have pushed him away.

Gabriel squeezes me tighter. "You'll find a way," he promises softly, his voice shaky but determined. "We both will."

I wish I could feel an ounce of the confidence he does. But all I feel is the searing ache of loss and regret.

I did this to us. He's walking away because of me. My fault. My mistake.

After a couple of minutes, he releases his hold and nudges me towards Felix. Some form of silent communication passes between them, and with one final look, he turns and walks away.

I take a step in his direction but Felix wraps a tentative arm around my shoulders, stopping me. "Let him go," he says as we both watch Gabriel climb onto his bike, turn on the ignition, and drive away.

I choke on a sob.

"Don't cry." He gives my shoulder a squeeze. "It'll be okay. He's hurting. Give him time to blow off some steam." I don't miss the fact that he doesn't say Gabriel will change his mind or that he'll come around.

Felix knows it's over, too.

Swiping at the tears on my face, I allow him to usher me to the passenger door of his car. A numbness settles over me as I slide onto the cool leather seat. Felix jogs around the car and climbs inside.

"What are you doing here?" I ask him once we've pulled onto the road. "How did you know—"

"Gabe texted me," he says.

"Oh." Of course he did. Even angry, Gabriel would never abandon me. Even when he has every right to.

We drive in silence and I stare down at my hands, wondering how everything went so horribly wrong. I feel awful about the wedding. I never meant to— I cut off the thought. Gabriel deserves better than this. If I'd known how awful of a woman his mother was, I never would have suggested we come. The last thing I ever wanted was to hurt Gabriel.

But that's all we seem capable of doing to one another lately. Hurting each other.

What if he never forgives me for this?

All of a sudden, I get a glimpse of the way he's been feeling these past few weeks.

I was wrong to blame him for what Austin did. I may have asked Gabriel to let me fight my own battles, but what happened that day, it wasn't his fault. He wasn't the one who attacked me and I had no right to blame him the way that I did.

"What did he tell you?" I ask, suddenly desperate to know what else Gabriel may have said when he messaged him.

"Nothing," he tells me, eyes trained on the road in front of him. "He dropped me the address and asked me to take you home."

"That was it?"

He nods.

"And you just dropped everything and came?" No need for clarity? No questions asked?

Felix shrugs. "That's what family does," he tells me. "We show up for one another. He wouldn't have asked me to take you home unless things got fucked up. So, here I am."

466

A fresh wave of tears blurs my vision because things are fucked up. They're so fucked up, and I don't know how we'll ever come out of this. He was so angry with me. So ... hurt. I did that to him. I put him in that position. I made him relive the feeling of loss and abandonment his parents put him through all over again.

"You wanna tell me what happened between the two of you?" he asks.

I open my mouth. Close it. Try again.

"I think I really messed up."

He sighs, his expression grim. "I like you, Cecilia. We all do." There's a "but" coming, and I brace myself for it. "But you're not helping him. Whatever this situationship the two of you guys have going on is, it's not healthy. Not for him. And probably not for you." I nod, hating the truth of his words. "Gabe cares too much. Loves too much. And all it's getting him is—"

"Hurt," I finish for him.

"Yeah."

We don't talk again after that.

43

GABRIEL

I ride alone with my thoughts for close to an hour before I find myself slowing as I reach Pier 39. The sight of the ocean shimmering beneath the sunset brings a sense of calmness to my turbulent mind.

With a deep breath, I dismount from my bike and walk toward the edge of the dock, the old wooden planks creaking beneath my weight.

My phone buzzes incessantly in my pocket, each vibration a jarring interruption to the solitude I seek. With a frustrated sigh, I finally reach into my pocket and turn the damn thing off, silencing the persistent notifications that have plagued me since parting ways with Cecilia.

As I gaze out at the vast expanse of the ocean, lost in my own thoughts, a voice interrupts my solitude.

"Gabriel?"

I stiffen at the sound, the hairs on the back of my neck standing on end. Turning, I see my father approach, his figure outlined against the soft glow of the setting sun.

His presence is both unexpected and unwelcome, but I suppress the urge to tell him to go away.

"What are you doing here?" I ask, my tone sharp and not at all respectful.

He grimaces as he draws closer, lingering only a few feet away from where I'm seated with my legs hanging over the dock's edge.

"I spotted your bike in the parking lot as I was driving by," he explains. "I just wanted to check on you. I know this is where you come when something's wrong."

I nod, a begrudging acknowledgment of his observation. Pier 39 has always been my sanctuary, a place to escape to when the chaos of my thoughts becomes too much. I don't come here often anymore. Lately only on the anniversaries of Carlos's death. But today, I don't know, today I needed the ocean to help clear my thoughts away.

"I'm fine," I reply curtly, turning my gaze back to the lapping waves.

My father sighs, his breath forming a cloud of mist in the chilly air. "You're dressed awfully nice," he says. "Almost like you just came from a wedding."

My jaw tightens.

"You knew about that?"

He sighs and moves a few steps closer. "I did. I've known about the wedding for a couple of months now," he says softly. "Today was the big day. Did you go?"

I tense at the mention of the wedding, the wound still raw in my chest. "Yeah," I mutter, my voice barely above a whisper. "I went."

"How was it?" he asks.

"How do you think it was?" I scoff. "She's replaced us with a new family. A new husband and two new sons now, in case you were wondering."

My father's expression darkens with sympathy. "I'm sorry, mijo." His voice is heavy with regret. "I tried calling you when I found out. I didn't want you to be blindsided."

His words offer little comfort.

Sighing, I lean back against the dock, the rough texture of the wood digging into my palms.

"Whatever. Not sure why I expected anything different."

He steps closer again before gingerly sitting down beside me.

"Your Mom and I, we were hurting after your brother passed away," he murmurs. "It's not an excuse," he adds when I open my mouth to respond. "Simply an observation. You didn't deserve what we did. You were hurting too, and we turned our backs on you when you needed us most." He stares up at the sky. "Nunca me perdonaré por cómo te tratamos." *I will never forgive myself for how we treated you.* "Pero si me lo permites, me gustaría intentar ganarme tu perdón." *But if you'll let me, I'd like to try earning your forgiveness.*

"No sé si pueda hacer eso, papá." *I don't know if I can do that, Dad.*

He nods. "Cuando estés listo." *Whenever you're ready.*

He sits with me in silence as we watch the sky turn from pink to purple as night begins to take over. He doesn't ask me any questions. He doesn't push. He just sits with me, lending me his strength with nothing more than his presence as we listen to the gentle lapping of the waves against the shore.

"I just ... I don't get it, papá," I admit, breaking the silence. "How could she move on like this? How could she just replace Carlos and me?" I'm still here, I want to tell him, but instead, I keep that last part to myself.

My father reaches out, placing a comforting hand on my shoulder. "I wish I had the answers, mijo," he says softly. "But sometimes, hurt people, hurt people. And your mamá, she's been hurting for a very long time."

I nod, his words sinking in despite my resistance.

"I should get going," my father says, breaking the quiet once again. "But I'm always here if you need to talk. I mean that."

I offer him another small nod, a silent acknowledgment of his offer. As he turns to leave, I'm left alone once again, the weight of his words lingering in the air. Hurt people, hurt people. That's exactly what I did to Cecilia today.

With a heavy sigh, I pull out my phone and power it back on. As soon as the screen illuminates a call comes in, and seeing Felix's name flash across the screen, I answer it.

"Where are you? I've called you at least a dozen fucking times," Felix says, his voice strained with concern.

I sigh, running a hand through my hair as I stride back toward my motorcycle.

"Relax. I'm just now leaving the pier," I tell him as I reach my CBR1000. "I'll be home soon."

"Have you heard from her at all? Cecilia?" he asks, a worried edge sharpening his tone. He has a right to worry after I dumped her on him with no explanation and refused to answer my phone for what's now been—I glance at the clock on my screen—roughly two hours.

But damn, give a guy some room to breathe. It's only been a few hours, and after the day I've had, a little alone time isn't unwarranted.

Rolling my eyes, I straddle my bike, prepping my helmet as I connect my phone to its built-in bluetooth speaker. "If I wasn't answering your calls, I sure as fuck wasn't answering hers either," I say tersely. I know I lashed out, and she didn't deserve it. I have some apologizing to do, but that doesn't mean my anger at today's events has been completely washed away.

Felix curses under his breath, and something in his tone makes the hair on the back of my neck stand on edge.

"What—" I begin right as he interrupts.

"You need to get your ass home. Now."

"What's wrong?" I demand, my grip tightening on the phone as I buckle my helmet and start the engine. "What happened?"

"Holt happened. He was released on bail an hour ago."

The fuck? "Are you shitting me right now?" I ask in disbelief, my jaw clenched. "The officers we spoke with said Holt didn't have a chance of being released before his trial." This shouldn't be happening. There has to be some kind of mistake.

Holt went after Cecilia before just for suspecting she was behind him getting suspended from the team. Who knows what that psycho will try now that he's facing attempted murder charges?

"How the hell did that asshole make bail?"

"I don't know, man. But he did. Time to end the pity party and get your ass back here so we can figure out our next move." Felix says, his voice grim.

"Does Cecilia know?" I ask, immediately worried as I peel out of the pier, weaving into late-night traffic. I take a left and head toward her place. I doubt she'll talk to me right now. Not after the way I acted, but that's fine. She doesn't need to talk to me. I just need to see her. To make sure she's home and safe.

"That's what I'm trying to tell you, Gabe. No one's been able to get a hold of Cecilia since he got out. She's not answering her phone, and I went by her place as soon as we got the news. She isn't home and her parents don't know where she is."

An icy dread trickles down my spine at his words, my pulse kicking up as I lean into a turn.

"Where did you drop her off?"

"Where you told me to," he snaps. "I took her straight home after you left. But that was more than two hours ago. I spoke with her dad when I stopped by and he said she wasn't there. She went out shortly after I dropped her off, but she didn't tell him where she was going. I don't know if she's somewhere on campus or in town on her own ignoring her phone or if—"

"If he took her," I finish grimly, adrenaline flooding my veins as I accelerate.

"Yeah," Felix confirms.

I clench my jaw, urging my bike faster through the streets. "Fuck."

Felix clears his throat. "You need to get back here so we can start looking for her. We need a plan—"

"No time to waste," I interject tersely. "I'm going to find her before that psycho can hurt her again." *Assuming it's not already too late*, a voice in my head whispers. I grit my teeth, forcing the thought away. "Call Adriana, see if Cecilia's with her. Then get to PacNorth. I'll meet you there."

I use the bluetooth control on my helmet to hang up with Felix before glancing at my phone's screen.

My fingers tap her name before I can stop myself, hoping that maybe, just maybe, if she's not answering Felix's call, she'll answer mine.

The line trills once. Twice.

"Come on, pick up," I mutter, weaving recklessly between cars.

Voicemail.

I hang up and hit redial, barely avoiding a sedan as it changes lanes.

Ringing echoes in my helmet. My pulse throbs in my temples.

Why isn't she answering?

"Cecilia!" I shout when her voicemail picks up again. "Call me back. Please! Holt made bail. Where are you? I need to know you're somewhere safe."

I redial again.

And again.

And again.

Each time, it goes straight to voicemail.

Fuck. I shove my phone into my pocket, hands gripping the bars of my bike so hard that my knuckles blanch.

She has to be okay. She has to ...

I lean forward on my bike, pushing it to dangerous speeds. Lamp posts streak by in a haze. Every one of my nerve endings is alight with fear.

Hold on, Cecilia. I'm coming.

I race into the night, the city flying by in a blur. There's a thrumming urgency in my veins screaming that if I don't find Cecilia soon, it'll be too late. The thought makes my chest constrict. I have to find her.

I can't be too late.

Oy! That was intese. Sorry to leave you hanging.
But try not to panic. Gabriel and Cecilia's story will conclude
in The Replay. Be sure to add The Replay to your Goodreads
TRB

Join my newsletter so you don't miss out on The Replay's
release announcement.

And remember Roman, and Allie? While you wait for the Replay's relase, jump into Wicked Devil where we get our first look at the boys in Richland.

ABOUT THE AUTHOR

Daniela Romero is a USA Today and Wall Street Journal bestselling author. She write steamy, new-adult and paranormal romance that delivers an emotional roller coaster sure to take your breath away.

Her books feature a diverse cast of characters with rich and vibrant cultures in an effort to effectively portray the world we all live in. One that is so beautifully colorful.

Daniela is a Bay Area native though she currently lives in Washington State with her sarcastic husband and their three tiny terrors.

In her free time, Daniela enjoys frequent naps, binge reading her favorite romance books, and is known to crochet while watching television because her ADHD brain can never do just one thing at a time.

Stop by her website to find all the fun and unique ways you can stalk her. And while you're there you can check out some free bonus scenes from your favorite books, learn about her Patreon, order signed copies of her books, and swoon over her gorgeous alternative cover editions.

www.daniela-romero.com

You can join my newsletter by visiting

https://hi.switchy.io/VIP

Printed in the USA
CPSIA information can be obtained
at www.ICGtesting.com
LVHW031207020724
784485LV00010B/583